JOHN VARLEY

"John Varley is the hottest writer in science fiction ... he radiates ideas the way an out-of-control reactor throws off electrons. In his short stories Varley routinely tosses off a dozen ideas, any one of which might provide material for a whole novel ..."
—*Houston Chronicle*

"No matter what Varley writes, he writes it well."
—*Amazing*

"John Varley is a strong-man of modern science fiction, a writer who manhandles us into the future ... with the heart and wit of prime Robert Heinlein ..."
—*Philadelphia Inquirer*

"Varley writes with wit and imagination."
—*San Francisco Examiner & Chronicle*

"One of the most outstanding science fiction writers alive today ... breathtakingly fresh and provocative."
—THRUST—*Science Fiction in Review*

"Varley is an exceptional writer, possessed of a seemingly boundless imagination and a real skill for transforming it into gripping stories."
—*St. Louis Post-Dispatch*

JOHN VARLEY

Blue Champagne

ACE BOOKS, NEW YORK

This Ace book contains the complete
text of the original hardcover edition.
It has been completely reset in a typeface
designed for easy reading, and was printed
from new film.

BLUE CHAMPAGNE

An Ace Book / published by arrangement with
the author

PRINTING HISTORY
Dark Harvest edition published 1986
Berkley edition / November 1986
Ace edition / September 1987

ISBN: 0-441-06868-5

Ace Books are published by The Berkley Publishing Group,
200 Madison Avenue, New York, New York 10016.
The name "ACE" and the "A" logo
are trademarks belonging to Charter Communications, Inc.

PRINTED IN THE UNITED STATES OF AMERICA

10   9   8   7   6   5   4   3   2   1

This book is dedicated to Ricia,
who did everything but write it.

Contents

Blue Champagne

The Pusher

Things change. Ian Haise expected that. Yet there are certain constants, dictated by function and use. Ian looked for those and he seldom went wrong.

The playground was not much like the ones he had known as a child. But playgrounds are built to entertain children. They will always have something to swing on, something to slide down, something to climb. This one had all those things, and more. Part of it was thickly wooded. There was a swimming hole. The stationary apparatus was combined with dazzling light sculptures that darted in and out of reality. There were animals, too: pygmy rhinoceros and elegant gazelles no taller than your knee. They seemed unnaturally gentle and unafraid.

But most of all, the playground had children.

Ian liked children.

He sat on a wooden park bench at the edge of the trees, in the shadows, and watched them. They came in all colors and all sizes, in both sexes. There were black ones like animated licorice jellybeans and white ones like bunny rabbits, and brown ones with curly hair and more brown ones with slanted eyes and straight black hair and some who had been white but were now toasted browner than some of the brown ones.

Ian concentrated on the girls. He tried with boys before, long ago, but it had not worked out.

He watched one black child for a time, trying to estimate her age. He thought it was around eight or nine. Too young. Another one was more like thirteen, judging from her skirt. A

1

possibility, but he'd prefer something younger. Somebody less sophisticated, less suspicious.

Finally he found a girl he liked. She was brown, but with startling blonde hair. Ten? Possibly eleven. Young enough, at any rate.

He concentrated on her, and did the strange thing he did when he had selected the right one. He didn't know what it was, but it usually worked. Mostly it was just a matter of looking at her, keeping his eyes fixed on her no matter where she went or what she did, not allowing himself to be distracted by anything. And sure enough, in a few minutes she looked up, looked around, and her eyes locked with his. She held his gaze for a moment, then went back to her play.

He relaxed. Possibly what he did was nothing at all. He had noticed, with adult women, that if one really caught his eye so he found himself staring at her she would usually look up from what she was doing and catch him. It never seemed to fail. Talking to other men, he had found it to be a common experience. It was almost as if they could feel his gaze. Women had told him it was nonsense, or if not, it was just reaction to things seen peripherally by people trained to alertness for sexual signals. Merely an unconscious observation penetrating to the awareness; nothing mysterious, like ESP.

Perhaps. Still, Ian was very good at this sort of eye contact. Several times he had noticed the girls rubbing the backs of their necks while he observed them, or hunching their shoulders. Maybe they'd developed some kind of ESP and just didn't recognize it as such.

Now he merely watched. He was smiling, so that every time she looked up to see him—which she did with increasing frequency—she saw a friendly, slightly graying man with a broken nose and powerful shoulders. His hands were strong, too. He kept them clasped in his lap.

Presently she began to wander in his direction.

No one watching her would have thought she was coming toward him. She probably didn't know it herself. On her way, she found reasons to stop and tumble, jump on the soft rubber mats, or chase a flock of noisy geese. But she was coming toward him, and she would end up on the park bench beside him.

He glanced around quickly. As before, there were few adults in this playground. It had surprised him when he arrived. Apparently the new conditioning techniques had reduced the numbers of the violent and twisted to the point that parents felt it safe to allow their children to run without supervision. The adults present were involved with each other. No one had given him a second glance when he arrived.

That was fine with Ian. It made what he planned to do much easier. He had his excuses ready, of course, but it could be embarrassing to be confronted with the questions representatives of the law ask single, middle-aged men who hang around playgrounds.

For a moment he considered, with real concern, how the parents of these children could feel so confident, even with mental conditioning. After all, no one was conditioned until he had first done something. New maniacs were presumably being produced every day. Typically, they looked just like everyone else until they proved their difference by some demented act.

Somebody ought to give those parents a stern lecture, he thought.

"Who are you?"

Ian frowned. Not eleven, surely, not seen up this close. Maybe not even ten. She might be as young as eight.

Would eight be all right? He tasted the idea with his usual caution, looked around again for curious eyes. He saw none.

"My name is Ian. What's yours?"

"*No*. Not your *name*. Who are *you?*"

"You mean what do I do?"

"Yes."

"I'm a pusher."

She thought that over, then smiled. She had her permanent teeth, crowded into a small jaw.

"You give away pills?"

He laughed. "Very good," he said. "You must do a lot of reading." She said nothing, but her manner indicated she was pleased.

"No," he said. "That's an old kind of pusher. I'm the other kind. But you knew that, didn't you?" When he smiled she broke into giggles. She was doing the pointless things with her hands that little girls do. He thought she had a pretty good idea of how cute she was, but no inkling of her forbidden eroticism. She was a ripe seed with sexuality ready to burst to the surface. Her body was a bony sketch, a framework on which to build a woman.

"How old are you?"

"That's a secret. What happened to your nose?"

"I broke it a long time ago. I'll bet you're twelve."

She giggled, then nodded. Eleven, then. And just barely.

"Do you want some candy?" He reached into his pocket and pulled out the pink and white striped paper bag.

She shook her head solemnly. "My mother says not to take candy from strangers."

"But we're not strangers. I'm Ian, the pusher."

She thought that over. While she hesitated he reached into the bag and picked out a chocolate thing so thick and gooey it was almost obscene. He bit into it, forcing himself to chew. He hated sweets.

"Okay," she said, and reached toward the bag. He pulled it away. She looked at him in innocent surprise.

"I just thought of something," he said. "I don't know your name, so I guess we *are* strangers."

She caught on to the game when she saw the twinkle in his eye. He'd practiced that. It was a good twinkle.

"My name is Radiant. Radiant Shiningstar Smith."

"A very fancy name," he said, thinking how names had changed. "For a very pretty girl." He paused, and cocked his head. "No. I don't think so. You're Radiant . . . Starr. With two *r's*. . . . *Captain* Radiant Starr, of the Star Patrol."

She was dubious for a moment. He wondered if he'd judged her wrong. Perhaps she was really Miss Radiant Faintingheart Belle, or Mrs. Radiant Motherhood. But her fingernails were a bit dirty for that.

She pointed a finger at him and made a Donald Duck sound as her thumb worked back and forth. He put his hand to his heart and fell over sideways, and she dissolved in laughter. She was careful, however, to keep her weapon firmly trained on him.

"And you'd better give me that candy or I'll shoot you again."

The playground was darker now, and not so crowded. She sat beside him on the bench, swinging her legs. Her bare feet did not quite touch the dirt.

She was going to be quite beautiful. He could see it clearly in her face. As for the body . . . who could tell?

Not that he really gave a damn.

She was dressed in a little of this and a little of that, worn here and there without much regard for his concepts of modesty. Many of the children wore nothing. It had been something of a shock when he arrived. Now he was almost used to it, but he still thought it incautious on the part of her parents. Did they really think the world was that safe, to let an eleven-year-old girl go practically naked in a public place?

He sat there listening to her prattle about her friends—the ones she hated and the one or two she simply adored—with only part of his attention.

He inserted um's and uh-huh's in the right places.

She was cute, there was no denying it. She seemed as sweet as a child that age ever gets, which can be very sweet and as poisonous as a rattlesnake, almost at the same moment. She had the capacity to be warm, but it was on the surface. Underneath, she cared mostly about herself. Her loyalty would be a transitory thing, bestowed easily, just as easily forgotten.

And why not? She was young. It was perfectly healthy for her to be that way.

But did he dare try to touch her?

It was crazy. It was insane as they all told him it was. It worked so seldom. Why would it work with her? He felt a weight of defeat.

"Are you okay?"

"Huh? Me? Oh, sure, I'm all right. Isn't your mother going to be worried about you?"

"I don't have to be in for hours and hours yet." For a moment she looked so grown up he almost believed the lie.

"Well, I'm getting tired of sitting here. And the candy's all gone." He looked at her face. Most of the chocolate had ended up in a big circle around her mouth, except where she had wiped it daintily on her shoulder or forearm. "What's back there?"

She turned.

"That? That's the swimming hole."

"Why don't we go over there? I'll tell you a story."

The promise of a story was not enough to keep her out of the water. He didn't know if that was good or bad. He knew she was smart, a reader, and she had an imagination. But she was also active. That pull was too strong for him. He sat far from the water, under some bushes, and watched her swim with the three other children still in the park this late in the evening.

Maybe she would come back to him, and maybe she wouldn't. It wouldn't change his life either way, but it might change hers.

She emerged dripping and infinitely cleaner from the murky water. She dressed again in her random scraps, for whatever good it did her, and came to him shivering.

"I'm cold," she said.

"Here." He took off his jacket. She looked at his hands as he wrapped it around her, and once she reached out and touched the hardness of his shoulder.

"You sure must be strong," she commented.

"Pretty strong. I work hard, being a pusher."

"Just what *is* a pusher?" she said, and stifled a yawn.

"Come sit on my lap, and I'll tell you."

He did tell her, and it was a very good story that no adventurous child could resist. He had practiced that story, refined it, told it many times into a recorder until he had the rhythms and cadences just right, until he found just the right words—not too difficult words, but words with some fire and juice in them.

And once more he grew encouraged. She had been tired when he started, but he gradually caught her attention. It was possible no one had ever told her a story in quite that way. She was used to sitting before the screen and having a story shoved into her eyes and ears. It was something new to be able to interrupt with questions and get answers. Even reading was not like that. It was the oral tradition of storytelling, and it could still mesmerize the nth generation of the electronic age.

"That sounds great," she said, when she was sure he was through.

"You liked it?"

"I really truly did. I think I want to be a pusher when I grow up. That was a really neat story."

"Well, that's not actually the story I was going to tell you. That's just what it's like to be a pusher."

"You mean you have another story?"

"Sure." He looked at his watch. "But I'm afraid it's getting late. It's almost dark, and everybody's gone home. You'd probably better go, too."

She was in agony, torn between what she was supposed to do and what she wanted. It really should be no contest, if she was who he thought she was.

"Well . . . but—but I'll come back here tomorrow and you—"

He was shaking his head.

"My ship leaves in the morning," he said. "There's no time."

"Then tell me now! I can stay out. Tell me now. Please please please?"

He coyly resisted, harrumphed, protested, but in the end allowed himself to be seduced. He felt very good. He had her like a five-pound trout on a twenty-pound line. It wasn't sporting. But then, he wasn't playing a game.

So at last he got to his specialty.

He sometimes wished he could claim the story for his own, but the fact was he could not make up stories. He no longer tried to. Instead, he cribbed from every fairy tale and fantasy story he could find. If he had a genius, it was in adapting some of the elements to fit the world she knew—while keeping it strange enough to enthrall her—and in ad libbing the end to personalize it.

It was a wonderful tale he told. It had enchanted castles sitting on mountains of glass, moist caverns beneath the sea, fleets of starships and shining riders astride horses that flew the galaxy. There were evil alien creatures, and others with much good in them. There were drugged potions. Scaled beasts roared out of hyperspace to devour planets.

Amid all the turmoil strode the Prince and Princess. They got into frightful jams and helped each other out of them.

The story was never quite the same. He watched her eyes. When they wandered, he threw away whole chunks of story. When they widened, he knew what parts to plug in later. He tailored it to her reactions.

The child was sleepy. Sooner or later she would surrender. He needed her in a trance state, neither awake nor asleep. That is when the story would end.

". . . and though the healers labored long and hard, they could not save the Princess. She died that night, far from her Prince."

Her mouth was a little round **o**. Stories were not supposed to end that way.

"Is that *all?* She died, and she never saw the Prince again?"

"Well, not quite all. But the rest of it probably isn't true, and I shouldn't tell it to you." Ian felt pleasantly tired. His throat was a little raw, making him hoarse. Radiant was a warm weight on his lap.

"You have to tell me, you know," she said, reasonably. He supposed she was right. He took a deep breath.

"All right. At the funeral, all the greatest people from that part of the galaxy were in attendance. Among them was the greatest Sorcerer who ever lived. His name . . . but I really shouldn't tell you his name. I'm sure he'd be very cross if I did.

"This Sorcerer passed by the Princess's bier . . . that's a—"

"I know, I *know*, Ian. Go on!"

"Suddenly he frowned, and leaned over her pale form. 'What is this?' he thundered. 'Why was I not told?' Everyone was very concerned. This Sorcerer was a dangerous man. One time when someone insulted him he made a spell that turned everyone's heads backwards so they had to walk around with rear-view mirrors. No one knew what he would do if he got really angry.

" 'This Princess is wearing the Starstone,' he said, and drew himself up and frowned all around as if he were surrounded by idiots. I'm sure he thought he was, and maybe he was right. Because he went on to tell them just what the Starstone was, and what it did, something no one there had ever heard before. And this is the part I'm not sure of. Because, though everyone knew the Sorcerer was a wise and powerful man, he was also known as a great liar.

"He said that the Starstone was capable of capturing the essence of a person at the moment of her death. All her wisdom, all her power, all her knowledge and beauty and strength would flow into the stone and be held there, timelessly."

"In suspended animation," Radiant breathed.

"Precisely. When they heard this, the people were amazed. They buffeted the Sorcerer with questions, to which he gave few answers, and those only grudgingly. Finally he left in a huff. When he was gone everyone talked long into the night

about the things he had said. Some felt the Sorcerer had held
out hope that the Princess might yet live on. That if her body
were frozen, the Prince, upon his return, might somehow
infuse her essence back within her. Others thought the Sorcerer had said that was impossible, that the Princess was
doomed to a half-life, locked in the stone.

"But the opinion that prevailed was this:

"The Princess would probably never come fully back to
life. But her essence might flow from the Starstone and into
another, if the right person could be found. All agreed this
person must be a young maiden. She must be beautiful, very
smart, swift of foot, loving, kind . . . oh, my, the list was
very long. Everyone doubted such a person could be found.
Many did not even want to try.

"But at last it was decided the Starstone should be given to
a faithful friend of the Prince. He would search the galaxy for
this maiden. If she existed, he would find her.

"So he departed with the blessings of many worlds behind
him, vowing to find the maiden and give her the Starstone."

He stopped again, cleared his throat, and let the silence
grow.

"Is that all?" she said, at last, in a whisper.

"Not quite all," he admitted. "I'm afraid I tricked you."

"Tricked me?"

He opened the front of his coat, which was still draped
around her shoulders. He reached in past her bony chest and
down into an inner pocket of the coat. He came up with the
crystal. It was oval, with one side flat. It pulsed ruby light as
it sat in the palm of his hand.

"It shines," she said, looking at it wide-eyed and open-
mouthed.

"Yes, it does. And that means you're the one."

"Me?"

"Yes. Take it." He handed it to her, and as he did so, he
nicked it with his thumbnail. Red light spilled into her hands,
flowed between her fingers, seemed to soak into her skin.
When it was over, the crystal still pulsed, but dimmed. Her
hands were trembling.

"It felt very, very hot," she said.

"That was the essence of the Princess."

"And the Prince? Is he still looking for her?"

"No one knows. I think he's still out there, and some day
he will come back for her."

"And what then?"

He looked away from her. "I can't say. I think, even though you are lovely, and even though you have the Starstone, that he will just pine away. He loved her very much."

"I'd take care of him," she promised.

"Maybe that would help. But I have a problem now. I don't have the heart to tell the Prince that she is dead. Yet I feel that the Starstone will draw him to it one day. If he comes and finds you, I fear for him. I think perhaps I should take the stone to a far part of the galaxy, some place he could never find it. Then at least he would never know. It might be better that way."

"But I'd help him," she said, earnestly. "I promise. I'd wait for him, and when he came, I'd take her place. You'll see."

He studied her. Perhaps she would. He looked into her eyes for a long time, and at last let her see his satisfaction.

"Very well. You can keep it then."

"I'll wait for him," she said. "You'll see."

She was very tired; almost asleep.

"You should go home now," he suggested.

"Maybe I could just lie down for a moment," she said.

"All right." He lifted her gently and placed her prone on the ground. He stood looking down at her, then knelt beside her and began to gently stroke her forehead. She opened her eyes with no alarm, then closed them again. He continued to stroke her.

Twenty minutes later he left the playground, alone.

He was always depressed afterwards. It was worse than usual this time. She had been much nicer than he had imagined at first. Who could have guessed such a romantic heart beat beneath all that dirt?

He found a phone booth several blocks away. Punching her name into information yielded a fifteen-digit number, which he called. He held his hand over the camera eye.

A woman's face appeared on his screen.

"Your daughter is in the playground, at the south end by the pool, under the bushes," he said. He gave the address of the playground.

"We were so worried! What . . . is she . . . who is—"

He hung up and hurried away.

• • •

Most of the other pushers thought he was sick. Not that it mattered. Pushers were a tolerant group when it came to other pushers, and especially when it came to anything a pusher might care to do to a puller. He wished he had never told anyone how he spent his leave time, but he had, and now he had to live with it.

So, while they didn't care if he amused himself by pulling the legs and arms off infant puller pups, they were all just back from ground leave and couldn't pass up an opportunity to get on each other's nerves. They ragged him mercilessly.

"How were the swing-sets this trip, Ian?"

"Did you bring me those dirty knickers I asked for?"

"Was it good for you, honey? Did she pant and slobber?"

" *'My ten-year-old baby, she's a pullin' me back home . . .'*"

Ian bore it stoically. It was in extremely bad taste and he was the brunt of it, but it really didn't matter. It would end as soon as they lifted again. They would never understand what he sought, but he felt he understood them. They hated coming to Earth. There was nothing for them there, and perhaps they wished there was.

And he was a pusher himself. He didn't care for pullers. He agreed with the sentiment expressed by Marian, shortly after lift-off. Marian had just finished her first ground leave after her first voyage, so naturally she was the drunkest of them all.

"Gravity sucks," she said, and threw up.

It was three months to Amity, and three months back. He hadn't the foggiest idea of how far it was in miles; after the tenth or eleventh zero his mind clicked off.

Amity. Shit City. He didn't even get off the ship. Why bother? The planet was peopled with things that looked a little like ten-ton caterpillars and a little like sentient green turds. Toilets were a revolutionary idea to the Amiti; so were ice cream bars, sherbets, sugar donuts, and peppermint. Plumbing had never caught on, but sweets had, so the ship was laden with plain and fancy desserts from every nation on Earth. In addition, there was a pouch of reassuring mail for the forlorn human embassy. The cargo for the return trip was some grayish sludge that Ian supposed someone on Earth found tremendously valuable, and a packet of desperate mail for the folks back home. Ian didn't need to read the letters to

know what was in them. They could all be summed up as
"Get me *out* of here!"

He sat at the viewport and watched an Amiti family lum-
bering and farting its way down the spaceport road. They
paused every so often to do something that looked like an
alien cluster-fuck. The road was brown. The land was brown,
and in the distance were brown, unremarkable hills. There
was a brown haze in the air, and the sun was yellow-brown.

He thought of castles perched on mountains of glass, of
Princes and Princesses, of shining white horses galloping
among the stars.

He spent the return trip just as he had on the way out:
sweating down in the gargantuan pipes of the stardrive. Just
beyond the metal walls unimaginable energies pulsed. And on
the walls themselves, tiny plasmoids grew into bigger
plasmoids. The process was too slow to see, but if left
unchecked the encrustations would soon impair the engines.
His job was to scrape them off.

Not everyone was cut out to be an astrogator.

And what of it? It was honest work. He had made his
choices long ago. You spent your life either pulling gees or
pushing *c*. And when you got tired, you grabbed some *z*'s. If
there was a pushers' code, that was it.

The plasmoids were red and crystalline, teardrop-shaped.
When he broke them free of the walls they had one flat side.
They were full of a liquid light that felt as hot as the center of
the sun.

It was always hard to get off the ship. A lot of pushers never
did. One day, he wouldn't either.

He stood for a few moments looking at it all. It was
necessary to soak it in passively at first, get used to the
changes. Big changes didn't bother him. Buildings were just
the world's furniture and he didn't care how it was arranged.
Small changes worried the shit out of him. Ears, for instance.
Very few of the people he saw had earlobes. Each time he
returned he felt a little more like an ape who has fallen from
his tree. One day he'd return to find everybody had three eyes
or six fingers, or that little girls no longer cared to hear stories
of adventure.

He stood there, dithering, getting used to the way people
were painting their faces, listening to what sounded like

Spanish being spoken all around him. Occasional English or Arabic words seasoned it. He grabbed a crewmate's arm and asked him where they were. The man didn't know so he asked the Captain, and she said it was Argentina, or it had been when they left.

The phone booths were smaller. He wondered why.

There were four names in his book. He sat there facing the phone, wondering which name to call first. His eyes were drawn to Radiant Shiningstar Smith, so he punched that name into the phone. He got a number and an address in Novosibirsk.

Checking the timetable he had picked up—putting off making the call—he found the antipodean shuttle left on the hour. Then he wiped his hands on his pants and took a deep breath and looked up to see her standing outside the phone booth. They regarded each other silently for a moment. She saw a man much shorter than she remembered, but powerfully built, with big hands and shoulders and a pitted face that would have been forbidding but for the gentle eyes. He saw a tall woman around forty years old who was fully as beautiful as he had expected she would be. The hand of age had just begun to touch her. He thought she was fighting that waistline and fretting about those wrinkles, but none of that mattered to him. Only one thing mattered, and he would know it soon enough.

"You *are* Ian Haise, aren't you?" she said, at last.

"It was sheer luck I remembered you again," she was saying. He noted the choice of words. She could have said coincidence.

"It was two years ago. We were moving again and I was sorting through some things and I came across that plasmoid. I hadn't thought about you in . . . oh, it must have been fifteen years."

He said something noncommittal. They were in a restaurant, away from most of the other patrons, at a booth near a glass wall beyond which spaceships were being trundled to and from the blast pits.

"I hope I didn't get you into trouble," he said.

She shrugged it away.

"You did, some, but that was so long ago. I certainly wouldn't bear a grudge that long. And the fact is, I thought it was all worth it at the time."

She went on to tell him of the uproar he had caused in her

family, of the visits by the police, the interrogation, puzzlement, and final helplessness. No one knew quite what to make of her story. They had identified him quickly enough, only to find he had left Earth and would not be back for a long, long time.

"I didn't break any laws," he pointed out.

"That's what no one could understand. I told them you had talked to me and told me a long story, and then I went to sleep. None of them seemed interested in what the story was about, so I didn't tell them. And I didn't tell them about the . . . the Starstone." She smiled. "Actually, I was relieved they hadn't asked. I was determined not to tell them, but I was a little afraid of holding it all back. I thought they were agents of the . . . who were the villains in your story? I've forgotten."

"It's not important."

"I guess not. But something is."

"Yes."

"Maybe you should tell me what it is. Maybe you can answer the question that's been in the back of my mind for twenty-five years, ever since I found out that thing you gave me was just the scrapings from a starship engine."

"Was it?" he said, looking into her eyes. "Don't get me wrong. I'm not saying it *was* more than that. I'm asking *you* if it wasn't more."

She looked at him again. He felt himself being appraised for the third or fourth time since they met. He still didn't know the verdict.

"Yes, I guess it was more," she said, at last.

"I'm glad."

"I believed in that story passionately for . . . oh, years and years. Then I stopped believing it."

"All at once?"

"No. Gradually. It didn't hurt much. Part of growing up, I guess."

"And you remembered me."

"Well, that took some work. I went to a hypnotist when I was twenty-five and recovered your name and the name of your ship. Did you know—"

"Yes. I mentioned them on purpose."

She nodded, and they fell silent again. When she looked at him now he saw more sympathy, less defensiveness. But there was still a question.

"Why?" she said.

He nodded, then looked away from her, out to the starships. He wished he was on one of them, pushing *c*. It wasn't working. He knew it wasn't. He was a weird problem to her, something to get straightened out, a loose end in her life that would irritate until it was made to fit in, then be forgotten.

To hell with it.

"Hoping to get laid," he said. When he looked up she was slowly shaking her head back and forth.

"Don't trifle with me, Haise. You're not as stupid as you look. You knew I'd be married, leading my own life. You knew I wouldn't drop it all because of some half-remembered fairy tale thirty years ago. *Why?*"

And how could he explain the strangeness of it all to her?

"What do you do?" He recalled something, and re-phrased it. "Who *are* you?"

She looked startled. "I'm a mysteliologist."

He spread his hands. "I don't even know what that is."

"Come to think of it, there was no such thing when you left."

"That's it, in a way," he said. He felt helpless again. "Obviously, I had no way of knowing what you'd do, what you'd become, what would happen to you that you had no control over. All I was gambling on was that'd you remember me. Because that way . . ." He saw the planet Earth looming once more out the viewport. So many, many years and only six months later. A planet full of strangers. It didn't matter that Amity was full of strangers. But Earth was home, if that word still had any meaning for him.

"I wanted somebody my own age I could talk to," he said. "That's all. All I want is a friend."

He could see her trying to understand what it was like. She wouldn't, but maybe she'd come close enough to think she did.

"Maybe you've found one," she said, and smiled. "At least I'm willing to get to know you, considering the efforts you've put into this."

"It wasn't much effort. It seems so long-term to you, but it wasn't to me. I held you on my lap six months ago."

She giggled in almost the same way she had six months before.

"How long is your leave?" she asked.

"Two months."

"Would you like to come stay with us for a while? We have room in our house."

"Will your husband mind?"

"Neither my husband nor my wife. That's them sitting over there, pretending to ignore us." Ian looked, caught the eye of a woman in her late twenties. She was sitting across from a man Ian's age, who now turned and looked at Ian with some suspicion but no active animosity. The woman smiled; the man reserved judgment.

Radiant had a wife. Well, times change.

"Those two in the red skirts are police," Radiant was saying. "So is that man over by the wall, and the one at the end of the bar."

"I spotted two of them," Ian said. When she looked surprised, he said, "Cops always have a look about them. That's one of the things that don't change."

"You go back quite a ways, don't you? I'll bet you have some good stories."

Ian thought about it, and nodded. "Some, I suppose."

"I should tell the police they can go home. I hope you don't mind that we brought them in."

"Of course not."

"I'll do that, and then we can go. Oh, and I guess I should call the children and tell them we'll be home soon." She laughed, reached across the table and touched his hand. "See what can happen in six months? I have three children, and Gillian has two."

He looked up, interested.

"Are any of them girls?"

Blue Champagne

Megan Galloway arrived in the Bubble with a camera crew of three. With her breather and her sidekick she was the least naked nude woman any of the lifeguards had ever seen.

"I bet she's carrying more hardware than any of her crew," Glen said.

"Yeah, but it hardly shows, you know?"

Q. M. Cooper was thinking back as he watched her accept the traditional bulb of champagne. "Isn't that some kind of record? Three people in her crew?"

"The President of Brazil brought twenty-nine people in with her," Anna-Louise observed. "The King of England had twenty-five."

"Yeah, but only one network pool camera."

"So that's the Golden Gypsy," Leah said.

Anna-Louise snorted. "More like the Brass Transistor."

They had all heard that one before, but laughed anyway. None of the lifeguards had much respect for Trans-sisters. Yet Cooper had to admit that in a profession which sought to standardize emotion, Galloway was the only one who was uniquely herself. The others were interchangeable as News Anchors.

A voice started whispering in their ears, over the channel reserved for emergency announcements and warnings.

"Entering the Bubble is Megan Galloway, representing the Feelie Corporation, a wholly-owned subsidiary of GWA Conglom. Feeliecorp: bringing you the best in experiential tapes and erotix. Blue Champagne Enterprises trusts you will not impede the taping, and regrets any disturbance."

"Commercials, yet," Glen said in disgust. To those who loved the Bubble—as all the lifeguards did—this was something like using the walls of the Taj Mahal for the Interconglomerate Graffiti Championship finals.

"Stick around for the yacht races," Cooper said. "They should have at least told us she was coming. What about that sidekick? Should we know anything about it if she gets into trouble?"

"Maybe she knows what she's doing," Leah said, earning sour looks from the other four. It was an article of faith that *nobody* on a first visit to the Bubble knew what they were doing.

"You think she'll take the sidekick into the water?"

"Well, since she can't move without it I sort of doubt she'll take it off," Cooper said. "Stu, you call operations and ask why we weren't notified. Find out about special precautions. The rest of you get back to work. A.L., you take charge here."

"What will *you* be doing, Q.M.?" Anna-Louise asked, arching one eyebrow.

"I'm going to get a closer look." He pushed off, and flew toward the curved inner surface of the Bubble.

The Bubble was the only thing Q. M. Cooper ever encountered which caught his imagination, held it for years, and did not prove a disappointment when he finally saw it. It was love at first sight.

It floated in lunar orbit with nothing to give it perspective. Under those conditions the eye can see the Earth or Luna as hunks of rock no bigger than golf balls, or a fleck of ice millimeters from the ship's window can seem to be a distant, tumbling asteroid. When Cooper first saw it the illusion was perfect: someone had left a champagne glass floating a few meters from the ship.

The constricted conic-shape was dictated by the mathematics of the field generators that held the Bubble. It was made of an intricate network of fine wires. No other configuration was possible; it was mere chance that the generator resembled the bowl and stem of a wine glass.

The Bubble itself had to be weightless, but staff and visitors needed a spin-gravity section. A disc was better than a wheel for that purpose, since it provided regions of varying gravity, from one gee at the rim to free-fall at the hub. The most logical place for the disc was at the base of the generator stem, which also made it the base of the glass. It was rumored that the architect of the Bubble had gone mad while designing it and that, since he favored martinis, he had included in the blueprints a mammoth toothpick spearing a giant green olive.

But that was only the station. It was beautiful enough in itself, but was nothing compared to the Bubble.

It floated in the shallow bowl of the generators, never touching them. It was two hundred million liters of water held between two concentric spherical fields of force, one of them one hundred meters in diameter, the other one hundred and forty. The fields contained a shell of water massing almost a million tonnes, with a five-hundred-thousand-cubic-meter bubble of air in the middle.

Cooper knew the relevant numbers by heart. Blue Champagne Enterprises made sure no one entered the Bubble without hearing them at least once. But numbers could not begin to tell what the Bubble was really like. To know that, one had to ride the elevator up through the glass swizzle stick that ended in the center of the air bubble, step out of the car, grab one of the monkeybar struts near the lifeguard station, and hold on tight until one's emotions settled down enough to be able to *believe* in the damn thing.

The lifeguards had established six classes of visitor. It was all unofficial; to BCE, everyone was an honored guest. The rankings were made by a guest's behavior and personal habits, but mostly by swimming ability.

Crustaceans clung to the monkeybars. Most never got their feet wet. They came to the Bubble to be seen, not to swim. Plankton thought they could swim, but it was no more than a fond hope. Turtles and frogs really could swim, but it was a comical business.

Sharks were excellent swimmers. If they had added brains to their other abilities the lifeguards would have loved them. Dolphins were the best. Cooper was a dolphin-class swimmer, which was why he had the job of chief lifeguard for the third shift.

To his surprise, Megan Galloway ranked somewhere between a frog and a shark. Most of her awkward moves were the result of being unaccustomed to the free-fall environment. She had obviously spent a lot of time in flat water.

He pulled ahead and broke through the outer surface of the Bubble with enough speed to carry him to the third field, which kept air in and harmful radiation out. On his way he twisted in the air to observe how she handled the breakthrough. He could see gold reflections from the metal bands of her sidekick while she was just an amorphous shape beneath the surface. The water around her was bright aquamarine from the camera lights. She had outdistanced her crew.

He had an immediate and very strong reaction: what a ghastly way to live. Working in the Bubble was very special to him. He griped about the clients, just like everyone did, complained when he had to ferry some damn crustacean who couldn't even get up enough speed to return to the monkeybars, or when he had to clean up one of the excretory nuisances that got loose in surprising numbers when somebody got disoriented and scared. But the basic truth was that, for him, it never got old. There was always some new way of looking at the place, some fresh magic to be found. He wondered if he could feel that way about it if he lived in the middle of a traveling television studio with the whole world watching.

He was starting to drift back toward the water when she burst free of it. She broke the surface like a golden mermaid, rising, trailing a plume of water that turned into a million quivering crystals as it followed her into the air. She tumbled in the middle of a cloud of water globes, a flesh and metal Aphrodite emerging from the foam.

Her mouthpiece fell from her lips to dangle from its airhose, and he heard her laugh. He did not think she had noticed him. He was fairly sure she thought she was alone, for once, if only for a few seconds. She sounded as delighted as a child, and her laughter went on until the camera crew came grumbling out of the water.

They made her go back and do it over.

"She's not worth the effort, Q.M."

"Who? Oh, you mean the Golden Gypsy."

"You want your bedroom technique studied by ninety million slobs?"

Cooper turned to look at Anna-Louise, who sat behind him on the narrow locker room bench, tying her shoelaces. She glanced over her shoulder and grinned. He knew he had a reputation as a starfucker. When he first came to work at the Bubble he had perceived one of the fringe benefits to be the opportunity to meet, hob-nob with, and bed famous women, and had done so with more than a few. But he was long over that.

"Galloway doesn't make heavy-breathers."

"Not yet. Neither did Lyshia Trumbull until about a year ago. Or that guy who works for ABS . . . Chin. Randall Chin."

"Neither did Salome Hassan," someone chimed in from across the room. Cooper looked around and saw the whole shift was listening.

"I thought you were all above that," he said. "Turns out we're a bunch of feelie-groupies."

"You can't help hearing the names," Stu said, defensively.

Anna-Louise pulled her shirt over her head and stood up. "There's no sense denying I've tried tapes," she said. "The trans-sisters have to make a living. She'll do them. Wet-dreams are the coming thing."

"They're coming, all right," Stu said, with an obscene gesture.

"Why don't you idiots knock it off and get out of here?" Cooper said.

They did, gradually, and the tiny locker room at the gee/10 level was soon empty but for Cooper and Anna-Louise. She stood at the mirror, rubbing a lotion over her scalp to make it shine.

"I'd like to move to the number two shift," she said.

"You're a crazy Loonie, you know that?" he shot back, annoyed.

She turned at the waist and glared at him.

"That's redundant and racist," she said. "If I wasn't such a sweet person I'd resent it."

"But it's true."

"That's the other reason I'm not going to resent it."

He got up and embraced her from behind, nuzzling her ear. "Hey, you're all wet," she laughed, but did not try to stop him, even when his hands lifted her shirt and went down under the waistband of her pants. She turned and he kissed her.

Cooper had never really understood Anna-Louise, even though he had bunked with her for six months. She was almost as big as he was, and he was not small. Her home was New Dresden, Luna. Though German was her native tongue, she spoke fluent, unaccented English. Her face would inspire adjectives like strong, healthy, glowing, and fresh, but never a word like glamorous. In short, she was physically just like all the other female lifeguards. She even shaved her head, but where the others did it in an attempt to recapture past glory, to keep that Olympic look, she had never done any competitive swimming. That alone made her unique in the group, and was probably what made her so refreshing. All the other women in the lifeguard force were uncomplicated jocks who liked two things: swimming, and sex, in that order.

Cooper did not object to that. It was a pretty fair description of himself. But he was creeping up on thirty, getting closer every day. That is never a good time for an athlete. He was surprised to find that it hurt when she told him she wanted to change shifts.

"Does this have anything to do with Yuri Feldman?" he asked, between kisses.

"Is that his shift?"

"Are we still going to be bunkmates?"

She drew back. "Are we going to talk? Is that why you're undressing me?"

"I just wanted to know."

She turned away, buckling her pants.

"Unless you want to move out, we're still bunkmates. I didn't think it really meant a hell of a lot. Was I wrong?"

"I'm sorry."

"It's just that it might be simpler to sleep alone, that's all." She turned back and patted his cheek. "Hell, Q.M. It's just sex. You're very good at it, and so long as you stay interested we'll do just fine. Okay?" Her hand was still on his cheek. Her expression changed as she peered intently into his eyes. "It *is* just sex, isn't it? I mean—"

"Sure, it's—"

"—if it *isn't* . . . but you've never said anything that would—"

"God, no," he said. "I don't want to get tied down."

"Me, either." She looked as if she might wish to say more, but instead touched his cheek again, and left him alone.

Cooper was so preoccupied that he walked past the table where Megan Galloway sat with her camera crew.

"Cooper! Your name is Cooper, right?"

When he turned he had his camera smile in place. Though

being recognized had by that time become a rare thing, the reflexes were still working. But the smile was quickly replaced by a more genuine expression of delight. He was surprised and flattered that she had known who he was.

Galloway had her hand to her forehead, looking up at him with comical intensity. She snapped her fingers, hit her forehead again.

"I've been trying to think of the name since I saw you in the water," she said. "Don't tell me . . . I'll get it . . . it was a nickname . . . " She trailed off helplessly, then plunked both elbows on the table and put her chin in her hands, glowering at him.

"I can't think of it."

"It's—"

"Don't *tell me.*"

He had been about to say it was not something he revealed, but instead he shrugged and said nothing.

"I'll get it, if you'll just give me time."

"She will, too," said the other woman, who then gestured to an empty seat and extended a hand to him. "I'm Consuela Lopez. Let me buy you a drink."

"I'm . . . Cooper."

Consuela leaned closer and murmured, "If she doesn't have the goddam name in ten minutes, tell her, huh? Otherwise she won't be worth a damn until she gets it. You're a lifeguard."

He nodded, and his drink arrived. He tried to conceal his amazement. It was *impossible* to impress the waiters at the promenade cafes. Yet Galloway's party did not even have to order.

"Fascinating profession. You must tell me all about it. I'm a producer, studying to be a pimp." She swayed slightly, and Cooper realized she was drunk. It didn't show in her speech. "That devilish fellow with the beard is Markham Montgomery, director and talent prostitute." Montgomery glanced at Cooper, made a gesture that could have been the step-outline for a nod. "And the person of debatable sex is Coco-89 (Praisegod), recordist, enigma, and devotee of a religiosexual cult so obscure even Coco isn't sure what it's about." Cooper had seen Coco in the water. He or she had the genitals of a man and the breasts of a woman, but androgynes were not uncommon in the Bubble.

"Cheers," Coco said, solemnly raising a glass. "Accly your am tance to deep make honored."

Everyone laughed but Cooper. He could not see the joke. Lopez had not bothered him—he had heard cute speeches from more rich/sophisticated people than he could count—but Coco sounded crazy.

Lopez lifted a small, silver tube over the edge of the table, squeezed a trigger, and a stream of glittering silver powder sprayed toward Coco. It burst in a thousand pinpoint scintillations. The androgyne inhaled with a foolish grin.

"Wacky Dust," Lopez said, and pointed the tube at Cooper. "Want some?" Without waiting for an answer she fired again. The stuff twinkled around his head. It smelled like one of the popular aphrodisiacs.

"What is it?" he asked.

"A mind-altering drug," she said, theatrically. When she saw his alarm she relented a little. "The trip is very short. In fact, I gave you such a little squirt you'll hardly notice it. Five minutes, tops."

"What does it do?"

She was eyeing him suspiciously. "Well, it should have done it already. Are you left-handed?"

"Yes."

"That explains it. Most of it's going to the wrong side of your head. What it does is scramble your speech center."

Montgomery roused himself enough to turn his head. He looked at Cooper with something less than total boredom. "It's like inhaling helium," he said. "You talk funny for a while."

"I didn't think that was possible," Cooper said, and everyone laughed. He found himself grinning reflexively, not knowing what was funny until he played his words back in his head and realized he had said something like "Pos that ib think unt I bull . . ."

He gritted his teeth and concentrated.

"I," he said, and thought some more. "Don't. Like. This." They seemed delighted. Coco babbled gibberish, and Lopez patted him on the back.

"Not many people figure it out that fast," she said. "Stick to one-word sentences and you're okay."

"The Wacky Dust scrambles the sentence-making capability of the brain," Montgomery said. He was sounding almost enthusiastic. Cooper knew from experience that the man was speaking of one of the few things that could excite him, that being his current ten-minute's wonder, the thing that everyone of any importance was doing today and would forget about tomorrow. "Complex thoughts are no longer—"

Cooper slammed his fist on the table and got the expected silence. Montgomery's eyes glazed and he looked away, bored by poor sportsmanship. Cooper stood.

"You," he said, pointing at all of them. "Stink."

"Quarter-meter!" Galloway shouted, pointing at Cooper. "Quarter-meter Cooper! Silver medal in Rio, bronze at Shanghai, 1500-meter freestyle, competed for United N.A., then for Ryancorp." She was grinning proudly, but when she looked around her face fell. "What's wrong?"

Cooper walked away from them. She caught him when he was almost out of sight around the curved promenade floor.

"Quarter-meter, please don't—"

"Don't me call that!" he shouted, jerking his arm away from her touch, not caring how the words came out. Her hand sprang back poised awkwardly, each joint of her fingers twinkling with its own golden band.

"Mr. Cooper, then." She let her hand fall, and her gaze with it, looked at her booted feet. "I want to apologize for her. She had no right to do that. She's drunk, if you hadn't—"

"I no . . . ticed."

"You'll be all right now," she said, touching his arm lightly, remembering, and pulling it away with a sheepish smile.

"There are no lasting effects?"

"We hope not. There haven't been so far. It's experimental."

"And illegal."

She shrugged. "Naturally. Isn't everything fun?"

He wanted to tell her how irresponsible that was, but he sensed she would be bored with him if he belabored it and while he did not care if Montgomery was bored with him, he did not want to be tiresome with her. So when she offered another tentative smile, he smiled back, and she grinned, showing him that gap between her front teeth which had made a fortune for the world's dentists when one hundred million girls copied it.

She had one of the most famous faces in the world, but she did not closely resemble herself as depicted on television. The screen missed most of her depth, which centered on her wide eyes and small nose, was framed by her short blonde curls. A faint series of lines around her mouth betrayed the fact that she was not twenty, as she looked at first glance, but well into her thirties. Her skin was pale, and she was taller than she seemed in pictures, and her arms and legs were even thinner.

"They compensate for that with camera angles," she said, and he realized she was not reading his mind but merely noticing where he was looking. He had given her a stock reaction, one she got every day, and he hated that. He resolved not to ask any questions about her sidekick. She had heard them all and was surely as sick of them as he was of his nickname.

"Will you join us?" she asked. "I promise we won't misbehave again."

He looked back at the three, just visible at their table before the curved roof cut off his view of the corridor promenade, gee/1 level.

"I'd rather not. Maybe I shouldn't say this, but those are pretty stock types. I always want to either sneer at them or run away from them."

She leaned closer.

"Me too. Will you rescue me?"

"What do you mean?"

"Those three could teach limpets a thing or two about clinging. That's their job, but the hell with them."

"What do you want to do?"

"How should I know? Whatever people do around here for a good time. Bob for apples, ride on the merry-go-round, screw, play cards, see a show."

"I'm interested in at least one of those."

"So you like cards, too?" She glanced back at her crew. "I think they're getting suspicious."

"Then let's go." He took her arm and started to walk away with her. Suddenly she was running down a corridor. He hesitated only a second, then was off after her.

He was not surprised to see her stumble. She recovered quickly, but it slowed her enough for him to catch her.

"What happened?" she said. "I thought I was falling—" She pulled back her sleeve and stared at the world's most complicated wristwatch. He realized it was some sort of monitor for her sidekick.

"It isn't your hardware," he said, leading her at a fast walk. "You were running with the spin. You got heavier. You should bear in mind that what you're feeling isn't gravity."

"But how will we get away if we can't run?"

"By going just a little faster than they do." He looked back, and as he had expected, Lopez was already down. Coco was wavering between turning back to help and following Montgomery, who was still coming, wearing a determined expression. Cooper grinned. He had finally succeeded in getting the man's attention. He was making off with the star.

Just beyond stairwell C Cooper pulled Galloway into an elevator whose door was closing. He had a glimpse of Montgomery's outraged face.

"What good will this do us?" Galloway wanted to know. "He'll just follow us up the stairs. These things are slow as the mid-town express."

"They're slow for a very good reason, known as coriolis force," Cooper said, reaching into his pocket for his keys. He inserted one in the control board of the elevator. "Since we're on the bottom level, Montgomery will go up. It's the only direction the stairs go." He twisted the key, and the elevator began to descend.

The two "basement" levels were the parts of the Champagne Hotel complex nearest hard vacuum. The car stopped on B level and he held the door for her. They walked among exposed pipes, structural cables, and beams not masked by the frothy decorations of the public levels. The only light came from bare bulbs spaced every five meters. The girders and the curved floor made the space resemble the innards of a zeppelin.

"How hard will they look for you?"

She shrugged. "They won't be fooling around. They'll keep it up until they find me. It's only a question of time."

"Can they get me in trouble?"

"They'd love to. But I won't let them."

"Thanks."

"It's the least I could do."

"So my room is out. First place they'd look."

"No, they'd check my room first. It's better equipped for playing cards."

He was mentally kicking himself. She was playing games with him, he knew that, but what was the game? If it was just sex, that was okay. He'd never made love with a woman in a sidekick.

"About your nickname . . ." she said, leaving the sentence unfinished to see how he would react. When he said nothing, she started over. "Is it your favorite swimming distance? I seem to recall you were accused of never exerting yourself more than the situation required."

"Wouldn't it be foolish if I did?" But the label still rankled. It was true he had never turned in a decent time just swimming laps, and that he seldom won a race by more than a meter. The sports media had never warmed to him because of that, even before he failed to win the gold. For some reason, they thought of him as lazy, and most people assumed his nickname meant he would prefer to swim races of no more than a quarter of a meter.

"No, that's not it," was all he would say, and she dropped the subject.

The silence gave him time to reflect, and the more he did, the less happy he was. She had said she could keep him out of trouble, but could she? When it came to a showdown, who had more clout with BCE? The Golden Gypsy, or her producers? He might be risking a lot, and she was risking nothing at all. He knew he should ditch her but, if he spurned her now, she might withdraw what protection she could offer.

"I sense you don't care for your nickname," she said, at last. "What should I call you? What's your real name?"

"I don't like that, either. Call me Q.M."

"Must I?" she sighed.

"Everybody else does."

He took her to Eliot's room because Eliot was in the infirmary and because Montgomery and company would not look for them there. They drank some of Eliot's wine, talked for a while, and made love.

The sex was pleasant, but nothing to shout about. He was surprised at how little the sidekick got in his way. Though it was all over her body, it was warm and most of it was flexible, and he soon forgot about it.

Finally she kissed him and got dressed. She promised to see him again soon. He thought she said something about love. It struck him as a grotesque thing to say, but by then he was not listening very hard. There was an invisible wall between them and most of it belonged to her. He had tried to penetrate it—not very hard, he admitted to himself—but a good ninety-nine percent of her was in a fiercely-guarded place he was sure he'd never see. He shrugged mentally. It was certainly her right.

He was left with a bad post-coital depression. It had not been one of his finer moments. The best thing to do about it was to put it behind him and try not to do it again. It was not long before he realized he was doing uncommonly well at that already. Reclining naked on the bed, gazing at the ceiling, he could not recall a single thing she had said.

What with one thing and another, he did not get back to his room until late. He did not turn on the light because he did not want to wake Anna-Louise. And he walked with extra care because he was not balancing as well as he might. There had been a few drinks.

Still, she woke up, as she always did. She pressed close to him under the covers, her body warm and humid and musky, her breath a little sour as she kissed him. He was half-drunk and she was half-awake, but when her hands began to pull and her hips to thrust forward insistently he found to his surprise that he was ready and so was she. She guided him, then eased over onto her side and let him nestle in behind her. She drew her knees up and hugged them. Her head was pillowed on his arm. He kissed the back of her smooth scalp and nibbled her ear, then let his head fall into the pillow and moved against her slowly for a peaceful few minutes. At last she stretched, squeezing him, making small fists, digging her toes into his thighs.

"How did you like her?" she mumbled.

"Who?"

"You know who."

He was pretty sure he could pull off a lie, because Anna-Louise couldn't be *that* sure, and then he frowned in the darkness, because he had never wanted to lie to her before.

So he said, "Do you know me that well?"

She stretched again, this time more sensually, to more of a purpose than simply getting the sleepiness out of her system.

"How should I know? My nose didn't give me a chance to find out. I smelled the liquor on your breath when you came in, but I smelled her on my fingers after I touched you."

"Come *on.*"

"Don't get mad." She reached around to pat his buttocks while at the same time pressing herself back against him. "Okay, so I guessed at the identity. It didn't take much intuition."

"It was lousy," he admitted.

"I'm so sorry." He knew she really was, and did not know if that made him happy or sad. It was a hell of a thing, he thought, not to know something as basic as that.

"It's a damn shame," she went on. "Fucking should never be lousy."

"I agree."

"If you can't have fun doing it, you shouldn't do it."

"You're one hundred per cent right."

He could just see her teeth in the darkness; he had to imagine the rest of her grin, but he knew it well.

"Do you have anything left for me?"

"There's a very good chance that I do."

"Then what do you say we just skip the next part and *wake up?*"

She shifted gears so fast he had a hard time keeping up at first; she was all over him and she was one of the strongest women he knew. She liked to wrestle. Luckily, there were no losers in her matches. It was everything the encounter with Galloway had not been. That was no surprise; it *always* was. Sex with Anna-Louise was very good indeed. For that matter, so was everything else.

He lay there in the dark long after she had gone to sleep, their bodies spooned together just as they had begun, and he thought long and hard and as clearly as he could. Why not? Why not Anna-Louise? She could care if he gave her the chance. And maybe he could, too.

He sighed, and hugged her tighter. She murmured like a big, happy cat, and began to snore.

He would talk to her in the morning, tell her what he had been thinking. They would begin the uncertain process of coming to know each other.

Except that he woke with a hangover, Anna-Louise had already showered, dressed, and gone, and someone was knocking on his door.

He stumbled out of bed and it was her, Galloway. He had a bad moment of disorientation, wishing that famous face would get back on the television screen where it belonged. But somehow she was in his room, though he did not recall standing aside to admit her. She was smiling, smiling, and talking so fast he could barely understand her. It was an inane rattle about how good it was to see him and how nice the room was, as her eyes swept him and the room from head to toe and corner to corner until he was sure she knew Anna-Louise better than he did himself, just from the faint traces she had left on the bare impersonal cubicle.

This was going to be difficult. He closed the door and padded to the bed, where he sank gratefully and put his face in his hands.

When she finally ran down he looked up. She was perched on the edge of the room's only chair, hands laced together on her knees. She looked so bright and chipper he wanted to puke.

"I quit my job," she said. It took a while for that to register. In time, he was able to offer a comment.

"Huh?" he said.

"I quit. Just said screw this and walked out. All over, ka-put, down the toilet. Fuck it." Her smile looked unhealthy.

"Oh." He thought about that, listening to the dripping of the bathroom faucet. "Ah . . . what will you do?"

"Oh, no problem, no problem." She was bouncing a little now. One knee bobbed in four-four time while the other waltzed. Perhaps that should have told him something. Her head jerked to the left, and there was a whine as it slowly straightened.

"I've had offers from all over," she went on. "CBS would sacrifice seven virgin vice-presidents on a stone altar to sign me up. NAAR and Telecommunion are fighting a pitched battle across Sixth Avenue at this very moment, complete with tanks and nerve gas. Shit, I'm already pulling down half the GNP of Costa Rica, and they all want to triple that."

"Sounds like you'll do all right," he ventured. He was alarmed. The head movement was repeating now, and her heels were hammering the floor. He had finally figured out that the whining noise was coming from her sidekick.

"Oh, bugger them, too," she said easily. "Independent production, that's for me. Doing my own thing. I'll show you some tapes. No more LCD, no more Trendex. Just me and a friend or two."

"LCD?"

"Lowest common denominator. My audience. Eight-year-old minds in thirty-one-point-three-six-year-old bodies. Demographics. Brain-cancer victims."

"Television made them that way," he said.

"Of course. And they loved it. Nobody could ever underestimate them, and nobody could ever give them enough crap. I'm not even going to try anymore.''

She stood up, turned·at the waist, and knocked the door off its hinges. It clattered into the hallway, teetering around the deep dimple her fist had made in the metal.

All that would have been bizarre enough, but when the noise had finally stopped she still stood there, arm extended, fist clenched, half turned at the waist. The whining sound was louder now, accompanied by something resembling the wail of a siren. She looked over her shoulder.

"Oh, darn it," she said, in a voice that rose in pitch with every word. "I think I'm stuck." And she burst into tears.

Cooper was no stranger to the ways of the super-rich and super-famous. He had thought he understood clout. He soon learned he knew nothing about it.

He got her calmed in a few minutes. She eventually noticed the small crowd that had gathered beyond the space where his door had been, whispering and pointing at the woman sitting on Cooper's bed with her arm stuck in an odd position. Her eyes grew cold, and she asked for his telephone.

Thirty seconds after her first call, eight employees of BCE arrived in the hallway outside. Guards herded the audience away and engineers erected a new door, having to remove two twisted hinges to do so. It was all done in less than four minutes, and by then Galloway had completed her second call.

She made three calls, none of them over two minutes long. In one, she merely chatted with someone at the Telecommunion. Network and mentioned, in passing, that she had a problem with her sidekick. She listened, thanked the person on the other end, and hung up. The call to GM&L, the conglom that owned Sidekick, Incorporated, was businesslike and short.

Two hours later a repairman from Sidekick knocked at the door. It was not until the next day that Cooper realized the man had been on the Earth's surface when he got the call, that his trip had involved a special ship boosting at one gee all the way and carrying no cargo but himself and his tool kit, which he opened and plugged into the wall computerminal before starting to work on the sidekick.

But in those two hours . . .

•   •   •

"If you'd like me to leave, I'll leave," she said, sipping her third glass of Cooper's wine.

"No, please."

She was still frozen like a frame from a violent film. Her legs worked and so did her right arm, but from her hips all the way up her back and down her left arm the sidekick had shorted out. It looked awfully uncomfortable. He asked if there was anything he could do.

"It's okay, really," she said, resting her chin on the arm that crossed in front of her.

"Will they be able to fix it?"

"Oh, sure." She tossed down the rest of the wine. "And if they can't, I'll just stay here and you'll have a real conversation piece. A human hatrack." She picked her shirt off the couch beside her and draped it over her frozen arm, then smiled at him. It was not a pretty smile.

He had helped her get the shirt off. It had been like undressing a statue. The idea had been to check the sidekick core for hot spots and visible cracks, which would necessitate the quick removal of the apparatus. It was clearly a project she did not relish. But as far as he had been able to see the thing was physically intact. The damage was on the electronic level.

It was the closest look he had yet taken at the technological marvel of the age, closer even than the night before, when he had made love to her. Then, manners had prevented him from staring. Now he had a perfect excuse, and he used it.

When he thought about it, it was frightening that they could pack so much power into a mechanism that, practically speaking, was hardly even there. The most massive part of the sidekick was the core, which was segmented, padded in flesh-toned soft plastic, and hugged her spine from the small of the back to the nape of her neck. Nowhere was it more than three centimeters thick.

Radiating from the core was an intricate network of gold chains, bands, and bracelets, making such a cunningly contrived system that one could almost believe it was all decoration rather than the conductors for energized fields that allowed her to move. Woven belts of fine gold wire criss-crossed like bandoliers between her breasts and just happened to connect, via a fragile gold chain, with the sinuous gooseneck that was concealed by her hair before it attached to the back of the golden tiara that made her look like Wonder Woman. Helical bands fashioned to look like snakes coiled down her arms, biting each other's tails until the last ones attached to thick, jewel-encrusted bracelets around her wrists, which in turn sprouted hair-fine wires that transformed themselves into finger rings, one for each joint, each inset with a single diamond. Elsewhere the effect was much the same. Each piece, taken by itself, was a beautiful piece of jewelry. The worst that could be said about Megan Galloway in the "nude" was that she was ostentatiously bejeweled. If one didn't mind that, she was absolutely stunning: a gilded Venus, or a fantasy artist's Amazon in full, impractical armor. Dressed, she was just like anyone else except for the tiara and the rings. There were no edges on her sidekick to savage clothes or poke out at unnatural angles. Cooper guessed this was as important to Galloway as the fact that the sidekick was a beautiful object, emphatically not an orthopedic appliance.

"It's unique," she said. "One of a kind."

"I didn't mean to stare."

"Heavens," she said. "You weren't staring. You are so pointedly *not* staring that your fascination must be intense. And no . . . don't say anything." She held up her free hand and waited for him to settle back in his chair. "Please, no more apologies. I've got a pretty good idea of the problem I present to somebody with both manners and curiosity, and it was shitty of me to say that about not staring. That puts you in the wrong whatever you do, huh?" She leaned back against the wall, getting comfortable as she could while waiting for the repairman to arrive.

"I'm proud of the damned thing, Cooper. That's probably obvious. And of course I've answered the same questions so many times that it bores me, but for you, since you're providing me a refuge in an embarrassing moment, I'll tell you anything you want to know."

"Is it really gold?"

"Twenty-four carat, solid."

"That's where your nickname comes from, I presume."

She looked puzzled for a moment, then her face cleared.

"Touché. I don't like that nickname any more than you like yours. And no, it's no more correct than yours is. At first, *I* wasn't the Golden Gypsy. The sidekick was. That was the name of this model sidekick. But they've still only made one of them, and before long, the name rubbed off on me. I discourage it."

Cooper understood that too well.

He asked more questions. Before long the explanations got too technical for him. He was surprised that she knew as much about it as she did. Her knowledge stopped short of the mathematics of Tunable Deformation Fields, but that was her only limit. TDF's were what had made the Bubble possible, since they could be made to resonate with particular molecular or atomic structures. The Bubble's fields were turned to attract or repel H_2O, while the fields generated by Galloway's sidekick influenced gold, Au^{197}, and left everything else alone. She went on to tell him far more than he could absorb about the ways in which the fields were generated in the sidekick core, shaped by wave guides buried in the jewelry, and deformated ("Physics terms are usually inelegant," she apologized), to the dictates of nanocomputers scattered throughout the hardware, operating by a process she called "augmented neuro-feedback holistitopology."

"The English of which is . . ." he pleaded.

". . . that I think of pressing the middle valve down, the music goes round and round and it comes out here." She held out her hand and depressed the middle finger. "You would weep to know how many decisions the core made to accomplish that simple movement."

"On the other hand," he said, and rushed on when he remembered what had happened to her other hand, "what goes on in my brain to do the same thing is complex, but I don't have to program it. It's done for me. Isn't it much the same with you?"

"Much. Not exactly. If they made one of these for you and plugged you in right now, you'd twitch a lot. In a few weeks you'd patty-cake pretty well. But in a year you'd not even think about it. The brain re-trains itself. Which is a simple way of saying you struggle day and night for six or seven months with something that feels totally unnatural and eventually you learn to do it. Having done it, you know that learning to tap-dance on the edge of a razor blade would be a snap."

"You say you've heard all the questions. What's your least favorite?"

"God, you're merciless, aren't you? There's no contest. 'How did you hurt yourself?' To answer the question you so cleverly didn't ask, I broke my fool neck when me and my hang-glider got into an argument with a tree. The tree won.

Many years later I went back and chopped that tree down, which just *may* be the stupidest thing I ever did, not counting today.'' She looked at him and raised one eyebrow. ''Aren't you going to ask me about that?''

He shrugged.

''The funny thing is, that's the question I *want* you to ask. Because it's tied up with what we did yesterday, and that's really what I came here to talk to you about.''

''So talk,'' he said, wondering what she could have to say about it beyond the fact that it had been hideous, and demeaning to both of them.

''It was the worst sexual experience I ever had,'' she said. ''And you bear zero percent responsibility for that. Please don't interrupt. There are things you don't know about.

''I know you don't think much of my profession—I *really* don't want you to interrupt, or I'll never get all this out; if you disagree you can tell me when I'm through.

''You'd be a pretty strange lifeguard if you were a fan of the trans-tapes, or if you didn't feel superior to the kind of people who buy them. You're young, fairly well-educated and fairly articulate, you've got a good body and an attractive face and the opposite sex neither terrifies nor intimidates you. You are out on the end of *all* the bell-curves, demographically. You are *not* my audience, and people who *aren't* my audience tend to *look down* on my audience, and usually on me and my kind, too. And I don't blame them. Me and my kind have taken what might have been a great art-form and turned it into something so exploitative that even Hollywood and Sixth Avenue gag at it.

''You know as well as I do that there are many, many people growing up now who wouldn't know an honest, geniune, self-originated emotion if it kicked them in the behind. If you take their Transers away from them they're practically zombies.

''For a long time I've flattered myself that I'm a little better than the industry in general. There are some tapes I've made that will back me up on that. Things I've taken a chance on, things that try to be more complex than the LCD would dictate. *Not* my bread-and-butter tapes. Those are as simple-headed as the worst hack travelogue. But I've tried to be like the laborers in other artistic sweatshops of the past. Those few who managed to turn out something with some merit, like some directors of Hollywood westerns which were never meant to be anything but crowd pleasers and who still produced some works of art, or a handful of television producers who . . . none of this is familiar to you, is it? Sorry, I didn't mean to get academic. I've made a study of it, of art in the mass culture.

"All those old art-forms had undergrounds, independents who struggled along with no financing and produced things of varying quality but with some *vision*, no matter how weird. Trans-tapes are more expensive than films or television but there is an underground. It's just so far under it practically never comes to light. Believe it or not, it's possible to produce great art in emotional recording. I could name names, but you will not have heard of any of them. And I'm not talking about the people who make tapes about how it feels to kill somebody; that's another underground entirely.

"But things are getting tight. It used to be that we could make a good living and still stay away from the sex tapes. Let me add that I don't feel contempt for the people who make sex tapes. Given the state of our audience, it has become necessary that many of them have their well-worn jerk-off cassette, so when they get horny they know what to do with it. Most of them wouldn't have the vaguest notion otherwise. I just didn't want to make them myself. It's axiomatic in the trade that love is the one emotion that cannot be recorded, and if I can't have—"

"I'm sorry," Cooper said, "but I have to interrupt there. I've never heard that. In fact, I've heard just the opposite."

"You've been listening to our commercials," she reproved. "Get that shit out of your head, Cooper. It's pure hype." She rubbed her forehead, and sighed. "Oh, all right. I wasn't precise enough. I can make a tape of how I love my mother or my father or anybody I'm already in love with. It's not easy to do—it's the less subtle emotions that are more readily transed. But nobody has ever recorded the process of falling in love. It's sort of a Heisenberg Principle of transing, and nobody's sure if the limitation is in the equipment or in the person being recorded, but it exists, and there are some very good reasons to think nobody will ever succeed in recording that kind of love."

"I don't see why not," Cooper confessed. "It's supposed to be very intense, isn't it? And you said the strong emotions are the easiest to tape."

"That's true. But . . . well, try to visualize it. I've got my job because I'm better at ignoring all the hardware involved in transing. It's because of my sidekick; I mean, if I can learn to forget I'm operating *that* I can ignore anything. That's why the nets scour the trauma wards of hospitals looking for potential stars. It's like . . . well, in the early days of sex research they had people fuck in laboratories, with wires taped to them. A lot of people just couldn't do it. They were too self-conscious. Hook most people up to a transcorder and what you get is 'Oh, how interesting it is to be making a tape, look at all those people watching me, look at all those cameras, how interesting, now I have to forget about them, I must forget about them I just *must* forget—' "

Cooper held up his hand, nodding. He was recalling seeing her burst from the water that first day in the Bubble, and his feelings as he watched her.

"So the essence of making a tape," she went on, "is the ability to ignore the fact that you're making one. To react just as you would have reacted if you *weren't* doing it. It calls for some of the qualities of an actor, but most actors can't do it. They think too much about the process. They can't be natural about it. That's my talent: to feel natural in unnatural circumstances.

"But there are limits. You can fuck up a storm while transing, and the tape will record how good everything feels and how goddam happy you are to be fucking. But it all falls apart when the machine is confronted with that moment of first falling in love. Either that, or the person being recorded just can't get into the *frame of mind* to fall in love while transing. The distraction of the transer itself makes that emotional state impossible.

"But I really got off on a tangent there. I'd appreciate it if you'd just hear me out until I've said what I have to say." She rubbed her forehead again, and looked away from him.

"We were talking economics. You have to make what sells. My sales have been dropping off. I've specialized in what we call 'elbow-rubbers.' 'You, too, can go to fancy places with fancy people. You, too, can be important, recognized, appreciated.' " She made a face. "I also do the sort of thing we've been making in the Bubble. Sensuals, short of sex. Those, frankly, are not selling so well anymore. The snob-tapes still do well, but everybody makes those. What you're marketing there is your celebrity, and mine is falling off. The competition has been intense.

"That's why I . . . well, it was Markham who talked me

into it. I've been on the verge of going into heavy-breathers."
She lifted her eyes. "I assume you know what those are."

Cooper nodded, remembering what Anna-Louise had said.
So even Galloway could not stay out of it.

She sighed deeply, but no longer looked away from him.

"Anyway, I wanted to make something just a *little bit*
better than the old tired in-and-outers. You know: 'Door-to-
door salesman enters living room; "I'd like to show you my
samples, ma'am." Woman rips open nightgown; "Take a
look at these samples, buster." Fade to bed.' I thought that
for my first sex-tape I'd try for something more erotic than
salacious. I wanted a romantic situation, and if I couldn't get
some love in it at least I'd try for affection. It would be with a
handsome guy I met unexpectedly. He'd have some aura of
romance about him. Maybe there'd be an argument at first,
but the irresistible attraction would bring us together in spite of
it, and we'd make love and part on a slightly tragic note since
we'd be from different worlds and it could never . . ."

Tears were running down her cheeks. Cooper realized his
mouth was open. He was leaning toward her, too astonished
at first to say anything.

"You and me . . ." he finally managed to say.

"Shit, Cooper, *obviously* you and me."

"And you thought that . . . that what we did last night . . .
did you really think that was worth a tape? I knew it was bad,
but I had no inkling *how* bad it could be. I knew you were
using me—hell, I was using you, too, and I didn't like that
any better—but I never thought it was so cynical—"

"No, no, *no, no, no!*" She was sobbing now. "It wasn't
that. It was *worse* than that! It was supposed to be *spontaneous*,
damn it! *I* didn't pick you out. *Markham* was going to do
that. He would find someone, coach him, arrange a meeting,
conceal cameras to tape the meeting and in the bedroom later.
I'd never really *know*. We've been studying an old show
called *Candid Camera* and using some of their techniques.
They're *always* throwing something unexpected at me, trying
to help me stay fresh. That's Markham's job. But how surprised can I be when you show up at my table? Just look at it:
in the romantic Bubble, the handsome lifeguard—*lifeguard*,
for pete's sake!—an Olympic athlete familiar to millions from
their television sets, gets pissed at my rich, decadent friends
. . . I couldn't have gotten a more clichéd script from the
most drug-brained writer in Television City!"

For a time there was no sound in the room but her quiet sobs. Cooper looked at it from all angles, and it didn't look pretty from any of them. But he had been just as eager to go along with the script as she had.

"I wouldn't have your job for anything," he said.

"Neither would I," she finally managed to say. "And I *don't,* damn it. You want to know what happened this morning? Markham showed me just how original he really is. I was eating breakfast and this guy—he was a lifeguard, are you ready?—he tripped over his feet and dropped his plate in my lap. Well, while he was cleaning me up he started dropping cute lines at a rate that would have made Neil Simon green. Sorry, getting historical again. Let's just say he sounded like he was reading from a script . . . he made that shitty little scene we played out together yesterday seem just wonderful. His smile was phony as a brass transistor. I realized what had happened, what I'd done to you, so I pushed the son of a bitch down into his French toast, went to find Markham, broke his fucking jaw for him, quit my job, and came here to apologize. And went a little crazy and broke your door. So I'm sorry, I really am, and I'd leave but I've busted my sidekick and I can't *stand* to have people staring at me like that, so I'd like to stay here a little longer, until the repairman gets here, and I don't have any notion of what I'm going to *do.*"

What composure she had managed to gather fell apart once again, and she wept bitterly.

By the time the repairman arrived Galloway was back in control.

The repairman's name was Snyder. He was a medical doctor as well as a cybertechnician, and Cooper supposed that combination allowed him to set any price he fancied for his services.

Galloway went into the bedroom and got all the clean towels. She spread them on the bed, then removed her clothes. She reclined, face down, with the towels making a thick pad from her knees to her waist. She made herself as comfortable as she could with her arm locked in the way, and waited.

Snyder fiddled with the controls in his tool kit, touched needle-sharp probes to various points on the sidekick core, and Galloway's arm relaxed. He made more connections, there was a high whine from the core, and the sidekick

opened like an iron maiden. Each bracelet, chain, amulet and
ring separated along invisible join lines. Snyder then went to
the bed, grasped the sidekick with one hand around the center
of the core, and lifted it away from her. He set it on its
"feet," where it promptly assumed a parade-rest stance.

There was an Escher print Cooper had seen, called "Rind,"
that showed the bust of a woman as if her skin had been
peeled off and arranged in space to suggest the larger thing
she had once been. Both the inner and outer surfaces of the
rind could be seen, like one barber-pole stripe painted over an
irregular, invisible surface. Galloway's sidekick, minus Galloway, looked much like that. It was one continuous, though
convoluted, entity, a thing of springs and wires, too fragile to
stand on its own but doing it somehow. He saw it shift
slightly to maintain its balance. It seemed all too alive.

Galloway, on the other hand, looked like a rag doll. Snyder
motioned to Cooper with his eyes, and the two of them turned
her on her back. She had some control of her arms, and her
head did not roll around as he had expected it to. There was a
metal wire running along her scarred spine.

"I was an athlete, too, before the accident," she said.

"Were you?"

"Well, not in your class. I was fifteen when I cracked my
neck, and I wasn't setting the world on fire as a runner. For a
girl that's already too old."

"Not strictly true," Cooper said. "But it's a lot harder
after that." She was reaching for the blanket with hands that
did not work very well. Coupled with her inability to raise
herself from the bed, it was a painful process to watch.
Cooper reached for the edge of the blanket.

"No," she said, matter-of-factly. "Rule number one. Don't
help a crip unless she asks for it. No matter how badly she's
doing something, just don't. She's got to learn to ask, and
you've got to learn to let her do what she *can* do."

"I'm afraid I've never known any crips."

"Rule number two. A nigger can call herself a nigger and a
cripple can call herself a cripple, but lord help the able-bodied
white who uses either word."

Cooper settled back in his chair.

"Maybe I'd better just shut up until you fill me in on all
the rules."

She grinned at him. "It'd take all day. And frankly, maybe
some of them are self-contradictory. We can be a pretty

prickly lot, but I ain't going to apologize for it. You've got your body and I don't have mine. That's not your fault, but I think I hate you a little because of it.''

Cooper thought about that. ''I think I probably would, too.''

''Yeah. It's nothing serious. I came to terms with it a long time ago, and so would you, after a bad couple of years.'' She still hadn't managed to reach the blanket, and at last she gave it up and asked him to do it for her. He tucked it around her neck.

There were other things he thought he would like to know, but he felt she must have reached the limits of questioning, no matter what she said. And he was no longer quite so eager to know the answers. He had been about to ask what the towels on the bed were for, then suddenly it was obvious what they were for and he couldn't imagine why he hadn't known it at once. He simply knew nothing about her, and nothing about disability. And he was a little ashamed to admit it, but he was not sure he *wanted* to know any more.

There was no way he could keep the day's events from Anna-Louise, even if he had wanted to. The complex was buzzing with the story of how the Golden Gypsy had blown a fuse, though the news about her quitting her job was still not general knowledge. He was told the story three different times during his next shift. Each story was slightly different, but all approximated the truth. Most of the tellers seemed to think it was funny. He supposed he would have, too, yesterday.

Anna-Louise inspected the door hinges when they got back from work.

''She must have quite a right hook,'' she said.

''Actually, she hit it with her left. Do you want to hear about it?''

''I'm all ears.''

So he told her the whole story. Cooper had a hard time figuring out how she was taking it. She didn't laugh, but she didn't seem too sympathetic, either. When he was through— mentioning Galloway's incontinence with some difficulty— Anna-Louise nodded, got up, and started toward the bathroom.

''You've led a sheltered life, Q.M.''

''What do you mean?''

She turned, and looked angry for the first time.

"I mean you sound as if incontinence was the absolute worst thing you'd ever heard of in your life."

"Well, what is it, then? No big thing?"

"It certainly isn't to *that* woman. For most people with her problem, it means catheters and feces bags. Or diapers. Like my grandfather wore for the last five years of his life. The operations she's had to fix it, and the hardware, implanted and external . . . well, it's damn expensive, Q.M. You can't afford it on the money grandfather was getting from the State, and Conglomerate health plans won't pay for it, either."

"Oh, so that's it. Just because she's rich and can afford the best treatment, her problems don't amount to anything. Just how would *you* like to—"

"Wait a minute, hold on . . ." She was looking at him with an expression that would not hold still, changing from sympathy to disgust. "I don't want to fight with you. I know it wouldn't be pleasant to have my neck broken, even if I was a trillionaire." She paused, and seemed to be choosing her words carefully.

"I'm bothered by something here," she said, at last. "I'm not even sure what it is. I'm concerned about you, for one thing. I still think it's a mistake to get involved with her. I like you. I don't want to see you hurt."

Cooper suddenly remembered his resolve of the night before, as she lay sleeping at his side. It confused him terribly. Just what *did* he feel for Anna-Louise? After the things Galloway had told him about love and the lies of the Transer commercials, he didn't know what to think. It was pitiful, when he thought about it, that he was as old as he was and hadn't the vaguest notion what love might be, that he had actually assumed the place to find it, when the time came, was on trans-tapes. It made him angry.

"What are you talking about, hurt?" he retorted. "She's not dangerous. I'll admit she lost control there for a moment, and she's strong, but—"

"Oh, help!" Anna-Louise moaned. "What am I supposed to do with these emotionally stunted smoggies who think nothing is real unless they've been told by somebody on the—"

"Smoggies? You called me a racist when—"

"Okay, I'm sorry." He complained some more but she just shook her head and wouldn't listen and he eventually sputtered to a stop.

"Finished? Okay. I'm getting crazy here. I've only got one more month before I go back home. And I do find most Earthlings—is that a neutral enough term for you?—I find them weird. *You're* not so bad, most of the time, except you don't seem to have much notion about what life is *for*. You like to screw and you like to swim. Even *that* is twice as much purpose as most sm—, Terrans seem to have."

"You . . . you're going?"

"Surprise!" Her tone dripped sarcasm.

"But why didn't you tell me?"

"You never asked. You never asked about a lot of things. I don't think you ever realized I might like to tell you about my life, or that it might be any different from yours."

"You're wrong. I sensed a difference."

She raised an eyebrow and seemed about to say something, but changed her mind. She rubbed her forehead, then took a deep, decisive breath.

"I'm almost sorry to hear that. But I'm afraid it's too late to start over. I'm moving out." And she began packing.

Cooper tried to argue with her but it did no good. She assured him she wasn't leaving because she was jealous; she even seemed amused that he thought that might be the reason. And she also claimed she was not going to move in with Yuri Feldman. She intended to live her last month in the Bubble alone.

"I'm going back to Luna to do what I planned to do all along," she said, tying the drawstring of her duffel bag. "I'm going to the police academy. I've saved enough now to put me through."

"Police?" Cooper could not have been more astonished if she had said she intended to fly to Mars by flapping her arms.

"You had no inkling, right? Well, why should you? You don't notice other people much unless you're screwing them. I'm not saying that's your fault; you've been trained to be that way. Haven't you ever wondered what I was doing here? It isn't the working conditions that drew me. I despise this place and all the people who come to visit. I don't even like water very much, and I *hate* that monstrous obscenity they call the Bubble."

Cooper was beyond shock. He had never imagined anyone could exist who would not be drawn by the magic of the Bubble.

"Then why? Why work here, and why do you hate it?"

"I hate it because people are starving in Pennsylvania," she said, mystifying him completely. "And I work here, God help me, because the pay is good, which you may not have noticed since you grew up comfortable. I would have said rich, but by now I know what real rich is. I grew up poor, Q.M. Another little detail you never bothered to learn. I've worked hard for everything, including the chance to come here to this disgusting pimp-city to provide a safety service for rich degenerates, because BCE pays in good, hard GWA Dollars. You probably never noticed, but Luna is having serious economic troubles because it's caught between a couple of your corporation-states . . . ah, forget it. Why worry your cute little head with things like that?"

She went to the door, opened it, then turned to look at him.

"Honestly, Q.M., I don't dislike you. I think I feel sorry for you. Sorry enough that I'm going to say once more you'd better watch out for Galloway. If you mess around with her right now, you're going to get hurt."

"I still don't understand how."

She sighed, and turned away.

"Then there's nothing more I can say. I'll see you around."

Megan Galloway had the Mississippi Suite, the best in the hotel. She didn't come to the door when Cooper knocked, but just buzzed him in.

She was sitting tailor-fashion on the bed, wearing a loose nightgown and a pair of wire-rimmed glasses and looking at a small box in front of her. The bed resembled a sternwheeler, with smoke and sparks shooting from the bedposts, and was larger than his entire room and bath. She put her glasses at the end of her nose and peered over them.

"Something I can do for you?"

He came around until he could see the box, which had a picture flickering dimly on one side of it.

"What's that?"

"Old-timey television," she said. "*Honey West*, circa 1965, American Broadcasting Company. Starring Anne Francis, John Ericson, and Irene Hervey, Friday nights at 2100. Spin-off from *Burke's Law*, died 1966. What's up?"

"What's wrong with the depth?"

"They didn't have it." She removed her glasses and began to chew absently on one rubber tip. "How are you doing?"

"I'm surprised to see you wear glasses."

"When you've had as many operations as I have, you skip the ones you think you can do without. Why is it I sense you're havng a hard time saying whatever it is you came here to say?"

"Would you like to go for a swim?"

"Pool's closed. Weekly filtering, or something like that."

"I know. Best possible time to go for a swim."

She frowned. "But I was told no one is admitted during the filtering."

"Yeah. It's illegal. Isn't everything that's fun?"

The Bubble was closed one hour in every twenty-four for accelerated filtering. At one time the place had been open all day, with filteration constantly operating, but then a client got past the three safety systems, where he was aerated, churned, irradiated, centrifuged, and eventually forced through a series of very fine screens. Most of him was still in the water in one form or another, and his legend had produced the station's first ghost.

But long before the Filtered Phantom first sloshed down the corridors the system had been changed. The filters never shut down completely, but while people were in the pool they were operated at slow speed. Once a day they were turned to full power.

It still wasn't enough. So every ten days BCE closed the pool for a longer period and gave the water an intensive treatment.

"I can't believe no one even watches it," Megan whispered.

"It's a mistake. Security is done by computer. There's twenty cameras in here but somebody forgot to tell the computer to squeal if it sees anybody enter during filteration. I got that from the computer itself, which thinks the whole fuck-up is very funny."

The hordes of swimmers had been gone for over two hours, and the clean-up crew had left thirty minutes before. Megan Galloway had probably thought she knew the Bubble pretty well, on the basis of her two visits. She was finding out now, as Cooper had done long ago, that she knew nothing. The difference between a resort beach on a holiday weekend and on a day in mid-winter was nothing compared to what she saw now.

It was perfectly still, totally clear: a crystal ball as big as the world.

"Oh, Cooper." He felt her hand tighten on his arm.

"Look. Down there. No, to the left." She followed his pointing finger and saw a school of the Bubble goldfish far below the surface, moving like lazy submarines, big and fat as watermelons and tame as park squirrels.

"Can I touch it, daddy?" she whispered, with the hint of a giggle. He pretended to consider it, then nodded. "I almost don't want to, you know?" she said. "Like a huge field covered in new snow, before anybody tracks across it."

"Yeah, I know." He sighed. "But it might as well be us. Hurry, before somebody beats you to it." He grinned at her, and pushed off slowly from his weightless perch on the sundeck tier that circled the rim of the champagne glass.

She pushed off harder and passed him before he was halfway there, as he had expected her to. The waves made by her entry spread out in perfect circles, then he broke the surface right behind her.

It was a different world.

When the Bubble had first been proposed, many years before, it had been suggested that it be a solid sphere of water, and that nothing but weightlessness and surface tension be employed to maintain it. Both forces came free of charge, which was a considerable factor in their favor.

But in the end, the builders had opted for TDF fields. This was because, while any volume of water would assume a spherical shape in free-fall, surface tension was not strong enough to keep it that way if it was disturbed. Such a structure would work fine so long as no swimmers entered to upset the delicate balance.

The TDF's provided the necessary unobtrusive force to keep things from getting messy. Tuned to attract or repel water, they also acted to force foreign matter toward either the inner or outer surfaces; in effect, making things that were *not* water float. A bar of lead floated better than a human body. Air bubbles also were pushed out. The fields were deliberately tuned to a low intensity. As a result, humans did not bob out of the water like corks but drifted toward a surface slowly, where they floated quite high in the water. As a further result, when the pool was open it was always churned by a billion bubbles.

When Cooper and Galloway entered the water the bubbles left behind by the happy throngs had long since merged with one of the larger volumes of air. The Bubble had become a magic lens, a piece of water with infinite curvature. It was nearly transparent with an aquamarine tint. Light was bent by it in enchanting ways, to the point that one could fancy the possibility of seeing all the way around it.

It distorted the world outside itself. The lifeguard station, cabanas, bar, and tanning chairs in the center were twisted almost beyond recognition, as if vanishing down the event horizon of a black hole. The rim of the glass, the deep violet field-dome that arched over it, and the circle of tanning chairs where patrons could brown themselves under genuine sunlight bent and flowed like a surrealist landscape. And everything, inside and outside the Bubble, oozed from one configuration to another as one changed position in the water. Nothing remained constant.

There was one exception to that rule. Objects in the water were not distorted. Galloway's body existed in a different plane, moved against the flowing, twisting background as an almost jarring intrusion of reality: pink flesh and golden metal, curly yellow hair, churning arms and legs. The stream of air ejected from her mouthpiece cascaded down the front of her body. It caressed her intimately, a thousand shimmering droplets of mercury, before it was thrashed to foam by her feet. She moved like a sleek aerial machine, streamlined, leaving a contrail behind her.

He customarily left his mouthpiece and collar-tank behind when he swam alone, but he was wearing it now, mostly so Galloway would not insist on removing hers, too. He felt the only decent way to swim was totally nude. He conceded the breathers were necessary for the crustaceans and plankton who did not understand the physical laws of the Bubble and who would never take the time to learn them. It was possible to get hopelessly lost, to become disoriented, unable to tell which was the shortest distance to air. Though bodies would float to a surface eventually, one could easily drown on the way out. The Bubble had no ends, deep or shallow. Thus the mouthpieces were required for all swimmers. They consisted of two semi-circular tanks that closed around the neck, a tube, a sensor that clipped to the ear, and the mouthpiece itself. Each contained fifteen minutes of oxygen, supplied on demand or when blood color changed enough to indicate it was needed. The devices automatically notified both the user and the lifeguard station when they were nearly empty.

It was a point of honor among the lifeguards to turn them in as full as they had been issued.

There were things one could do in the Bubble that were simply impossible in flat water. Cooper showed her some of the tricks, soon had her doing them herself. They burst from the water together, described long, lazy parabolas through the air, trailing comet tails of water. The TDF fields acted on the water in their bodies at all times, but it was such a lackadaisical force that it was possible to remain in the air for several minutes before surrendering to the inexorable center-directed impulse. They laced the water with their trails of foam, be-spattered the air with fine mist. They raced through the water, cutting across along a radial line, building up speed until they emerged on the inner surface to barrel across the width of the Bubble and re-enter, swam some more, and came up outside in the sunlight. If they went fast enough their momentum would carry them to the dark sun-field, which was solid enough to stand on.

He had had grave misgivings about asking her to come here with him. In fact, it had surprised him when he heard himself asking. For hours he had hesitated, coming to her door, going away, never knocking. Once inside it hadn't seemed possible to talk to her, particularly since he was far from sure he knew what he wanted to say. So he had brought her here, where talking was unnecessary. And the biggest surprise was that he was glad. It was fun to share this with someone. He wondered why he had never done it before. He wondered why he had never brought Anna-Louise, remembered the revelation of her real opinions of the place, and then turned away from thoughts of her.

It was strenuous play. He was in pretty good shape but was getting tired. He wondered if Galloway ever got tired. If she did, she seemed sustained by the heady joy of being there. She summed it up to him in a brief rest period at the outer rim.

"Cooper, you're a genius. We've just hijacked a swimming pool!"

The big clock at the lifeguard station told him it was time to quit, not so much because he needed the rest as because there was something he wanted her to see, something she would not expect. So he swam up to her and took her hand, motioned toward the rim of the glass, and saw her nod. He followed her as she built up speed.

He got her to the rim just in time. He pointed toward the sun, shielding his eyes, just as the light began to change. He squinted, and there it was. The Earth had appeared as a black disc, beginning to swallow the sun.

It ate more and more of it. The atmosphere created a light show that had no equal. Arms of amber encircled the black hole in the sky, changing colors quickly through the entire spectrum: pure, luminous colors against the deepest black imaginable. The sun became a brilliant point, seemed to flare sharply, and was gone. What was left was one side of the corona, the halo of Earth's air, and stars.

Millions of stars. If tourists ever complained about anything at the Bubble, it was usually that. There were no stars. The reason was simple: space was flooded with radiation. There was enough of it to fry an unprotected human. Any protection that could shut out that radiation would have to shut out the faint light of the stars as well. But now, with the sun in eclipse, the sensors in the field turned it clear as glass. It was still opaque to many frequencies, but that did not matter to the human eye. It simply vanished, and they were naked in space.

Cooper could not imagine a better time or place to make love, and that is exactly what they did.

"Enjoyed that a little more, did you?" she said.

"Uh." He was still trying to catch his breath. She rested her head against his chest and sighed in contentment.

"I can still hear your heart going crazy."

"My heart has seldom had such a workout."

"Nor a certain quarter of a meter, from the look of things."

He laughed. "So you figured that out. It's exaggerated."

"But a fifth of a meter would be an understatement, wouldn't you say?"

"I suppose so."

"So what's between? Nine fortieths? Who the hell needs a nickname like 'Nine-fortieths-of-a-meter Cooper'? That is about right, isn't it?"

"Close enough for rock and roll."

She thought about that for a time, then kissed him. "I'll bet you know, *exactly*. To the goddamn tenth of a millimeter. You'd *have* to, with a nickname like that." She laughed again, and moved in his arms. He opened his eyes and she was looking into them.

"This time I rock, and *you* roll," she suggested.

"I guess I'm getting older," he admitted, at last.

"You'd be a pretty odd fellow if you weren't."

He had to smile at that, and he kissed her again. "I only regret that we didn't get to see t' e sun come out."

"Well, I regret a little more than *that*." She studied his face closely, and seemed puzzled by what she found. "Damn. I never would have expected it, but I don't think you're really upset. For some reason, I don't feel the need to soothe your wounded ego."

He shrugged. "I guess not."

"What's your secret?"

"Just that I'm a realist, I guess. I never claimed to be superman. And I had a fairly busy night." He shut his eyes, not wanting to remember it. But the truth was that something *was* bothering him, and something else was warning him not to ask about it. He did, anyway.

"Not only did I have a rather full night," he said, "but I think I sensed a certain . . . well, you were less than totally enthusiastic, the second time. I think that put me off slightly."

"Did it, now?"

He looked at her face, but she did not seem angry, only amused.

"Was I right?"

"Certainly."

"What was wrong?"

"Not much. Only that I have absolutely no sensation from my toes to . . . right about here." She was holding her arm over her chest, just below her shoulders.

It was too much for him to take in all at once. When he began to understand what she was saying, he felt a terror beside which fear of impotence would have been a very minor annoyance.

"You can't mean . . . nothing I did had . . . you were faking it? Faking everything, the whole time? You felt—"

"That first night, yes, I was. Totally. Not very well, I presume, from your reaction."

". . . but just now . . ."

"Just now, it was something different. I really don't know if I could explain it to you."

"Please try." It was very important that she try, because he felt despair such as he had never imagined. "Can you . . .

is it all going through the motions? Is that it? You can't have sex, really?''

"I have a full and satisfying sex life,'' she assured him. "It's different than yours, and it's different from other women's. There are a lot of adaptations, a lot of new techniques my lovers must learn.''

"Will you—'' Cooper was interrupted by high-pitched, chittering squeals from the water. He glanced behind him, saw Charlie the Dolphin had been allowed to re-enter the Bubble, signaling the end of their privacy. Charlie knew about Cooper, was in on the joke, and always warned him when people were coming.

"We have to go now. Can we go back to your room, and . . . and will you teach me how?''

"I don't know if it's a good idea, friend. Listen, I enjoyed it, I loved it. Why don't we leave it that way?''

"Because I'm very ashamed. It never occurred to me.''

She studied him, all trace of levity gone from her face. At last, she nodded. He wished she looked more pleased about it.

But when they returned to her room she had changed her mind. She did not seem angry. She would not even talk about it. She just kept putting him off each time he tried to start something, not unkindly, but firmly, until he finally stopped pursuing the matter. She asked him then if he wanted to leave. He said no, and he thought her smile grew a little warmer at that.

So they built a fire in her fireplace with logs of real wood brought up from Earth. (''This fireplace must be the least energy-efficient heater humans have ever built,'' she said.) They curled up on the huge pillows scattered on the rug, and they talked. They talked long into the night, and this time Cooper had no trouble at all remembering what she said. Yet he would have been hard put to relate the conversation to anyone else. They spoke of trivia and of heartbreaks, sometimes in the same sentence, and it was hard to know what it all meant.

They popped popcorn, drank hot buttered rum from her autobar until they were both feeling silly, kissed a few times, and at last fell asleep, chaste as eight-year-olds at a slumber party.

• • •

For a week they were separated only when Cooper was on duty. He did not get much sleep, and he got no sex at all. It was his longest period of abstinence since puberty, and he was surprised at how little he felt the lack. There was another surprise, too. Suddenly he found himself watching the clock while he was working. The shift could not be over soon enough to suit him.

She was educating him, he realized that, and he did not mind. There was nothing dry or boring about the things they did together, nor did she demand that he share all her interests. In the process he expanded his tastes more in a week than he had in the previous ten years.

The outer, promenade level of the station was riddled with hole-in-the-wall restaurants, each featuring a different ethnic cuisine. She showed him there was more to food than hamburgers, steaks, potato chips, tacos, and fried chicken. She never ate *anything* that was advertised on television, yet her diet was a thousand times more varied than his.

"Look around you," she told him one night, in a Russian restaurant she assured him was better than any to be found in Moscow. "These are the people who own the companies that make the food you've been eating all your life. They pay the chemists who formulate the glop-of-the-month, they hire the advertising agencies who manufacture a demand for it, and they bank the money the proles pay for it. They do everything with it but *eat* it."

"Is there really something wrong with it?"

She shrugged. "Some of it used to cause problems, like cancer. Most of it's not very nutritious. They watched for carcinogens, but that's because a consumer with cancer eats less. As for nutrition, the more air the better. My rule of thumb is if they have to flog the stuff on television it *has* to be bad."

"Is everything on television bad, then?"

"Yes. Even me."

He was indifferent to clothes but liked to shop for them. She did not patronize the couturiers but put her wardrobe together from unlikely sources.

"Those high-priced designers work according to ancient laws," she told him. "They all work more or less together— though they don't plan it that way. I've decided that trite ideas are born simultaneously in mediocre minds. A fashion designer or a television writer or a studio executive cannot really be said to possess a mind at all. They're hive mentalities; they eat the sewage that floats on the surface of the mass culture, digest it, and then get creative diarrhea—all at once. The turds look and smell exactly alike, and we call them this year's fashions, hit shows, books, and movies. The key to dressing is to look at what everyone else is wearing then avoid it. Find a creative person who had never thought of designing clothes, and ask her to come up with something."

"You don't look like that on television," he pointed out.

"Ah, my *dear*. That's my job. A Celebrity must be homogenized with the culture that believes she *is* a Celebrity. I couldn't even get *on* the television dressed like I am now; the Taste Arbiter would consult its trendex and throw up its hands and have a screaming snit. But take note; the way I'm dressed now is the way everyone will be dressed in about a month."

"Do you like that?"

"Better than I like getting into costume for a guest spot on the *Who's Hot, Who's Shit?* show. This way the designers are watching me instead of the other way around." She laughed, and nudged him with her elbow. "Remember drop-seat pajamas, about a year and a half ago? That was mine. I wanted to see how far they'd go. They ate it up. Didn't you think that was funny?"

Cooper did recall thinking they were funny when they first came around. But then, somehow, they looked sexy. Soon a girl looked frumpy without that rectangle of flannel flapping against the backs of her thighs. Later, another change had happened, the day he realized the outfits were old-fashioned.

"Remember tail-fins on shoes? That was mine too."

One night she took him through part of her library of old tapes.

After her constant attacks on television, he was not prepared for her fondness, her genuine love, for the buried antiques of the medium.

"Television is the mother that eats its young," she said, culling through a case of thumbnail-sized cassettes. "A television show is senile about two seconds after the phosphor dots stop glowing. It's dead after one re-run, and it doesn't go to heaven." She came back to the couch with her selection and dumped them on the table beside the ancient video device.

"My library is hit-and-miss," she said. "But it's one of

the best there is. In the real early days they didn't even save the shows. They made some films, lost most of those, then went to tape and erased most of them after a few years in the vault. Shows you how valuable the product was, in their own estimation. Here, take a look at this.''

What she now showed him lacked not only depth, but color as well. It took him a few minutes to reliably perceive the picture, it was so foreign to him. It flickered, jumped, it was all shades of gray, and the sound was tinny. But in ten minutes he was hypnotized.

"This is called *Faraway Hill*," she said. "It was the first net soap. It came on Wednesday nights at 2100, on the DuMont Net, and it ran for twelve weeks. This is, so far as I know, the only existing episode, and it didn't surface until 1990.''

She took him back, turning the tiny glass screen into a time machine. They sampled *Toast of the Town, One Man's Family, My Friend Irma, December Bride, Pete and Gladys, Petticoat Junction, Ball Four, Hunky & Dora, Black Vet, Kunklowitz, Kojak,* and *Koonz*. She showed him wonderfully inventive game shows, serials that made him deeply involved after only one episode, adventures so civilized and restrained he could barely believe they were on television. Then she went on to the Golden Age of the Sitcom for *Gilligan's Island* and *Family Affair*.

"What I can't get over," he said, "is how good it is. It's so much better than what we see today. And they did it all with no sex and practically no violence.''

"No nudity, even," she said. "There was no frontal nudity on network TV until *Koonz*. Next season, *every* show had it, naturally. There was no actual intercourse until much later, in *Kiss My Ass*.'' She looked away from him, but not before he caught a hint of sadness in her eyes. He asked her what was wrong.

"I don't know, Q.M. I mean . . . I don't know exactly. Part of it is knowing that most of these shows were panned by the critics when they came out. And I've showed you some flops, but mostly these were hits. And I *can't tell the difference*. They all look good. I mean, none of them have people you'd expect to meet in real life, but they're all recognizably human, they act more or less like humans act. You can care for the characters in the dramas, and the comedies are witty.''

"So those critics just had their heads up their asses.''

She sighed. "No. What I fear is that it's *us*. If you're brought up eating shit, rotten soyaloid tastes great. I really do think that's what's happened. It's possible to do the moral equivalent of the anatomical impossibility you just mentioned. I know, because I'm one of the contortionists who does it. What frightens me is that I've been kidding myself all along, that I'm *stuck* in that position. That none of us can unbend our spines any longer."

She had other tapes.

It was not until their second week together that she brought them out, rather shyly, he thought. Her mother had been a fanatic home vidmaker; she had documented Megan's life in fine detail.

What he saw was a picture of lower-upper-class life, not too different in its broad outlines from his own upper-middle milieu. Cooper's family had never had any financial troubles. Galloway's were not fabulously wealthy, though they brought in twenty times the income of Cooper's. The house that appeared in the background shots was much larger than the one Cooper had grown up in. Where his family had biked, hers had private automobiles. There was a woman in the early tapes that Megan identified as her nurse; he did not see any other servants. But the only thing he saw that really impressed him was a sequence of her receiving a pony for her tenth birthday. Now, there was class.

Little Megan Galloway, pre-sidekick, emerged as a precocious child, perhaps a trifle spoiled. It was easy to see where at least part of her composure before the Transer came from; her mother had been everywhere, aiming her vidicam. Her life was *cinema verité*, with Megan either totally ignoring the camera or playing to it expertly, as her mood dictated. There were scenes of her reading fluently in three languages at the age of seven, others showing her hamming it up in amateur theatricals staged in the back yard.

"Are you sure you want to see more?" she asked, for the third or fourth time.

"I tell you, I'm fascinated. I forgot to ask you where all this is happening. California, isn't it?"

"No, I grew up in *La Barrio Cercada, Veintiuno,* one of the sovereign enclaves the congloms carved out of Mexico for exec families. Dual United States and GWA citizenship. I never saw a real Mexican the whole time I lived there. I just thought I ought to ask you," she went on, diffidently. "Home vids can be deadly boring."

"Only if you don't care about the subject. Show me more."

Somewhere during the next hour of tapes, control of the camera was wrested from Megan's mother and came to reside primarily with Megan herself and with her friends. They were as camera-crazy as her mother had been, but not quite so restrained in subject matter. The children used their vidicams as virtually every owner had used them since the invention of the device: they made dirty tapes. The things they did could usually better be described as horseplay than as sex, and they generally stopped short of actual intercourse, at least while the tape was rolling.

"My god," Megan sighed, rolling her eyes. "I must have a million kilometers of this sort of kiddie-porn. You'd think we invented it."

He observed that she and her crowd were naked a lot more than he and his friends had been. The students at his school had undressed at the beach, to participate in athletics, and to celebrate special days like Vernal Equinox and The Last Day of School. Megan's friends did not seem to dress at all. Most of them were Caucasian, but all were brown as coffee beans.

"It's true," she said. "I never wore *anything* but a pair of track shoes."

"Even to school?"

"They didn't believe in dictating things like that to us."

He watched her develop as a woman in a sequence that lap-dissolved her from the age of ten, like those magic time-lapses of flowers blooming.

"I call this 'The Puberieties of 2073,' " she said, with a self-deprecating laugh. "I put it together years ago, for something to do."

He had already been aware of the skilled hand which had assembled these pieces into a whole which was integrated, yet not artificially slick. The arts learned during her years in the business had enabled her to produce an extended program which entranced him far longer than its component parts, seen raw, could ever have done. He remembered Anna-Louise's accusations, and wondered what she would think if she could see him now, totally involved in someone else's life.

A hand-lettered title card appeared on the screen: "The Broken Blossom: An Act of Love. By Megan Allegra Galloway and Reginald Patrick Thomas." What followed had none

of the smooth flow of what had gone before. The cuts were
jerky. The camera remained stationary at all times, and there
were no fades. He knew this bit of tape had been left untouched from the time a young girl had spliced it together
many years ago. The children ran along the beach in slow-
motion, huge waves breaking silently behind them. They
walked along a dirt road, holding hands, stopping to kiss. The
music swelled behind them. They sat in an infinite field of
yellow flowers. They laughed, tenderly fondled each other.
The boy covered Megan with showers of petals.

They ran through the woods, found a waterfall and a deep
pool. They embraced under the waterfall. The kisses became
passionate and they climbed out onto a flat rock where—
coincidentally—there was an inflatable mattress. ("When we
rehearsed it," Megan explained, "that damn rock didn't feel
half as romantic as it looked.") The act was consummated. The
sequence was spliced from three camera angles; in some of
the shots Cooper could see the legs of one of the other
tripods. The lovers lay in each other's arms, spent, and more
ocean breakers were seen. Fade to black.

Galloway turned off the tape player. She sat for a time
examining her folded hands.

"That was my first time," she said.

Cooper frowned. "I was sure I saw—"

"No. Not with me, you didn't. The other girls, yes. And
you saw me doing a lot of other things. But I was 'saving'
that." She chuckled. "I'd read too many old romances. My
first time was going to be with someone I loved. I know it's
silly."

"And you loved him?"

"Hopelessly." She brushed her eyes with the back of her
hand, then sighed. "He wanted to pull out at the end and
ejaculate on my belly, because that's the way they always do
it on television. I had to argue with him for hours to talk him
out of that. He was an idiot." She considered that for a
moment. "We were both idiots. He believed real life should
imitate television, and I believed it wasn't real unless it was
on television. So I had to record it, or it might all fade away.
I guess I'm still doing that."

"But you know it's not true. You do it for a living."

She regarded him bleakly. "This makes it better?"

When he did not answer she fell silent for a long time,

studying her hands again. When she spoke, she did not look up.

"There are more tapes."

He knew what she meant, knew it would no longer be fun, and knew just as certainly that he must view them. He told her to go on.

"My mother shot this."

It began with a long shot of a silver hang-glider. Cooper heard Megan's mother shout for her daughter to be careful. In response, the glider banked sharply upward, almost stalled, then came around to pass twenty meters overhead. The camera followed. Megan was waving and smiling. There was a chaotic moment—shots of the ground, of the sky, a blurred glimpse of the glider nearing the tree—then it steadied.

"I don't know what was going through her mind," Megan said, quietly. "But she responded like an old pro. It must have been reflex."

Whatever it was, the camera was aimed unerringly as the glider turned right, grazed the tree, and flipped over. It went through the lower branches, and impaled itself. The image was jerky as Megan's mother ran. There was a momentary image of Megan dangling from her straps. Her head was at a horrifying angle. Then the sky filled one half of the screen and the ground the other as the camera continued to record after being flung aside.

Things were not nearly so comprehensive after that. The family at last had no more inclination to tape things. There were some hasty shots of a bed with a face—Megan, so wrapped and strapped and tucked that nothing else showed—pictures of doctors, of the doors of operating rooms and the bleak corridors of hospitals. And suddenly a girl with ancient eyes was sitting in a wheelchair, feeding herself laboriously with a spoon strapped to her fist.

"Things pick up a little now," Megan said. "I told them to start taping again. I was going to contrast these tapes with the ones they would make a year from now, when I was walking again."

"They told you you would walk?"

"They told me I would *not*. But everyone thinks they're the exception. The doctors tell you you'll regain some function, and hell, if you can regain some you can regain it all, right? You start to believe in mind over matter, and you're sure God will smile on you alone. Oh, by the way, there's trans-tape material with some of these.''

The implications of the casual statement did not hit him for a moment. When he understood, he knew she would not mention it again. It was an invitation she would never make more directly than she had just done.

''I'd like to run them, if you wouldn't mind.'' He had hoped for a tone of voice as casual as hers had been, and was not sure he had pulled it off. When she looked at him her eyes were measuring.

''It would be bad form for me to protest,'' she said, at last. ''Obviously, I want very much for you to try them. But I'm not sure you can handle them. I should warn you, they're—''

''—not much fun? Damn it, Megan, don't insult me.''

''All right.'' She got up and went to a cabinet, removed a very small, very expensive Transer unit and helmet. As she helped him mount it she would not look into his eyes, but babbled nervously about how the Feelie Corporation people had showed up in the hospital one day, armed with computer printouts that had rated her a good possibility for a future contract with the company. She had turned them away the first time, but they were used to that. Transing had still been a fairly small industry at the time. They were on the verge of breakthroughs that would open the mass market, but neither Feelie-corp nor Megan knew that. When she finally agreed to make some tapes for them it was not in the belief that they would lead to stardom. It was to combat her growing fear that there was very little she could do with her life. They were offering the possibility of a job, something she had never worried about when she was rich and un-injured. Suddenly, any job looked good.

''I'll start you at low intensity,'' she said. ''You don't have a tolerance for transing, I presume, so there's no need for power boosters. This is fragmented stuff. Some of the tapes have trans-tracks, and others don't, so you'll—''

''Will you get on with it, please?''

She turned on the machine.

On the screen, Megan was in a therapy pool. Two nurses stood beside her, supporting her, stretching her thin limbs. There were more scenes of physical therapy. He was wondering when the transing would begin. It should start with a shifting of perspectives, as though he had *(The television expanded; he passed through the glass and into the world beyond.)* actually *entered*—

"Are you all right?"

Cooper was holding his face in his hands. He looked up, and shook his head, realized that she would misinterpret the gesture, and nodded.

"A touch of vertigo. It's been a while."

"We could wait. Do it another time."

"No. Let's go."

He was sitting in the wheelchair, dressed in a fine lace gown that covered him from his neck to his toes. The toes were already beginning to look different. There was no more muscle tone in them. Most important, he could no longer feel them.

He felt very little sensation. There was a gray area just above his breasts where everything began to fade. He was a floating awareness, suspended above the wheelchair and the body attached to it.

He was aware af all this, but he was not thinking about it. It was already a common thing. The awful novelty was long gone.

Spring had arrived outside his window. (Where was he? This was not Mexico, he was sure, but his precise location eluded him. No matter.) He watched a squirrel climbing a tree just outside his window. It might be nice to be a squirrel.

Someone was coming to visit real soon. It would only be a few more hours. He felt good about that. He was looking forward to it. Nothing much had happened today. There had been therapy (his shoulders still ached from it) and a re-training session (without thinking about it, he made the vast, numb mittens that used to be his hands close together strongly— which meant he had exerted almost enough force to hold a sheet of paper between thumb and bunched fingers). Pretty soon there would be lunch. He wondered what it would be.

Oh, yes. There had been that unpleasantness earlier in the day. He had been screaming hysterically and the doctor had come with the needle. That was all still down there. There was enough sadness to drown in, but he didn't feel it. He felt the sunlight on his arm and was grateful for it. He felt pretty good. Wonder what's for lunch?

"You still okay?"

"I'm fine." He rubbed his eyes, trying to uncross them. It was the transition that always made him dizzy; that feeling as

though a taut rubber band had snapped and he had popped out
of the set and back into his own head, his own body. He
rubbed his arms, which felt as though they had gone to sleep.
On the screen, Megan still sat in her wheelchair, looking out
the window with a vague expression. The scene changed.

*He sat as still as he could so he wouldn't disturb the
sutures in the back of his neck, but it was worth a little pain.
On the table in front of him, the tiny metal bug shuddered,
jerked forward, then stopped. He concentrated, telling it to
make a right turn. He thought about how he would have
turned right while driving a car. Foot on the accelerator,
hands on the wheel. Shoulder muscles holding the arms up,
fingers curled, thumbs . . . what had he done with his
thumbs? But then he had them, he felt the muscles of his arms
as he began turning the wheel. He tapped the brake with his
foot, trying to feel the tops of his toes against the inside of his
shoe as his foot lifted, the steady pressure on the sole as he
pushed down. He took his right hand off the wheel as his left
crossed in front of him . . .*

*On the table, the metal bug whirred as it turned to the
right. There was applause from the people he only vaguely
sensed standing around him. Sweat dripped down his neck as
he guided the device through a left turn, then another right. It
was too much. The bug reached the edge of the table and try
as he might, he could not get it straightened out. One of the
doctors caught it and placed it in the center of the table.*

"Would you like to rest, Megan?"

*"No," he said, not allowing himself to relax. "Let me try
again." Behind him, an entire wall flashed and blinked as the
computer found itself taxed to its limits, sorting the confusing
neural impulses that gathered on the stump of his spinal cord,
translating the information, and broadcasting it to the servos
in the remotalog device. He made it start, then stopped it
before it reached the edge of the table. Just how he had done
it was still mostly mysterious, but he felt he was beginning to
get a handle on it. Sometimes it worked best if he tried to
trick himself into thinking he could still walk and then just did
it. Other times the bug just sat there, not fooled. It knew he
could not walk. It knew he was never going to—*

*A white-sheeted form was being wheeled down the corridor
toward the door to the operating room. Inside, from the
gallery, he saw them transfer the body onto the table. The
lights were very bright. He blinked, confused by them. But*

they were turning him over now, and that made it much better. Something cool touched the back of his neck—

"A thousand pardons, sir," Megan said, briskly fast-forwarding the tape. "You're not ready for that. *I'm* not ready for that."

He was not sure what she was talking about. He knew he needed the operation. It was going to improve the neural interfaces, which would make it easier for him to operate the new remotes they were developing. It was exciting to be involved in the early stages of . . .

"Oh. Right. I'm . . ."

"Q.M. Cooper," she said, and looked dubiously into his eyes. "Are you sure you wouldn't rather wait?"

"No. Show me more."

The nights were the worst. Not all of them, but when it was bad it was very bad. During the day there was acceptance, or some tough armor that contained the real despair. For days at a time he could be happy, he could accept what had happened, know that he must struggle but that the struggle was worth it. For most of his life he knew that what had happened was not the end of the world, that he could lead a full, happy life. There were people who cared about him. His worst fears had not been realized. Pleasure was still possible, happiness could be attained. Even sexual pleasures had not vanished. They were different and sometimes awkward, but he didn't mind.

But alone at night, it could all fall apart. The darkness stripped his defenses and he was helpless, physically and emotionally.

He could not move. His legs were dead meat. He was repulsive, disgusting, rotting away, a hideous object no one could ever love. The tube had slipped out and the sheets were soaked with urine. He was too ashamed to buzz for the nurse.

He wept silently. When he was through, he coldly began plotting the best way to end his life.

She held him until the worst of the shaking passed. He cried like a child who cannot understand the hurt, and like a weary old man. For the longest time he could not seem to make his eyes open. He did not want to see anything.

"Do I . . . do I have to see the next part?" He heard the whine in his voice.

She covered his face with kisses, hugging him, giving him

wordless reassurance that everything would be all right. He accepted it gratefully.

"No. You don't have to see anything. I don't know why I showed you as much as I have, but I can't show you that part even if I wanted to because I destroyed it. It's too dangerous. I'm no more suicidal now than anybody else, but transing that next tape would strip me naked and maybe drive me crazy, or anybody who looked at it. The strongest of us is pretty fragile, you know. There is so much primal despair just under our surfaces that you don't dare fool around with it."

"How close did you come?"

"Gestures," she said, easily. "Two attempts, both discovered in plenty of time." She kissed him again, looked into his eyes and gave him a tentative smile. She seemed satisfied with what she saw, for she patted his cheek and reached for the transer controls again.

"One more little item," she said, "and we'll call it a night. This is a happy tape. I think we could both use it."

There was a girl in a sidekick. This machine was to the Golden Gypsy what a Wright Brothers Flyer was to a supersonic jet. Megan was almost invisible. Chromed struts stuck out all over, hydraulic cylinders hissed. There were welds visible where the thing had been bashed into shape. When she moved, the thing whined like a sick dog. Yet she was moving, and under her own control, placing one foot laboriously in front of the other, biting her tongue in concentration as she pondered her next step. Quick cut to—

—next year's model. It was still ponderous, it poked through her clothes, it was hydraulic and no-nonsense orthopedic. But she was moving well. She was able to walk naturally; the furrows of concentration were gone from her brow. This one had hands. They were heavy metal gauntlets, but she could move each finger separately. The smile she gave the camera had more genuine warmth than Cooper had seen from her since the accident.

"The new Mark Three," said an off-camera voice, and Cooper saw Megan running. She did high kicks, jumped up and down. And yet this new model was actually bulkier than the Mark Two had been. There was a huge bulge on her back, containing computers which had previously been external to the machine. It was the first self-contained sidekick. No one would ever call it pretty, but he could imagine the feeling of freedom it must have given Megan, and wondered why she wasn't playing the trans-track. He started to look away from the screen *but this was no time to worry about things like that. He was free!*

He held his hands before his face, turning them, looking at the trim leather gloves he would always have to wear, and not caring, because they were so much better than the mailed fists, or the fumbling hooks before that. It was the first day in his new sidekick, and it was utterly glorious. He ran, he shouted and jumped and cavorted, and everyone laughed with him and applauded his every move. He was powerful! He was going to change the world. Nothing could stop him. Some day, everyone would know the name of Me(Q.M.)gan Gallo (Cooper)way. There was nothing, nothing in the world he couldn't do. He would—

"Oh!" He clapped his hands to his face in shock. "Oh! You turned it off!"

"Sort of coitus interruptus, huh?" she said, smugly.

"But I want more!"

"That would be a mistake. It's not good to get too deeply into someone else's joy or sadness. Besides, how do you know it stays that good?"

"How could it not? You have everything now, you—" He stopped, and looked into her face. She was smiling. He would come back to the moment many times in days to come, searching for a hint of mockery, but he would never find it. The walls were gone. She had showed him everything there was to know about her, and he knew his life would never be the same.

"I love you," he said.

Her expression changed so slightly he might have missed it had he not been so exquisitely attuned to her emotions. Her lower lip quivered, and sadness outlined her eyes. She drew a ragged breath.

"This is sudden. Maybe you should wait until you've recovered from—"

"No." He touched her face with his hands and made her look at him. "No. I could only put it into words just now, in that crazy moment. It wasn't an easy thing for me to say."

"Oh boy," she said, in a quiet monotone.

"What's the matter?" When she wouldn't talk, he shook her head gently back and forth between his hands. "You don't love me, is that it? I'd rather you came out and said it now.''

"That's not it. I do love you. You've never been in love before, have you?"

"No. I wondered if I'd know what it would feel like. Now I know."

"You don't know the half of it. Sometimes, you almost wish it was a more rational thing, that it wouldn't hit you when you feel you can least cope with it."

"I guess we're really helpless, aren't we?"

"You said it." She sighed again, then rose and took his hand. She pulled him toward the bed.

"Come on. You're going to have to learn to make love."

He had feared it would be bizarre. It was not. He had thought about it a great deal in the last weeks and had come up with no answers. What would she do? If she could feel nothing below the collarbone, how could any sexual activity have any meaning for her?

One answer should have been obvious. She still felt with her shoulders, her neck, her face, lips, and ears. A second answer had been there for him to see, but he had not made the connection. She was still capable of erection. Sensation from her genitals never reached her brain, but the nerves from her clitoris to her spinal cord were undamaged. Complex things happened, things she never explained completely, involving secondary and tertiary somatic effects, hormones, transfer arousal, the autonomic and vascular systems of the body.

"Some of it is natural adaptation," she said, "and some of it has been augmented by surgery and microprocessors. Quadraplegics could do this before the kind of nerve surgery we can do today, but not as easily as I can. It's like a blind person, whose sense of hearing and touch sharpen in compensation. The areas of my body I can still feel are now more sensitive, more responsive. I know a woman who can have an orgasm from having her elbow stimulated. With me, elbows are not so great."

"With all they can do, why can't they bridge the gap where your spinal cord was cut? If they can make a machine to read the signals your brain sends out, why can't they make one to put new signals into the rest of your body, and take the signals that come from your lower body and put them into—''

"It's a different problem. They're working on it. Maybe in fifteen or twenty years."

"Here?"

"More around here. All around my neck, from ear to ear . . . that's it. Keep doing that. And why don't you find something for your hands to do?"

"But you can't feel this. Can you?"

"Not directly. But nice things are happening. Just look."

"Yeah."

"Then don't worry about it. Just keep doing it."

"What about this?"

"Not particularly."

"This?"

"You're getting warmer."

"But I thought you—"

"Why don't you do a little less thinking? Come on, put it in. I want this to be good for you, too. And don't think it won't do something for me."

"Whatever you say. Oh, lord, that feels . . . hey, how did you do that?"

"You ask a lot of questions."

"Yeah, but you can't move any muscles down there."

"A simple variation on the implants that keep me from making a mess of myself. Now, honestly, Q.M. Don't you think the time for questions is over?"

"I think you're right."

"You want to see something funny?" she asked.

They were sprawled in each other's arms, looking at the smoke belching from her ridiculous bedposts. She had flipped on the holo generators, and her bedroom had vanished in a Mark Twain illusion. They floated down the Mississippi River. The bed rocked gently. Cooper felt indecently relaxed.

"Sure."

"Promise you won't laugh?"

"Not unless it's funny."

She rolled over and spread her arms and legs, face down on the bed. The sidekick released her, stood up, found the holo control, and turned off the river. It put one knee on the bed, carefully turned Megan onto her back, crossed her legs for her, then sat beside her on the edge of the bed and crossed its own legs, swinging them idly. By then he was laughing, as she had intended. It sat beside her and encased her left forearm and hand, lit a cigarette and placed it in her mouth, then released her hand again. It went to a chair across the room and sat down.

He jumped when she touched him. He turned and saw a thin hand on his elbow, not able to grasp him, not strong enough to do more than nudge.

"Will you put this out?" She inclined her head toward him. He carefully removed the cigarette from her lips, cupping his hand under the ash. When he turned back to her, her eyes were guarded.

"This is me, too," she said.

"I know that." He frowned, and tried to get closer to the truth, for his own sake as well as hers. "I hadn't thought about it much. You look very helpless like this."

"I *am* very helpless."

"Why are you doing it?"

"Because *nobody* sees me like this, except doctors. I wanted to know if it made any difference."

"No. No difference at all. I've seen you this way before. I'm surprised you asked."

"You shouldn't be. I hate myself like this. I disgust myself. I expect everyone else to react the way I do."

"You expect wrong." He hugged her, then drew back and studied her face. "Do you . . . would you like to make love again? Not this second, I mean, but a little later. Like this."

"God, no. But thanks for offering." When she was inside the sidekick again she touched his face with her be-ringed hand. Her expression was an odd mixture of satisfaction and uncertainty.

"You keep passing the tests, Cooper. As fast as I can throw them at you. I wonder what I'm going to do with you?"

"Are there more tests?"

She shook her head. "No. Not for you."

"You're going to be late for work," Anna-Louse said, as Cooper lifted one of her suitcases and followed her out of the shuttleport waiting room.

"I don't care." Anna-Louise gave him an odd look. He knew why. When they had been together he had always been eager for his shift to begin. By now he was starting to hate it. When he worked he could not be with Megan.

"You've really got it bad, don't you?" she said.

He smiled at her. "I sure do. This is the first time I've been away from her in weeks. I hope you aren't angry."

"Me? No. I'm flattered that you came to see me off. You . . . well, you wouldn't have thought of something like that a month ago. Sorry."

"You're right." He put the suitcase down beside the things she had been carrying. A porter took them through the lock and into the shuttle. Cooper leaned against the sign that announced "New Dresden, Clavius, Tycho Under." "I didn't know if you'd be angry, but I thought I ought to be here."

Anna-Louise smiled wryly. "Well, she's certainly changed you. I'm happy for you. Even though I still think she's going to hurt you, you'll gain something from it. You've come alive since the last time I saw you."

"I wanted to ask you about that," he said, slowly. "Why do you think she'll hurt me?"

She hesitated, hitching at her pants and awkwardly scuffing her shoes on the deck.

"You don't like your work as much as you did. Right?"

"Well . . . yeah. I guess not. Mostly because I'd like to spend more time with her."

She looked at him, cocking her head.

"Why don't you quit?"

"What . . . you mean—"

"Just quit. She wouldn't even notice the money she spent to support you."

He grinned at her. "You've got the wrong guy, A.L. I don't have any objections to being supported by a woman. Did you really think I was that old-fashioned?"

She shook her head.

"But you think money will be a problem."

She nodded. "Not the fact that she has it. The fact that you don't."

"Come on. She doesn't care that I'm not rich."

Anna-Louise looked at him a long time, then smiled.

"Good," she said, and kissed him. She hurried into the shuttle, waving over her shoulder.

Megan received a full sack of mail every day. It was the tip of the iceberg; she employed a staff on Earth to screen it,

answer fan mail with form letters, turn down speaking en-
gagements, and repel parasites. The remainder was sent on,
and fell into three categories. The first, and by far the largest,
was the one out of a thousand matters that came in unsolicited
and, after sifting, seemed to have a chance of meriting her
attention. She read some, threw most away, unopened.

The last two categories she always read. One was job
offers, and the other was material from facilities on Earth
doing research into the nervous system. Often the latter was
accompanied by requests for money. She usually sent a check.

At first she tried to keep him up on the new developments
but she soon realized he would never have her abiding and
personal interest in matters neurological. She was deeply
involved with what is known as the cutting edge of the
research. Nothing new was discovered, momentous or trivial,
that did not end up on her desk the next day. There were odd
side effects: The Wacky Dust which had figured in their first
meeting had been sent by a lab which had stumbled across it
and didn't know what to do with it.

Her computer was jammed with information on neurosur-
gery. She could call up projections of when certain milestones
might be reached, from minor enhancements all the way up to
complete regeneration of the neuron net. Most of the ones
Cooper saw looked dismal. The work was not well funded.
Most money for medical research went to the study of radiation disease.

Reading the mail in the morning was far from the high
point of the day. The news was seldom good. But he was not
prepared for her black depression one morning two weeks
after Anna-Louise's departure.

"Did someone die?" he asked, sitting down and reaching
for the coffee.

"Me. Or I'm in the process."

When she looked up and saw his face she shook her head.

"No, it's not medical news. Nothing so straightforward."
She tossed a sheet of paper across the table at him. "It's from
Allgemein Fernsehen Gesellschaft. They will pay any price . . .
if I'll do essentially what I've been doing all along for
Feeli–corp. They regret that the board of directors will not
permit the company to enter any agreement wherein AFG has
less than total creative control of the product."

"How many does that make now?"

"That you've seen? Seventeen. There have been many more that never got past the preliminary stage."

"So independent production isn't going to be as easy as you thought."

"I never said it would be easy."

"Why not use your own money? Start your own company."

"We've looked into it, but the answers are all bad. The war between GWA and Royal Dutch Shell makes the tax situation . . ." She looked at him, quickly shifted gears. "It's hard to explain."

That was a euphemism for "you wouldn't understand." He did not mind it. She had tried to explain her business affairs to him and all it did was frustrate them both. He had no head for it.

"Okay. So what do you do now?"

"Oh, there's no crisis yet. My investments are doing all right. Some war losses, but I'm getting out of GWA. The bank balance is in fair shape." That was another euphemism. She had begun using it when she realized he was baffled by the baroque mechanism that was *Gitano de Oro*, her corporate self. He had seen some astounding bills from Sidekick Inc., but if she said she was not hurting he would believe her.

She had been toying with the salt shaker while her eggs benedict grew cold. Now she gave a derisive snort, and glanced at him.

"The funny thing is, I've just proved all the theoreticians wrong. I've made a breakthrough no one believed was possible. I could set the whole industry on its ear, and I can't get a job."

It was the first he heard of it. He raised one eyebrow in polite inquiry.

"Damn it, Cooper. I've been wondering how to tell you this. The problem is I didn't realize until something you said a few days ago that you didn't know my transcorder is built in to my sidekick."

"I thought your camera crew—"

"I know you did, now. I swear I didn't realize that. No, the crew makes nothing but visual tapes. It's edited into the trans-tape which is made by my sidekick. I leave it on all the time."

He chewed on that one for a while, and frowned at her.

"You're saying you got love on tape."

"The moment of falling in love. I got it all."

"Why didn't you tell me?"

She sighed. "Trans-tapes have to be developed. They aren't like viddies. They just came back from the lab yesterday. I transed them last night, while you slept."

"I'd like to see them."

"Maybe someday," she hedged. "For right now, it's too personal. I want to keep this just for myself. Can you understand that? God knows I've never sought privacy very hard in my life, but this . . ." She looked helpless.

"I guess so." He considered it a little longer. "But if you sell them, it'll hardly be personal then, will it?"

"I don't want to sell them, Q.M."

He said nothing, but he had been hoping for something a little stronger than that. For the first time, he began to feel alarmed.

He did not think about money, or about trans-tapes, in the next two weeks. There was too much else to do. He took his accumulated vacation and sick leave and the two of them traveled to Earth. It might as well have been a new planet.

It was not only that he went to places he had never seen. They went there in a style to which he was not accustomed. It was several steps above what most people thought of as first class. Problems did not exist on this planet. Luggage took care of itself. He never saw any money. There was no schedule that had to be met. Cars and planes and hypersonic shuttles were always ready to whisk them anywhere they wanted to go. When he mentioned that all this might be costing too much she explained that she was paying for none of it. Everything was provided by eager corporate suitors. Cooper thought they behaved worse than any love-smitten adolescent. They were as demonstrative as puppies, and as easily forgiving when she snubbed them while accepting their gifts.

She did not seem afraid of kidnapping, either, though he saw little in the way of security. When he asked, she told him that security one kept tripping over was just amateur gun-toting. She advised him never to think of it again, that it was all taken care of.

"You wouldn't market that tape, would you?" There, he finally had it out in the open.

"Well, let me put it this way. When I first came to you, I

was near a nervous breakdown from just thinking about going into the sex tape business. This is much more personal, much dearer to me than plain old intercourse.''

"Ah. I feel better."

She reached across the bed and squeezed his hand, looked at him fondly.

"You really don't want me to market it, do you?"

"No. I really don't. The first day I saw you, a good friend warned me that if I got into bed with you my technique would be seen by ninety million slobs."

She laughed. "Well, Anna-Louise was wrong. You can put that possibility right out of your mind. For one thing, there were no vidicams around, so no one will ever see you making love to me. For another, they wouldn't use my sensations while I'm making love if I ever get into the sex-tape business. Those are a little esoteric for my audience. That would all be put together in the editing room. There would be visuals and emotionals from me—showing me making love in the regular way—and there'd be a stand-in for the physical sensations."

"Pardon my asking," he said, "but wasn't your reaction that first day a little overblown, then?"

She laughed. "Much ado about nothing?"

"Yeah. I mean, it'd be your body on the screen—"

"—but I've already shown you I don't care about that."

"And if you were making love in the conventional way, you'd hardly be emotionally transported—"

"It would register as sheer boredom."

"—so I presume you'd splice in the emotional track from some other source, too." He frowned, no longer sure of what he was trying to say.

"You're catching on. I told you this business was all fake. And I can't really explain why it bothers me so much, except to say I don't want to surrender that part of myself, even a little bit. I *taped* my first intercourse, but I didn't show it to anybody until you saw it. And what about you? You're worried that I might sell a tape of falling in love with you. You wouldn't be on it at all.''

"Well, it was something we shared."

"Exactly. I don't want to share it with anyone else."

"I'm glad you don't plan to sell it."

"My darling, I would hate that as much as you would."

It was not until later that he realized she had never ruled out the possibility.

• • •

They went back to the Bubble when Cooper's vacation time
was over. She never suggested he quit his job. They checked
into a different suite. She said the cost had little to do with it,
but this time he was not so sure. He had begun to see a
haunted expression around her eyes as she read letter after
letter rejecting increasingly modest proposals.

"They really know the game," she told him bitterly, one
night. "Every one of those companies will give me any salary
I want to name, but I have to sign their contract. You begin to
think it's a conspiracy."

"Is it?"

"I really don't know. It may be just shrewdness. I talk
about how stupid they are, and artistically they live up to that
description. Morally, there's not one of them who wouldn't
pay to have his daughter gang-raped if it meant a tenth-point
ratings jump. But financially, you can't fault them. These are
the folks who have suppressed the cures for a dozen diseases
because they didn't cost enough to use. I'm speaking of the
parent congloms, of course, the real governments. If they
ever find a way to profit off nuclear war we'll be having them
every other week. And they have obviously decided that
television outside their control is dangerous."

"So what does it mean to you and me?"

"I got into the business by accident. I won't go crazy if
I'm not working."

"And the money?"

"We'll get along."

"Your expenses must be pretty high."

"They are. No sense lying about that. I can cut out a lot,
but the sidekick is never going to be cheap."

As if to underscore her words of the night before, the Golden
Gypsy chose the next morning to get temperamental. The
middle finger of Megan's right hand was frozen in the extended position. She joked about it.

"As they say, 'The perversity of the universe tends toward
the maximum.' Why the *middle* finger? Can you answer me
that?"

"I guess you'll have the repairman up here before I get
back."

"Not this time," she decided. "It'll be hard, but I'll

struggle through. I'll wait until we return to Earth, and drop by the factory.''

She called Sidekick while he dressed for work. He could hear her without being able to make out the words. She was still on the phone when he came out of the bathroom and started for the door. She punched the hold button and caught him, turned him around, and kissed him hard.

''I love you very much,'' she said.

''I love you, too.''

She was not there when he returned. She had left a tape playing. When he went to turn it off he found the switch had been sealed. On the screen, a younger Megan moved through the therapy room in her Mark One sidekick. It was a loop, repeating the same scene.

He waited for almost an hour, then went to look for her. Ten minutes later he learned she had taken the 0800 shuttle for Earth.

A day later he realized he was not going to be able to get her on the telephone. That same day he heard the news that she had signed a contract with Telecommunion, and as he turned off the set he saw the trans-tape which had been sitting on top of it, unnoticed.

He got out the Transer she had left behind, donned the headset, inserted the cassette, turned on the machine. Half an hour later it turned itself off, and he came back to reality with a beatific smile on his face.

Then he began to scream.

They released him from the hospital in three days. Still numb from sedation, he went to the bank and closed his account. He bought a ticket for New Dresden.

He located Anna-Louise in the barracks of the police academy. She was surprised to see him, but not as much as he had expected. She took him to a lunar park—an area of trees with a steel roof and corridors radiating in all directions—sat him down, and let him talk.

''. . . and you were the only one who seemed to have understood her. You warned me the first day. I want to know how you did that, and I want to know if you can explain it to me.''

She did not seem happy, but he could see it was not directed at him.

"You say the tape really did what she claimed? It captured love?"

"I don't think anyone could doubt it."

She shivered. "That frightens me more than anything I've heard in a long time." He waited, not knowing exactly what she meant by that. When she spoke again, it was not about her fears. "Then it proved to your satisfaction that she really *was* in love with you."

"Absolutely."

She studied his face. "I'll take your word for it. You look like someone who would recognize it." She got up and began to walk, and he followed her. "Then I've done her an injustice. I thought at first that you were just a plaything to her. From what you said, I changed my mind, even before I left the station."

"But you were still sure she'd hurt me. Why?"

"Cooper, have you studied much history? Don't answer that. Whatever you learned, you got from corporate-run schools. Have you heard of the great ideological struggles of the last century?"

"What the *hell* does that have to do with me?"

"Do you want my opinions or not? You came a long way to hear them." When she was sure he'd listen, she went on.

"This is very simplified. I don't have time to give you a history lesson, and I'm pretty sure you aren't in the mood for one. But there was capitalism, and there was communism. Both systems were run, in the end, by money. The capitalists said money was really a good thing. The communists kept trying to pretend that money didn't actually exist. They were both wrong, and money won in the end. It left us where we are now. The institutions wholly devoted to money swallowed up *all* political philosophies."

"Listen, I know you're a crazy Loonie and you think Earth is—"

"Shut up!" He was caught off guard when she spun him around. For a moment he thought she would hit him. "Damn you, that might have been funny in the Bubble, but now you're on *my* territory and *you're* the crazy one. I don't have to listen to your smoggie *shit!*"

"I'm sorry."

"Forget it!" she shouted, then ran her hand through her short hair. "Forget the history lesson, too. Megan Galloway is trying to make it as best she can in a world that rewards nothing so well as it rewards total self-interest. So am I, and so are you. Today or yesterday, Earth or Luna, it doesn't really matter. It's probably always been like that. It'll be that way tomorrow. I am *very sorry,* Q.M., I was right about her, but *she had no choice,* and I could see that from the start."

"That's what I want you to explain to me."

"If she was anybody but the Golden Gypsy, she might have gone with you to the ends of the world, endured any poverty. She might not have cared that you were never going to be rich. I'm not saying you wouldn't have had your problems, but you'd have had the same chance anyone else has to overcome them. But there is only one Golden Gypsy, and there's a reason for that."

"You're talking about the machine now. The sidekick."

"Yes. She called me yesterday. She was crying. I didn't know what to say to her, so I just listened. I felt sorry for her, and I don't even *like* her. I guess she knew you'd seek me out. She wanted you to hear some things she was ashamed to tell you. I *really* don't like her for that, but what can I do?

"There is only one Golden Gypsy. It is not owned by Megan Galloway. Rich as she is, she couldn't afford that. She leases it, at a monthly fee that is more than you or I will ever see in our lives, and she pays for a service contract that is almost that much money again. She had not been on television for over a month. Babe, it's not like there aren't other people who would like to use a machine like that. There must be a million of them or more. If you ran a conglom that owned that machine, who would you rent it to? Some nobody, or someone who will wear it in ten billion homes every night, along with a promo for your company?"

"That's what they told her on the phone? That they were going to take the machine away."

"The way she put it was they threatened to take her *body* away."

"But that's not enough!" He was weeping again, and he had thought he was past that stage. "I would have understood that. I told her I didn't care if she was in a sidekick, in a wheelchair, in bed, or whatever."

"Your opinion is hardly the one that matters, there," Anna-Louise pointed out.

"No, what I'm saying is, I don't *care* if she had to sign a contract she didn't like to do things she hates. Not if it means that much to her. If having the Golden Gypsy is that important. That wasn't enough reason to walk out on me.''

"Well, I think she gave you credit for that much. She was less certain you'd forgive her for the other thing she had to do, which was sell the tape she made of her falling in love with you. But maybe she'd have tried to make you understand why she had to do that, too . . . except that wasn't her real problem. The thing is, *she* couldn't live with it, not with her betrayal of herself, if you were around to remind her of the magnitude of the thing she had sold.''

He looked at it from all angles, taking his time. He thought it would be too painful to put into words, but he gave it a try.

"She could keep me, or she could keep her body. She couldn't keep both.''

"I'm afraid that's the equation. There's a rather complex question of self-respect in there, too. I don't think she figured she could save much of that either way.''

"And she chose the machine.''

"You might have, too.''

"But she *loved* me. Love is supposed to be the strongest thing there is.''

"Get your brain out of the television set, Q.M.''

"I think I hate her.''

"That would be a big mistake.''

But he was no longer listening.

He tried to kill her, once, shortly after the tape came out, more because it seemed like the right thing to do than because he really wanted to. He never got within a mile of her. Her security had his number, all right.

The tape was a smash, the biggest thing ever to hit the industry. Within a year, all the other companies had imitations, mostly bootlegged from the original. Copyright skirmishes were fought in Hollywood and Tokyo.

He spent his time beachcombing, doing a lot of swimming. He found that he now preferred flat water. He roamed, with no permanent address, but the checks found him, no matter where he was. The first was accompanied with a detailed royalty statement showing that he was getting fifty percent of the profits from sales of the tape. He tore it up and mailed it back. The second one was for the original amount plus interest plus the new royalties. He smeared it with his blood and paid to have it hand-delivered to her.

• • •

The tape she had left behind continued to haunt him. He had kept it, and viewed it when he felt strong enough. Again and again the girl in the wheezing sidekick walked across the room, her face set in determination. He remembered her feeling of triumph to be walking, even so awkwardly.

Gradually, he came to focus on the last few meters of the tape. The camera panned away from Megan and came to rest on the face of one of the nurses. There was an odd expression there, as subtle and elusive as the face of the Mona Lisa. He knew this was what Megan had wanted him to see, this was her last statement to him, her final plea for understanding. He willed himself to supply a trans-track for the nurse, to see with her eyes and feel with her skin. He could let no nuance escape him as he watched Megan's triumphant walk, the thing the girl had worked so long and hard to achieve. And at last he was sure that what the woman was feeling was an uglier thing than mere pity. That was the image Megan had chosen to leave him with: the world looking at Megan Galloway. It was an image to which she would never return, no matter what the price.

In a year he allowed himself to view the visual part of the love tape. They had used an actor to stand in for him, re-playing the scene in the Bubble and in the steam-boat bed. He had to admit it: she had never lied to him. The man did not even resemble Cooper. No one would be studying his lovemaking.

It was some time later before he actually transed the tape again. It was both calming and sobering. He wondered what they could sell using this new commodity, and the thought frightened him as much as it had Anna-Louise. But he was probably the only spurned lover in history who knew, beyond a doubt, that she actually *had* loved him.

Surely that counted for something.

His hate died quickly. His hurt lasted much longer, but a day came when he could forgive her.

Much later, he knew she had done nothing that needed his forgiveness.

Tango Charlie
and Foxtrot Romeo

The police probe was ten kilometers from Tango Charlie's Wheel when it made rendezvous with the unusual corpse. At this distance, the wheel was still an imposing presence, blinding white against the dark sky, turning in perpetual sunlight. The probe was often struck by its beauty, by the myriad ways the wheel caught the light in its thousand and one windows. It had been composing a thought-poem around that theme when the corpse first came to its attention.

There was a pretty irony about the probe. Less than a meter in diameter, it was equipped with sensitive radar, very good visible-light camera eyes, and a dim awareness. Its sentient qualities came from a walnut-sized lump of human brain tissue cultured in a lab. This was the cheapest and simplest way to endow a machine with certain human qualities that were often useful in spying devices. The part of the brain used was the part humans use to appreciate beautiful things. While the probe watched, it dreamed endless beautiful dreams. No one knew this but the probe's control, which was a computer that had not bothered to tell anyone about it. The computer did think it was rather sweet, though.

There were many instructions the probe had to follow. It did so religiously. It was never to approach the wheel more closely than five kilometers. All objects larger than one centimeter leaving the wheel were to be pursued, caught, and examined. Certain categories were to be reported to higher authorities. All others were to be vaporized by the probe's small battery of lasers. In thirty years of observation, only a dozen objects had needed reporting. All of them proved to be large structural components of the wheel which had broken away under the stress of rotation. Each had been destroyed by the probe's larger brother, on station five hundred kilometers away.

When it reached the corpse, it immediately identified it that far: it was a dead body, frozen in a vaguely fetal position. From there on, the probe got stuck.

Many details about the body did not fit the acceptable parameters for such a thing. The probe examined it again, and still again, and kept coming up with the same unacceptable answers. It could not tell what the body was . . . and yet it was a body.

The probe was so fascinated that its attention wavered for some time, and it was not as alert as it had been these previous years. So it was unprepared when the second falling object bumped gently against its metal hide. Quickly the probe leveled a camera eye at the second object. It was a single, long-stemmed, red rose, of a type that had once flourished in the wheel's florist shop. Like the corpse, it was frozen solid. The impact had shattered some of the outside petals, which rotated slowly in a halo around the rose itself.

It was quite pretty. The probe resolved to compose a thought-poem about it when this was all over. The probe photographed it, vaporized it with its lasers—all according to instruction—then sent the picture out on the airwaves along with a picture of the corpse, and a frustrated shout.

"Help!" the probe cried, and sat back to await developments.

"A puppy?" Captain Hoeffer asked, arching one eyebrow dubiously.

"A Shetland Sheepdog puppy, sir," said Corporal Anna-Louise Bach, handing him the batch of holos of the enigmatic orbiting object, and the single shot of the shattered rose. He took them, leafed through them rapidly, puffing on his pipe.

"And it came from Tango Charlie?"

"There is no possible doubt about it, sir."

Bach stood at parade rest across the desk from her seated superior and cultivated a detached gaze. I'm only awaiting orders, she told herself. I have no opinions of my own. I'm brimming with information, as any good recruit should be, but I will offer it only when asked, and then I will pour it forth until asked to stop.

That was the theory, anyway. Bach was not good at it. It

was her ineptitude at humoring incompetence in superiors that had landed her in this assignment, and put her in contention for the title of oldest living recruit/apprentice in the New Dresden Police Department.

"A Shetland . . ."

"Sheepdog, sir." She glanced down at him, and interpreted the motion of his pipestem to mean he wanted to know more. "A variant of the Collie, developed on the Shetland Isles of Scotland. A working dog, very bright, gentle, good with children."

"You're an authority on dogs, Corporal Bach?"

"No, sir. I've only seen them in the zoo. I took the liberty of researching this matter before bringing it to your attention, sir."

He nodded, which she hoped was a good sign.

"What else did you learn?"

"They come in three varieties: black, blue merle, and sable. They were developed from Icelandic and Greenland stock, with infusions of Collie and possible Spaniel genes. Specimens were first shown at Cruft's in London in 1906, and in American—"

"No, no. I don't give a damn about Shelties."

"Ah. We have confirmed that there were four Shelties present on Tango Charlie at the time of the disaster. They were being shipped to the zoo at Clavius. There were no other dogs of any breed resident at the station. We haven't determined how it is that their survival was overlooked during the investigation of the tragedy."

"Somebody obviously missed them."

"Yes, sir."

Hoeffer jabbed at a holo with his pipe.

"What's this? Have you researched *that* yet?"

Bach ignored what she thought might be sarcasm. Hoeffer was pointing to the opening in the animal's side.

"The computer believes it to be a birth defect, sir. The skin is not fully formed. It left an opening into the gut."

"And what's this?"

"Intestines. The bitch would lick the puppy clean after birth. When she found this malformation, she would keep licking as long as she tasted blood. The intestines were pulled out, and the puppy died."

"It couldn't have lived anyway. Not with that hole."

"No, sir. If you'll notice, the forepaws are also mal-formed. The computer feels the puppy was stillborn."

Hoeffer studied the various holos in a blue cloud of pipe smoke, then sighed and leaned back in his chair.

"It's fascinating, Bach. After all these years, there are dogs alive on Tango Charlie. And breeding, too. Thank you for bringing it to my attention."

Now it was Bach's turn to sigh. She *hated* this part. Now it was her job to explain it to him.

"It's even more fascinating than that, sir. We knew Tango Charlie was largely pressurized. So it's understandable that a colony of dogs could breed there. But, barring an explosion, which would have spread a large amount of debris into the surrounding space, this dead puppy must have left the station through an airlock."

His face clouded, and he looked at her in gathering outrage.

"Are you saying . . . there are humans alive aboard Tango Charlie?"

"Sir, it has to be that . . . or some *very* intelligent dogs."

Dogs can't count.

Charlie kept telling herself that as she knelt on the edge of forever and watched little Albert dwindling, hurrying out to join the whirling stars. She wondered if he would become a star himself. It seemed possible.

She dropped the rose after him and watched it dwindle, too. Maybe it would become a rosy star.

She cleared her throat. She had thought of things to say, but none of them sounded good. So she decided on a hymn, the only one she knew, taught her long ago by her mother, who used to sing it for her father, who was a spaceship pilot. Her voice was clear and true.

> *Lord guard and guide all those who fly*
> *Through Thy great void above the sky.*
> *Be with them all on ev'ry flight,*
> *In radiant day or darkest night.*
> *Oh, hear our prayer, extend Thy grace*
> *To those in peril deep in space.*

She knelt silently for a while, wondering if God was listening, and if the hymn was good for dogs, too. Albert sure was flying through the void, so it seemed to Charlie he ought to be deserving of some grace.

Charlie was perched on a sheet of twisted metal on the bottom, or outermost layer of the wheel. There was no gravity anywhere in the wheel, but since it was spinning, the farther down you went the heavier you felt. Just beyond the sheet of metal was a void, a hole ripped in the wheel's outer skin, fully twenty meters across. The metal had been twisted out and down by the force of some long-ago explosion, and this part of the wheel was a good place to walk carefully, if you had to walk here at all.

She picked her way back to the airlock, let herself in, and sealed the outer door behind her. She knew it was useless, knew there was nothing but vacuum on the other side, but it was something that had been impressed on her very strongly. When you go through a door, you lock it behind you. Lock it tight. If you don't, the breathsucker will get you in the middle of the night.

She shivered, and went to the next lock, which also led only to vacuum, as did the one beyond that. Finally, at the fifth airlock, she stepped into a tiny room that had breathable atmosphere, if a little chilly. Then she went through yet another lock before daring to take off her helmet.

At her feet was a large plastic box, and inside it, resting shakily on a scrap of bloody blanket and not at all at peace with the world, were two puppies. She picked them up, one in each hand—which didn't make them any happier—and nodded in satisfaction.

She kissed them, and put them back in the box. Tucking it under her arm, she faced another door. She could hear claws scratching at this one.

"Down, Fuchsia," she shouted. "Down, momma-dog." The scratching stopped, and she opened the last door and stepped through.

Fuchsia O'Charlie Station was sitting obediently, her ears pricked up, her head cocked and her eyes alert with that total, quivering concentration only a mother dog can achieve.

"I've got 'em, Foosh," Charlie said. She went down on one knee and allowed Fuchsia to put her paws up on the edge of the box. "See? There's Helga, and there's Conrad, and there's Albert, and there's Conrad, and Helga. One, two, three, four, eleventy-nine and six makes twenty-seven. See?"

Fuchsia looked at them doubtfully, then leaned in to pick one up, but Charlie pushed her away.

"I'll carry them," she said, and they set out along the darkened corridor. Fuchsia kept her eyes on the box, whimpering with the desire to get to her pups.

Charlie called this part of the wheel The Swamp. Things had gone wrong here a long time ago, and the more time went by, the worse it got. She figured it had been started by the explosion—which, in its turn, had been an indirect result of The Dying. The explosion had broken important pipes and wires. Water had started to pool in the corridor. Drainage pumps kept it from turning into an impossible situation. Charlie didn't come here very often.

Recently plants had started to grow in the swamp. They were ugly things, corpse-white or dental-plaque-yellow or mushroom gray. There was very little light for them, but they didn't seem to mind. She sometimes wondered if they were plants at all. Once she thought she had seen a fish. It had been white and blind. Maybe it had been a toad. She didn't like to think of that.

Charlie sloshed through the water, the box of puppies under one arm and her helmet under the other. Fuchsia bounced unhappily along with her.

At last they were out of it, and back into regions she knew better. She turned right and went three flights up a staircase—dogging the door behind her at every landing—then out into the Promenade Deck, which she called home.

About half the lights were out. The carpet was wrinkled and musty, and worn in the places Charlie frequently walked. Parts of the walls were streaked with water stains, or grew mildew in leprous patches. Charlie seldom noticed these things unless she was looking through her pictures from the old days, or was coming up from the maintenance levels, as she was now. Long ago, she had tried to keep things clean, but the place was just too big for a little girl. Now she limited her housekeeping to her own living quarters—and like any little girl, sometimes forgot about that, too.

She stripped off her suit and stowed it in the locker where she always kept it, then padded a short way down the gentle curve of the corridor to the Presidential Suite, which was hers. As she entered, with Fuchsia on her heels, a long-dormant television camera mounted high on the wall stuttered

to life. Its flickering red eye came on, and it turned jerkily on
its mount.

Anna-Louise Bach entered the darkened monitoring room,
mounted the five stairs to her office at the back, sat down,
and put her bare feet up on her desk. She tossed her uniform
cap, caught it on one foot, and twirled it idly there. She laced
her fingers together, leaned her chin on them, and thought
about it.

Corporal Steiner, her number two on C Watch, came up to
the platform, pulled a chair close, and sat beside her.

"Well? How did it go?"

"You want some coffee?" Bach asked him. When he
nodded, she pressed a button in the arm of her chair. "Bring
two coffees to the Watch Commander's station. Wait a minute . . . bring a pot, and two mugs." She put her feet down
and turned to face him.

"He did figure out there had to be a human aboard."

Steiner frowned. "You must have given him a clue."

"Well, I mentioned the airlock angle."

"See? He'd never have seen it without that."

"All right. Call it a draw."

"So then what did our leader want to do?"

Bach had to laugh. Hoeffer was unable to find his left
testicle without a copy of *Gray's Anatomy*.

"He came to a quick decision. We had to send a ship out
there *at once,* find the survivors and bring them to New
Dresden with all possible speed."

"And then you reminded him . . ."

". . . that no ship had been allowed to get within five
kilometers of Tango Charlie for thirty years. That even our
probe had to be small, slow, and careful to operate in the
vicinity, and that if it crossed the line it would be destroyed,
too. He was all set to call the Oberluftwaffe headquarters and
ask for a cruiser. I pointed out that A, we already *had* a robot
cruiser on station under the reciprocal trade agreement with
Allgemein Fernsehen Gesellschaft: B, that it was perfectly
capable of defeating Tango Charlie without any more help;
but C, any battle like that would *kill* whoever was on Charlie;
but that in any case, D, even if a ship *could* get to Charlie
there was a good reason for not doing so."

Emil Steiner winced, pretending pain in the head.

"Anna, Anna, you should never list things to him like that, and if you do, you should *never* get to point D."

"Why not?"

"Because you're lecturing him. If you have to make a speech like that, make it a set of options, which I'm sure you've already seen, sir, but which I will list for you, sir, to get all our ducks in a row. Sir."

Bach grimaced, knowing he was right. She was too impatient.

The coffee arrived, and while they poured and took the first sips, she looked around the big monitoring room. This is where impatience gets you.

In some ways, it could have been a lot worse. It *looked* like a good job. Though only a somewhat senior Recruit/Apprentice Bach was in command of thirty other R/A's on her watch, and had the rank of Corporal. The working conditions were good: clean, high-tech surroundings, low job stress, the opportunity to command, however fleetingly. Even the coffee was good.

But it was a dead-end, and everyone knew it. It was a job many rookies held for a year or two before being moved on to more important and prestigious assignments: part of a routine career. When a R/A stayed in the monitoring room for five years, even as a watch commander, someone was sending her a message. Bach understood the message, had realized the problem long ago. But she couldn't seem to do anything about it. Her personality was too abrasive for routine promotions. Sooner or later she angered her commanding officers in one way or another. She was far too good for anything overtly negative to appear in her yearly evaluations. But there were ways such reports could be written, good things left un-said, a lack of excitement on the part of the reporting officer . . . all things that added up to stagnation.

So here she was in Navigational Tracking, not really a police function at all, but something the New Dresden Police Department had handled for a hundred years and would probably handle for a hundred more.

It was a necessary job. So is garbage collection. But it was not what she had signed up for, ten years ago.

Ten years! God, it sounded like a long time. Any of the skilled guilds were hard to get into, but the average apprenticeship in New Dresden was six years.

She put down her coffee cup and picked up a hand mike.

"Tango Charlie, this is Foxtrot Romeo. Do you read?"

She listened, and heard only background hiss. Her troops were trying every available channel with the same message, but this one had been the main channel back when TC-38 had been a going concern.

"Tango Charlie, this is Foxtrot Romeo. Come in, please."

Again, nothing.

Steiner put his cup close to hers, and leaned back in his chair.

"So did he remember what the reason was? Why we can't approach?"

"He did, eventually. His first step was to slap a top-priority security rating on the whole affair, and he was confident the government would back him up."

"We got that part. The alert came through about twenty minutes ago."

"I figured it wouldn't do any harm to let him send it. He needed to do something. And it's what I would have done."

"It's what you *did,* as soon as the pictures came in."

"You know I don't have the authority for that."

"Anna, when you get that look in your eye and say, 'If one of you bastards breathes a word of this to *anyone,* I will cut out your tongue and eat it for breakfast,' . . . well, people listen."

"Did I say that?"

"Your very words."

"No wonder they all love me so much."

She brooded on that for a while, until T/A3 Klosinski hurried up the steps to her office.

"Corporal Bach, we've finally seen something," he said.

Bach looked at the big semicircle of flat television screens, over three hundred of them, on the wall facing her desk. Below the screens were the members of her watch, each at a desk/console, each with a dozen smaller screens to monitor. Most of the large screens displayed the usual data from the millions of objects monitored by Nav/Track radar, cameras, and computers. But fully a quarter of them now showed curved, empty corridors where nothing moved, or equally lifeless rooms. In some of them skeletons could be seen.

The three of them faced the largest screen on Bach's desk, and unconsciously leaned a little closer as a picture started to form. At first it was just streaks of color. Klosinski consulted a datapad on his wrist.

"This is from camera 14/P/delta. It's on the Promenade

Deck. Most of that deck was a sort of PX, with shopping areas, theaters, clubs, so forth. But one sector had VIP suites, for when people visited the station. This one's just outside the Presidential Suite."

"What's wrong with the picture?"

Klosinski sighed.

"Same thing wrong with all of them. The cameras are old. We've got about five percent of them in some sort of working order, which is a miracle. The Charlie computer is fighting us for every one."

"I figured it would."

"In just a minute . . . there! Did you see it?"

All Bach could see was a stretch of corridor, maybe a little fancier than some of the views already up on the wall, but not what Bach thought of as VIP. She peered at it, but nothing changed.

"No, nothing's going to happen now. This is a tape. We got it when the camera first came on." He fiddled with his data pad, and the screen resumed its multi-colored static. "I rewound it. Watch the door on the left."

This time Klosinski stopped the tape on the first recognizable image on the screen.

"This is someone's leg," he said, pointing. "And this is the tail of a dog."

Bach studied it. The leg was bare, and so was the foot. It could be seen from just below the knee.

"That looks like a Sheltie's tail," she said.

"We thought so, too."

"What about the foot?"

"Look at the door," Steiner said. "In relation to the door, the leg looks kind of small."

"You're right," Bach said. *A child?* she wondered. "Okay. Watch this one around the clock. I suppose if there was a camera in that room, you'd have told me about it."

"I guess VIP's don't like to be watched."

"Then carry on as you were. Activate every camera you can, and tape them *all*. I've got to take this to Hoeffer."

She started down out of her wall-less office, adjusting her cap at an angle she hoped looked smart and alert.

"Anna," Steiner called. She looked back.

"How did Hoeffer take it when you reminded him Tango Charlie only has six more days left?"

"He threw his pipe at me."

• • •

Charlie put Conrad and Helga back in the whelping box, along with Dieter and Inga. All four of them were squealing, which was only natural, but the quality of their squeals changed when Fuchsia jumped in with them, sat down on Dieter, then plopped over on her side. There was nothing that sounded or looked more determined than a blind, hungry, newborn puppy, Charlie thought.

The babies found the swollen nipples, and Fuchsia fussed over them, licking their little bottoms. Charlie held her breath. It almost looked as if she was counting her brood, and that certainly wouldn't do.

"Good dog, Fuchsia," she cooed, to distract her, and it did. Fuchsia looked up, said I haven't got time for you now, Charlie, and went back to her chores.

"How was the funeral?" asked Tik-Tok the Clock.

"Shut up!" Charlie hissed. "You . . . you big idiot! It's okay, Foosh."

Fuchsia was already on her side, letting the pups nurse and more or less ignoring both Charlie and Tik-Tok. Charlie got up and went into the bathroom. She closed and secured the door behind her.

"The funeral was very beautiful," she said, pushing the stool nearer the mammoth marble washbasin and climbing up on it. Behind the basin the whole wall was a mirror, and when she stood on the stool she could see herself. She flounced her blonde hair out and studied it critically. There were some tangles.

"Tell me about it," Tik-Tok said. "I want to know *every* detail."

So she told him, pausing a moment to sniff her armpits. Wearing the suit always made her smell so gross. She clambered up onto the broad marble counter, went around the basin and goosed the 24-karat gold tails of the two dolphins who cavorted there, and water began gushing out of their mouths. She sat with her feet in the basin, touching one tail or another when the water got too hot, and told Tik-Tok all about it.

Charlie used to bathe in the big tub. It was so big it was more suited for swimming laps than bathing. One day she slipped and hit her head and almost drowned. Now she usually bathed in the sink, which was not quite big enough, but a lot safer.

"The rose was the most wonderful part," she said. "I'm glad you thought of that. It just turned and turned and turned . . ."

"Did you say anything?"

"I sang a song. A hymn."

"Could I hear it?"

She lowered herself into the basin. Resting the back of her neck on a folded towel, the water came up to her chin, and her legs from the knees down stuck out the other end. She lowered her mouth a little, and made burbling sounds in the water.

"Can I hear it? I'd like to hear."

"Lord, guide and guard all those who fly . . ."

Tik-Tok listened to it once, then joined in harmony as she sang it again, and on the third time through added an organ part. Charlie felt the tears in her eyes again, and wiped them with the back of her hand.

"Time to scrubba-scrubba-scrubba," Tik-Tok suggested.

Charlie sat on the edge of the basin with her feet in the water, and lathered a washcloth.

"Scrubba-scrub beside your nose," Tik-Tok sang.

"Scrubba-scrub beside your nose," Charlie repeated, and industriously scoured all around her face.

"Scrubba-scrub between your toes. Scrub all the jelly out of your belly. Scrub your butt, and your you-know-what."

Tik-Tok led her through the ritual she'd been doing so long she didn't even remember how long. A couple times he made her giggle by throwing in a new verse. He was always making them up. When she was done, she was about the cleanest little girl anyone ever saw, except for her hair.

"I'll do that later," she decided, and hopped to the floor, where she danced the drying-off dance in front of the warm air blower until Tik-Tok told her she could stop. Then she crossed the room to the vanity table and sat on the high stool she had installed there.

"Charlie, there's something I wanted to talk to you about," Tik-Tok said.

Charlie opened a tube called "Coral Peaches" and smeared it all over her lips. She gazed at the thousand other bottles and tubes, wondering what she'd use this time.

"Charlie, are you listening to me?"

"Sure," Charlie said. She reached for a bottle labeled "The Glenlivet, Twelve Years Old," twisted the cork out of it, and put it to her lips. She took a big swallow, then another, and wiped her mouth on the back of her arm.

"Holy mackerel! That's real sippin' whiskey!" she shouted, and set the bottle down. She reached for a tin of rouge.

"Some people have been trying to talk to me," Tik-Tok said. "I believe they may have seen Albert, and wondered about him."

Charlie looked up, alarmed—and, doing so, accidentally made a solid streak of rouge from her cheekbone to her chin.

"Do you think they shot at Albert?"

"I don't think so. I think they're just curious."

"Will they hurt me?"

"You never can tell."

Charlie frowned, and used her finger to spread black eye-liner all over her left eyelid. She did the same for the right, then used another jar to draw violent purple frown lines on her forehead. With a thick pencil she outlined her eyebrows.

"What do they want?"

"They're just prying people, Charlie. I thought you ought to know. They'll probably try to talk to you, later."

"Should I talk to them?"

"That's up to you."

Charlie frowned even deeper. Then she picked up the bottle of Scotch and had another belt.

She reached for the Rajah's Ruby and hung it around her neck.

Fully dressed and made up now, Charlie paused to kiss Fuchsia and tell her how beautiful her puppies were, then hurried out to the Promenade Deck.

As she did, the camera on the wall panned down a little, and turned a few degrees on its pivot. That made a noise in the rusty mechanism, and Charlie looked up at it. The speaker beside the camera made a hoarse noise, then did it again. There was a little puff of smoke, and an alert sensor quickly directed a spray of extinguishing gas toward it, then itself gave up the ghost. The speaker said nothing else.

Odd noises were nothing new to Charlie. There were places on the wheel where the clatter of faltering mechanisms behind the walls was so loud you could hardly hear yourself think.

She thought of the snoopy people Tik-Tok had mentioned. That camera was probably just the kind of thing they'd like.

So she turned her butt to the camera, bent over, and farted at it.

She went to her mother's room, and sat beside her bed telling her all about little Albert's funeral. When she felt she'd been there long enough she kissed her dry cheek and ran out of the room.

Up one level were the dogs. She went from room to room, letting them out, accompanied by a growing horde of barking jumping Shelties. Each was deliriously happy to see her, as usual, and she had to speak sharply to a few when they kept licking her face. They stopped on command; Charlie's dogs were all good dogs.

When she was done there were seventy-two almost identical dogs yapping and running along with her in a sable-and-white tide. They rushed by another camera with a glowing red light, which panned to follow them up, up, and out of sight around the gentle curve of Tango Charlie.

Bach got off the slidewalk at the 34strasse intersection. She worked her way through the crowds in the shopping arcade, then entered the Intersection-park, where the trees were plastic but the winos sleeping on the benches were real. She was on Level Eight. Up here, 34strasse was taprooms and casinos, second-hand stores, missions, pawn shops, and cheap bordellos. Free-lance whores, naked or in elaborate costumes according to their specialty, eyed her and sometimes propositioned her. Hope springs eternal; these men and women saw her every day on her way home. She waved to a few she had met, though never in a professional capacity.

It was a kilometer and a half to Count Otto Von Zeppelin Residential Corridor. She walked beside the slidewalk. Typically, it operated two days out of seven. Her own quarters were at the end of Count Otto, apartment 80. She palmed the printpad, and went in.

She knew she was lucky to be living in such large quarters on a T/A salary. It was two rooms, plus a large bath and a tiny kitchen. She had grown up in a smaller place, shared by a lot more people. The rent was so low because her bed was only ten meters from an arterial tubeway; the floor vibrated loudly every thirty seconds as the capsules rushed by. It didn't bother her. She had spent her first ten years sleeping within a meter of a regional air-circulation station, just beyond a thin metal apartment wall. It left her with a hearing loss she had been too poor to correct until recently.

For most of her ten years in Otto 80 she had lived alone. Five times, for periods varying from two weeks to six months, she shared with a lover, as she was doing now.

When she came in, Ralph was in the other room. She could hear the steady huffing and puffing as he worked out. Bach went to the bathroom and ran a tub as hot as she could stand it, eased herself in, and stretched out. Her blue paper uniform brief floated to the surface; she skimmed, wadded up, and tossed the soggy mass toward the toilet.

She missed. It had been that sort of day.

She lowered herself until her chin was in the water. Beads of sweat popped out on her forehead. She smiled, and mopped her face with a washcloth.

After a while Ralph appeared in the doorway. She could hear him, but didn't open her eyes.

"I didn't hear you come in," he said.

"Next time I'll bring a brass band."

He just kept breathing heavy, gradually getting it under control. That was her most vivid impression of Ralph, she realized: heavy breathing. That, and lots and lots of sweat. And it was no surprise he had nothing to say. Ralph was oblivious to sarcasm. It made him tiresome, sometimes, but with shoulders like his he didn't need to be witty. Bach opened her eyes and smiled at him.

Luna's low gravity made it hard for all but the most fanatical to aspire to the muscle mass one could develop on the Earth. The typical Lunarian was taller than Earth-normal, and tended to be thinner.

As a much younger woman Bach had become involved, very much against her better judgment, with an earthling of the species "jock." It hadn't worked out, but she still bore the legacy in a marked preference for beefcake. This doomed her to consorting with only two kinds of men: well-muscled mesomorphs from Earth, and single-minded Lunarians who thought nothing of pumping iron for ten hours a day. Ralph was one of the latter.

There was no rule, so far as Bach could discover, that such specimens had to be mental midgets. That was a stereotype. It also happened, in Ralph's case, to be true. While not actually mentally defective, Ralph Goldstein's idea of a tough intellectual problem was how many kilos to bench press. His spare time was spent brushing his teeth or shaving his chest or looking at pictures of himself in bodybuilding magazines. Bach knew for a fact that Ralph thought the Earth and Sun revolved around Luna.

He had only two real interests: lifting weights, and making love to Anna-Louise Bach. She didn't mind that at all.

Ralph had a swastika tattooed on his penis. Early on, Bach had determined that he had no notion of the history of the symbol; he had seen it in an old film and thought it looked nice. It amused her to consider what his ancestors might have thought of the adornment.

He brought a stool close to the tub and sat on it, then stepped on a floor button. The tub was Bach's chief luxury. It did a lot of fun things. Now it lifted her on a long rack until she was half out of the water. Ralph started washing that half. She watched his soapy hands.

"Did you go to the doctor?" he asked her.

"Yeah, I finally did."

"What did he say?"

"Said I have cancer."

"How bad?"

"Real bad. It's going to cost a bundle. I don't know if my insurance will cover it all." She closed her eyes and sighed. It annoyed her to have him be right about something. He had nagged her for months to get her medical check-up.

"Will you get it taken care of tomorrow?"

"No, Ralph, I don't have time tomorrow. Next week, I promise. This thing has come up, but it'll be all over next week, one way or another."

He frowned, but didn't say anything. He didn't have to. The human body, its care and maintenance, was the one subject Ralph knew more about than she did, but even she knew it would be cheaper in the long run to have the work done now.

She felt so lazy he had to help her turn over. Damn, but he was good at this. She had never asked him to do it; he seemed to enjoy it. His strong hands dug into her back and found each sore spot, as if by magic. Presently, it wasn't sore anymore.

"What's this thing that's come up?"

"I . . . can't tell you about it. Classified, for now."

He didn't protest, nor did he show surprise, though it was

the first time Bach's work had taken her into the realm of secrecy.

It was annoying, really. One of Ralph's charms was that he was a good listener. While he wouldn't understand the technical side of anything, he could sometimes offer surprisingly good advice on personal problems. More often, he showed the knack of synthesizing and expressing things Bach had already known, but had not allowed herself to see.

Well, she could tell him part of it.

"There's this satellite," she began. "Tango Charlie. Have you ever heard of it?"

"That's a funny name for a satellite."

"It's what we call it on the tracking logs. It never really had a name—well, it did, a long time ago, but GWA took it over and turned it into a research facility and an Exec's retreat, and they just let it be known as TC-38. They got it in a war with Telecommunion, part of the peace treaty. They got Charlie, the Bubble, a couple other big wheels.

"The thing about Charlie . . . it's coming down. In about six days, it's going to spread itself all over the Farside. Should be a pretty big bang."

Ralph continued to knead the backs of her legs. It was never a good idea to rush him. He would figure things out in his own way, at his own speed, or he wouldn't figure them out at all.

"Why is it coming down?"

"It's complicated. It's been derelict for a long time. For a while it had the capacity to make course corrections, but it looks like it's run out of reaction mass, or the computer that's supposed to stabilize it isn't working anymore. For a couple of years it hasn't been making corrections."

"Why does it—"

"A Lunar orbit is never stable. There's the Earth tugging on the satellite, the solar wind, mass concentrations of Luna's surface . . . a dozen things that add up, over time. Charlie's in a very eccentric orbit now. Last time it came within a kilometer of the surface. Next time it's gonna miss us by a gnat's whisker, and the time after that, it hits."

Ralph stopped massaging. When Bach glanced at him, she saw he was alarmed. He had just understood that a very large object was about to hit his home planet, and he didn't like the idea.

"Don't worry," Bach said, "there's a surface installation

that might get some damage from the debris, but Charlie won't come within a hundred kilometers of any settlements. We got nothing to worry about on that score."

"Then why don't you just . . . push it back up . . . you know, go up there and do . . ." Whatever it is you do, Bach finished for him. He had no real idea what kept a satellite in orbit in the first place, but knew there were people who handled such matters all the time.

There were other questions he might have asked, as well. Why leave Tango Charlie alone all these years? Why not salvage it? Why allow things to get to this point at all?

All those questions brought her back to classified ground.

She sighed, and turned over.

"I wish we could," she said, sincerely. She noted that the swastika was saluting her, and that seemed like a fine idea, so she let him carry her into the bedroom.

And as he made love to her she kept seeing that incredible tide of Shelties with the painted child in the middle.

After the run, ten laps around the Promenade Deck, Charlie led the pack to the Japanese Garden and let them run free through the tall weeds and vegetable patches. Most of the trees in the Garden were dead. The whole place had once been a formal and carefully tended place of meditation. Four men from Tokyo had been employed full time to take care of it. Now the men were buried under the temple gate, the ponds were covered in green scum, the gracefully arched bridge had collapsed, and the flower beds were choked with dog turds.

Charlie had to spend part of each morning in the flower beds, feeding Mister Shitface. This was a cylindrical structure with a big round hole in its side, an intake for the wheel's recycling system. It ate dog feces, weeds, dead plants, soil, scraps . . . practically anything Charlie shoveled into it. The cylinder was painted green, like a frog, and had a face painted on it, with big lips outlining the hole. Charlie sang The Shit-Shoveling Song as she worked.

Tik-Tok had taught her the song, and he used to sing it with her. But a long time ago he had gone deaf in the Japanese Garden. Usually, all Charlie had to do was talk, and Tik-Tok would hear. But there were some places—and more of them every year—where Tik-Tok was deaf.

" '. . . *Raise dat laig,*' " Charlie puffed. " '*Lif' dat tail, If I gets in trouble will you go my bail?*' "

She stopped, and mopped her face with a red bandanna. As usual, there were dogs sitting on the edge of the flowerbed watching Charlie work. Their ears were lifted. They found this *endlessly* fascinating. Charlie just wished it would be over. But you took the bad with the good. She started shoveling again.

" *'I gets weary, O' all dis shovelin' . . .'* "

When she was finished she went back on the Promenade.

"What's next?" she asked.

"Plenty," said Tik-Tok. "The funeral put you behind schedule."

He directed her to the infirmary with the new litter. There they weighed, photographed, X-rayed, and catalogued each puppy. The results were put on file for later registration with the American Kennel Club. It quickly became apparent that Conrad was going to be a cull. He had an overbite. With the others it was too early to tell. She and Tik-Tok would examine them weekly, and their standards were an order of magnitude more stringent than the AKC's. Most of her *culls* would easily have best of breed in a show, and as for her breeding animals . . .

"I ought to be able to write Champion on most of these pedigrees."

"You must be patient."

Patient, yeah, she'd heard that before. She took another drink of Scotch. *Champion Fuchsia O'Charlie Station,* she thought. *Now* that *would really make a breeder's day.*

After the puppies, there were two from an earlier litter who were now ready for a final evaluation. Charlie brought them in, and she and Tik-Tok argued long and hard about points so fine few people would have seen them at all. In the end, they decided both would be sterilized.

Then it was noon feeding. Charlie never enforced discipline here. She let them jump and bark and nip at each other, as long as it didn't get *too* rowdy. She led them all to the cafeteria (and was tracked by three wall cameras), where the troughs of hard kibble and soft soyaburger were already full. Today it was chicken-flavored, Charlie's favorite.

Afternoon was training time. Consulting the records Tik-Tok displayed on a screen, she got the younger dogs one at a time and put each of them through thirty minutes of leash work, up and down the Promenade, teaching them Heel, Sit, Stay, Down, Come according to their degree of progress and

Tik-Tok's rigorous schedules. The older dogs were taken to the Ring in groups, where they sat obediently in a line as she put them, one by one, through free-heeling paces.

Finally it was evening meals, which she hated. It was all human food.

"Eat your vegetables," Tik-Tok would say. "Clean up your plate. People are starving in New Dresden." It was usually green salads and yucky broccoli and beets and stuff like that. Tonight it was yellow squash, which Charlie liked about as much as a root canal. She gobbled up the hamburger patty and then dawdled over the squash until it was a yellow-ish mess all over her plate like baby shit. Half of it ended up on the table. Finally Tik-Tok relented and let her get back to her duties, which, in the evening, was grooming. She brushed each dog until the coats shone. Some of the dogs had already settled in for the night, and she had to wake them up.

At last, yawning, she made her way back to her room. She was pretty well plastered by then. Tik-Tok, who was used to it, made allowances and tried to jolly her out of what seemed a very black mood.

"There's *nothing* wrong!" she shouted at one point, tears streaming from her eyes. Charlie could be an ugly drunk.

She staggered out to the Promenade Deck and lurched from wall to wall, but she never fell down. Ugly or not, she knew how to hold her liquor. It had been ages since it made her sick.

The elevator was in what had been a commercial zone. The empty shops gaped at her as she punched the button. She took another drink, and the door opened. She got in.

She hated this part. The elevator was rising up through a spoke, toward the hub of the wheel. She got lighter as the car went up, and the trip did funny things to the inner ear. She hung on to the hand rail until the car shuddered to a stop.

Now everything was fine. She was almost weightless up here. Weightlessness was great when you were drunk. When there was no gravity to worry about, your head didn't spin—and if it did, it didn't matter.

This was one part of the wheel where the dogs never went. They could never get used to falling, no matter how long they were kept up here. But Charlie was an expert in falling. When she got the blues she came up here and pressed her face to the huge ballroom window.

People were only a vague memory to Charlie. Her mother

didn't count. Though she visited every day, mom was about as lively as V.I. Lenin. Sometimes Charlie wanted to be held so much it hurt. The dogs were good, they were warm, they licked her, they loved her . . . but they couldn't hold her.

Tears leaked from her eyes, which was really a bitch in the ballroom, because tears could get *huge* in here. She wiped them away and looked out the window.

The moon was getting bigger again. She wondered what it meant. Maybe she would ask Tik-Tok.

She made it back as far as the Garden. Inside, the dogs were sleeping in a huddle. She knew she ought to get them back to their rooms, but she was far too drunk for that. And Tik-Tok couldn't do a damn thing about it in here. He couldn't see, and he couldn't hear.

She lay down on the ground, curled up, and was asleep in seconds.

When she started to snore, the three or four dogs who had come over to watch her sleep licked her mouth until she stopped. Then they curled up beside her. Soon they were joined by others, until she slept in the middle of a blanket of dogs.

A crisis team had been assembled in the monitoring room when Bach arrived the next morning. They seemed to have been selected by Captain Hoeffer, and there were so many of them that there was not enough room for everyone to sit down. Bach led them to a conference room just down the hall, and everyone took seats around the long table. Each seat was equipped with a computer display, and there was a large screen on the wall behind Hoeffer, at the head of the table. Bach took her place on his right, and across from her was Deputy Chief Zeiss, a man with a good reputation in the department. He made Bach very nervous. Hoeffer, on the other hand, seemed to relish his role. Since Zeiss seemed content to be an observer, Bach decided to sit back and speak only if called upon.

Noting that every seat was filled, and that what she assumed were assistants had pulled up chairs behind their principles, Bach wondered if this many people were really required for this project. Steiner, sitting at Bach's right, leaned over and spoke quietly.

"Pick a time," he said.

"What's that?"

"I said pick a time. We're running an office pool. If you come closest to the time security is broken, you win a hundred Marks."

"Is ten minutes from now spoken for?"

They quieted when Hoeffer stood up to speak.

"Some of you have been working on this problem all night," he said. "Others have been called in to give us your expertise in the matter. I'd like to welcome Deputy Chief Zeiss, representing the Mayor and the Chief of Police. Chief Zeiss, would you like to say a few words?"

Zeiss merely shook his head, which seemed to surprise Hoeffer. Bach knew he would never have passed up an opportunity like that, and probably couldn't understand how anyone else could.

"Very well. We can start with Doctor Blume."

Blume was a sour little man who affected wire-rimmed glasses and a cheap toupee over what must have been a completely bald head. Bach thought it odd that a medical man would wear such clumsy prosthetics, calling attention to problems that were no harder to cure than a hangnail. She idly called up his profile on her screen, and was surprised to learn he had a Nobel Prize.

"The subject is a female caucasoid, almost certainly Earthborn."

On the wall behind Hoeffer and on Bach's screen, tapes of the little girl and her dogs were being run.

"She displays no obvious abnormalities. In several shots she is nude, and clearly has not yet reached puberty. I estimate her age between seven and ten years old. There are small discrepancies in her behavior. Her movements are economical—except when playing. She accomplishes various hand-eye tasks with a maturity beyond her apparent years." The doctor sat down abruptly.

It put Hoeffer off balance.

"Ah . . . that's fine, doctor. But, if you recall, I just asked you to tell me how old she is, and if she's healthy."

"She appears to be eight. I said that."

"Yes, but—"

"What do you want from me?" Blume said, suddenly angry. He glared around at many of the assembled experts. "There's something badly wrong with that girl. I say she is eight. Fine! Any fool could see that. I say I can observe no health problems visually. For this, you need a doctor? Bring her to me, give me a few days, and I'll give you six volumes on her health. But videotapes . . . ?'' He trailed off, his silence as eloquent as his words.

"Thank you, Doctor Blume," Hoeffer said. "As soon as—"

"I'll tell you one thing, though," Blume said, in a low, dangerous tone. "It is a disgrace to let that child drink liquor like that. The effects in later life will be terrible. I have seen large men in their thirties and forties who could not hold half as much as I saw her drink . . . *in one day!*'' He glowered at Hoeffer for a moment. "I was sworn to silence. But I want to know who is responsible for this."

Bach realized he didn't know where the girl was. She wondered how many of the others in the room had been filled in, and how many were working only on their own part of the problem.

"It will be explained," Zeiss said, quietly. Blume looked from Zeiss to Hoeffer, and back, then settled into his chair, not mollified but willing to wait.

"Thank you, Doctor Blume," Hoeffer said again. "Next we'll hear from . . . Ludmilla Rossnikova, representing the GMA Conglomerate."

Terrific, thought Bach. He's brought GMA into it. No doubt he swore Ms. Rossnikova to secrecy, and if he really thought she would fail to mention it to her supervisor then he was even dumber than Bach had thought. She had worked for them once, long ago, and though she was just an employee she had learned something about them. GMA had its roots deep in twentieth-century Japanese industry. When you went to work on the executive level at GMA, you were set up for life. They expected, and received, loyalty that compared favorably with that demanded by the Mafia. Which meant that, by telling Rossnikova his "secret," Hoeffer had insured that three hundred GMA execs knew about it three minutes later. They could be relied on to keep a secret, but only if it benefited GMA.

"The computer on Tango Charlie was a custom-designed array," Rossnikova began. "That was the usual practice in those days, with BioLogic computers. It was designated the same as the station: BioLogic TC-38. It was one of the largest installations of its time.

"At the time of the disaster, when it was clear that everything had failed, the TC-38 was given its final instructions. Because of the danger, it was instructed to impose an interdiction zone around the station, which you'll find described under the label Interdiction on your screens."

Rossnikova paused while many of those present called up this information.

"To implement the zone, the TC-38 was given command of certain defensive weapons. These included ten bevawatt lasers . . . and other weapons which I have not been authorized to name or describe, other than to say they are at least as formidable as the lasers."

Hoeffer looked annoyed, and was about to say something, but Zeiss stopped him with a gesture. Each understood that the lasers were enough in themselves.

"So while it is possible to destroy the station," Rossnikova went on, "there is no chance of boarding it—assuming anyone would even want to try."

Bach thought she could tell from the different expressions around the table which people knew the whole story and which knew only their part of it. A couple of the latter seemed ready to ask a question, but Hoeffer spoke first.

"How about canceling the computer's instructions?" he said. "Have you tried that?"

"That's been tried many times over the last few years, as this crisis got closer. We didn't expect it to work, and it did not. Tango Charlie won't accept a new program."

"Oh my God," Doctor Blume gasped. Bach saw that his normally florid face had paled. "Tango Charlie. She's on Tango Charlie."

"That's right, doctor," said Hoeffer. "And we're trying to figure out how to get her off. Doctor Wilhelm?"

Wilhelm was an older woman with the stocky build of the Earthborn. She rose, and looked down at some notes in her hand.

"Information's under the label Neurotropic Agent X on your machines," she muttered, then looked up at them. "But you needn't bother. That's about as far as we got, naming it. I'll sum up what we know, but you don't need an expert for this; there *are* no experts on Neuro-X.

"It broke out on August 9, thirty years ago next month. The initial report was five cases, one death. Symptoms were progressive paralysis, convulsions, loss of motor control, numbness.

"Tango Charlie was immediately quarantined as a standard procedure. An epidemiological team was dispatched from Atlanta, followed by another from New Dresden. All ships which had left Tango Charlie were ordered to return, except for one on its way to Mars and another already in parking orbit around Earth. The one in Earth orbit was forbidden to land.

"By the time the teams arrived, there were over a hundred reported cases, and six more deaths. Later symptoms included blindness and deafness. It progressed at different rates in different people, but it was always quite fast. Mean survival time from onset of symptoms was later determined to be forty-eight hours. Nobody lived longer than four days.

"Both medical teams immediately came down with it, as did a third, and a fourth team. *All* of them came down with it, each and every person. The first two teams had been using class three isolation techniques. It didn't matter. The third team stepped up the precautions to class two. Same result. Very quickly we had been forced into class one procedures—which involves isolation as total as we can get it: no physical contact whatsoever, no sharing of air supplies, all air to the investigators filtered through a sterilizing environment. They *still* got it. Six patients and some tissue samples were sent to a class one installation two hundred miles from New Dresden, and more patients were sent, with class one precautions, to a hospital ship close to Charlie. Everyone at both facilities came down with it. We *almost* sent a couple of patients to Atlanta."

She paused, looking down and rubbing her forehead. No one said anything.

"I was in charge," she said, quietly. "I can't take credit for not shipping anyone to Atlanta. We were going to . . . and suddenly there wasn't anybody left on Charlie to load patients aboard. All dead or dying.

"We backed off. Bear in mind this all happened in five days. What we had to show for those five days was a major space station with all aboard dead, three ships full of dead people, and an epidemiological research facility here on Luna full of dead people.

"After that, politicians began making most of the decisions—but I advised them. The two nearby ships were landed by robot control at the infected research station. The derelict ship going to Mars was . . . I think it's still classified, but what the hell? It was blown up with a nuclear weapon. Then we started looking into what was left. The station here was easiest. There was one cardinal rule: *nothing* that went into that station was to come out. Robot crawlers brought in remote manipulators and experimental animals. Most of the animals died. Neuro-X killed most mammals: monkeys, rats, cats—''

"Dogs?" Bach asked. Wilhelm glanced at her.

"It didn't kill *all* the dogs. Half of the ones we sent in lived.''

"Did you know that there were dogs alive on Charlie?''

"No. The interdiction was already set up by then. Charlie Station was impossible to land, and too close and too visible to nuke, because that would violate about a dozen corporate treaties. And there seemed no reason not to just leave it there. We had our samples isolated here at the Lunar station. We decided to work with that, and forget about Charlie.''

"Thank you, doctor.''

"As I was saying, it was by far the most virulent organism we had ever seen. It seemed to have a taste for all sorts of neural tissue, in almost every mammal.

"The teams that went in never had time to learn anything. They were all disabled too quickly, and just as quickly they were dead. We didn't find out much, either . . . for a variety of reasons. My guess is it was a virus, simply because we would certainly have seen anything larger almost immediately. But we never *did* see it. It was fast getting in—we don't know how it was vectored, but the only reliable shield was several miles of vacuum—and once it got in, I suspect it worked changes on genetic material of the host, setting up a secondary agent which I'm almost sure we isolated . . . and then it went away and hid very well. It was still in the host, in some form, it *had* to be, but we think its active life in the nervous system was on the order of one hour. But by then it had already done its damage. It set the system against itself, and the host was consumed in about two days.''

Wilhelm had grown increasingly animated. A few times Bach thought she was about to get incoherent. It was clear the nightmare of Neuro-X had not diminished for her with the passage of thirty years. But now she made an effort to slow down again.

"The other remarkable thing about it was, of course, its infectiousness. Nothing I've ever seen was so persistent in evading our best attempts at keeping it isolated. Add that to its mortality rate, which, at the time, seemed to be one hundred percent . . . and you have the second great reason why we learned so little about it.''

"What was the first?" Hoeffer asked. Wilhelm glared at him.

"The difficulty of investigating such a subtle process of infection by remote control.''

"Ah, of course.''

"The other thing was simply fear. Too many people had died for there to be any hope of hushing it up. I don't know if anyone tried. I'm sure those of you who were old enough remember the uproar. So the public debate was loud and long, and the pressure for extreme measures was intense . . . and, I should add, not unjustified. The argument was simple. Everyone who got it was dead. I believe that if those patients had been sent to Atlanta, everyone on *Earth* would have died. Therefore . . . what was the point of taking a chance by keeping it alive and studying it?''

Doctor Blume cleared his throat, and Wilhelm looked at him.

"As I recall, doctor,'' he said, "there were two reasons raised. One was the abstract one of scientific knowledge. Though there might be no point in studying Neuro-X since no one was afflicted with it, we might learn something by the study itself.''

"Point taken,'' Wilhelm said, "and no argument.''

"And the second was, we never found out where Neuro-X came from . . . there were rumors it was a biological warfare agent.'' He looked at Rossnikova, as if asking her what comment GMA might want to make about *that*. Rossnikova said nothing. "But most people felt it was a spontaneous mutation. There have been several instances of that in the high-radiation environment of a space station. And if it happened once, what's to prevent it from happening again?''

"Again, you'll get no argument from me. In fact, I supported both those positions when the question was being debated.'' Wilhelm grimaced, then looked right at Blume. "But the fact is, I didn't support them very hard, and when the Lunar station was sterilized, I felt a lot better.''

Blume was nodding.

"I'll admit it. I felt better, too.''

"And if Neuro-X were to show up again,'' she went on,

quietly, "my advice would be to sterilize immediately. Even if it meant losing a city."

Blume said nothing. Bach watched them both for a while in the resulting silence, finally, understanding just how much Wilhelm feared this thing.

There was a lot more. The meeting went on for three hours, and everyone got a chance to speak. Eventually, the problem was outlined to everyone's satisfaction.

Tango Charlie could not be boarded. It could be destroyed. (Some time was spent debating the wisdom of the original interdiction order—beating a dead horse, as far as Bach was concerned—and questioning whether it might be possible to countermand it.)

But things could *leave* Tango Charlie. It would only be necessary to withdraw the robot probes that had watched so long and faithfully, and the survivors could be evacuated.

That left the main question. *Should* they be evacuated?

(The fact that only one survivor had been sighted so far was not mentioned. Everyone assumed others would show up sooner or later. After all, it was simply not possible that just one eight-year-old girl could be the only occupant of a station no one had entered or left for thirty years.)

Wilhelm, obviously upset but clinging strongly to her position, advocated blowing up the station at once. There was some support for this, but only about ten percent of the group.

The eventual decision, which Bach had predicted before the meeting even started, was to do nothing at the moment.

After all, there were almost five whole days to keep thinking about it.

"There's a call waiting for you," Steiner said, when she got back to the monitoring room. "The switchboard says it's important."

Bach went into her office—wishing yet again for one with walls—flipped a switch.

"Bach," she said. Nothing came on the vision screen.

"I'm curious," said a woman's voice. "Is this the Anna-Louise Bach who worked in The Bubble ten years ago?"

For a moment, Bach was too surprised to speak, but she felt a wave of heat as blood rushed to her face. She knew the voice.

"Hello? Are you there?"

"Why no vision?" she asked.

"First, are you alone? And is your instrument secure?"

"The instrument is secure, if yours is." Bach flipped another switch, and a privacy hood descended around her screen. The sounds of the room faded as a sonic scrambler began operating. "And I'm alone."

Megan Galloway's face appeared on the screen. One part of Bach's mind noted that she hadn't changed much, except that her hair was curly and red.

"I thought you might not wish to be seen with me," Galloway said. Then she smiled. "Hello, Anna-Louise. How are you?"

"I don't think it really matters if I'm seen with you," Bach said.

"No? Then would you care to comment on why the New Dresden Police Department, among other government agencies, is allowing an eight-year-old child to go without the rescue she so obviously needs?"

Bach said nothing.

"Would you comment on the rumor that the NDPD does not intend to effect the child's rescue? That, if it can get away with it, the NDPD will let the child be smashed to pieces?"

Still Bach waited.

Galloway sighed, and ran a hand through her hair.

"You're the most exasperating woman I've ever known, Bach," she said. "Listen, don't you even want to *try* to talk me out of going with the story?"

Bach almost said something, but decided to wait once more.

"If you want to, you can meet me at the end of your shift. The Mozartplatz. I'm on the *Great Northern*, suite 1, but I'll see you in the bar on the top deck."

"I'll be there," Bach said, and broke the connection.

Charlie sang the Hangover Song most of the morning. It was not one of her favorites.

There was penance to do, of course. Tik-Tok made her drink a foul glop that—she had to admit—did do wonders for her headache. When she was done she was drenched in sweat, but her hangover was gone.

"You're lucky," Tik-Tok said. "Your hangovers are never severe."

"They're severe enough for *me*," Charlie said.

He made her wash her hair, too.

After that, she spent some time with her mother. She always valued that time. Tik-Tok was a good friend, mostly, but he was so *bossy*. Charlie's mother never shouted at her, never scolded or lectured. She simply listened. True, she wasn't very active. But it was nice to have somebody just to talk to. One day, Charlie hoped, her mother would walk again. Tik-Tok said that was unlikely.

Then she had to round up the dogs and take them for their morning run.

And everywhere she went, the red camera eyes followed her. Finally she had enough. She stopped, put her fists on her hips, and shouted at a camera.

"You stop that!" she said.

The camera started to make noises. At first she couldn't understand anything, then some words started to come through.

". . . lie, Tango . . . Foxtrot . . . in, please. Tango Charlie . . ."

"Hey, that's my name."

The camera continued to buzz and spit noise at her.

"Tik-Tok, is that you?"

"I'm afraid not, Charlie."

"What's going on, then?"

"It's those nosy people. They've been watching you, and now they're trying to talk to you. But I'm holding them off. I don't think they'll bother you, if you just ignore the cameras."

"But why are you fighting them?"

"I didn't think you'd want to be bothered."

Maybe there was some of that hangover still around. Anyway, Charlie got real angry at Tik-Tok, and called him some names he didn't approve of. She knew she'd pay for it later, but for now Tik-Tok was pissed, and in no mood to reason with her. So he let her have what she wanted, on the principle that getting what you want is usually the worst thing that can happen to anybody.

"*Tango Charlie, this is Foxtrot Romeo. Come in, please. Tango—*"

"Come in *where?*" Charlie asked, reasonably. "And my name isn't Tango."

Bach was so surprised to have the little girl actually reply that for a moment she couldn't think of anything to say.

"Uh . . . it's just an expression," Bach said. "Come in . . . that's radio talk for 'please answer.' "

"Then you should say please answer," the little girl pointed out.

"Maybe you're right. My name is Bach. You can call me Anna-Louise, if you'd like. We've been trying to—"

"Why should I?"

"Excuse me?"

"Excuse you for what?"

Bach looked at the screen and drummed her fingers silently for a short time. Around her in the monitoring room, there was not a sound to be heard. At last, she managed a smile.

"Maybe we started off on the wrong foot."

"Which foot would that be?"

The little girl just kept staring at her. Her expression was not amused, not hostile, not really argumentative. Then why was the conversation suddenly so maddening?

"Could I make a statement?" Bach tried.

"I don't know. Can you?"

Bach's fingers didn't tap this time; they were balled up in a fist.

"I shall, anyway. My name is Anna-Louise Bach. I'm talking to you from New Dresden, Luna. That's a city on the moon, which you can probably see—"

"I know where it is."

"Fine. I've been trying to contact you for many hours, but your computer has been fighting me all the time."

"That's right. He said so."

"Now, I can't explain why he's been fighting me, but—"

"I know why. He thinks you're nosy."

"I won't deny that. But we're trying to help you."

"Why?"

"Because . . . it's what we do. Now if you could—"

"Hey. Shut up, will you?"

Bach did so. With forty-five other people at their scattered screens, Bach watched the little girl—the *horrible* little girl, as she was beginning to think of her—take a long pull from the green glass bottle of Scotch whiskey. She belched, wiped her mouth with the back of her hand, and scratched between her legs. When she was done, she smelled her fingers.

She seemed about to say something, then cocked her head, listening to something Bach couldn't hear.

"That's a good idea," she said, then got up and ran away.

She was just vanishing around the curve of the deck when Hoeffer burst into the room, trailed by six members of his advisory team. Bach leaned back in her chair, and tried to fend off thoughts of homicide.

"I was told you'd established contact," Hoeffer said, leaning over Bach's shoulder in a way she absolutely *detested*. He peered at the lifeless scene. "What happened to her?"

"I don't know. She said, 'That's a good idea,' got up, and ran off."

"I told you to keep her here until I got a chance to talk to her."

"I tried," Bach said.

"You should have—"

"I have her on camera nineteen," Steiner called out.

Everyone watched as the technicians followed the girl's progress on the working cameras. They saw her enter a room to emerge in a moment with a big-screen monitor. Bach tried to call her each time she passed a camera, but it seemed only the first one was working for incoming calls. She passed through the range of four cameras before coming back to the original, where she carefully unrolled the monitor and tacked it to a wall, then payed out the cord and plugged it in very close to the wall camera Bach's team had been using. She unshipped this camera from its mount. The picture jerked around for awhile, and finally steadied. The girl had set it on the floor.

"Stabilize that," Bach told her team, and the picture on her monitor righted itself. She now had a worm's-eye view of the corridor. The girl sat down in front of the camera, and grinned.

"Now I can see you," she said. Then she frowned. "If you send me a picture."

"Bring a camera over here," Bach ordered.

While it was being set up, Hoeffer shouldered her out of the way and sat in her chair.

"There you are," the girl said. And again, she frowned. "That's funny. I was sure you were a girl. Did somebody cut your balls off?"

Now it was Hoeffer's turn to be speechless. There were a few badly suppressed giggles; Bach quickly silenced them with her most ferocious glare, while giving thanks no one would ever know how close she had come to bursting into laughter.

"Never mind that," Hoeffer said. "My name is Hoeffer. Would you go get your parents? We need to talk to them."

"No," said the girl. "And no."

"What's that?"

"No, I won't get them," the girl clarified, "and no, you don't need to talk to them."

Hoeffer had little experience dealing with children.

"Now, please be reasonable," he began, in a wheedling tone. "We're trying to help you, after all. We have to talk to your parents, to find out more about your situation. After that, we're going to help get you out of there."

"I want to talk to the lady," the girl said.

"She's not here."

"I think you're lying. She talked to me just a minute ago."

"I'm in charge."

"In charge of what?"

"Just in charge. Now, go get your parents!"

They all watched as she got up and moved closer to the camera. All they could see at first was her feet. Then water began to splash on the lens.

Nothing could stop the laughter this time, as Charlie urinated on the camera.

For three hours Bach watched the screens. Every time the girl passed the prime camera Bach called out to her. She had thought about it carefully. Bach, like Hoeffer, did not know a lot about children. She consulted briefly with the child psychologist on Hoeffer's team and the two of them outlined a tentative game plan. The guy seemed to know what he was talking about and, even better, his suggestions agreed with what Bach's common sense told her should work.

So she never said anything that might sound like an order. While Hoeffer seethed in the background, Bach spoke quietly and reasonably every time the child showed up. "I'm still here," she would say. "We could talk," was a gentle suggestion. "You want to play?"

She longed to use one line the psychologist suggested, one that would put Bach and the child on the same team, so to speak. The line was "The idiot's gone. You want to talk now?"

Eventually the girl began glancing at the camera. She had a different dog every time she came by. At first Bach didn't realize this, as they were almost completely identical. Then she noticed they came in slightly different sizes.

"That's a beautiful dog," she said. The girl looked up, then started away. "I'd like to have a dog like that. What's its name?"

"This is Madam's Sweet Brown Sideburns. Say *hi*, Brownie." The dog yipped. "Sit up for mommy, Brownie. Now roll over. Stand tall. Now go in a circle, Brownie, that's a good doggy, walk on your hind legs. Now *jump*, Brownie. Jump, jump, *jump!*" The dog did exactly as he was told, leaping into the air and turning a flip each time the girl commanded it. Then he sat down, pink tongue hanging out, eyes riveted on his master.

"I'm impressed," Bach said, and it was the literal truth. Like other citizens of Luna, Bach had never seen a wild animal, had never owned a pet, knew animals only from the municipal zoo, where care was taken not to interfere with natural behaviors. She had had no idea animals could be so smart, and no inkling of how much work had gone into the exhibition she had just seen.

"It's nothing," the girl said. "You should see his father. Is this Anna-Louise again?"

"Yes, it is. What's your name?"

"Charlie. You ask a lot of questions."

"I guess I do. I just want to—"

"I'd like to ask some questions, too."

"All right. Go ahead."

"I have six of them, to start off with. One, why should I call you Anna-Louise? Two, why should I excuse you? Three, what is the wrong foot? Four . . . but that's not a question, really, since you already proved you *can* make a statement, if you wish, by doing so. Four, why are you trying to help me? Five, why do you want to see my parents?"

It took Bach a moment to realize that these were the questions Charlie had asked in their first, maddening conversation, questions she had not gotten answers for. And they were in their original order.

And they didn't make a hell of a lot of sense.

But the child psychologist was making motions with his hands, and nodding his encouragement to Bach, so she started in.

"You should call me Anna-Louise because . . . it's my first name, and friends call each other by their first names."

"Are we friends?"

"Well, I'd like to be your friend."

"Why?"

"Look, you don't have to call me Anna-Louise if you don't want to."

"I don't mind. Do I have to be your friend?"

"Not if you don't want to."

"Why should I want to?"

And it went on like that. Each question spawned a dozen more, and a further dozen sprang from each of those. Bach had figured to get Charlie's six—make that five—questions out of the way quickly, then get to the important things. She soon began to think she'd never answer even the *first* question.

She was involved in a long and awkward explanation of friendship, going over the ground for the tenth time, when words appeared at the bottom of her screen.

Put your foot down, they said. She glanced up at the child psychologist. He was nodding, but making quieting gestures with his hands. "But gently," the man whispered.

Right, Bach thought. Put your foot down. And get off on the wrong foot again.

"That's enough of that," Bach said abruptly.

"Why?" asked Charlie.

"Because I'm tired of that. I want to do something else."

"All right," Charlie said. Bach saw Hoeffer waving frantically, just out of camera range.

"Uh . . . Captain Hoeffer is still here. He'd like to talk to you."

"That's just too bad for him. I don't want to talk to him."

Good for you, Bach thought. But Hoeffer was still waving.

"Why not? He's not so bad." Bach felt ill, but avoided showing it.

"He lied to me. He said you'd gone away."

"Well, he's in charge here, so—"

"I'm warning you," Charlie said, and waited a dramatic moment, shaking her finger at the screen. "You put that poo-poo-head back on, and I won't come in ever again."

Bach looked helplessly at Hoeffer, who at last nodded.

"I want to talk about dogs," Charlie announced.

So that's what they did for the next hour. Bach was thankful she had studied up on the subject when the dead puppy first appeared. Even so, there was no doubt as to who was the authority. Charlie knew everything there was to know about dogs. And of all the experts Hoeffer had called in, not one could tell Bach anything about the goddamn animals. She wrote a note and handed it to Steiner, who went off to find a zoologist.

Finally Bach was able to steer the conversation around to Charlie's parents.

"My father is dead," Charlie admitted.

"I'm sorry," Bach said. "When did he die?"

"Oh, a long time ago. He was a spaceship pilot, and one day he went off in his spaceship and never came back." For a moment she looked far away. Then she shrugged. "I was real young."

Fantasy, the psychologist wrote at the bottom of her screen, but Bach had already figured that out. Since Charlie had to have been born many years after the Charlie Station Plague, her father could not have flown any spaceships.

"What about your mother?"

Charlie was silent for a long time, and Bach began to wonder if she was losing contact with her. At last, she looked up.

"You want to talk to my mother?"

"I'd like that very much."

"Okay. But that's all for today. I've got work to do. You've already put me way behind."

"Just bring your mother here, and I'll talk to her, and you can do your work."

"No. I can't do that. But I'll take you to her. Then I'll work, and I'll talk to you tomorrow."

Bach started to protest that tomorrow was not soon enough, but Charlie was not listening. The camera was picked up, and the picture bounced around as she carried it with her. All Bach could see was a very unsteady upside-down view of the corridor.

"She's going into Room 350," said Steiner. "She's been in there twice, and she stayed a while both times."

Bach said nothing. The camera jerked wildly for a moment, then steadied.

"This is my mother," Charlie said. "Mother, this is my friend, Anna-Louise."

The Mozartplatz had not existed when Bach was a child. Construction on it had begun when she was five, and the first phase was finished when she was fifteen. Tenants had begun

moving in soon after that. During each succeeding year new
sectors had been opened, and though a structure as large as
the Mozartplatz would never be finished—two major sectors
were currently under renovation—it had been essentially completed six years ago.

It was a virtual copy of the Soleri-class arcology atriums
that had spouted like mushrooms on the Earth in the last four
decades, with the exception that on Earth you built up, and on
Luna you went down.

First dig a trench fifteen miles long and two miles deep.
Vary the width of the trench, but never let it get narrower
than one mile, nor broader than five. In some places make the
base of the trench wider than the top, so the walls of rock
loom outward. Now put a roof over it, fill it with air, and
start boring tunnels into the sides. Turn those tunnels into
apartments and shops and everything else humans need in a
city. You end up with dizzying vistas, endless terraces that
reach higher than the eye can see, a madness of light and
motion and spaces too wide to echo.

Do all that, and you still wouldn't have the Mozartplatz.
To approach that ridiculous level of grandeur there were still
a lot of details to attend to. Build four mile-high skyscrapers
to use as table legs to support the mid-air golf course. Criss-
cross the open space with bridges having no visible means of
support, and encrusted with shops and homes that cling like
barnacles. Suspend apartment buildings from silver balloons
that rise half the day and descend the other half, reachable
only by glider. Put in a fountain with more water than Niag-
ara, and a ski slope on a huge spiral ramp. Dig a ten-mile
lake in the middle, with a bustling port at each end for the
luxury ships that ply back and forth, attach runways to balco-
nies so residents can fly to their front door, stud the interior
with zeppelin ports and railway stations and hanging gardens
. . . and you still don't have Mozartplatz, but you're getting
closer.

The upper, older parts of New Dresden, the parts she had
grown up in, were spartan and claustrophobic. Long before
her time Lunarians had begun to build larger when they could
afford it. The newer, lower parts of the city were studded
with downscale versions of the Mozartplatz, open spaces half
a mile wide and maybe fifty levels deep. This was just a logical
extension.

She felt she ought to dislike it because it was so overdone, so fantastically huge, such a waste of space . . . and, oddly, so standardized. It was a taste of the culture of old Earth, where Paris looked just like Tokyo. She had been to the new Beethovenplatz at Clavius, and it looked just like this place. Six more arco-malls were being built in other Lunar cities.

And Bach liked it. She couldn't help herself. One day she'd like to live here.

She left her tube capsule in the bustling central station, went to a terminal and queried the location of the *Great Northern*. It was docked at the southern port, five miles away.

It was claimed that any form of non-animal transportation humans had ever used was available in the Mozartplatz. Bach didn't doubt it. She had tried most of them. But when she had a little time, as she did today, she liked to walk. She didn't have time to walk five miles, but compromised by walking to the trolley station a mile away.

Starting out on a brick walkway. she moved to cool marble, then over a glass bridge with lights flashing down inside. This took her to a boardwalk, then down to a beach where machines made four-foot breakers, each carrying a new load of surfers. The sand was fine and hot between her toes. Mozartplatz was a sensual delight for the feet. Few Lunarians ever wore shoes, and they could walk all day through old New Dresden and feel nothing but different types of carpeting and composition flooring.

The one thing Bach didn't like about the place was the weather. She thought it was needless, preposterous, and inconvenient. It began to rain and, as usual, caught her off guard. She hurried to a shelter where, for a tenthMark, she rented an umbrella, but it was too late for her paper uniform. As she stood in front of a blower, drying off, she wadded it up and threw it away, then hurried to catch the trolley, nude but for her creaking leather equipment belt and police cap. Even this stripped down, she was more dressed than a quarter of the people around her.

The conductor gave her a paper mat to put on the artificial leather seat. There were cut flowers in crystal vases attached to the sides of the car. Bach sat by an open window and leaned one arm outside in the cool breeze, watching the passing scenery. She craned her neck when the *Graf Zeppelin* muttered by overhead. They said it was an exact copy of the

first world-girdling dirigible, and she had no reason to doubt
it.

It was a great day to be traveling. If not for one thing, it
would be perfect. Her mind kept coming back to Charlie and
her mother.

She had forgotten just how big the *Great Northern* was. She
stopped twice on her way down the long dock to board it,
once to buy a lime sherbet ice cream cone, and again to
purchase a skirt. As she fed coins into the clothing machine,
she looked at the great metal wall of the ship. It was painted
white, trimmed in gold. There were five smokestacks and six
towering masts. Midships was the housing for the huge
paddlewheel. Multi-colored pennants snapped in the breeze
from the forest of rigging. It was quite a boat.

She finished her cone, punched in her size, then selected a
simple above-the-knee skirt in a gaudy print of tropical fruit
and palm trees. The machine hummed as it cut the paper to
size, hemmed it and strengthened the waist with elastic, then
rolled it out into her hand. She held it up against herself. It
was good, but the equipment belt spoiled it.

There were lockers along the deck. She used yet another
coin to rent one. In it went the belt and cap. She took the pin
out of her hair and shook it down around her shoulders,
fussed with it for a moment, then decided it would have to do.
She fastened the skirt with its single button, wearing it low on
her hips, south-seas style. She walked a few steps, studying
the effect. The skirt tended to leave one leg bare when she
walked, which felt right.

"Look at you," she chided herself, under her breath.
"You think you look all right to meet a worlds-famous,
glamorous tube personality? Who you happen to despise?"
She thought about reclaiming her belt, then decided that
would be foolish. The fact was it was a glorious day, a
beautiful ship, and she was feeling more alive than she had in
months.

She climbed the gangplank and was met at the top by a
man in an outlandish uniform. It was all white, covered everything but his face, and was festooned with gold braid and
black buttons. It looked hideously uncomfortable, but he
didn't seem to mind it. That was one of the odd things about
Mozartplatz. In jobs at places like the *Great Northern,* people

often worked in period costumes, though it meant wearing shoes or things even more grotesque.

He made a small bow and tipped his hat, then offered her a hibiscus, which he helped her pin in her hair. She smiled at him. Bach was a sucker for that kind of treatment—and knew it—perhaps because she got so little of it.

"I'm meeting someone in the bar on the top deck."

"If madame would walk this way . . ." He gestured, then led her along the side rail toward the stern of the ship. The deck underfoot was gleaming, polished teak.

She was shown to a wicker table near the rail. The steward held the chair out for her, and took her order. She relaxed, looking up at the vast reaches of the arco-mall, feeling the bright sunlight washing over her body, smelling the salt water, hearing the lap of waves against wood pilings. The air was full of bright balloons, gliders, putt-putting nano-lights, and people in muscle-powered flight harnesses. Not too far away, a fish broke the surface. She grinned at it.

Her drink arrived, with sprigs of mint and several straws and a tiny parasol. It was good. She looked around. There were only a few people out here on the deck. One couple was dressed in full period costume, but the rest looked normal enough. She settled on one guy sitting alone across the deck. He had a good pair of shoulders on him. When she caught his eye, she made a hand signal that meant "I might be available." He ignored it, which annoyed her for a while, until he was joined by a tiny woman who couldn't have been five feet tall. She shrugged. No accounting for taste.

She knew what was happening to her. It was silly, but she felt like going on the hunt. It often happened to her when something shocking or unpleasant happened at work. The police headshrinker said it was compensation, and not that uncommon.

With a sigh, she turned her mind away from that. It seemed there was no place else for it to go but back into that room on Charlie Station, and to the thing in the bed.

Charlie knew her mother was very sick. She had been that way "a long, long time." She left the camera pointed at her mother while she went away to deal with her dogs. The doctors had gathered around and studied the situation for quite some time, then issued their diagnosis.

She was dead, of course, by any definition medical science had accepted for the last century.

Someone had wired her to a robot doctor, probably during the final stages of the epidemic. It was capable of doing just about anything to keep a patient alive and was not programmed to understand brain death. That was a decision left to the human doctor, when he or she arrived.

The doctor had never arrived. The doctor was dead, and the thing that had been Charlie's mother lived on. Bach wondered if the verb "to live" had ever been so abused.

All of its arms and legs were gone, victims of gangrene. Not much else could be seen of it, but a forest of tubes and wires entered and emerged. Fluids seeped slowly through the tissue. Machines had taken over the function of every vital organ. There were patches of greenish skin here and there, including one on the side of its head which Charlie had kissed before leaving. Bach hastily took another drink as she recalled that, and signaled the waiter for another.

Blume and Wilhelm had been fascinated. They were dubious that any part of it could still be alive, even in the sense of cell cultures. There was no way to find out, because the Charlie Station computer—Tik-Tok, to the little girl—refused access to the autodoctor's data outputs.

But there was a very interesting question that emerged as soon as everyone was convinced Charlie's mother *had* died thirty years ago.

"Hello, Anna-Louise. Sorry I'm late."

She looked up and saw Megan Galloway approaching.

Bach had not met the woman in just over ten years, though she, like almost everyone else, had seen her frequently on the tube.

Galloway was tall, for an Earth woman, and not as thin as Bach remembered her. But that was understandable, considering the recent change in her life. Her hair was fiery red and curly, which it had not been ten years ago. It might even be her natural color; she was almost nude, and the colors matched, though that didn't have to mean much. But it looked right on her.

She wore odd-looking silver slippers, and her upper body was traced by a quite lovely filigree of gilded, curving lines. It was some sort of tattoo, and it was all that was left of the machine called the Golden Gypsy. It was completely symbolic. Being the Golden Gypsy was worth a lot of money to Galloway.

Megan Galloway had broken her neck while still in her teens. She became part of the early development of a powered exoskeleton, research that led to the hideously expensive and beautiful Golden Gypsy, of which only one was ever built. It abolished wheelchairs and crutches for her. It returned her to life, in her own mind, and it made her a celebrity.

An odd by-product to learning to use an exoskeleton was the development of skills that made it possible to excel in the new technology of emotional recording: the "feelies." The world was briefly treated to the sight of quadriplegics dominating a new art form. It made Galloway famous as the best of the Trans-sisters. It made her rich, as her trans-tapes out-sold everyone else's. She made herself extremely rich by investing wisely, then she and a friend of Bach's had made her fabulously rich by being the first to capture the experience of falling in love on a trans-tape.

In a sense, Galloway had cured herself. She had always donated a lot of money to neurological research, never really expecting it to pay off. But it did, and three years ago she had thrown the Golden Gypsy away forever.

Bach had thought her cure was complete, but now she wondered. Galloway carried a beautiful crystal cane. It didn't seem to be for show. She leaned on it heavily, and made her way through the tables slowly. Bach started to get up.

"No, no, don't bother," Galloway said. "It takes me a while but I get there." She flashed that famous smile with the gap between her front teeth. There was something about the woman; the smile was so powerful that Bach found herself smiling back. "It's so good to walk I don't mind taking my time."

She let the waiter pull the chair back for her, and sat down with a sigh of relief.

"I'll have a Devil's Nitelite," she told him. "And get another of whatever that was for her."

"A banana Daquiri," Bach said, surprised to find her own drink was almost gone, and a little curious to find out what a Devil's Nitelite was.

Galloway stretched as she looked up at the balloons and gliders.

"It's great to get back to the moon," she said. She made a small gesture that indicated her body. "Great to get out of my clothes. I always feel so free in here. Funny thing, though. I just *can't* get used to not wearing shoes." She lifted one foot to display a slipper. "I feel too vulnerable without them. Like I'm going to get stepped on."

"You can take your clothes off on Earth, too," Bach pointed out.

"Some places, sure. But aside from the beach, there's no place where it's *fashionable*, don't you see?"

Bach didn't, but decided not to make a thing out of it. She knew social nudity had evolved in Luna because it never got hot or cold, and that Earth would never embrace it as fully as Lunarians had.

The drinks arrived. Bach sipped hers, and eyed Galloway's, which produced a luminous smoke ring every ten seconds. Galloway chattered on about nothing in particular for a while.

"Why did you agree to see me?" Galloway asked, at last.

"Shouldn't that be my question?"

Galloway raised an eyebrow, and Bach went on.

"You've got a hell of a story. I can't figure out why you didn't just run with it. Why arrange a meeting with someone you barely knew ten years ago, and haven't seen since, and never liked even back then?"

"I always liked you, Anna-Louise," Galloway said. She looked up at the sky. For a while she watched a couple pedaling a skycycle, then she looked at Bach again. "I feel like I owe you something. Anyway, when I saw your name I thought I should check with you. I don't want to cause you any trouble." Suddenly she looked angry. "I don't *need* the story, Bach. I don't need *any* story, I'm too big for that. I can let it go or I can use it, it makes no difference."

"Oh, that's cute," Bach said. "Maybe I don't understand how you pay your debts. Maybe they do it different on Earth."

She thought Galloway was going to get up and leave. She had reached for her cane, then thought better of it.

"I gather it doesn't matter, then, if I go with the story."

Bach shrugged. She hadn't come here to talk about Charlie, anyway.

"How is Q.M., by the way?" she said.

Galloway didn't look away this time. She sat in silence for almost a minute, searching Bach's eyes.

"I thought I was ready for that question," she said at last. "He's living in New Zealand, on a commune. From what my agents tell me, he's happy. They don't watch television, they don't marry. They worship and they screw a lot.''

"Did you really give him half of the profits on that . . . that tape?''

"Did give him, am giving him, and will continue to give him until the day I die. And it's half the *gross*, my dear, which is another thing entirely. He gets half of every Mark that comes in. He's made more money off it than I have . . . and he's never touched a tenthMark. It's piling up in a Swiss account I started in his name.''

"Well, he never sold anything.''

Bach hadn't meant that to be as harsh as it came out, but Galloway did not seem bothered by it. The thing she had sold . . .

Had there ever been anyone as thoroughly betrayed as Q.M. Cooper? Bach wondered. She might have loved him herself, but he fell totally in love with Megan Galloway.

And Galloway fell in love with him. There could be no mistake about that. Doubters are referred to *Gitana de Oro* catalog #1, an emotional recording entitled, simply, "Love." Put it in your trans-tape player, don the headset, punch PLAY, and you will experience just how hard and how completely Galloway fell in love with Q.M. Cooper. But have your head examined first. GDO #1 had been known to precipitate suicide.

Cooper had found this an impediment to the course of true love. He had always thought that love was something between two people, something exclusive, something private. He was unprepared to have Galloway mass-produce it, put it in a box with liner notes and a price tag of LM14.95, and hawk copies in every trans-tape shop from Peoria to Tibet.

The supreme irony of it to the man, who eventually found refuge in a minor cult in a far corner of the Earth, was that the tape itself, the means of his betrayal, his humiliation, was proof that Galloway had returned his love.

And Galloway had sold it. Never mind that she had her reasons, or that they were reasons with which Bach could find considerable sympathy.

She had sold it.

All Bach ever got out of the episode was a compulsion to seek lovers who looked like the Earth-muscled Cooper. Now it seemed she might get something else. It was time to change the subject.

"What do you know about Charlie?'' she asked.

"You want it all, or just a general idea?" Galloway didn't wait for an answer. "I know her real name is Charlotte Isolde Hill Perkins-Smith. I know her father is dead, and her mother's condition is open to debate. Leda Perkins-Smith has a lot of money—if she's alive. Her daughter would inherit, if she's dead. I know the names of ten of Charlie's dogs. And, oh yes, I know that, appearances to the contrary, she is thirty-seven years old."

"Your source is very up-to-date."

"It's a very good source."

"You want to name him?"

"I'll pass on that, for the moment." She regarded Bach easily, her hands folded on the table in front of her. "So. What do you want me to do?"

"Is it really that simple?"

"My producers will want to kill me, but I'll sit on the story for at least twenty-four hours if you tell me to. By the way," she turned in her seat and crooked a finger at another table. "It's probably time you met my producers."

Bach turned slightly, and saw them coming toward her table.

"These are the Myers twins, Joy and Jay. Waiter, do you know how to make a Shirley Temple and a Roy Rogers?"

The waiter said he did, and went off with the order while Joy and Jay pulled up chairs and sat in them, several feet from the table but very close to each other. They had not offered to shake hands. Both were armless, with no sign of amputation, just bare, rounded shoulders. Both wore prosthetics made of golden, welded wire and powered by tiny motors. The units were one piece, fitting over their backs in a harness-like arrangement. They were quite pretty—light and airy, perfectly articulated, cunningly wrought—and also creepy.

"You've heard of amparole?" Galloway asked. Bach shook her head. "That's the slang word for it. It's a neo-Moslem practice. Joy and Jay were convicted of murder."

"I have heard of it." She hadn't paid much attention to it, dismissing it as just another hare-brained Earthling idiocy.

"Their arms are being kept in cryonic suspension for twenty years. The theory is, if they sin no more, they'll get them back. Those prosthetics won't pick up a gun, or a knife. They won't throw a punch."

Joy and Jay were listening to this with complete stolidity. Once Bach got beyond the arms, she saw another unusual thing about them. They were dressed identically, in loose bell-bottomed trousers. Joy had small breasts, and Jay had a small mustache. Other than that, they were absolutely identical in face and body. Bach didn't care for the effect.

"They also took slices out of the cerebrums and they're on a maintenance dosage of some drug. Calms them down. You don't want to know who they killed, or how. But they were proper villains, these two."

No, I don't think I do, Bach decided. Like many cops, she looked at eyes. Joy and Jay's were calm, placid . . . and deep inside was a steel-gray coldness.

"If they try to get naughty again, the amparole units go on strike. I suppose they might find a way to kill with their feet."

The twins glanced at each other, held each other's gaze for a moment, and exchanged wistful smiles. At least, Bach hoped they were just wistful.

"Yeah, okay," Bach said.

"Don't worry about them. They can't be offended with the drugs they're taking."

"I wasn't worried," Bach said. She couldn't have cared less what the freaks felt; she wished they'd been executed.

"Are they really twins?" she finally asked, against her better judgment.

"Really. One of them had a sex change, I don't know which one. And to answer your next question, yes they do, but only in the privacy of their own room."

"I wasn't—"

"And your other question . . . they are *very* good at what they do. Who am I to judge about the other? And I'm in a highly visible industry. It never hurts to have conversation pieces around. You need to get noticed."

Bach was starting to get angry, and she was not quite sure why. Maybe it was the way Galloway so cheerfully admitted her base motives, even when no one had accused her of having them.

"We were talking about the story," she said.

"We need to go with it," Joy said, startling Bach. Somehow, she had not really expected the cyborg-thing to talk. "Our source is good and the security on the story is tight—"

"—but it's dead certain to come out in twenty-four hours," Jay finished for her.

"Maybe less," Joy added.

"Shut up," Galloway said, without heat. "Anna-Louise, you were about to tell me your feeling on the matter."

Bach finished her drink as the waiter arrived with more. She caught herself staring as the twins took theirs. The metal hands were marvels of complexity. They moved just as cleverly as real hands.

"I was considering leaking the story myself. It looked like things were going against Charlie. I thought they might just let the station crash and then swear us all to secrecy."

"It strikes me," Galloway said, slowly, "that today's developments give her an edge."

"Yeah. But I don't envy her."

"Me, either. But it's not going to be easy to neglect a girl whose body may hold the secret of eternal life. If you do, somebody's bound to ask awkward questions later."

"It may not be eternal life," Bach said.

"What do you call it, then?" Jay asked.

"Why do you say that?" Joy wanted to know.

"All we know is she's lived thirty years without growing any older—externally. They'd have to examine her a lot closer to find out what's actually happening."

"And there's pressure to do so."

"Exactly. It might be the biggest medical breakthrough in a thousand years. What I think has happened to her is not eternal life, but extended youth."

Galloway looked thoughtful. "You know, of the two, I think extended youth would be more popular."

"I think you're right."

They brooded over that in silence for a while. Bach signaled the waiter for another drink.

"Anyway," she went on, "Charlie doesn't seem to need protection just now. But she may, and quickly."

"So you aren't in favor of letting her die."

Bach looked up, surprised and beginning to be offended, then she remembered Doctor Wilhelm. The good Doctor was not a monster, and Galloway's question was a reasonable one, given the nature of Neuro-X.

"There has to be a way to save her, *and* protect ourselves from her. That's what I'm working toward, anyway."

"Let me get this straight, then. You were thinking of leaking the story so the public outcry would force the police to save her?"

"Sure, I thought . . ." Bach trailed off, suddenly realizing what Galloway was saying. "You mean you think—"

Galloway waved her hand impatiently.

"It depends on a lot of things, but mostly on how the story is handled. If you start off with the plague story, there could be pressure to blast her out of the skies and have done with it." She looked at Jay and Joy, who went into a trance-like state.

"Sure, sure," Jay said. "The plague got big play. Almost everybody remembers it. Use horror show tapes of the casualties . . ."

". . . line up the big brains to start the scare," Joy said.

"You can even add sob stuff, after it gets rolling."

"What a tragedy, this little girl has to die for the good of us all."

"Somber commentary, the world watches as she cashes in."

"You could make it play. No problem."

Bach's head had been ping-ponging between the two of them. When Galloway spoke, it was hard to swing around and look at her.

"Or you could start off with the little girl," Galloway prompted.

"*Much* better," Joy said. "Twice the story there. Indignant exposé stuff: 'Did you know, fellow citizens . . .' "

" ' . . . there's this little girl, this innocent child, swinging around up there in space and she's going to *die!* ' "

"A *rich* little girl, too, and her dying mother."

"Later, get the immortality angle."

"Not too soon," Joy cautioned. "At first, she's ordinary. Second lead is, she's got money."

"Third lead, she holds the key to eternal youth."

"Immortality."

"Youth, honey, youth. Who the fuck knows what living forever is like? Youth you can sell. It's the *only* thing you can sell."

"Megan, this is the biggest story since Jesus."

"Or at least we'll *make* it the biggest story."

"See why they're so valuable?" Galloway said. Bach hardly heard her. She was re-assessing what she had thought she knew about the situation.

"I don't know what to do," she finally confessed. "I don't

know what to ask you to do, either. I guess you ought to go with what you think is best.''

Galloway frowned.

''Both for professional and personal reasons, I'd rather try to help her. I'm not sure why. She is dangerous, you know.''

''I realize that. But I can't believe she can't be handled.''

''Neither can I.'' She glanced at her watch. ''Tell you what, you come with us on a little trip.''

Bach protested at first, but Galloway would not be denied, and Bach's resistance was at a low ebb.

By speedboat, trolley, and airplane they quickly made their way on the top of Mozartplatz, where Bach found herself in a four-seat PTP—or point-to-point—ballistic vehicle.

She had never ridden in a PTP. They were rare, mostly because they wasted a lot of energy for only a few minutes' gain in travel time. Most people took the tubes, which reached speeds of three thousand miles per hour, hovering inches above their induction rails in Luna's excellent vacuum.

But for a celebrity like Galloway, the PTP made sense. She had trouble going places in public without getting mobbed. And she certainly had the money to spare.

There was a heavy initial acceleration, then weightlessness. Bach had never liked it, and enjoyed it even less with a few drinks in her.

Little was said during the short journey. Bach had not asked where they were going, and Galloway did not volunteer it. Bach looked out one of the wide windows at the fleeting moonscape.

As she counted the valleys, rilles, and craters flowing past beneath her, she soon realized her destination. It was a distant valley, in the sense that no tube track ran through it. In a little over an hour, Tango Charlie would come speeding through, no more than a hundred meters from the surface.

The PTP landed itself in a cluster of transparent, temporary domes. There were over a hundred of them, and more PTP's than Bach had ever seen before. She decided most of the people in and around the domes fell into three categories. There were the very wealthy, owners of private spacecraft, who had erected most of these portable Xanadus and filled them with their friends. There were civic dignitaries in city-owned domes. And there were the news media.

This last category was there in its teeming hundreds. It was not what they would call a *big* story, but it was a very visual one. It should yield spectacular pictures for the evening news.

A long, wide black stripe had been created across the sundrenched plain, indicating the path Tango Charlie would take. Many cameras and quite a few knots of pressure-suited spectators were situated smack in the middle of that line, with many more off to one side, to get an angle on the approach. Beyond it were about a hundred large glass-roofed touring buses and a motley assortment of private crawlers, sunskimmers, jetsleds, and even some hikers: the common people, come to see the event.

Bach followed along behind the uncommon people: Galloway, thin and somehow spectral in the translucent suit, leaning on her crystal cane; the Myers twins, whose amparolee arms would not fit in the suits, so that the empty sleeves stuck out, bloated, like crucified ghosts; and most singular of all, the wire-sculpture arm units themselves, walking independently, on their fingertips, looking like some demented, disjointed mechanical camel as they lurched through the dust.

They entered the largest of the domes, set on the edge of the gathering nearest the black line, which put it no more than a hundred meters from the expected passage.

The first person Bach saw, as she was removing her helmet, was Hoeffer.

He did not see her immediately. He, and many of the other people in the dome, were watching Galloway. So she saw his face as his gaze moved from the celebrity to Joy and Jay . . . and saw amazement and horror, far too strong to be simple surprise at their weirdness. It was a look of recognition.

Galloway had said she had an excellent source.

She noticed Bach's interest, smiled, and nodded slightly. Still struggling to remove her suit, she approached Bach.

"That's right. The twins heard a rumor something interesting might be going on at NavTrack, so they found your commander. Turns out he has rather odd sexual tastes, though it's probably fairly pedestrian to Joy and Jay. They scratched his itch, and he spilled everything."

"I find that . . . rather interesting," Bach admitted.

"I thought you would. Were you planning to make a career out of being a R/A in Navigational Tracking?"

"That wasn't my intention."

"I didn't think so. Listen, don't touch it. I can handle it

without there being any chance of it backfiring on you. Within the week you'll be promoted out of there.''

"I don't know if . . ."

"If what?" Galloway was looking at her narrowly.

Bach hesitated only a moment.

"I may be stiff-necked, but I'm not a fool. Thank you."

Galloway turned away a little awkwardly, then resumed struggling with her suit. Bach was about to offer some help, when Galloway frowned at her.

"How come you're not taking off your pressure suit?"

"That dome up there is pretty strong, but it's only one layer. Look around you. Most of the natives have just removed their helmets, and a lot are carrying those around. Most of the Earthlings are out of their suits. They don't understand vacuum."

"You're saying it's not safe?"

"No. But vacuum doesn't forgive. It's trying to kill you *all* the time."

Galloway looked dubious, but stopped trying to remove her suit.

Bach wandered the electronic wonderland, helmet in hand.

Tango Charlie would not be visible until less than a minute before the close encounter, and then would be hard to spot as it would be only a few seconds of arc above the horizon line. But there were cameras hundreds of miles downtrack which could already see it, both as a bright star, moving visibly against the background, and as a jittery image in some very long lenses. Bach watched as the wheel filled one screen until she could actually see furniture behind one of the windows.

For the first time since arriving, she thought of Charlie. She wondered if Tik-Tok—no, dammit, if the Charlie Station Computer had told her of the approach, and if so, would Charlie watch it. Which window would she choose? It was shocking to think that, if she chose the right one, Bach might catch a glimpse of her.

Only a few minutes to go. Knowing it was stupid, Bach looked along the line indicated by the thousand cameras, hoping to catch the first glimpse.

She saw Megan Galloway doing a walk-around, followed by a camera crew, no doubt saying bright, witty things to her huge audience. Galloway was here less for the event itself than for the many celebrities who had gathered to witness it.

Bach saw her approach a famous TV star, who smiled and embraced her, making some sort of joke about Galloway's pressure suit.

You can meet him if you want, she told herself. She was a little surprised to discover she had no interest in doing so.

She saw Joy and Jay in heated conversation with Hoeffer. The twins seemed distantly amused.

She saw the countdown clock, ticking toward one minute.

Then the telescopic image in one of the remote cameras began to shake violently. In a few seconds, it had lost its fix on Charlie Station. Bach watched as annoyed technicians struggled to get it back.

"Seismic activity," one of them said, loud enough for Bach to hear.

She looked at the other remote monitor, which showed Tango Charlie as a very bright star sitting on the horizon. As she watched, the light grew visibly, until she could see it as a disc. And in another part of the screen, at a site high in the lunar hills, there was a shower of dust and rock. That must be the seismic activity, she thought. The camera operator zoomed in on this eruption, and Bach frowned. She couldn't figure out what sort of lunar quake could cause such a commotion. It looked more like an impact. The rocks and dust particles were fountaining up with lovely geometrical symmetry, each piece, from the largest boulder to the smallest mote, moving at about the same speed and in a perfect mathematical trajectory, unimpeded by any air resistance, in a way that could never be duplicated on Earth. It was a dull gray expanding dome shape, gradually flattening on top.

Frowning, she turned her attention to the spot on the plain where she had been told Charlie would first appear. She saw the first light of it, but more troubling, she saw a dozen more of the expanding domes. From here, they seemed no larger than soap bubbles.

Then another fountain of rock erupted, not far from the impromptu parking lot full of tourist buses.

Suddenly she knew what was happening.

"It's shooting at us!" she shouted. Everyone fell silent, and as they were still turning to look at her, she yelled again. "Suit up."

Her voice was drowned out by the sound every Lunarian dreads: the high, haunting shriek of escaping air.

Step number one, she heard a long-ago instructor say. See

to *your own* pressure integrity *first*. You can't help anybody, man, woman or child, if you pass out before you get into your suit.

It was a five-second operation to don and seal her helmet, one she had practiced a thousand times as a child. She glimpsed a great hole in the plastic roof. Debris was pouring out of it, swept up in the sudden wind: paper, clothing, a couple of helmets . . .

Sealed up, she looked around and realized many of these people were doomed. They were not in their suits, and there was little chance they could put them on in time.

She remembered the next few seconds in a series of vivid impressions.

A boulder, several tons of dry lunar rock, crashed down on a bank of television monitors.

A chubby little man, his hands shaking, unable to get his helmet over his bald head. Bach tore it from his hands, slapped it in place, and gave it a twist hard enough to knock him down.

Joy and Jay, as good as dead, killed by the impossibility of fitting the mechnical arms into their suits, holding each other calmly in metallic embrace.

Beyond the black line, a tour bus rising slowly in the air, turning end over end. A hundred of the hideous gray domes of explosions growing like mushrooms all through the valley.

And there was Galloway. She was going as fast as she could, intense concentration on her face as she stumbled along after her helmet, which was rolling on the ground. Blood had leaked from one corner of her nose. It was almost soundless in the remains of the dome now.

Bach snagged the helmet, and hit Galloway with a flying tackle. Just like a drill: put helmet in place, twist, hit three snap-interlocks, then the emergency pressurization switch. She saw Galloway howl in pain and try to put her hands to her ears.

Lying there she looked up as the last big segment of the dome material lifted in a dying wind to reveal . . . Tango Charlie.

It was a little wheel rolling on the horizon. No bigger than a coin.

She blinked.

And it was *here*. Vast, towering, coming directly at her through a hell of burning dust.

It was the dust that finally made the lasers visible. The great spokes of light were flashing on and off in millisecond bursts, and in each pulse a trillion dust motes were vaporized in an eyeball-frying purple light.

It was impossible that she saw it for more than a tenth of a second, but it seemed much longer. The sight would remain with her, and not just in memory. For days afterward her vision was scored with a spiderweb of purple lines.

But much worse was the awesome grandeur of the thing, the whirling menace of it as it came rushing out of the void. That picture would last much longer than a few days. It would come out only at night, in dreams that would wake her for years, drenched in sweat.

And the last strong image she would carry away from the valley was of Galloway, turned over now, pointing her crystal cane at the wheel, already far away on the horizon. A line of red laser light came out of the end of the cane and stretched away into infinity.

"Wow!" said Charlotte Isolde Hill Perkins-Smith. "Wow, Tik-Tok, that was great! Let's do it again."

Hovering in the dead center of the hub, Charlie had watched all of the encounter. It had been a lot like she imagined a roller-coaster would be when she watched the films in Tik-Tok's memory. If it had a fault—and she wasn't complaining, far from it—it was that the experience had been too short. For almost an hour she had watched the moon get bigger, until it no longer seemed round and the landscape was rolling by beneath her. But she'd seen that much before. This time it just got larger and larger, and faster and faster, until she was scooting along at about a zillion miles an hour. Then there was a lot of flashing lights . . . and gradually, the ground got farther away again. It was still back there, dwindling, no longer very interesting.

"I'm glad you liked it," Tik-Tok said.

"Only one thing. How come I had to put on my pressure suit?"

"Just a precaution."

She shrugged, and made her way to the elevator.

When she got out at the rim, she frowned. There were alarms sounding, far around the rim on the wheel.

"We got a problem?" she asked.

"Minor," Tik-Tok said.

"What happened?"

"We got hit by some rocks."

"We must of passed *real* close!"

"Charlie, if you'd been down here when we passed, you could have reached out and written your name on a rock."

She giggled at that idea, then hurried off to see to the dogs.

It was about two hours later that Anna-Louise called. Charlie was inclined to ignore it, she had so much to do, but in the end, she sat down in front of the camera. Anna-Louise was there, and sitting beside her was another woman.

"Are you okay, Charlie?" Anna wanted to know.

"Why shouldn't I be?" Damn, she thought. She wasn't supposed to answer a question with another question. But then, what right did Anna have to ask her to do that?

"I was wondering if you were watching a little while ago, when you passed so close to the moon."

"I sure was. It was great."

There was a short pause. The two women looked at each other, then Anna-Louise sighed, and faced Charlie again.

"Charlie, there are a few things I have to tell you."

As in most disasters involving depressurization, there was not a great demand for first aid. Most of the bad injuries were fatal.

Galloway was not hearing too well and Bach still had spots before her eyes; Hoeffer hadn't even bumped his head.

The body-count was not complete, but it was going to be high.

For a perilous hour after the passage, there was talk of shooting Tango Charlie out of the sky.

Much of the advisory team had already gathered in the meeting room by the time Bach and Hoeffer arrived—with Galloway following closely behind. A hot debate was in progress. People recognized Galloway, and a few seemed inclined to question her presence here, but Hoeffer shut them up quickly. A deal had been struck in the PTP, on the way back from the disaster. The fix was in, and Megan Galloway was getting an exclusive on the story. Galloway had proved to Hoeffer that Joy and Jay had kept tapes of his security lapse.

The eventual explanation for the unprovoked and insane attack was simple. The Charlie Station Computer had been instructed to fire upon any object approaching within five kilometers. It had done so, faithfully, for thirty years, not that it ever had much to shoot at. The close approach of Luna must have been an interesting problem. Tik-Tok was no fool. Certainly he would know the consequences of his actions. But a computer did not think at all like a human, no matter how much it might sound like one. There were rigid hierarchies in a brain like Tik-Tok. One part of him might realize something was foolish, but be helpless to over-ride a priority order.

Analysis of the pattern of laser strikes helped to confirm this. The hits were totally random. Vehicles, domes, and people had not been targeted; however, if they were in the way, they were hit.

The one exception to the randomness concerned the black line Bach had seen. Tik-Tok had found a way to avoid shooting directly ahead of himself without violating his priority order. Thus, he avoided stirring up debris that Charlie Station would be flying through in another few seconds.

The decision was made to take no reprisals on Tango Charlie. Nobody was happy about it, but no one could suggest anything short of total destruction.

But action had to be taken now. Very soon the public was going to wonder why this dangerous object had not been destroyed before the approach. The senior police present and the representatives of the Mayor's office all agreed that the press would have to be let in. They asked Galloway if they could have her cooperation in the management of this phase.

And Bach watched as, with surprising speed, Megan Galloway took over the meeting.

"You need time right now," she said, at one point. "The best way to get it is to play the little-girl angle, and play it hard. You were not so heartless as to endanger the little girl—and you had no reason to believe the station was any kind of threat. What you have to do now is tell the truth about what we know, and what's been done."

"How about the immortality angle?" someone asked.

"What about it? It's going to leak someday. Might as well get it out in front of us."

"But it will prejudice the public in favor of . . ." Wilhelm looked around her, and decided not to finish her objection.

"It's a price we have to pay," Galloway said, smoothly. "You folks will do what you think is right. I'm sure of that. You wouldn't let public opinion influence your decision."

Nobody had anything to say to that. Bach managed not to laugh.

"The big thing is to answer the questions before they get asked. I suggest you get started on your statements, then call in the press. In the meantime, Corporal Bach has invited me to listen in on her next conversation with Charlie Perkins-Smith, so I'll leave you now."

Bach led Galloway down the corridor toward the operations room, shaking her head in admiration. She looked over her shoulder.

"I got to admit it. You're very smooth."

"It's my profession. You're pretty smooth, yourself."

"What do you mean?"

"I mean I owe you. I'm afraid I owe you more than I'll be able to repay."

Bach stopped, honestly bewildered.

"You saved my *life*," Galloway shouted. *"Thank you!"*

"So what if I did? You don't owe me anything. It's not the custom."

"What's not the custom?"

"You can be grateful, sure. I'd be, if somebody pressurized me. But it would be an insult to try to pay me back for it. Like on the desert, you know, you have to give water to somebody dying of thirst."

"Not in the deserts I've been to," Galloway said. They were alone in the hallway. Galloway seemed distressed, and Bach felt awkward. "We seem to be at a cultural impasse. I feel I owe you a lot, and you say it's nothing."

"No problem," Bach pointed out. "You were going to help me get promoted out of this stinking place. Do that, and we'll call it even."

Galloway was shaking her head.

"I don't think I'll be able to, now. You know that fat man you stuffed into a helmet, before you got to me? He asked me about you. He's the Mayor of Clavius. He'll be talking to the Mayor of New Dresden, and you'll get the promotion and a couple of medals and maybe a reward, too."

They regarded each other uneasily. Bach knew that gratitude could equal resentment. She thought she could see some of that in Galloway's eyes. But there was determination, too. Megan Galloway paid her debts. She had been paying one to Q.M. Cooper for ten years.

By unspoken agreement they left it at that, and went to talk to Charlie.

Most of the dogs didn't like the air blower. Mistress Too White O'Hock was the exception. 2-White would turn her face into the stream of warm air as Charlie directed the hose over her sable pelt, then she would let her tongue hang out in an expression of such delight that Charlie would usually end up laughing at her.

Charlie brushed the fine hair behind 2-White's legs, the hair that was white almost an inch higher than it should be on a champion Sheltie. Just one little inch, and 2-White was sterilized. She would have been a fine mother. Charlie had seen her looking at puppies whelped by other mothers, and she knew it made 2-White sad.

But you can't have everything in this world. Tik-Tok had said that often enough. And you can't let all your dogs breed, or pretty soon you'll be knee deep in dogs. Tik-Tok said that, too.

In fact, Tik-Tok said a lot of things Charlie wished were not true. But he had never lied to her.

"Were you listening?" she asked.

"During your last conversation? Of course I was."

Charlie put 2-White down on the floor, and summoned the next dog. This was Engelbert, who wasn't a year old yet, and still inclined to be frisky when he shouldn't be. Charlie had to scold him before he would be still.

"Some of the things she said," Tik-Tok began. "It seemed like she disturbed you. Like how old you are."

"That's silly," Charlie said, quickly. "I knew how old I am." This was the truth . . . and yet it wasn't everything. Her first four dogs were all dead. The oldest had been thirteen. There had been many dogs since then. Right now, the oldest dog was sixteen, and sick. He wouldn't last much longer.

"I just never added it up," Charlie said, truthfully.

"There was never any reason to."

"But I don't grow up," she said, softly. "Why is that, Tik-Tok?"

"I don't know, Charlie."

"Anna said if I go down to the moon, they might be able to find out."

Tik-Tok didn't say anything.

''Was she telling the truth? About all those people who got hurt?''

''Yes.''

''Maybe I shouldn't have got mad at her.''

Again, Tik-Tok was silent. Charlie had been very angry. Anna and a new woman, Megan, had told her all these awful things, and when they were done Charlie knocked over the television equipment and went away. That had been almost a day ago, and they had been calling back almost all the time.

''Why did you do it?'' she said.

''I didn't have any choice.''

Charlie accepted that. Tik-Tok was a mechanical man, not like her at all. He was a faithful guardian and the closest thing she had to a friend, but she knew he was different. For one thing, he didn't have a body. She had sometimes wondered if this inconvenienced him any, but she had never asked.

''Is my mother really dead?''

''Yes.''

Charlie stopped brushing. Engelbert looked around at her, then waited patiently until she told him he could get down.

''I guess I knew that.''

''I thought you did. But you never asked.''

''She was someone to talk to,'' Charlie explained. She left the grooming room and walked down the promenade. Several dogs followed behind her, trying to get her to play.

She went into her mother's room and stood for a moment looking at the thing in the bed. Then she moved from machine to machine, flipping switches, until everything was quiet. And when she was done, that was the only change in the room. The machines no longer hummed, rumbled, and clicked. The thing on the bed hadn't changed at all. Charlie supposed she could keep on talking to it, if she wanted to, but she suspected it wouldn't be the same.

She wondered if she ought to cry. Maybe she should ask Tik-Tok, but he'd never been very good with those kind of questions. Maybe it was because he couldn't cry himself, so he didn't know when people ought to cry. But the fact was, Charlie had felt a lot sadder at Albert's funeral.

In the end, she sang her hymm again, then closed and locked the door behind her. She would never go in there again.

*   *   *

"She's back," Steiner called across the room. Bach and Galloway hastily put down their cups of coffee and hurried over to Bach's office.

"She just plugged this camera in," Steiner explained, as they took their seats. "Looks a little different, doesn't she?"

Bach had to agree. They had glimpsed her in other cameras as she went about her business. Then, about an hour ago, she had entered her mother's room again. From there, she had gone to her own room, and when she emerged, she was a different girl. Her hair was washed and combed. She wore a dress that seemed to have started off as a woman's blouse. The sleeves had been cut off and bits of it had been inexpertly taken in. There was red polish on her nails. Her face was heavily made up. It was overdone, and completely wrong for someone of her apparent age, but it was not the wild, almost tribal paint she had worn before.

Charlie was seated behind a huge wooden desk, facing the camera.

"Good morning, Anna and Megan," she said, solemnly.

"Good morning, Charlie," Galloway said.

"I'm sorry I shouted at you," Charlie said. Her hands were folded carefully in front of her. There was a sheet of paper just to the left of them; other than that, the desk was bare. "I was confused and upset, and I needed some time to think about the things you said."

"That's all right," Bach told her. She did her best to conceal a yawn. She and Galloway had been awake for a day and a half. There had been a few catnaps, but they were always interrupted by sightings of Charlie.

"I've talked things over with Tik-Tok," Charlie went on. "And I turned my mother off. You were right. She was dead, anyway."

Bach could think of nothing to say to that. She glanced at Galloway, but could read nothing in the other woman's face.

"I've decided what I want to do," Charlie said. "But first I—"

"Charlie," Galloway said, quickly, "could you show me what you have there on the table?"

There was a brief silence in the room. Several people turned to look at Galloway, but nobody said anything. Bach was about to, but Galloway was making a motion with her hand, under the table, where no one but Bach was likely to see it. Bach decided to let it ride for the moment.

Charlie was looking embarrassed. She reached for the paper, glanced at it, then looked back at the camera.

"I drew this picture for you," she said. "Because I was sorry I shouted."

"Could I see it?"

Charlie jumped down off the chair and came around to hold the picture up. She seemed proud of it, and she had every right to be. Here at last was visual proof that Charlie was not what she seemed to be. No eight-year-old could have drawn this fine pencil portrait of a Sheltie.

"This is for Anna," she said.

"That's very nice, Charlie," Galloway said. "I'd like one, too."

"I'll draw you one!" Charlie said happily . . . and ran out of the picture.

There was angry shouting for a few moments. Galloway stood her ground, explaining that she had only been trying to cement the friendship, and how was she to know Charlie would run off like that?

Even Hoeffer was emboldened enough to take a few shots, pointing out—logically, in Bach's opinion—that time was running out and if anything was to be done about her situation every second was valuable.

"All right, all right, so I made a mistake. I promise I'll be more careful next time. Anna, I hope you'll call me when she comes back." And with that, she picked up her cane and trudged from the room.

Bach was surprised. It didn't seem like Galloway to leave the story before it was over, even if nothing was happening. But she was too tired to worry about it. She leaned back in her chair, closed her eyes, and was asleep in less than a minute.

Charlie was hard at work on the picture for Megan when Tik-Tok interrupted her. She looked up in annoyance.

"Can't you see I'm busy?"

"I'm sorry, but this can't wait. There's a telephone call for you."

"There's a . . . *what?*"

But Tik-Tok said no more. Charlie went across the room to the phone, silent these thirty years. She eyed it suspiciously, then pressed the button. As she did, dim memories flooded through her. She saw her mother's face. For the first time, she felt like crying.

"This is Charlotte Perkins-Smith," she said, in a childish voice. "My mother isn't . . . my mother . . . may I ask who's calling, please?"

There was no picture on the screen, but after a short pause, there was a familiar voice.

"This is Megan Galloway, Charlie. Can we talk?"

When Steiner shook Bach's shoulder, she opened her eyes to see Charlie sitting on the desk once more. Taking a quick sip of the hot coffee Steiner had brought, she tried to wipe the cobwebs from her mind and get back to work. The girl was just sitting there, hands folded once more.

"Hello, Anna," the girl said. "I just wanted to call and tell you I'll do whatever you people think is best. I've been acting silly. I hope you'll forgive me; it's been a long time since I had to talk to other people."

"That's okay, Charlie."

"I'm sorry I pissed on Captain Hoeffer. Tik-Tok said that was a bad thing to do, and that I ought to be more respectful to him, since he's the guy in charge. So if you'll get him, I'll do whatever he says."

"All right, Charlie. I'll get him."

Bach got up and watched Hoeffer take her chair.

"You'll be talking just to me from now on," he said, with what he must have felt was a friendly smile. "Is that all right?"

"Sure," Charlie said, indifferently.

"You can go get some rest now, Corporal Bach," Hoeffer said. She saluted, and turned on her heel. She knew it wasn't fair to Charlie to feel betrayed, but she couldn't help it. True, she hadn't talked to the girl all that long. There was no reason to feel a friendship had developed. But she felt sick watching Hoeffer talk to her. The man would lie to her, she was sure of that.

But then, could she have done any different? It was a disturbing thought. The fact was, there had as yet been no orders on what to do about Charlie. She was all over the news, the public debate had begun, and Bach knew it would be another day before public officials had taken enough soundings to know which way they should leap. In the meantime, they had Charlie's cooperation, and that was good news.

Bach wished she could be happier about it.

"Anna, there's a phone call for you."

She took it at one of the vacant consoles. When she pushed the Talk button, a light came on, indicating the other party wanted privacy, so she picked up the handset and asked who was calling.

"Anna," said Galloway, "come at once to room 569 in the Pension Kleist. That's four corridors from the main entrance to NavTrack, level—"

"I can find it. What's this all about? You got your story."

"I'll tell you when you get there."

The first person Bach saw in the small room was Ludmilla Rossnikova, the computer expert from GMA. She was sitting in a chair across the room, looking uncomfortable. Bach shut the door behind her, and saw Galloway sprawled in another chair before a table littered with electronic gear.

"I felt I had to speak to Tik-Tok privately," Galloway began, without preamble. She looked about as tired as Bach felt.

"Is that why you sent Charlie away?"

Galloway gave her a truly feral grin, and for a moment did not look tired at all. Bach realized she loved this sort of intrigue, loved playing fast and loose, taking chances.

"That's right. I figured Ms. Rossnikova was the woman to get me through, so now she's working for me."

Bach was impressed. It would not have been cheap to hire Rossnikova away from GMA. She would not have thought it possible.

"GMA doesn't know that, and it won't know, if you can keep a secret," Galloway went on. "I assured Ludmilla that you could."

"You mean she's spying for you."

"Not at all. She's not going to be working against GMA's interests, which are quite minimal in this affair. We're just not going to tell them about her work for me, and next year Ludmilla will take early retirement and move into a dacha in Georgia she's coveted all her life."

Bach looked at Rossnikova, who seemed embarrassed. So everybody has her price, Bach thought. So what else is new?

"Turns out she had a special code which she withheld from the folks back at NavTrack. I suspected she might. I wanted to talk to him without anyone else knowing I was doing it.

Your control room was a bit crowded for that. Ludmilla, you want to take it from there?''

She did, telling Bach the story in a low voice, with reserved, diffident gestures. Bach wondered if she would be able to live with her defection, decided she'd probably get over it soon enough.

Rossnikova had raised Charlie Station, which in this sense was synonymous with Tik-Tok, the station computer. Galloway had talked to him. She wanted to know what he knew. As she suspected, he was well aware of his own orbital dynamics. He knew he was going to crash into the moon. So what did he intend to do about Charlotte Perkins-Smith? Galloway wanted to know.

What are you offering? Tik-Tok responded.

"The important point is, he doesn't want Charlie to die. He can't do anything about his instruction to fire on intruders. But he claims he would have let Charlie go years ago but for one thing.''

"Our quarantine probes,'' Bach said.

"Exactly. He's got a lifeboat in readiness. A few minutes from impact, if nothing has been resolved, he'll load Charlie in it and blast her away, after first killing both your probes. He knows it's not much of a chance, but impact on the lunar surface is no chance at all.''

Bach finally sat down. She thought it over for a minute, then spread her hands.

"Great,'' she said. "It sounds like all our problems are solved. We'll just take this to Hoeffer, and we can call off the probes.''

Galloway and Rossnikova were silent. As last, Galloway sighed.

"It may not be as simple as that.''

Bach stood again, suddenly sure of what was coming next.

"I've got good sources, both in the news media and in city hall. Things are not looking good for Charlie.''

"I can't *believe* it!'' Bach shouted. "They're ready to let a little girl die? They're not even going to try to save her?''

Galloway made soothing motions, and Bach gradually calmed down.

"It's not definite yet. But the trend is there. For one thing, she is *not* a little girl, as you well know. I was counting on the public perception of her as a little girl, but that's not working out so well.''

"But all your stories have been so positive."

"I'm not the only newscaster. And . . . the public doesn't always determine it anyway. Right now, they're in favor of Charlie, seventy-thirty. But that's declining, and a lot of that seventy percent is soft, as they say. Not sure. The talk is, the decision makers are going to make it look like an unfortunate accident. Tik-Tok will be a great help there; it'll be easy to provoke an incident that could kill Charlie."

"It's just not right," Bach said, gloomily. Galloway leaned forward and looked at her intently.

"That's what I wanted to know. Are you still on Charlie's side, all the way? And if you are, what are you willing to risk to save her?"

Bach met Galloway's intent stare. Slowly, Galloway smiled again.

"That's what I thought. Here's what I want to do."

Charlie was sitting obediently by the telephone in her room at the appointed time, and it rang just when Megan had said it would. She answered it as she had before.

"Hi there, kid. How's it going?"

"I'm fine. Is Anna there too?"

"She sure is. Want to say hi to her?"

"I wish you'd tell her it was you that told me to—"

"I already did, and she understands. Did you have any trouble?"

Charlie snorted.

"With *him?* What a doo-doo-head. He'll believe anything I tell him. Are you sure he can't hear us in here?"

"Positive. Nobody can hear us. Did Tik-Tok tell you what all you have to do?"

"I think so. I wrote some of it down."

"We'll go over it again, point by point. We can't have any mistakes."

When they got the final word on the decision, it was only twelve hours to impact. None of them had gotten any sleep since the close approach. It seemed like years ago to Bach.

"The decision is to have an accident," Galloway said, hanging up the phone. She turned to Rossnikova who bent, hollow-eyed, over her array of computer keyboards. "How's it coming with the probe?"

"I'm pretty sure I've got it now," she said, leaning back. "I'll take it through the sequence one more time." She sighed, then looked at both of them. "Every time I try to re-program it, it wants to tell me about this broken rose blossom and the corpse of a puppy and the way the wheel looks with all the lighted windows." She yawned hugely. "Some of it's kind of pretty, actually."

Bach wasn't sure what Rossnikova was talking about, but the important thing was the probe was taken care of. She looked at Galloway.

"My part is all done," Galloway said. "In record time, too."

"I'm not even going to guess what it cost you," Bach said.

"It's only money."

"What about Doctor Blume?"

"He's with us. He wasn't even very expensive. I think he wanted to do it, anyway." She looked from Bach to Rossnikova, and back again. "What do you say? Are we ready to go? Say in one hour?"

Neither of them raised an objection. Silently, they shook each other's hands. They knew it would not go easy with them if they were discovered, but that had already been discussed and accepted and there seemed no point in mentioning it again.

Bach left them in a hurry.

The dogs were more excited than Charlie had ever seen them. They sensed something was about to happen.

"They're probably just picking it up from you," Tik-Tok ventured.

"That could be it," Charlie agreed. They were leaping and running all up and down the corridor. It had been *hell* getting them all down here, by a route Tik-Tok had selected that would avoid all the operational cameras used by Captain Hoeffer and those other busybodies. But here they finally were, and there was the door to the lifeboat, and suddenly she realized that Tik-Tok could not come along.

"What are you going to do?" she finally asked him.

"That's a silly question, Charlie."

"But you'll *die!*"

"Not possible. Since I was never alive, I can't die."

"Oh, you're just playing with words." She stopped, and

couldn't think of anything good to say. Why didn't they have more words? There ought to be more words, so some of them would be useful for saying goodbye.

"Did you scrubba-scrub?" Tik-Tok asked. "You want to look nice."

Charlie nodded, wiping away a tear. Things were just happening so *fast*.

"Good. Now you remember to do all the things I taught you to do. It may be a long time before you can be with people again, but I think you will, someday. And in the meantime, Anna-Louise and Megan have promised me that they'll be very strict with little girls who won't pick up their rooms and wash their hair."

"I'll be good," Charlie promised.

"I want you to obey them just like you've obeyed me."

"I will."

"Good. You've been a very good little girl, and I'll expect you to continue to be a good girl. Now get in that lifeboat, and get going."

So she did, along with dozens of barking Shelties.

There was a guard outside the conference room and Bach's badge would not get her past him, so she assumed that was where the crime was being planned.

She would have to be very careful.

She entered the control room. It was understaffed, and no one was at her old chair. A few people noticed her as she sat down, but no one seemed to think anything of it. She settled down, keeping an eye on the clock.

Forty minutes after her arrival, all hell broke loose.

It had been an exciting day for the probe. New instructions had come. Any break in the routine was welcome, but this one was doubly good, because the new programmer wanted to know *everything*, and the probe finally got a chance to transmit its poetry. It was a hell of a load off one's mind.

When it finally managed to assure the programmer that it understood and would obey, it settled back in a cybernetic equivalent of wild expectation.

The explosion was everything it could have hoped for. The wheel tore itself apart in a ghastly silence and began spreading itself wildly to the blackness. The probe moved in, listening, listening . . .

And there it was. The soothing song it had been told to listen for, coming from a big oblong hunk of the station that moved faster than the rest of it. The probe moved in close, though it had not been told to. As the oblong flashed by the probe had time to catalog it (LIFEBOAT, type 4A; functioning) and to get just a peek into one of the portholes.

The face of a dog peered back, ears perked alertly.

The probe filed the image away for later contemplation, and then moved in on the rest of the wreckage, lasers blazing in the darkness.

Bach had a bad moment when she saw the probe move in on the lifeboat, then settled back and tried to make herself inconspicuous as the vehicle bearing Charlie and the dogs accelerated away from the cloud of wreckage.

She had been evicted from her chair, but she had expected that. As people ran around, shouting at each other, she called room 569 at the Kleist, then patched Rossnikova into her tracking computers. She was sitting at an operator's console in a corner of the room, far from the excitement.

Rossnikova was a genius. The blip vanished from her screen. If everything was going according to plan, no data about the lifeboat was going into the memory of the tracking computer.

It would be like it never existed.

Everything went so smoothly, Bach thought later. You couldn't help taking it as a good omen, even if, like Bach, you weren't superstitious. She knew nothing was going to be easy in the long run, that there were bound to be problems they hadn't thought of . . .

But all in all, you just had to be optimistic.

The remotely-piloted PTP made rendezvous right on schedule. The transfer of Charlie and the dogs went like clockwork. The empty lifeboat was topped off with fuel and sent on a solar escape orbit, airless and lifeless, its only cargo a barrel of radioactive death that should sterilize it if anything would.

The PTP landed smoothly at the remote habitat Galloway's agents had located and purchased. It had once been a biological research station, so it was physically isolated in every way from lunar society. Some money changed hands, and all records of the habitat were erased from computer files.

All food, air, and water had to be brought in by crawler, over a rugged mountain pass. The habitat itself was large enough to accommodate a hundred people in comfort. There was plenty of room for the dogs. A single dish antenna was the only link to the outside world.

Galloway was well satisfied with the place. She promised Charlie that one of these days she would be paying a visit. Neither of them mentioned the reason that no one would be coming out immediately. Charlie settled in for a long stay, privately wondering if she would *ever* get any company.

One thing they hadn't planned on was alcohol. Charlie was hooked bad, and not long after her arrival she began letting people know about it.

Blume reluctantly allowed a case of whiskey to be brought in on the next crawler, reasoning that a girl in full-blown withdrawal would be impossible to handle remotely. He began a program to taper her off, but in the meantime Charlie went on a three-day bender that left her bleary-eyed.

The first biological samples sent in all died within a week. These were a guinea pig, a rhesus monkey, and a chicken. The symptoms were consistent with Neuro-X, so there was little doubt the disease was still alive. A dog, sent in later, lasted eight days.

Blume gathered valuable information from all these deaths, but they upset Charlie badly. Bach managed to talk him out of further live animal experiments for at least a few months.

She had taken accumulated vacation time, and was living in a condominium on a high level of the Mozartplatz, bought by Galloway and donated to what they were coming to think of as the Charlie Project. With Galloway back on Earth and Rossnikova neither needed nor inclined to participate further, Charlie Project was Bach and Doctor Blume. Security was essential. Four people knowing about Charlie was already three too many, Galloway said.

Charlie seemed cheerful, and cooperated with Blume's requests. He worked through robotic instruments, and it was frustrating. But she learned to take her own blood and tissue samples and prepare them for viewing. Blume was beginning to learn something of the nature of Neuro-X, though he admitted that, working alone, it might take him years to reach a breakthrough. Charlie didn't seem to mind.

The isolation techniques were rigorous. The crawler brought supplies to within one hundred yards of the habitat and left them sitting there on the dust. A second crawler would come out to bring them in. Under no circumstances was anything allowed to leave the habitat, nor to come in contact with anything that was going back to the world—and, indeed, the crawler was the only thing in the latter category.

Contact was strictly one-way. Anything could go in, but nothing could come out. That was the strength of the system, and its final weakness.

Charlie had been living in the habitat for fifteen days when she started running a fever. Doctor Blume prescribed bed rest and aspirin, and didn't tell Bach how worried he was.

The next day was worse. She coughed a lot, couldn't keep food down. Blume was determined to go out there in an isolation suit. Bach had to physically restrain him at one point, and be very firm with him until he finally calmed down and saw how foolish he was being. It would do Charlie no good for Blume to die.

Bach called Galloway, who arrived by express liner the next day.

By then Blume had some idea what was happening.

"I gave her a series of vaccinations," he said, mournfully. "It's so standard . . . I hardly gave it a thought. Measles-D1, the Manila-strain mumps, all the normal communicable diseases we have to be so careful of in a Lunar environment. Some of them were killed viruses, some were weakened . . . and they seem to be attacking her."

Galloway raged at him for a while. He was too depressed to fight back. Bach just listened, withholding her own judgment.

The next day he learned more. Charlie was getting things he had not inoculated her against, things that could have come in as hitch-hikers on the supplies, or that might have been lying dormant in the habitat itself.

He had carefully checked her thirty-year-old medical record. There had been no hint of any immune system deficiency, and it was not the kind of syndrome that could be missed. But somehow she had acquired it.

He had a theory. He had several of them. None would save his patient.

"Maybe the Neuro-X destroyed her immune system. But you'd think she would have succumbed to stray viruses there on the station. Unless the Neuro-X attacked the viruses, too, and changed them."

He mumbled things like that for hours on end as he watched Charlie waste away on his television screen.

"For whatever reason . . . she was in a state of equilibrium there on the station. Bringing her here destroyed that. If I could understand how, I still might save her . . ."

The screen showed a sweating, gaunt-faced little girl. Much of her hair had fallen out. She complained that her throat was very dry and she had trouble swallowing. She just keeps fighting, Bach thought, and felt the tightness in the back of her own throat.

Charlie's voice was still clear.

"Tell Megan I finally finished her picture," she said.

"She's right here, honey," Bach said. "You can tell her yourself."

"Oh." Charlie licked her lips with a dry tongue, and her eyes wandered around. "I can't see much. Are you there, Megan?"

"I'm here."

"Thanks for trying." She closed her eyes, and for a moment Bach thought she was gone. Then the eyes opened again.

"Anna-Louise?"

"I'm still right here, darling."

"Anna, what's going to happen to my dogs?"

"I'll take care of them," she lied. "Don't you worry." Somehow she managed to keep her voice steady. It was the hardest thing she had ever done.

"Good. Tik-Tok will tell you which ones to breed. They're good dogs, but you can't let them take advantage of you."

"I won't."

Charlie coughed, and seemed to become a little smaller when she was through. She tried to lift her head, could not, and coughed again. Then she smiled, just a little bit, but enough to break Bach's heart.

"I'll go see Albert," she said. "Don't go away."

"We're right here."

She closed her eyes. She continued breathing raggedly for over an hour, but her eyes never opened again.

Bach let Galloway handle the details of cleaning up and covering up. She felt listless, uninvolved. She kept seeing Charlie as she had first seen her, a painted savage in a brown tide of dogs.

When Galloway went away, Bach stayed on at the Mozart-platz, figuring the woman would tell her if she had to get out. She went back to work, got the promotion Galloway had predicted, and began to take an interest in her new job. She evicted Ralph and his barbells from her old apartment, though she continued to pay the rent on it. She grew to like Mozartplatz even more than she had expected she would, and dreaded the day Galloway would eventually sell the place. There was a broad balcony with potted plants where she could sit with her feet propped up and look out over the whole insane buzz and clatter of the place, or prop her elbows on the rail and spit into the lake, over a mile below. The weather was going to take some getting used to, though, if she ever managed to afford a place of her own here. The management sent rainfall and windstorm schedules in the mail and she faithfully posted them in the kitchen, then always forgot and got drenched.

The weeks turned into months. At the end of the sixth month, when Charlie was no longer haunting Bach's dreams, Galloway showed up. For many reasons Bach was not delighted to see her, but she put on a brave face and invited her in. She was dressed this time, Earth fashion, and she seemed a lot stronger.

"Can't stay long," she said, sitting on the couch Bach had secretly begun to think of as her own. She took a document out of her pocket and put it on a table near Bach's chair. "This is the deed to this condo. I've signed it over to you, but I haven't registered it yet. There are different ways to go about it, for tax purposes, so I thought I'd check with you. I told you I always pay my debts. I was hoping to do it with Charlie, but that turned out . . . well, it was more something I was doing for myself, so it didn't count."

Bach was glad she had said that. She had been wondering if she would be forced to hit her.

"This won't pay what I owe you, but it's a start." She looked at Bach and raised one eyebrow. "It's a start, whether or not you accept it. I'm hoping you won't be too stiff-necked, but with loonies—or should I say Citizens of Luna? —I've found you can never be too sure.''

Bach hesitated, but only for a split second.

''Loonies, Lunarians . . . who cares?'' She picked up the deed. ''I accept.''

Galloway nodded, and took an envelope out of the same pocket the deed had been in. She leaned back, and seemed to search for words.

''I . . . thought I ought to tell you what I've done.'' She waited, and Bach nodded. They both knew, without mentioning Charlie's name, what she was talking about.

''The dogs were painlessly put to sleep. The habitat was depressurized and irradiated for about a month, then reactivated. I had some animals sent in and they survived. So I sent in a robot on a crawler and had it bring these out. Don't worry, they've been checked out a thousand ways and they're absolutely clean.''

She removed a few sheets of paper from the envelope and spread them out on the table. Bach leaned over and looked at the pencil sketches.

''You remember she said she'd finally finished that picture for me? I've already taken that one out. But there were these others, one with your name on it, and I wondered if you wanted any of them?''

Bach had already spotted the one she wanted. It was a self-portrait, just the head and shoulders. In it, Charlie had a faint smile . . . or did she? It was that kind of drawing; the more she looked at it, the harder it was to tell just what Charlie had been thinking when she drew this. At the bottom it said ''To Anna-Louise, my friend.''

Bach took it and thanked Galloway, who seemed almost as anxious to leave as Bach was to have her go.

Bach fixed herself a drink and sat back in ''her'' chair in ''her'' home. That was going to take some getting used to, but she looked forward to it.

She picked up the drawing and studied it, sipping her drink. Frowning, she stood and went through the sliding glass doors onto her balcony. There, in the brighter light of the atrium, she held the drawing up and looked closer.

There was somebody behind Charlie. But maybe that wasn't right, either, maybe it was just that she had started to draw one thing, had erased it and started again. Whatever it was, there was another network of lines in the paper that were very close to the picture that was there, but slightly different.

The longer Bach stared at it, the more she was convinced she was seeing the older woman Charlie had never had a chance to become. She seemed to be in her late thirties, not a whole lot older than Bach.

Bach took a mouthful of liquor and was about to go back inside when a wind came up and snatched the paper from her hand.

"Goddamn weather!" she shouted as she made a grab for it. But it was already twenty feet away, turning over and over and falling. She watched it dwindle past all hope of recovery.

Was she relieved?

"Can I get that for you?"

She looked up, startled, and saw a man in a flight harness, flapping like crazy to remain stationary. Those contraptions required an amazing amount of energy, and this fellow showed it, with bulging biceps and huge thigh muscles and a chest big as a barrel. The metal wings glittered and the leather straps creaked and the sweat poured off him.

"No thanks," she said, then she smiled at him. "But I'd be proud to make you a drink."

He smiled back, asked her apartment number, and flapped off toward the nearest landing platform. Bach looked down, but the paper with Charlie's face on it was already gone, vanished in the vast spaces of Mozartplatz.

Bach finished her drink, then went to answer the knock on her door.

Options

Cleo hated breakfast.

Her energy level was lowest in the morning, but not so the children's. There was always some school crisis, something that had to be located at the last minute, some argument that had to be settled.

This morning it was a bowl of cereal spilled in Lilli's lap. Cleo hadn't seen it happen; her attention had been diverted momentarily by Feather, her youngest.

And of course it had to happen *after* Lilli was dressed.

"Mom, this was the *last* outfit I *had*."

"Well, if you wouldn't use them so hard they might last more than three days, and if you didn't . . ." She stopped before she lost her temper. "Just take it off and go as you are."

"But Mom, nobody goes to school naked. *No*body. Give me some money and I'll stop at the store on—"

Cleo raised her voice, something she tried never to do. "Child, I know there are kids in your class whose parents can't afford to buy clothes at all."

"All right, so the poor kids don't—"

"That's enough. You're late already. Get going."

Lilli stalked from the room. Cleo heard the door slam.

Through it all Jules was an island of calm at the other end of the table, his nose in his newspad, sipping his second cup of coffee. Cleo glanced at her own bacon and eggs cooling on the plate, poured herself a first cup of coffee, then had to get up and help Paul find his other shoe.

By then Feather was wet again, so she put her on the table and peeled off the sopping diaper.

"Hey, listen to this," Jules said. " 'The City Council today passed without objection an ordinance requiring—' "

"Jules, aren't you a little behind schedule?"

He glanced at his thumbnail. "You're right. Thanks." He finished his coffee, folded his newspad and tucked it under his arm, bent over to kiss her, then frowned.

"You really ought to eat more, honey," he said, indicating the untouched eggs. "Eating for two, you know. 'Bye now."

"Good-bye," Cleo said, through clenched teeth. "And if I hear that 'eating for two' business again, "I'll . . ." But he was gone.

She had time to scorch her lip on the coffee, then was out the door, hurrying to catch the train.

There were seats on the sun car, but of course Feather was with her and the UV wasn't good for her tender skin. After a longing look at the passengers reclining with the dark cups strapped over their eyes—and a rueful glance down at her own pale skin—Cleo boarded the next car and found a seat by a large man wearing a hardhat. She settled down in the cushions, adjusted the straps on the carrier slung in front of her, and let Feather have a nipple. She unfolded her newspad and spread it out in her lap.

"Cute," the man said. "How old is he?"

"She," Cleo said, without looking up. "Eleven days." And five hours and thirty-six minutes . . .

She shifted in the seat, pointedly turning her shoulder to him, and made a show of activating her newspad and scanning the day's contents. She did not glance up as the train left the underground tunnel and emerged on the gently rolling, airless plain of Mendeleev. There was little enough out there to interest her, considering she made the forty-minute commute to Hartman Crater twice a day. They had discussed moving to Hartman, but Jules liked living in King City near his work, and of course the kids would have missed all their school friends.

There wasn't much in the news storage that morning. When the red light flashed, she queried for an update. The pad printed some routine city business. Three sentences into the story she punched the reject key.

There was an Invasion Centennial parade listed for 1900

hours that evening. Parades bored her, and so did the Centennial. If you've heard one speech about how liberation of Earth is just around the corner if we all pull together, you've heard them all. Semantic content zero, nonsense quotient high.

She glanced wistfully at sports, noting that the J Sector jumpball team was doing poorly without her in the intracity tournament. Cleo's small stature and powerful legs had served her well as a starting sprint-wing in her playing days, but it just didn't seem possible to make practices anymore.

As a last resort, she called up the articles, digests, and analysis listings, the newspad's *Sunday Supplement* and Op-Ed department. A title caught her eye, and she punched it up.

Changing: The Revolution in Sex Roles
(Or, Who's on Top?)

Twenty years ago, when cheap and easy sex changes first became available to the general public, it was seen as the beginning of a revolution that would change the shape of human society in ways impossible to foresee. Sexual equality is one thing, the sociologists pointed out, but certain residual inequities—based on biological imperatives or on upbringing, depending on your politics—have proved impossible to weed out. Changing was going to end all that. Men and women would be able to see what it was like from the other side of the barrier that divides humanity. How could sex roles survive that?

Ten years later the answer is obvious. Changing had appealed only to a tiny minority. It was soon seen as a harmless aberration, practiced by only 1 per cent of the population. Everyone promptly forgot about the tumbling of barriers.

But in the intervening ten years a quieter revolution has been building. Almost unnoticed on the broad scale because it is an invisible phenomenon (how do you know the next woman you meet was not a man last week?), changing has been gaining growing, matter-of-fact acceptance among the children of the generation that rejected it. The chances are now better than even that you know someone who has had at least one sex change. The chances are better than one out of fifteen that you yourself have changed; if you are under twenty, the chance is one in three.

The article went on to describe the underground society which was springing up around changing. Changers tended to band together, frequenting their own taprooms, staging their own social events, remaining aloof from the larger society which many of them saw as outmoded and irrelevant. Changers tended to marry other changers. They divided the child-bearing equally, each preferring to mother only one child. The author viewed this tendency with alarm, since it went against the socially approved custom of large families. Changers reported that the time for that was the past, pointing out that Luna had been tamed long ago. They quoted statistics proving that at present rates of expansion, Luna's population would be in the billions in an amazingly short time.

There were interviews with changers, and psychological profiles. Cleo read that the males had originally been the heaviest users of the new technology, stating sexual reasons for their decision, and the change had often been permanent. Today, the changer was slightly more likely to have been born female, and to give social reasons, the most common of which was pressure to bear children. But the modern changer committed him/herself to neither role. The average time between changes in an individual was two years, and declining.

Cleo read the whole article, then thought about using some of the reading references at the end. Not that much of it was really new to her. She had been aware of changing, without thinking about it much. The idea had never attracted her, and Jules was against it. But for some reason it had struck a chord this morning.

Feather had gone to sleep. Cleo carefully pulled the blanket down around the child's face, then wiped milk from her nipple. She folded her newspad and stowed it in her purse, then rested her chin on her palm and looked out the window for the rest of the trip.

Cleo was chief on-site architect for the new Food Systems, Inc., plantation that was going down in Hartman. As such, she was in charge of three junior architects, five construction bosses, and an army of drafters and workers. It was a big project, the biggest Cleo had ever handled.

She liked her work, but the best part had always been being there on the site when things were happening, actually supervising construction instead of running a desk. That had been difficult in the last months of carrying Feather, but at least there were maternity pressure suits. It was even harder now.

She had been through it all before, with Lilli and Paul.

Everybody works. That had been the rule for a century, since the Invasion. There was no labor to spare for babysitters, so having children meant the mother or father must do the same job they had been doing before, but do it while taking care of the child. In practice, it was usually the mother, since she had the milk.

Cleo had tried leaving Feather with one of the women in the office, but each had her own work to do, and not unreasonably felt Cleo should bear the burden of her own offspring. And Feather never seemed to respond well to another person. Cleo would return from her visit to the site to find the child had been crying the whole time, disrupting everyone's work. She had taken Feather in a crawler a few times, but it wasn't the same.

That morning was taken up with a meeting. Cleo and the other section chiefs sat around the big table for three hours, discussing ways of dealing with the cost overrun, then broke for lunch only to return to the problem in the afternoon. Cleo's back was aching and she had a headache she couldn't shake, so Feather chose that day to be cranky. After ten minutes of increasingly hostile looks, Cleo had to retire to the booth with Leah Farnham, the accountant, and her three-year-old son, Eddie. The two of them followed the proceedings through earphones while trying to cope with their children and make their remarks through throat mikes. Half the people at the conference table either had to turn around when she spoke, or ignore her, and Cleo was hesitant to force them to that choice. As a result, she chose her remarks with extreme care. More often, she said nothing.

There was something at the core of the world of business that refused to adjust to children in the board room, while appearing to make every effort to accommodate the working mother. Cleo brooded about it, not for the first time.

But what did she want? Honestly, she could not see what else could be done. It certainly wasn't fair to disrupt the entire meeting with a crying baby. She wished she knew the answer. Those were her friends out there, yet her feeling of alienation was intense, staring through the glass wall that Eddie was smudging with his dirty fingers.

Luckily, Feather was a perfect angel on the trip home. She gurgled and smiled toothlessly at a woman who had stopped to admire her, and Cleo warmed to the infant for the first time that day. She spent the trip playing games with her, surrounded by the approving smiles of other passengers.

"Jules, I read the most interesting article on the pad this morning." There, it was out, anyway. She had decided the direct approach would be best.

"Hmm?"

"It was about changing. It's getting more and more popular."

"Is that so?" He did not look up from his book.

Jules and Cleo were in the habit of sitting up in bed for a few hours after the children were asleep. They spurned the video programs that were designed to lull workers after a hard day, preferring to use the time to catch up on reading, or to talk if either of them had anything to say. Over the last few years, they had read more and talked less.

Cleo reached over Feather's crib and got a packet of dopesticks. She flicked one to light with her thumbnail, drew on it, and exhaled a cloud of lavender smoke. She drew her legs up under her and leaned back against the wall.

"I just thought we might talk about it. That's all."

Jules put his book down. "All right. But what's to talk about? We're not into that."

She shrugged and picked at a cuticle. "I know. We did talk about it, way back. I just wondered if you still felt the same, I guess." She offered him the stick and he took a drag.

"As far as I know, I do," he said easily. "It's not something I spend a great deal of thought on. What's the matter?" He looked at her suspiciously. "You weren't having any thoughts in that direction, were you?"

"Well, no, not exactly. No. But you really ought to read the article. More people are doing it. I just thought we ought to be aware of it."

"Yeah, I've heard that," Jules conceded. He laced his hands behind his head. "No way to tell unless you've worked with them and suddenly one day they've got a new set of equipment." He laughed "First time it was sort of hard for me to get used to. Now I hardly ever think about it."

"Me, either."

"They don't cause any problem," Jules said with an air of finality. "Live and let live."

"Yeah." Cleo smoked in silence for a time and let Jules get back to his reading, but she still felt uncomfortable. "Jules?"

"What is it now?"

"Don't you ever wonder what it would be like?"

He sighed and closed his book, then turned to face her.

"I don't quite understand you tonight," he said.

"Well, maybe I don't either, but we could talk—"

"Listen. Have you thought about what it would do to the kids? I mean, even if I was willing to seriously consider it, which I'm not."

"I talked to Lilli about that. Just theoretically, you understand. She said she had two teachers who changed, and one of her best friends used to be a boy. There's quite a few kids at school who've changed. She takes it in stride."

"Yes, but she's older. What about Paul? What would it do to his concept of himself as a young man? I'll tell you, Cleo, in the back of my mind I keep thinking this business is a little sick. I feel it would have a bad effect on the children."

"Not according to—"

"Cleo, Cleo. Let's not get into an argument. Number one, I have no intention of getting a change, now or in the future. Two, if only one of us was changed, it would sure play hell with our sex life, wouldn't it? And three, I like you too much as you are." He leaned over and began to kiss her.

She was more than a little annoyed, but said nothing as his kisses became more intense. It was a damnably effective way of shutting off debate. And she could not stay angry: she was responding in spite of herself, easily, naturally.

It was as good as it always was with Jules. The ceiling, so familiar, once again became a calming blankness that absorbed her thoughts.

No, she had no complaints about being female, no sexual dissatisfactions. It was nothing as simple as that.

Afterward she lay on her side with her legs drawn up, her knees together. She faced Jules, who absently stroked her leg with one hand. Her eyes were closed, but she was not sleepy. She was savoring the warmth she cherished so much after sex; the slipperiness between her legs, holding his semen inside.

She felt the bed move as he shifted his weight.

"You did make it, didn't you?"

She opened one eye enough to squint at him.

"Of course I did. I always do. You know I never have any trouble in that direction."

He relaxed back onto the pillow. "I'm sorry for . . . well, for springing on you like that."

"It's okay. It was nice."

"I had just thought you might have been . . . faking it. I'm not sure why I would think that."

She opened the other eye and patted him gently on the cheek.

"Jules, I'd never be that protective of your poor ego. If you don't satisfy me, I promise you'll be the second to know."

He chuckled, then turned on his side to kiss her.

"Good night, babe."

"G'night."

She loved him. He loved her. Their sex life was good—with the slight mental reservation that he always seemed to initiate it—and she was happy with her body.

So why was she still awake three hours later?

Shopping took a few hours on the vidphone Saturday morning. Cleo bought the household necessities for delivery that afternoon, then left the house to do the shopping she fancied: going from store to store, looking at things she didn't really need.

Feather was with Jules on Saturdays. She savored a quiet lunch alone at a table in the park plaza, then found herself walking down Brazil Avenue in the heart of the medical district. On impulse, she stepped into the New Heredity Body Salon.

It was only after she was inside that she admitted to herself she had spent most of the morning arranging for the impulse.

She was on edge as she was taken down a hallway to a consulting room, and had to force a smile for the handsome young man behind the desk. She sat, put her packages on the floor, and folded her hands in her lap. He asked what he could do for her.

"I'm not actually here for any work," she said. "I wanted to look into the costs, and maybe learn a little more about the procedures involved in changing."

He nodded understandingly, and got up.

"There's no charge for the initial consultation," he said. "We're happy to answer your questions. By the way, I'm Marion, spelled with an 'O' this month." He smiled at her and motioned for her to follow him. He stood her in front of a full-length mirror mounted on the wall.

"I know it's hard to make that first step. It was hard for me, and I do it for a living. So we've arranged this demonstration that won't cost you anything, either in money or worry. It's a nonthreatening way to see some of what it's all about, but it might startle you a little, so be prepared." He touched a button in the wall beside the mirror, and Cleo saw her clothes fade away. She realized it was not really a mirror, but a holographic screen linked to a computer.

The computer introduced changes in the image. In thirty seconds she faced a male stranger. There was no doubt the face was her own, but it was more angular, perhaps a little larger in its underlying bony structure. The skin on the stranger's jaw was rough, as if it needed shaving.

The rest of the body was as she might expect, though overly muscled for her tastes. She did little more than glance at the penis; somehow that didn't seem to matter so much. She spent more time studying the hair on the chest, the tiny nipples, and the ridges that had appeared on the hands and feet. The image mimicked her every movement.

"Why all the brawn?" she asked Marion. "If you're trying to sell me on this, you've taken the wrong approach."

Marion punched some more buttons. "I didn't choose this image," he explained. "The computer takes what it sees, and extrapolates. You're more muscular than the average woman. You probably exercise. This is what a comparable amount of training would have produced with male hormones to fix nitrogen in the muscles. But we're not bound by that."

The image lost about eight kilos of mass, mostly in the shoulders and thighs. Cleo felt a little more comfortable, but still missed the smoothness she was accustomed to seeing in her mirror.

She turned from the display and went back to her chair. Marion sat across from her and folded his hands on the desk.

"Basically, what we do is produce a cloned body from one of your own cells. Through a process called Y-Recombinant Viral Substitution we remove one of your X chromosomes and replace it with a Y.

"The clone is forced to maturity in the usual way, which takes about six months. After that, it's just a simple non-rejection-hazard brain transplant. You walk in as a woman, and leave an hour later as a man. Easy as that."

Cleo said nothing, wondering again what she was doing here.

"From there we can modify the body. We can make you taller or shorter, rearrange your face, virtually anything you like." He raised his eyebrows, then smiled ruefully and spread his hands.

"All right, Ms. King," he said. "I'm not trying to pressure you. You'll need to think about it. In the meantime, there's a process that would cost you very little, and might be just the thing to let you test the waters. Am I right in thinking your husband opposes this?"

She nodded, and he looked sympathetic.

"Not uncommon, not uncommon at all," he assured her. "It brings out castration fears in men who didn't even suspect they had them. Of course, we do nothing of the sort. His male body would be kept in a tank, ready for him to move back into whenever he wanted to."

Cleo shifted in her chair. "What was this process you were talking about?"

"Just a bit of minor surgery. It can be done in ten minutes, and corrected in the same time before you even leave the office if you find you don't care for it. It's a good way to get husbands thinking about changing; sort of a signal you can send him. You've heard of the androgenous look. It's in all the fashion tapes. Many women, especially if they have large breasts like you do, find it an interesting change."

"You say it's cheap? And reversible?"

"All our processes are reversible. Changing the size or shape of breasts is our most common body operation."

Cleo sat on the examining table while the attendant gave her a quick physical.

"I don't know if Marion realized you're nursing," the woman said. "Are you sure this is what you want?"

How the hell should I know? Cleo thought. She wished the feeling of confusion and uncertainty would pass.

"Just do it."

Jules hated it.

He didn't yell or slam doors or storm out of the house; that had never been his style. He voiced his objections coldly and quietly at the dinner table, after saying practically nothing since she walked in the door.

"I just would like to know why you thought you should do this without even talking to me about it. I don't demand that you *ask* me, just discuss it with me."

Cleo felt miserable, but was determined not to let it show. She held Feather in her arm, the bottle in her other hand, and ignored the food cooling on her plate. She was hungry but at least she was not eating for two.

"Jules, I'd ask you before I rearrange the furniture. We both own this apartment. I'd ask you before I put Lilli or Paul in another school. We share the responsibility for their upbringing. But I don't ask you when I put on lipstick or cut my hair. It's my body."

"I like it, Mom," Lilli said. "You look like me."

Cleo smiled at her, reached over and tousled her hair.

"What do you like?" Paul asked, around a mouthful of food.

"See?" said Cleo. "It's not that important."

"I don't see how you can say that. And I said you didn't have to ask me. I just would . . . you should have . . . I should have *known*."

"It was an impulse, Jules."

"An impulse. An *impulse*." For the first time, he raised his voice, and Cleo knew how upset he really was. Lilli and Paul fell silent, and even Feather squirmed.

But Cleo liked it. Oh, not forever and ever: as an interesting change. It gave her a feeling of freedom to be that much in control of her body, to be able to decide how large she wished her breasts to be. Did it have anything to do with changing? She really didn't think so. She didn't feel the least bit like a man.

And what was a breast, anyway? It was anything from a nipple sitting flush with the rib cage to a mammoth hunk of fat and milk gland. Cleo realized Jules was suffering from the more-is-better syndrome, thinking of Cleo's action as the removal of her breasts, as if they had to be large to exist at all. What she had actually done was reduce their size.

No more was said at the table, but Cleo knew it was for the children's sake. As soon as they got into bed, she could feel the tension again.

"I can't understand why you did it *now*. What about Feather?"

"What about her?"

"Well, do you expect me to nurse her?"

Cleo finally got angry. "Damn it, that's *exactly* what I expect you to do. Don't tell me you don't know what I'm talking about. You think it's all fun and games, having to carry a child around all day because she needs the milk in your breasts?"

"You never complained before."

"I . . ." She stopped. He was right, of course. It amazed even Cleo that this had all come up so suddenly, but here it was, and she had to deal with it. *They* had to deal with it.

"That's because it isn't an awful thing. It's great to nourish another human being at your breast. I loved every minute of it with Lilli. Sometimes it was a headache, having her there all the time, but it was worth it. The same with Paul." She sighed. "The same with Feather, too, most of the time. You hardly think about it."

"Then why the revolt now? With no warning?"

"It's not a revolt, honey. Do you see it as that? I just . . . I'd like you to try it. Take Feather for a few months. Take her to work like I do. Then you'd . . . you'd see a little of what I go through." She rolled on her side and playfully punched his arm, trying to lighten it in some way. "You might even like it. It feels real good."

He snorted. "I'd feel silly."

She jumped from the bed and paced toward the living room, then turned, more angry than ever. "Silly? Nursing is silly? Breasts are silly? Then why the hell do you wonder why I did what I did?"

"Being a *man* is what makes it silly," he retorted. "It doesn't look right. I almost laugh every time I see a man with breasts. The hormones mess up your system, I heard, and—"

"That's *not true!* Not anymore. You can lactate—"

"—and besides, it's my body, as you pointed out. I'll do with it what pleases me."

She sat on the edge of the bed with her back to him. He reached out and stroked her, but she moved away.

"All right," she said. "I was just suggesting it. I thought you might like to try it. *I'm* not going to nurse her. She goes on the bottle from now on."

"If that's the way it has to be."

"It is. I want you to start taking Feather to work with you. Since she's going to be a bottle baby, it hardly matters which of us cares for her. I think you owe it to me, since I carried the burden alone with Lilli and Paul."

"All right."

She got into bed and pulled the covers up around her, her back to him. She didn't want him to see how close she was to tears.

But the feeling passed. The tension drained from her, and she felt good. She thought she had won a victory, and it was worth the cost. Jules would not stay angry at her.

She fell asleep easily, but woke up several times during the night as Jules tossed and turned.

He did adjust to it. It was impossible for him to say so all at once, but after a week without lovemaking he admitted grudgingly that she looked good. He began to touch her in the mornings and when they kissed after getting home from work. Jules had always admired her slim muscularity, her athlete's arms and legs. The slim chest looked so natural on her, it fit the rest of her so well that he began to wonder what all the fuss had been about.

One night while they were clearing the dinner dishes, Jules touched her nipples for the first time in a week. He asked her if it felt any different.

"There is very little feeling anywhere but the nipples," she pointed out, "no matter how big a woman is. You know that."

"Yeah, I guess I do."

She knew they would make love that night and determined it would be on her terms.

She spent a long time in the bathroom, letting him get settled with his book, then came out and took it away. She got on top of him and pressed close, kissing and tickling his nipples with her fingers.

She was aggressive and insistent. At first he seemed reluctant, but soon he was responding as she pressed her lips hard against his, forcing his head back into the pillow.

"I love you," he said, and raised his head to kiss her nose. "Are you ready?"

"I'm ready." He put his arms around her and held her close, then rolled over and hovered above her.

"Jules. *Jules*. Stop it." She squirmed onto her side, her legs held firmly together.

"What's wrong?"

"I want to be on top tonight."

"Oh. All right." He turned over again and reclined passively as she repositioned herself. Her heart was pounding. There had been no reason to think he would object—they had made love in any and all positions, but basically the exotic ones were a change of pace from the "natural" one with her on her back. Tonight she had wanted to feel in control.

"Open your legs, darling," she said, with a smile. He did, but didn't return the smile. She raised herself on her hands and knees and prepared for the tricky insertion.

"Cleo."

"What is it? This will take a little effort, but I think I can make it worth your while, so if you'd just—"

"Cleo, what the hell is the purpose of this?"

She stopped dead and let her head sag between her shoulders.

"What's the matter? Are you feeling silly with your feet in the air?"

"Maybe. Is that what you wanted?"

"Jules, humiliating you was the farthest thing from my mind."

"Then what *was* on your mind? It's not like we've never done it this way before. It's—"

"Only when *you* chose to do so. It's always your decision."

"It's not degrading to be on the bottom."

"Then why were you feeling silly?"

He didn't answer, and she wearily lifted herself away from him, sitting on her knees at his feet. She waited, but he didn't seem to want to talk about it.

"I've never complained about the position," she ventured. "I don't *have* any complaints about it. It works pretty well." Still he said nothing. "All right. I wanted to see what it looked like from up there. I was tired of looking at the ceiling. I was curious."

"And *that's* why I felt *silly*. I never minded you being on top before, have I? But before . . . well, it's never been in the context of the last couple of weeks. I *know* what's on your mind."

"And you feel threatened by it. By the fact that I'm curious about changing, that I want to know what it's like to take charge. You know I can't—and wouldn't if I could—force a change on you."

"But your curiosity is wrecking our marriage."

She felt like crying again, but didn't let it show except for a trembling of the lower lip. She didn't want him to try and soothe her; that was all too likely to work, and she would find herself on her back with her legs in the air. She looked down at the bed and nodded slowly, then got up. She went to the mirror and took the brush, began running it through her hair.

"What are you doing now? Can't we talk about this?"

"I don't feel much like talking right now." She leaned forward and examined her face as she brushed, then dabbed at the corners of her eyes with a tissue. "I'm going out. I'm still curious."

He said nothing as she started for the door.

"I may be a little late."

The place was called Oophyte. The capital "O" had a plus sign hanging from it, and an arrow in the upper right side. The sign was built so that the symbols revolved; one moment the plus was inside and the arrow out, the next moment the reverse.

Cleo moved in a pleasant haze across the crowded dance floor, pausing now and then to draw on her dopestick. The air in the room was thick with lavender smoke, illuminated by flashing blue lights. She danced when the mood took her. The music was so loud that she didn't have to think about it; the noise gripped her bones, animated her arms and legs. She glided through a forest of naked skin, feeling the occasional roughness of a paper suit and, rarely, expensive cotton clothing. It was like moving underwater, like wading through molasses.

She saw him across the floor, and began moving in his direction. He took no notice of her for some time, though she danced right in front of him. Few of the dancers had partners in more than the transitory sense. Some were celebrating life, others were displaying themselves, but all were looking for partners, so eventually he realized she had been there an unusual length of time. He was easily as stoned as she was.

She told him what she wanted.

"Sure. Where do you want to go? Your place?"

She took him down the hall in back and touched her credit bracelet to the lock on one of the doors. The room was simple, but clean.

He looked a lot like her phantom twin in the mirror, she noted with one part of her mind. It was probably why she had chosen him. She embraced him and lowered him gently to the bed.

"Do you want to exchange names?" he asked. The grin on his face kept getting sillier as she toyed with him.

"I don't care. Mostly I think I want to use you."

"Use away. My name's Saffron."

"I'm Cleopatra. Would you get on your back, please?"

He did, and they did. It was hot in the little room, but neither of them minded it. It was healthy exertion, the physical sensations were great, and when Cleo was through she had learned nothing. She collapsed on top of him. He did not seem surprised when tears began falling on his shoulder.

"I'm sorry," she said, sitting up and getting ready to leave.

"Don't go," he said, putting his hand on her shoulder. "Now that you've got that out of your system, maybe we can make love."

She didn't want to smile, but she had to, then she was crying harder, putting her face to his chest and feeling the warmth of his arms around her and the hair tickling her nose. She realized what she was doing, and tried to pull away.

"For God's sake, don't be ashamed that you need someone to cry on."

"It's weak. I . . . I just didn't want to be weak."

"We're all weak."

She gave up struggling and nestled there until the tears stopped. She sniffed, wiped her nose, and faced him.

"What's it like? Can you tell me?" She was about to explain what she meant, but he seemed to understand.

"It's like . . . nothing special."

"You were born female, weren't you? I mean, I thought I might be able to tell."

"It's no longer important how I was born. I've been both. It's still me, on the inside. You understand?"

"I'm not sure I do."

They were quiet for a long time. Cleo thought of a thousand things to say, questions to ask, but could do nothing.

"You've been coming to a decision, haven't you?" he said, at last. "Are you any closer after tonight?"

"I'm not sure."

"It's not going to solve any problems, you know. It might even create some."

She pulled away from him and got up. She shook her hair and wished for a comb.

"Thank you, Cleopatra," he said.

"Oh. Uh, thank you . . ." She had forgotten his name. She smiled again to cover her embarrassment, and shut the door behind her.

"Hello?"

"Yes. This is Cleopatra King. I had a consultation with one of your staff. I believe it was ten days ago."

"Yes, Ms. King. I have your file. What can I do for you?"

She took a deep breath. "I want you to start the clone. I left a tissue sample."

"Very well, Ms. King. Did you have any instructions concerning the chromosome donor?"

"Do you need consent?"

"Not as long as there's a sample in the bank."

"Use my husband, Jules La Rhin. Security number 4454390."

"Very good. We'll be in contact with you."

Cleo hung up the phone and rested her forehead against the cool metal. She should never get this stoned, she realized. What had she done?

But it was not final. It would be six months before she had to decide if she would ever use the clone. Damn Jules. Why did he have to make such a big thing of it?

Jules did *not* make a big thing of it when she told him what she had done. He took it quietly and calmly, as if he had been expecting it.

"You know I won't follow you in this?"

"I know you feel that way. I'm interested to see if you change your mind."

"Don't count on it. I want to see if you change yours."

"I haven't *made up* my mind. But I'm giving myself the option."

"All I ask is that you bear in mind what this could do to our relationship. I love you, Cleo. I don't think that will ever change. But if you walk into this house as a man, I don't think I'll be able to see you as the person I've always loved."

"You could if you were a woman."

"But I won't be."

"And I'll be the same person I always was." But would she be? What the hell was *wrong?* What had Jules ever done that he should deserve this? She made up her mind never to go through with it, and they made love that night and it was very, very good.

But somehow she never got around to calling the vivarium and telling them to abort the clone. She made the decision not to go through with it a dozen times over the next six months, and never had the clone destroyed.

Their relationship in bed became uneasy as time passed. At first, it was good. Jules made no objections when she initiated sex, and was willing to do it any way she preferred. Once that was accomplished she no longer cared whether she was on top or underneath. The important thing had been having the option of making love when she wanted to, the way she wanted to.

"That's what this is all about," she told him one night, in a moment of clarity when everything seemed to make sense except his refusal to see things from her side. "It's the option I want. I'm not unhappy being a female. I don't like the feeling that there's *anything* I *can't* be. I want to know how much of me is hormones, how much is genetics, how much is upbringing. I want to know if I feel more secure being aggressive as a man, because I don't most of the time, as a woman. Or do men feel the same insecurities I feel? Would Cleo the man feel free to cry? I don't know any of those things."

"But you said it yourself. You'll still be the same person."

They began to drift apart in small ways. A few weeks after her outing to Oophyte she returned home one Sunday afternoon to find him in bed with a woman. It was not like him to do it like that; their custom had been to bring lovers home and introduce them, to keep it friendly and open. Cleo was amused, because she saw it as his way of getting back at her for her trip to the encounter bar.

So she was the perfect hostess, joining them in bed, which seemed to disconcert Jules. The woman's name was Harriet, and Cleo found herself liking her. She was a changer—something Jules had not known or he certainly would not have chosen her to make Cleo feel bad. Harriet was uncomfortable when she realized why she was there. Cleo managed to put her at ease by making love to her, something that surprised Cleo a little and Jules considerably, since she had never done it before.

Cleo enjoyed it; she found Harriet's smooth body to be a whole new world. And she felt she had neatly turned the tables on Jules, making him confront once more the idea of his wife in the man's role.

The worst part was the children. They had discussed the possible impending change with Lilli and Paul.

Lilli could not see what all the fuss was about; it was a part of her life, something that was all around her which she took for granted as something she herself would do when she was old enough. But when she began picking up the concern from her father, she drew subtly closer to her mother. Cleo was tremendously relieved. She didn't think she could have held to it in the face of Lilli's displeasure. Lilli was her first born, and though she hated to admit it and did her best not to play favorites, her darling. She had taken a year's leave from her job at appalling expense to the household budget so she could devote all her time to her infant daughter. She often wished she could somehow return to those simpler days, when motherhood had been her whole life.

Feather, of course, was not consulted. Jules had assumed the responsibility for her nurture without complaint, and seemed to be enjoying it. It was fine with Cleo, though it maddened her that he was so willing about taking over the mothering role without being willing to try it as a female. Cleo loved Feather as much as the other two, but sometimes had trouble recalling why they had decided to have her. She felt she had gotten the procreative impulse out of her system with Paul, and yet there Feather was.

Paul was the problem.

Things could get tense when Paul expressed doubts about how he would feel if his mother were to become a man. Jules's face would darken and he might not speak for days. When he did speak, often in the middle of the night when neither of them could sleep, it would be in a verbal explosion that was as close to violence as she had ever seen him.

It frightened her, because she was by no means sure of herself when it came to Paul. Would it hurt him? Jules spoke of gender identity crises, of the need for stable role models, and finally, in naked honesty, of the fear that his son would grow up to be somehow less than a man.

Cleo didn't know, but cried herself to sleep over it many nights. They had read articles about it and found that psychologists were divided. Traditionalists made much of the importance of sex roles, while changers felt sex roles were important only to those who were trapped in them; with the breaking of the sexual barrier, the concept of roles vanished.

The day finally came when the clone was ready. Cleo still did not know what she should do.

"Are you feeling comfortable now? Just nod if you can't talk."

"Wha . . ."

"Relax. It's all over. You'll be feeling like walking in a few minutes. We'll have someone take you home. You may feel drunk for a while, but there's no drugs in your system."

"Wha . . . happen?"

"It's over. Just relax."

Cleo did, curling up in a ball. Eventually he began to laugh.

Drunk was not the word for it. He sprawled on the bed, trying on pronouns for size. It was all so funny. *He* was on *his* back with *his* hands in *his* lap. He giggled and rolled back and forth, over and over, fell on the floor in hysterics.

He raised his head.

"Is that you, Jules?"

"Yes, it's me." He helped Cleo back onto the bed, then sat on the edge, not too near, but not unreachably far away. "How do you feel?"

He snorted. "Drunker 'n a skunk." He narrowed his eyes, forced them to focus on Jules. "You must call me Leo now. Cleo is a woman's name. You shouldn't have called me Cleo then."

"All right, I didn't call you Cleo, though."

"You didn't? Are you *sure?*"

"I'm very sure it's something I wouldn't have said."

"Oh. Okay." He lifted his head and looked confused for a moment. "You know what? I'm gonna be sick."

Leo felt much better an hour later. He sat in the living room with Jules, both of them on the big pillows that were the only furniture.

They spoke of inconsequential matters for a time, punctuated by long silences. Leo was no more used to the sound of his new voice than Jules was.

"Well," Jules said, finally, slapping his hands on his knees and standing up. "I really don't know what your plans are from here. Did you want to go out tonight? Find a woman, see what it's like?''

Leo shook his head. ''I tried that out as soon as I got home,'' he said. ''The male orgasm, I mean.''

''What was it like?''

He laughed. ''Certainly you know that by now.''

''No, I meant, after being a woman—''

''I know what you mean.'' He shrugged. ''The erection is interesting. So much larger than what I'm used to. Otherwise . . .'' He frowned for a moment. ''A lot the same. Some different. More localized. Messier.''

''Um.'' Jules looked away, studying the electric fireplace as if seeing it for the first time. ''Had you planned to move out? It isn't necessary, you know. We could move people around. I can go in with Paul, or we could move him in with me in . . . in our old room. You could have his.'' He turned away from Leo, and put his hand to his face.

Leo ached to get up and comfort him, but felt it would be exactly the wrong thing to do. He let Jules get himself under control.

''If you'll have me, I'd like to continue sleeping with you.''

Jules said nothing, and didn't turn around.

''Jules, I'm perfectly willing to do whatever will make you most comfortable. There doesn't have to be any sex. Or I'd be happy to do what I used to do when I was in late pregnancy. You wouldn't have to do anything at all.''

''No sex,'' he said.

''Fine, fine. Jules, I'm getting awfully tired. Are you ready to sleep?''

There was a long pause, then he turned and nodded.

They lay quietly, side by side, not touching. The lights were out; Leo could barely see the outline of Jules's body.

After a long time, Jules turned on his side.

''Cleo, are you in there? Do you still love me?''

''I'm here,'' she said. ''I love you. I always will.''

Jules jumped when Leo touched him, but made no objection. He began to cry, and Leo held him close. They fell asleep in each other's arms.

The Oophyte was as full and noisy as ever. It gave Leo a headache.

He did not like the place any more than Cleo had, but it was the only place he knew to find sex partners quickly and easily, with no emotional entanglements and no long process of seduction. Everyone there was available; all one needed to do was ask. They used each other for sexual calisthenics just one step removed from masturbation, cheerfully admitted the fact, and took the position that if you didn't approve, what were you doing there? There were plenty of other places for romance and relationships.

Leo didn't normally approve of it—not for himself, though he cared not at all what other people did for amusement. He preferred to know someone he bedded.

But he was here tonight to learn. He felt he needed the practice. He did not buy the argument that he would know just what to do because he had been a woman and knew what they liked. He needed to know how people reacted to him as a male.

Things went well. He approached three women and was accepted each time. The first was a mess—so *that's* what they meant by too soon!—and she was rather indignant about it until he explained his situation. After that she was helpful and supportive.

He was about to leave when he was propositioned by a woman who said her name was Lynx. He was tired, but decided to go with her.

Ten frustrating minutes later she sat up and moved away from him. "What are you here for, if that's all the interest you can muster? And don't tell me it's my fault."

"I'm sorry," he said. "I forgot. I thought I could . . . well, I didn't realize I had to be really interested before I could perform."

"Perform? That's a funny way to put it."

"I'm sorry." He told her what the problem was, how many times he had made love in the last two hours. She sat on the edge of the bed and ran her hands through her hair, frustrated and irritable.

"Well, it's not the end of the world. There's plenty more out there. But you could give a girl a warning. You didn't have to say yes back there."

"I know. It's my fault. I'll have to learn to judge my capacity, I guess. It's just that I'm used to being *able* to, even if I'm not particularly—"

Lynx laughed. "What am I saying? Listen to me. Honey, I

used to have the same problem myself. *Weeks* of not getting it up. And I know it hurts.''

"Well," Leo said. "I know what you're feeling like, too. It's no fun.''

Lynx shrugged. "In other circumstances, yeah. But like I said, the woods are full of 'em tonight. I won't have any problem.'' She put her hand on his cheek and pouted at him. "Hey, I didn't hurt your poor male ego, did I?''

Leo thought about it, probed around for bruises, and found none.

"No.''

She laughed. "I didn't think so. Because you don't have one. Enjoy it, Leo. A male ego is something that has to be grown carefully, when you're young. People have to keep pointing out what you have to do to be a man, so you can recognize failure when you can't 'perform.' How come you used that word?''

"I don't know. I guess I was just thinking of it that way.''

"Trying to be a quote *man* unquote. Leo, you don't have enough emotional investment in it. And you're *lucky*. It took me over a year to shake mine. Don't be a man. Be a male human, instead. The switchover's a lot easier that way.''

"I'm not sure what you mean.''

She patted his knee. "Trust me. Do you see me getting all upset because I wasn't sexy enough to turn you on, or some such garbage? No. I wasn't brought up to worry that way. But reverse it. If I'd done to you what you just did to me, wouldn't something like that have occurred to you?''

"I think it would. Though I've always been pretty secure in that area.''

"The most secure of us are whimpering children beneath it, at least some of the time. You understand that I got upset because you said yes when you weren't ready? And that's *all I* was upset about? It was impolite, Leo. A male human shouldn't do that to a female human. With a man and a woman, it's different. The poor fellow's got a lot of junk in his head, and so does the woman, so they shouldn't be held responsible for the tricks their egos play on them.''

Leo laughed. "I don't know if you're making sense at all. But I like the sound of it. 'Male human.' Maybe I'll see the difference one day.''

· · ·

Some of the expected problems never developed.

Paul barely noticed the change. Leo had prepared himself for a traumatic struggle with his son, and it never came. If it changed Paul's life at all, it was in the fact that he could now refer to his maternal parent as Leo instead of mother.

Strangely enough, it was Lilli who had the most trouble at first. Leo was hurt by it, tried not to show it, and did everything he could to let her adjust gradually. Finally she came to him one day about a week after the change. She said she had been silly, and wanted to know if she could get a change, too, since one of her best friends was getting one. Leo talked her into remaining female until after the onset of puberty. He told her he thought she might enjoy it.

Leo and Jules circled each other like two tigers in a cage, unsure if a fight was necessary but ready to start clawing out eyes if it came to it. Leo didn't like the analogy; if he had still been a female tiger, he would have felt sure of the outcome. But he had no wish to engage in a dominance struggle with Jules.

They shared an apartment, a family, and a bed. They were elaborately polite, but touched each other only rarely, and Leo always felt he should apologize when they did. Jules would not meet his eyes; their gazes would touch, then rebound like two cork balls with identical static charges.

But eventually Jules accepted Leo. He was "that guy who's always around" in Jules' mind. Leo didn't care for that, but saw it as progress. In a few more days Jules began to discover that he liked Leo. They began to share things, to talk more. The subject of their previous relationship was taboo for a while. It was as if Jules wanted to know Leo from scratch, not acknowledging there had ever been a Cleo who had once been his wife.

It was not that simple; Leo would not let it be. Jules sometimes sounded like he was mourning the passing of a loved one when he hesitantly began talking about the hurt inside him. He was able to talk freely to Leo, and it was in a slightly different manner from the way he had talked to Cleo. He poured out his soul. It was astonishing to Leo that there were so many bruises on it, so many defenses and insecurities. There was buried hostility which Jules had never felt free to tell a woman.

Leo let him go on, but when Jules started a sentence with,

"I could never tell this to Cleo," or, "Now that she's gone," Leo would go to him, take his hand, and force him to look.

"I'm Cleo," he would say. "I'm right here, and I love you."

They started doing things together. Jules took him to places Cleo had never been. They went out drinking together and had a wonderful time getting sloshed. Before, it had always been dinner with a few drinks or dopesticks, then a show or concert. Now they might come home at 0200 harmonizing loud enough to get thrown in jail. Jules admitted he hadn't had so much fun since his college days.

Socializing was a problem. Few of their old friends were changers, and neither of them wanted to face the complications of going to a party as a couple. They couldn't make friends among changers, because Jules correctly saw he would be seen as an outsider.

So they saw a lot of men. Leo had thought he knew all of Jules' close friends, but found he had been wrong. He saw a side of Jules he had never seen before: more relaxed in ways, some of his guardedness gone, but with other defenses in place. Leo sometimes felt like a spy, looking in on a stratum of society he had always known was there, but he had never been able to penetrate. If Cleo had walked into the group its structure would have changed subtly; she would have created a new milieu by her presence, like light destroying the atom it was meant to observe.

After his initial outing to the Oophyte, Leo remained celibate for a long time. He did not want to have sex casually; he wanted to love Jules. As far as he knew, Jules was abstaining, too.

But they found an acceptable alternative in double-dating. They shopped around together for a while, taking out different women and having a lot of fun without getting into sex, until each settled on a woman he could have a relationship with. Jules was with Diane, a woman he had known at work for many years. Leo went out with Harriet.

The four of them had great times together. Leo loved being a pal to Jules, but would not let it remain simply that. He took to reminding Jules that he could do this with Cleo, too. What Leo wanted to emphasize was that he could be a companion, a buddy, a confidant no matter which sex he was. He wanted to combine the best of being a woman and being a man, be both things for Jules, fulfill all his needs. But it hurt to think that Jules would not do the same for him.

"Well, hello, Leo. I didn't expect to see you today."

"Can I come in, Harriet?"

She held the door open for him.

"Can I get you anything? Oh, yeah, before you go any further, that 'Harriet' business is finished. I changed my name today. It's Joule from now on. That's spelled j-o-u-l-e."

"Okay, Joule. Nothing for me, thanks." He sat on her couch.

Leo was not surprised at the new name. Changers had a tendency to get away from "name" names. Some did as Cleo had done by choosing a gender equivalent or a similar sound. Others ignored gender connotations and used the one they had always used. But most eventually chose a neutral word, according to personal preference.

"Jules, Julia," he muttered.

"What was that?" Joule's brow wrinkled slightly.

"Did you come here for mothering? Things going badly?"

Leo slumped down and contemplated his folded hands.

"I don't know. I guess I'm depressed. How long has it been now? Five months? I've learned a lot, but I'm not sure just what it is. I feel like I've grown. I see the world . . . well, I see things differently, yes. But I'm still basically the same person."

"In the sense that you're the same person at thirty-three as you were at ten?"

Leo squirmed. "Okay. Yeah, I've changed. But it's not any kind of reversal. Nothing turned topsy-turvy. It's an expansion. It's not a new viewpoint. It's like filling something up, moving out into unused spaces. Becoming . . ." His hands groped in the air, then fell back into his lap. "It's like a completion."

Joule smiled. "And you're disappointed? What more could you ask?"

Leo didn't want to get into that just yet. "Listen to this, and see if you agree. I always saw male and female—whatever that is, and I don't know if the two *really* exist other than physically and don't think it's important anyway . . . I saw those qualities as separate. Later, I thought of them like Siamese twins in everybody's head. But the twins were usually fighting, trying to cut each other off. One would beat the other down, maim it, throw it in a cell, and never feed it, but they were always connected and the beaten-down one would make the winner pay for the victory.

"So I wanted to try and patch things up between them. I thought I'd just introduce them to each other and try to referee, but they got along a lot better than I expected. In fact, they turned into one whole person, and found they could be very happy together. I can't tell them apart anymore. Does that make any sense?"

Joule moved over to sit beside him.

"It's a good analogy, in its way. I feel something like that, but I don't think about it anymore. So what's the problem? You just told me you feel whole now."

Leo's face controlled. "Yes. I do. And if I am, what does that make Jules?" He began to cry, and Joule let him get it out, just holding his hand. She thought he'd better face it alone, this time. When he had calmed down, she began to speak quietly.

"Leo, Jules is happy as he is. I think he could be much happier, but there's no way for us to show him that without having him do something he fears so much. It's possible that he will do it someday, after more time to get used to it. And it's possible that he'll hate it and run screaming back to his manhood. Sometimes the maimed twin can't be rehabilitated."

She sighed heavily, and got up to pace the room.

"There's going to be a lot of this in the coming years," she said. "A lot of broken hearts. We're not really very much like them, you know. We get along better. We're not angels, but we may be the most civilized, considerate group the race has yet produced. There are fools and bastards among us, just like the one-sexers, but I think we tend to be a little less foolish, and a little less cruel. I think changing is here to stay.

"And what you've got to realize is that you're lucky. And so is Jules. It could have been much worse. I know of several broken homes just among my own friends. There's going to be many more before society has assimilated this. But your love for Jules and his for you has held you together. He's made a tremendous adjustment, maybe as big as the one you made. He *likes* you. In either sex. Okay, so you don't make love to him as Leo. You may never reach that point."

"We did. Last night." Leo shifted on the couch. "I . . . I got mad. I told him if he wanted to see Cleo, he had to learn to relate to me, because I'm *me*, dammit."

"I think that might have been a mistake."

Leo looked away from her. "I'm starting to think so, too."

"But I think the two of you can patch it up, if there's any damage. You've come through a lot together."

"I didn't mean to force anything on him, I just got mad."

"And maybe you *should* have. It might have been just the thing. You'll have to wait and see."

Leo wiped his eyes and stood up.

"Thanks, Harr . . . sorry. Joule. You've helped me. I . . . uh, I may not be seeing you as often for a while."

"I understand. Let's stay friends, okay?" She kissed him, and he hurried away.

She was sitting on a pillow facing the door when he came home from work, her legs crossed, elbows resting on her knee with a dopestick in her hand. She smiled at him.

"Well, you're home early. What happened?"

"I stayed home from work." She nearly choked, trying not to laugh. He threw his coat to the closet and hurried into the kitchen. She heard something being stirred, then the sound of glass shattering. He burst through the doorway.

"Cleo!"

"Darling, you look so handsome with your mouth hanging open."

He shut it, but still seemed unable to move. She went to him, feeling tingling excitement in her loins like the return of an old friend. She put her arms around him, and he nearly crushed her. She loved it.

He drew back slightly and couldn't seem to get enough of her face, his eyes roaming every detail.

"How long will you stay this way?" he asked. "Do you have any idea?"

"I don't know. Why?"

He smiled, a little sheepishly. "I hope you won't take this wrong. I'm so *happy* to see you. Maybe I shouldn't say it . . . but no, I think I'd better. I like Leo. I think I'll miss him, a little."

She nodded. "I'm not hurt. How could I be?" She drew away and led him to a pillow. "Sit down, Jules. We have to have a talk." His knees gave way under him and he sat, looking up expectantly.

"Leo isn't gone, and don't you ever think that for a minute. He's right here." She thumped her chest and looked at him defiantly. "He'll always be here. He'll never go away."

"I'm sorry, Cleo, I—"

"No, don't talk yet. It was my own fault, but I didn't know any better. I never should have called myself Leo. It gave you an easy out. You didn't have to face Cleo being a male. I'm changing all that. My name is Nile. N-i-l-e. I won't answer to anything else."

"All right. It's a nice name."

"I thought of calling myself Lion. For Leo the lion. But I decided to be who I always was, the queen of the Nile, Cleopatra. For old time's sake."

He said nothing, but his eyes showed his appreciation.

"What you have to understand is that they're both gone, in a sense. You'll never be with Cleo again. I look like her now. I resemble her inside, too, like an adult resembles the child. I have a tremendous amount in common with what she was. But I'm not her."

He nodded. She sat beside him and took his hand.

"Jules, this isn't going to be easy. There are things I want to do, people I want to meet. We're not going to be able to share the same friends. We could drift apart because of it. I'm going to have to fight resentment because you'll be holding me back. You won't let me explore your female side like I want to. You're going to resent me because I'll be trying to force you into something you think is wrong for you. But I want to try and make it work."

He let out his breath. "God, Cl . . . Nile. I've never been so scared in my life. I thought you were leading up to leaving me."

She squeezed his hand. "Not if I can help it. I want each of us to try and accept the other as they are. For me, that includes being male whenever I feel like it. It's all the same to me, but I know it's going to be hard for *you*."

They embraced, and Jules wiped his tears on her shoulder, then faced her again.

"I'll do anything and everything in my power, up to—"

She put her finger to her lips. "I know. I accept you that way. But I'll keep trying to convince you."

Lollipop
and the Tar Baby

"Zzzzello. Zzz. Hello. Hello." Someone was speaking to Xanthia from the end of a ten-kilometer metal pipe, shouting to be heard across a roomful of gongs and cymbals being knocked over by angry giant bees. She had never heard such interference.

"Hello?" she repeated. "What are you doing on my wavelength?"

"Hello." The interference was still there, but the voice was slightly more distinct. "Wavelength. Searching, searching wavelength . . . get best reception with . . . Hello? Listening?"

"Yes, I'm listening. You're talking over . . . My radio isn't even . . ." She banged the radio panel with her palm in the ancient ritual humans employ when their creations are being balky. "My goddamn *radio* isn't even on. Did you know that?" It was a relief to feel anger boiling up inside her. Anything was preferable to feeling lost and silly.

"Not neccessary."

"What do you mean not—who are you?"

"Who. Having . . . *I'm*, pronoun, yes, I'm having difficulty. Bear with. Me? Yes, pronoun. Bear with me. I'm not who. What. *What* am I?"

"All right. *What* are you?"

"Spacetime phenomenon. I'm gravity and causality-sink. Black hole."

Xanthia did not need black holes explained to her. She had spent her entire eighteen years hunting them, along with her

183

clone-sister, Zoetrope. But she was not used to having them talk to her.

"Assuming for the moment that you really are a black hole," she said, beginning to wonder if this might be some elaborate trick played on her by Zoe, "just taking that as a tentative hypothesis—how are you able to talk to me?"

There was a sound like an attitude thruster going off, a rumbling pop. It was repeated.

"I manipulate spacetime framework . . . no, please hold line . . . *the* line. I manipulate the spacetime framework with controlled gravity waves projected in narrow . . . a narrow cone. I direct at the speaker in your radio. You hear. Me."

"What was that again?" It sounded like a lot of crap to her.

"I elaborate. I will elaborate. I cut through space itself, through—hold the line, hold the line, reference." There was a sound like a tape reeling rapidly through playback heads. "This is the BBC," said a voice that was recognizably human, but blurred by static. The tape whirred again, "gust the third, in the year of our Lord nineteen fifty-seven. Today in—" Once again the tape hunted.

"Chelson-Morley experiment disproved the existence of the ether, by ingeniously arranging a rotating prism—" Then the metallic voice was back.

"Ether. I cut through space itself, through a—hold the line." This time the process was shorter. She heard a fragment of what sounded like a video adventure serial. "Through a spacewarp made through the ductile etheric continuum—"

"Hold on there. That's not what you said before."

"I was elaborating."

"Go on. Wait, what were you doing? With that tape business?"

The voice paused, and when the answer came the line had cleared up quite a bit. But the voice still didn't sound human. Computer?

"I am not used to speech. No need for it. But I have learned your language by listening to your radio transmissions. I speak to you through use of indeterminate statistical concatenations. Gravity waves and probability, which is not the same thing in a causality singularity, enables a nonrational event to take place."

"Zoe, this is really you, isn't it?"

Xanthia was only eighteen Earth-years old, on her first

long orbit into the space beyond Pluto, the huge cometary zone where space is truly flat. Her whole life had been devoted to learning how to find and capture black holes, but one didn't come across them very often. Xanthia had been born a year after the beginning of the voyage and had another year to go before the end of it. In her whole life she had seen and talked to only one other human being, and that was Zoe, who was one hundred and thirty-five years old and her identical twin.

Their home was the *Shirley Temple*, a fifteen-thousand-tonne fusion-drive ship registered out of Lowell, Pluto. Zoe owned *Shirley* free and clear; on her first trip, many years ago, she had found a scale-five hole and had become instantly rich. Most hole hunters were not so lucky.

Zoe was also unusual in that she seemed to thrive on solitude. Most hunters who made a strike settled down to live in comfort, buy a large company or put the money into safe investments and live off the interest. They were unwilling or unable to face another twenty years alone. Zoe had gone out again, and a third time after the second trip had proved fruitless. She had found a hole on her third trip, and was now almost through her fifth.

But for some reason she had never adequately explained to Xanthia, she had wanted a companion this time. And what better company than herself? With the medical facilities aboard *Shirley* she had grown a copy of herself and raised the little girl as her daughter.

Xanthia squirmed around in the control cabin of *The Good Ship Lollipop*, stuck her head through the hatch leading to the aft exercise room, and found nothing. What she had expected, she didn't know. Now she crouched in midair with a screwdriver, attacking the service panels that protected the radio assembly.

"What are you doing by yourself?" the voice asked.

"Why don't *you* tell *me*, Zoe?" she said, lifting the panel off and tossing it angrily to one side. She peered into the gloomy interior, wrinkling her nose at the smell of oil and paraffin. She shone her pencil beam into the space, flicking it from one component to the next, all as familiar to her as neighborhood corridors would be to a planet-born child. There was nothing out of place, nothing that shouldn't be there.

Most of it was sealed into plastic blocks to prevent moisture or dust from getting to critical circuits. There was no tampering.

"I am failing to communicate. I am not your mother. I am a gravity and causality—"

"She's not my mother," Xanthia snapped.

"My records show that she would dispute you."

Xanthia didn't like the way the voice said that. But she was admitting to herself that there was no way Zoe could have set this up. That left her with the alternative: she really was talking to a black hole.

"She's not my mother," Xanthia repeated. "And if you've been listening in, you *know* why I'm out here in a lifeboat. So why do you ask?"

"I wish to help you. I have heard tension building between the two of you these last years. You are growing up."

Xanthia settled back in the control chair. Her head did not feel so good.

Hole hunting was a delicate economic balance, a tightrope walked between the needs of survival and the limitations of mass. The initial investment was tremendous and the return was undependable, so the potential hole hunter had to have a line to a source of speculative credit or be independently wealthy.

No consortium or corporation had been able to turn a profit at the business by going at it in a big way. The government of Pluto maintained a monopoly on the use of one-way robot probes, but they had found over the years that when a probe succeeded in finding a hole, a race usually developed to see who would reach it and claim it first. Ships sent after such holes had a way of disappearing in the resulting fights, far from law and order.

The demand for holes was so great that an economic niche remained which was filled by the solitary prospector, backed by people with tax writeoffs to gain. Prospectors had a ninety percent bankruptcy rate. But as with gold and oil in earlier days, the potential profits were huge, so there was never a lack of speculators.

Hole hunters would depart Pluto and accelerate to the limits of engine power, then coast for ten to fifteen years, keeping an eye on the mass detector. Sometimes they would be half a light-year from Sol before they had to decelerate and turn around. Less mass equaled more range, so the solitary hunter was the rule.

Teaming of ships had been tried, but teams that discovered a hole seldom came back together. One of them tended to have an accident. Hole hunters were a greedy lot, self-centered and self-sufficient.

Equipment had to be reliable. Replacement parts were costly in terms of mass, so the hole hunter had to make an agonizing choice with each item. Would it be better to leave it behind and chance a possibly fatal failure, or take it along, decreasing the range, and maybe miss the glory hole that is sure to be lurking just one more AU away? Hole hunters learned to be handy at repairing, jury-rigging, and bashing, because in twenty years even fail-safe triplicates can be on their last legs.

Zoe had sweated over her faulty mass detector before she admitted it was beyond her skills. Her primary detector had failed ten years into the voyage, and the second one had begun to act up six years later. She tried to put together one functioning detector with parts cannibalized from both. She nursed it along for a year with the equivalents of bobby pins and bubblegum. It was hopeless.

But *Shirley Temple* was a palace among prospecting ships. Having found two holes in her career, Zoe had her own money. She had stocked spare parts, beefed up the drive, even included that incredible luxury, a lifeboat.

The lifeboat was sheer extravagance, except for one thing. It had a mass detector as part of its astrogational equipment. She had bought it mainly for that reason, since it had only an eighteen-month range and would be useless except at the beginning and end of the trip, when they were close to Pluto. It made extensive use of plug-in components, sealed in plastic to prevent tampering or accidents caused by inexperienced passengers. The mass detector on board did not have the range or accuracy of the one on *Shirley*. It could be removed or replaced, but not recalibrated.

They had begun a series of three-month loops out from the mother ship. Xanthia had flown most of them earlier, when Zoe did not trust her to run *Shirley*. Later they had alternated.

"And that's what I'm doing out here by myself," Xanthia said. "I have to get out beyond ten million kilometers from *Shirley* so its mass doesn't affect the detector. My instrument is calibrated to ignore only the mass of this ship, not *Shirley*.

I stay out here for three months, which is a reasonably safe time for the life systems on *Lollipop,* and time to get pretty lonely. Then back for refueling and supplying.''

"The *Lollipop*?''

Xanthia blushed. "Well, I named this lifeboat that, after I started spending so much time on it. We have a tape of Shirley Temple in the library, and she sang this song, see—''

"Yes, I've heard it. I've been listening to radio for a very long time. So you no longer believe this is a trick by your mother?''

"She's *not . . .*'' Then she realized she had referred to Zoe in the third person again.

"I don't know what to think,'' she said, miserably. "Why are you doing this?''

"I sense that you are still confused. You'd like some proof that I am what I say I am. Since you'll think of it in a minute, I might as well ask you this question. Why do you suppose I haven't yet registered on your mass detector?''

Xanthia jerked in her seat, then was brought up short by the straps. It was true, there was not the slightest wiggle on the dials of the detector.

"All right, why haven't you?'' She felt a sinking sensation. She was sure the punchline came now, after she'd shot off her mouth about *Lollipop*—her secret from Zoe—and made such a point of the fact that Zoe was not her mother. It was her own private rebellion, one that she had not had the nerve to face Zoe with. Now she's going to reveal herself and tell me how she did it, and I'll feel like a fool, she thought.

"It's simple,'' the voice said. "You weren't in range of me yet. But now you are. Take a look.''

The needles were dancing, giving the reading of a scale-seven hole. A scale seven would mass about a tenth as much as the asteroid Ceres.

"Mommy, what *is* a black hole?''

The little girl was seven years old. One day she would call herself Xanthia, but she had not yet felt the need for a name and her mother had not seen fit to give her one. Zoe reasoned that you needed two of something before you needed names. There was only one other person on *Shirley.* There was no possible confusion. When the girl thought about it at all, she assumed her name must be Hey, or Darling.

She was a small child, as Zoe had been. She was recapitulating the growth Zoe had already been through a hundred years ago. Though she didn't know it, she was pretty: dark eyes with an oriental fold, dark skin, and kinky blonde hair. She was a genetic mix of Chinese and Negro, with dabs of other races thrown in for seasoning.

"I've tried to explain that before." Zoe said. "You don't have the math for it yet. I'll get you started on spacetime equations, then in about a year you'll be able to understand."

"But I want to know now." Black holes were a problem for the child. From her earliest memories the two of them had done nothing but hunt them, yet they never found one. She'd been doing a lot of reading—there was little else to do—and was wondering if they might inhabit the same category where she had tentatively placed Santa Claus and leprechauns.

"If I try again, will you go to sleep?"

"I promise."

So Zoe launched into her story about the Big Bang, the time in the long-ago when little black holes could be formed.

"As far as we can tell, all the little black holes like the ones we hunt were made in that time. Nowadays other holes can be formed by the collapse of very large stars. When the fires burn low and the pressures that are trying to blow the star apart begin to fade, gravity takes over and starts to pull the star in on itself." Zoe waved her hands in the air, forming cups to show bending space, flailing out to indicate pressures of fusion. These explanations were almost as difficult for her as stories of sex had been for earlier generations. The truth was that she was no relativist and didn't really grasp the slightly incredible premises behind black-hole theory. She suspected that no one could really visualize one, and if you can't do that, where are you? But she was practical enough not to worry about it.

"And what's gravity? I forgot." The child was rubbing her eyes to stay awake. She struggled to understand but already knew she would miss the point yet another time.

"Gravity is the thing that holds the universe together. The glue, or the rivets. It pulls everything toward everything else, and it takes energy to fight it and overcome it. It feels like when we boost the ship, remember I pointed that out to you?"

"Like when everything wants to move in the same direction?"

"That's right. So we have to be careful, because we don't think about it much. We have to worry about where things are because when we boost, everything will head for the stern. People on planets have to worry about that all the time. They have to put something strong between themselves and the center of the planet, or they'll go down."

"Down." The girl mused over that word, one that had been giving her trouble as long as she could remember, and thought she might finally have understood it. She had seen pictures of places where down was always the same direction, and they were strange to the eye. They were full of tables to put things on, chairs to sit in, and funny containers with no tops. Five of the six walls of the rooms on planets could hardly be used at all. One, the "floor," was called on to take all the use.

"So they use their legs to fight gravity with?" She was yawning now.

"Yes. You've seen pictures of the people with the funny legs. They're not so funny when you're in gravity. Those flat things on the ends are called feet. If they had peds like us, they wouldn't be able to walk so good. They always have to have one foot touching the floor, or they'd fall toward the surface of the planet."

Zoe tightened the strap that held the child to her bunk, and fastened the velcro patch on the blanket to the side of the sheet, tucking her in. Kids needed a warm, snug place to sleep. Zoe preferred to float free in her own bedroom, tucked into a fetal position and drifting.

"G'night, Mommy."

"Good night. You get some sleep, and don't worry about black holes."

But the child dreamed of them, as she often did. They kept tugging at her, and she would wake breathing hard and convinced that she was going to fall into the wall in front of her.

"You don't mean it? I'm rich!"

Xanthia looked away from the screen. It was no good pointing out that Zoe had always spoken of the trip as a partnership. She owned *Shirley* and *Lollipop*.

"Well, you too, of course. Don't think you won't be getting a real big share of the money. I'm going to set you up

so well that you'll be able to buy a ship of your own, and
raise little copies of yourself if you want to."

Xanthia was not sure that was her idea of heaven, but said
nothing.

"Zoe, there's a problem, and I . . . well, I was—" But
she was interrupted again by Zoe, who would not hear Xanthia's
comment for another thirty seconds.

"The first data is coming over the telemetry channel right
now, and I'm feeding it into the computer. Hold on a second
while I turn the ship. I'm going to start decelerating in about
one minute, based on these figures. You get the refined data
to me as soon as you have it."

There was a brief silence.

"What problem?"

"It's talking to me, Zoe. The hole is talking to me."

This time the silence was longer than the minute it took the
radio signal to make the round trip between ships. Xanthia
furtively thumbed the contrast knob, turning her sister-mother
down until the screen was blank. She could look at the
camera and Zoe wouldn't know the difference.

Damn, damn, she thinks I've flipped. But I had to tell her.

"I'm not sure what you mean."

"Just what I *said*. I don't understand it, either. But it's
been talking to me for the last hour, and it says the *damnedest*
things."

There was another silence.

"All right. When you get there, don't do anything, repeat,
anything, until I arrive. Do you understand?"

"Zoe, I'm not crazy. I'm *not.*"

"Of course you're not, baby, there's an explanation for
this and I'll find out what it is as soon as I get there. You just
hang on. My first rough estimate puts me alongside you about
three hours after you're stationary relative to the hole."

Shirley and *Lollipop,* traveling parallel courses, would both
be veering from their straight-line trajectories to reach the
hole. But Xanthia was closer to it; Zoe would have to move at
a more oblique angle and would be using more fuel. Xanthia
thought four hours was more like it.

"I'm signing off," Zoe said. "I'll call you back as soon as
I'm in the groove."

Xanthia hit the off button on the radio and furiously
unbuckled her seatbelt. Damn Zoe, damn her, damn her,

damn her. Just sit tight, she says. I'll be there to explain the unexplainable. It'll be all right.

She knew she should start her deceleration, but there was something she must do first.

She twisted easily in the air, grabbing at braces with all four hands, and dived through the hatch to the only other living space in *Lollipop:* the exercise area. It was cluttered with equipment that she had neglected to fold into the walls, but she didn't mind; she liked close places. She squirmed through the maze like a fish gliding through coral, until she reached the wall she was looking for. It had been taped over with discarded manual pages, the only paper she could find on *Lollipop*. She started ripping at the paper, wiping tears from her cheeks with one ped as she worked. Beneath the paper was a mirror.

How to test for sanity? Xanthia had not considered the question; the thing to do had simply presented itself and she had done it. Now she confronted the mirror and searched for . . . what? Wild eyes? Froth on the lips?

What she saw was her mother.

Xanthia's life had been a process of growing slowly into the mold Zoe represented. She had known her pug nose would eventually turn down. She had known that baby fat would melt away. Her breasts had grown just into the small cones she knew from her mother's body and no farther.

She hated looking in mirrors.

Xanthia and Zoe were small women. Their most striking feature was the frizzy dandelion of yellow hair, lighter than their bodies. When the time had come for naming, the young clone had almost opted for Dandelion until she came upon the word *xanthic* in a dictionary. The radio call-letters for *Lollipop* happened to be X-A-N, and the word was too good to resist. She knew, too, that Orientals were thought of as having yellow skin, though she could not see why.

Why had she come here, of all places? She strained toward the mirror, fighting her repulsion, searching her face for signs of insanity. The narrow eyes were a little puffy, and as deep and expressionless as ever. She put her hands to the glass, startled in the silence to hear the multiple clicks as the long nails just missed touching the ones on the other side. She was always forgetting to trim them.

Sometimes, in mirrors, she knew she was not seeing herself. She could twitch her mouth, and the image would not

move. She could smile, and the image would frown. It had
been happening for two years, as her body put the finishing
touches on its eighteen-year process of duplicating Zoe. She
had not spoken of it, because it scared her.

"And this is where I come to see if I'm sane," she said
aloud, noting that the lips in the mirror did not move. "Is she
going to start talking to me now?" She waved her arms
wildly, and so did Zoe in the mirror. At least it wasn't that
bad yet; it was only the details that failed to match: the small
movements, and especially the facial expressions. Zoe was
inspecting her dispassionately and did not seem to like what
she saw. That small curl at the edge of the mouth, the almost
brutal narrowing of the eyes . . .

Xanthia clapped her hands over her face, then peeked out
through the fingers. Zoe was peeking out, too. Xanthia began
rounding up the drifting scraps of paper and walling her twin
in again with new bits of tape.

The beast with two backs and legs at each end writhed, came
apart, and resolved into Xanthia and Zoe, drifting, breathing
hard. They caromed off the walls like monkeys, giving up
their energy, gradually getting breath back under control.
Golden, wet hair and sweaty skin brushed against each other
again and again as they came to rest.

Now the twins floated in the middle of the darkened bedroom. Zoe was already asleep, tumbling slowly with that total
looseness possible only in free fall. Her leg rubbed against
Xanthia's belly and her relative motion stopped. The leg was
moist. The room was close, thick with the smell of passion.
The recirculators whined quietly as they labored to clear the
air.

Pushing one finger gently against Zoe's ankle, Xanthia
turned her until they were face to face. Frizzy blonde hair
tickled her nose, and she felt warm breath on her mouth.

Why can't it always be like this?

"You're not my mother," she whispered. Zoe had no
reaction to this heresy. "You're *not*."

Only in the last year had Zoe admitted the relationship was
much closer. Xanthia was now fifteen.

And what was different? Something, there had to be something beyond the mere knowledge that they were not mother
and child. There was a new quality in their relationship,
growing as they came to the end of the voyage. Xanthia

would look into those eyes where she had seen love and now see only blankness, coldness.

"Oriental inscrutability?" she asked herself, half-seriously. She knew she was hopelessly unsophisticated. She had spent her life in a society of two. The only other person she knew had her own face. But she had thought she knew Zoe. Now she felt less confident with every glance into Zoe's face and every kilometer passed on the way to Pluto.

Pluto.

Her thoughts turned gratefully away from immediate problems and toward that unimaginable place. She would be there in only four more years. The cultural adjustments she would have to make were staggering. Thinking about that, she felt a sensation in her chest that she guessed was her heart leaping in anticipation. That's what happened to characters in tapes when they got excited, anyway. Their hearts were forever leaping, thudding, aching, or skipping beats.

She pushed away from Zoe and drifted slowly to the viewport. Her old friends were all out there, the only friends she had ever known, the stars. She greeted them all one by one, reciting childhood mnemonic riddles and rhymes like bedtime prayers.

It was a funny thought that the view from her window would terrify many of those strangers she was going to meet on Pluto. She'd read that many tunnel-raised people could not stand open spaces. What it was that scared them, she could not understand. The things that scared her were crowds, gravity, males, and mirrors.

"Oh, damn. Damn! I'm going to be just *hopeless*. Poor little idiot girl from the sticks, visiting the big city." She brooded for a time on all the thousands of things she had never done, from swimming in the gigantic underground disneylands to seducing a boy.

"To *being* a boy." It had been the source of their first big argument. When Xanthia had reached adolescence, the time when children want to begin experimenting, she had learned from Zoe that *Shirley Temple* did not carry the medical equipment for sex changes. She was doomed to spend her critical formative years as a sexual deviate, a unisex.

"It'll stunt me forever," she had protested. She had been reading a lot of pop psychology at the time.

"Nonsense," Zoe had responded, hard-pressed to explain why she had not stocked a viro-genetic imprinter and the companion Y-alyzer. Which, as Xanthia pointed out, *any* self-respecting home surgery kit should have.

"The human race got along for millions of years without sex changing," Zoe had said. "Even after the Invasion. We were a highly technological race for hundreds of years before changing. Billions of people lived and died in the same sex."

"Yeah, and look what they were like."

Now, for another of what seemed like an endless series of nights, sleep was eluding her. There was the worry of Pluto, and the worry of Zoe and her strange behavior, and no way to explain anything in her small universe which had become unbearably complicated in the last years.

I wonder what it would be like with a man?

Three hours ago Xanthia had brought *Lollipop* to a careful rendezvous with the point in space her instruments indicated contained a black hole. She had long since understood that even if she ever found one she would never see it, but she could not restrain herself from squinting into the starfield for some evidence. It was silly; though the hole massed ten to the fifteenth tonnes (the original estimate had been off one order of magnitude) it was still only a fraction of a millimeter in diameter. She was staying a good safe hundred kilometers from it. Still, you ought to be able to sense something like that, you ought to be able to *feel* it.

It was no use. This hunk of space looked exactly like any other.

"There is a point I would like explained," the hole said. "What will be done with me after you have captured me?"

The question surprised her. She still had not got around to thinking of the voice as anything but some annoying aberration like her face in the mirror. How was she supposed to deal with it? Could she admit to herself that it existed, that it might even have feelings?

"I guess we'll just mark you, in the computer, that is. You're too big for us to haul back to Pluto. So we'll hang around you for a week or so, refining your trajectory until we know precisely where you're going to be, then we'll leave you. We'll make some maneuvers on the way in so no one could retrace our path and find out where you are, because they'll know we found a big one when we get back."

"How will they know that?"

"Because we'll be renting . . . well, *Zoe* will be chartering one of those big monster tugs, and she'll come out here and put a charge on you and tow you . . . say, how do you feel about this?''

''Are you concerned with the answer?''

The more Xanthia thought about it, the less she liked it. If she really was not hallucinating this experience, then she was contemplating the capture and imprisonment of a sentient being. An innocent sentient being who had been wandering around the edge of the system, suddenly to find him or herself . . .

''Do you have sex?''

''No.''

''All right, I guess I've been kind of short with you. It's just because you *did* startle me, and I *didn't* expect it, and it was all a little alarming.''

The hole said nothing.

''You're a strange sort of person, or whatever,'' she said.

Again there was silence.

''Why don't you tell me more about yourself? What's it like being a black hole, and all that?'' She still couldn't fight down the ridiculous feeling those words gave her.

''I live much as you do, from day to day. I travel from star to star, taking about ten million years for the trip. Upon arrival, I plunge through the core of the star. I do this as often as is necessary, then I depart by a slingshot maneuver through the heart of a massive planet. The Tunguska Meteorite, which hit Siberia in 1908, was a black hole gaining momentum on its way to Jupiter, where it could get the added push needed for solar escape velocity.''

One thing was bothering Xanthia. ''What do you mean, 'as often as is necessary'?''

''Usually five or six thousand passes is sufficient.''

''No, no. What I meant is *why* is it necessary? What do you get out of it?''

''Mass,'' the hole said. ''I need to replenish my mass. The Relativity Laws state that nothing can escape from a black hole, but the Quantum Laws, specifically the Heisenberg Uncertainty Principle, state that below a certain radius the position of a particle cannot be determined. I lose mass constantly through tunneling. It is not all wasted, as I am able to control the direction and form of the escaping mass, and to use the energy that results to perform functions that your present-day physics says are impossible.''

"Such as?" Xanthia didn't know why, but she was getting nervous.

"I can exchange inertia for gravity, and create energy in a variety of ways."

"So you can move yourself."

"Slowly."

"And you eat . . ."

"Anything."

Xanthia felt a sudden panic, but she didn't know what was wrong. She glanced down at her instruments and felt her hair prickle from her wrists and ankles to the nape of her neck.

The hole was ten kilometers closer than it had been.

"How could you *do* that to me?" Xanthia raged. "I trusted you, and that's how you repaid me, by trying to sneak up on me and . . . and—"

"It was not intentional. I speak to you by means of controlled gravity waves. To speak to you at all, it is necessary to generate an attractive force between us. You were never in any danger."

"I don't believe that," Xanthia said angrily. "I think you're doubletalking me. I don't think gravity works like that, and I don't think you really tried very hard to tell me how you talk to me, back when we first started." It occurred to her now, also, that the hole was speaking much more fluently than in the beginning. Either it was a very fast learner, or that had been intentional.

The hole paused. "This is true," it said.

She pressed her advantage. "Then why did you do it?"

"It was a reflex, like blinking in a bright light, or drawing one's hand back from a fire. When I sense matter, I am attracted to it."

"The proper cliché would be 'like a moth to a flame.' But you're not a moth, and I'm not a flame. I don't believe you. I think you could have stopped yourself if you wanted to."

Again the hole hesitated. "You are correct."

"So you were trying to . . . ?"

"I was trying to eat you."

"Just like *that?* Eat someone you've been having a conversation with?"

"Matter is matter," the hole said, and Xanthia thought she detected a defensive note in its voice.

"What do you think of what I said we're going to do with

you? You were going to tell me, but we got off on that story about where you came from."

"As I understand it, you propose to return for me. I will be towed to near Pluto's orbit, sold, and eventually come to rest in the heart of an orbital power station, where your species will feed matter into my gravity well, extracting power cheaply from the gravitational collapse."

"Yeah, that's pretty much it."

"It sounds ideal. My life is struggle. Failing to find matter to consume would mean loss of mass until I am smaller than an atomic nucleus. The loss rate would increase exponentially, and my universe would disappear. I do not know what would happen beyond that point. I have never wished to find out."

How much could she trust this thing? Could it move very rapidly? She toyed with the idea of backing off still further. The two of them were now motionless relative to each other, but they were both moving slowly away from the location she had given Zoe.

It didn't make sense to think it could move in on her fast. If it could, why hadn't it? Then it could eat her and wait for Zoe to arrive—Zoe, who was helpless to detect the hole with her broken mass detector.

She should relay the new vectors to Zoe. She tried to calculate where her twin would arrive, but was distracted by the hole speaking.

"I would like to speak to you now of what I initially contacted you for. Listening to Pluto radio, I have become aware of certain facts that you should know, if, as I suspect, you are not already aware of them. Do you know of Clone Control Regulations?"

"No, what are they?" Again, she was afraid without knowing why.

The genetics statutes, according to the hole, were the soul of simplicity. For three hundred years, people had been living just about forever. It had become necessary to limit the population. Even if everyone had only one child—the Birthright—population would still grow. For a while, clones had been a loophole. No more. Now, only one person had the right to any one set of genes. If two possessed them, one was excess, and was summarily executed.

"Zoe has priority property rights to her genetic code," the

hole concluded. "This is backed up by a long series of court decisions."

"So I'm—"

"Excess."

Zoe met her at the airlock as Xanthia completed the docking maneuver. She was smiling, and Xanthia felt the way she always did when Zoe smiled these days: like a puppy being scratched behind the ears. They kissed, then Zoe held her at arm's length.

"Let me look at you. Can it only be three months? You've *grown*, my baby."

Xanthia blushed. "I'm not a baby anymore, Mother." But she was happy. Very happy.

"No. I should say not." She touched one of Xanthia's breasts, then turned her around slowly. "I should say not. Putting on a little weight in the hips, aren't we?"

"And the bosom. One inch while I was gone. I'm almost there." And it was true. At sixteen, the young clone was almost a woman.

"Almost there," Zoe repeated, and glanced away from her twin. But she hugged her again, and they kissed, and began to laugh as the tension was released.

They made love, not once and then to bed, but many times, feasting on each other. One of them remarked—Xanthia could not remember who because it seemed so accurate that either of them might have said it—that the only good thing about these three-month separations was the homecoming.

"You did very well," Zoe said, floating in the darkness and sweet exhausted atmosphere of their bedroom many hours later. "You handled the lifeboat like it was part of your body. I watched the docking. I *wanted* to see you make a mistake, I think, so I'd know I still have something on you." Her teeth showed in the starlight, rows of lights below the sparkles of her eyes and the great dim blossom of her hair.

"Ah, it wasn't that hard," Xanthia said, delighted, knowing full well that it *was* that hard.

"Well, I'm going to let you handle it again the next swing. From now on, you can think of the lifeboat as *your* ship. You're the skipper."

It didn't seem like the time to tell her that she already thought of it that way. Nor that she had christened the ship.

Zoe laughed quietly. Xanthia looked at her.

"I remember the day I first boarded my own ship," she said. "It was a big day for me. My own ship."

"This is the way to live," Xanthia agreed. "Who needs all those people? Just the two of us. And they say hole hunters are crazy. I . . . wanted to . . ." The words stuck in her throat, but Xanthia knew this was the time to get them out, if there ever would be a time. "I don't want to stay too long at Pluto, Mother. I'd like to get right back out here with you." There, she'd said it.

Zoe said nothing for a long time.

"We can talk about that later."

"I love you, Mother," Xanthia said, a little too loudly.

"I love you, too, baby," Zoe mumbled. "Let's get some sleep, okay?"

She tried to sleep, but it wouldn't happen. What *was* wrong?

Leaving the darkened room behind her, she drifted through the ship, looking for something she had lost, or was losing, she wasn't sure which. What had happened, after all? Certainly nothing she could put her finger on. She loved her mother, but all she knew was that she was choking on tears.

In the water closet, wrapped in the shower bag with warm water misting around her, she glanced in the mirror.

"Why? Why would she do a thing like that?"

"Loneliness. And insanity. They appear to go together. This is her solution. You are not the first clone she has made."

She had thought herself beyond shock, but the clarity that simple declarative sentence brought to her mind was explosive. Zoe had always needed the companionship Xanthia provided. She needed a child for diversion in the long, dragging years of a voyage, she needed someone to talk to. *Why couldn't she have brought a dog?* She saw herself now as a shipboard pet, and felt sick. The local leash laws would necessitate the destruction of the animal before landing. Regrettable, but there it was. Zoe had spent the last year working up the courage to do it.

How many little Xanthias? They might even have chosen that very name; they would have been that much like her. Three, four? She wept for her forgotten sisters. Unless . . .

"How do I know you're telling me the truth about this? How could she have kept it from me? I've seen tapes of Pluto. I never saw any mention of this."

"She edited those before you were born. She has been careful. Consider her position: there can be only one of you, but the law does not say which it has to be. With her death, you become legal. If you had known that, what would life have been like in *Shirley Temple*?"

"I don't believe you. You've got something in mind, I'm sure of it."

"Ask her when she gets here. But be careful. Think it out, all the way through."

She had thought it out. She had ignored the last three calls from Zoe while she thought. All the options must be considered, all the possibilities planned for. It was an impossible task; she knew she was far too emotional to think clearly, and there wasn't time to get herself under control.

But she had done what she could. Now *The Good Ship Lollipop*, outwardly unchanged, was a ship of war.

Zoe came backing in, riding the fusion torch and heading for a point dead in space relative to Xanthia. The fusion drive was too dangerous for *Shirley* to complete the rendezvous; the rest of the maneuver would be up to *Lollipop*.

Xanthia watched through the telescope as the drive went off. She could see *Shirley* clearly on her screen, though the ship was fifty kilometers away.

Her screen lit up again, and there was Zoe. Xanthia turned her own camera on.

"There you are," Zoe said. "Why wouldn't you talk to me?"

"I didn't think the time was ripe."

"Would you like to tell me how come this nonsense about talking black holes? What's gotten into you?"

"Never mind about that. There never was a hole, anyway. I just needed to talk to you about something you forgot to erase from the tape library in the *Lol*— . . . in the lifeboat. You were pretty thorough with the tapes in *Shirley*, but you forgot to take the same care here. I guess you didn't think I'd ever be using it. Tell me, what are Clone Control Regulations?"

The face on the screen was immobile. Or was it a mirror, and was she smiling? Was it herself, or Zoe she watched? Frantically, Xanthia thumbed a switch to put her telescope image on the screen, wiping out the face. Would Zoe try to talk her way out of it? If she did, Xanthia was determined to do nothing at all. There was no way she could check out any lie Zoe might tell her, nothing she could confront Zoe with except a fantastic story from a talking black hole.

Please say something. Take responsibility out of my hands. She was willing to die, tricked by Zoe's fast talk, rather than accept the hole's word against Zoe's.

But Zoe was acting, not talking, and the response was exactly what the hole had predicted. The attitude control jets were firing, *Shirley Temple* was pitching and yawing slowly, the nozzles at the stern hunting for a speck in the telescope screen. When the engines were aimed, they would surely be fired, and Xanthia and the whole ship would be vaporized.

But she was ready. Her hands had been poised over the thrust controls. *Lollipop* had a respectable acceleration, and every gee of it slammed her into the couch as she scooted away from the danger spot.

Shirley's fusion engines fired, and began a deadly hunt. Xanthia could see the thin, incredibly hot stream playing around her as Zoe made finer adjustments in her orientation. She could only evade it for a short time, but that was all she needed.

Then the lights went out. She saw her screen flare up as the telescope circuit became overloaded with an immense burst of energy. And it was over. Her radar screen showed nothing at all.

"As I predicted," the hole said.

"Why don't you shut up?" Xanthia sat very still, and trembled.

"I shall, very soon. I did not expect to be thanked. But what you did, you did for yourself."

"And you, too, you . . . you *ghoul!* Damn you, damn you to hell." She was shouting through her tears. "Don't think you've fooled me, not completely, anyway. I know what you did, and I know how you did it."

"Do you?" The voice was unutterably cool and distant.

She could see that now the hole was out of danger, it was rapidly losing interest in her.

"Yes, I do. Don't tell me it was a coincidence that when you changed direction it was just enough to be near Zoe when she got here. You had this planned from the start."

"From much further back than you know," the hole said. "I tried to get you both, but it was impossible. The best I could do was take advantage of the situation as it was."

"Shut up, shut up."

The hole's voice was changing from the hollow, neutral tones to something that might have issued from a tank of liquid helium. She would never have mistaken it for human.

"What I did, I did for my own benefit. But I saved your life. She was going to try to kill you. I maneuvered her into such a position that, when she tried to turn her fusion drive on you, she was heading into a black hole she was powerless to detect."

"You *used* me."

"You used me. You were going to imprison me in a power station."

"But you said you wouldn't *mind*! You said it would be the perfect place."

"Do you believe that eating is all there is to life? There is more to do in the wide universe than you can even suspect. I am slow. It is easy to catch a hole if your mass detector is functioning: Zoe did it three times. But I am beyond your reach now."

"What do you mean? What are you going to do? What am *I* going to do?" That question hurt so much that Xanthia almost didn't hear the hole's reply.

"I am on my way out. I converted *Shirley* into energy; I absorbed very little mass from her. I beamed the energy very tightly, and am now on my way out of your system. You will not see me again. You have two options. You can go back to Pluto and tell everyone what happened out here. It would be necessary for scientists to rewrite natural laws if they believe you. It has been done before, but usually with more persuasive evidence. There will be questions asked concerning the fact that no black hole has ever evaded capture, spoken, or changed velocity in the past. You can explain that when a hole has a chance to defend itself, the hole hunter does not survive to tell the story."

"I will. I *will* tell them what happened!" Xanthia was eaten by a horrible doubt. Was it possible there had been a solution to her problem that did not involve Zoe's death? Just how badly had the hole tricked her?

"There is a second possibility," the hole went on, relentlessly. "Just what *are* you doing out here in a lifeboat?"

"What am I . . . I told you, we had . . ." Xanthia stopped. She felt herself choking.

"It would be easy to see you as crazy. You discovered something in *Lollipop*'s library that led you to know you must kill Zoe. This knowledge was too much for you. In defense, you invented me to trick you into doing what you had to do. Look in the mirror and tell me if you think your story will be believed. Look closely, and be honest with yourself."

She heard the voice laugh for the first time, from down in the bottom of its hole, like a voice from a well. It was an extremely unpleasant sound.

Maybe Zoe had died a month ago, strangled or poisoned or slashed with a knife. Xanthia had been sitting in her lifeboat, catatonic, all that time, and had constructed this episode to justify the murder. It *had* been self-defense, which was certainly a good excuse, and a very convenient one.

But she knew. She was sure, as sure as she had ever been of anything, that the hole was out there, that everything had happened as she had seen it happen. She saw the flash again in her mind, the awful flash that had turned Zoe into radiation. But she also knew that the other explanation would haunt her for the rest of her life.

"I advise you to forget it. Go to Pluto, tell everyone that your ship blew up and you escaped and you are Zoe. Take her place in the world, and never, *never* speak of talking black holes."

The voice faded from her radio. It did not speak again.

After days of numb despair and more tears and recriminations than she cared to remember, Xanthia did as the hole had predicted. But life on Pluto did not agree with her. There were too many people, and none of them looked very much like her. She stayed long enough to withdraw Zoe's money from the bank and buy a ship, which she named *Shirley Temple*. It was massive, with power to blast to the stars if necessary. She had left something out there, and she meant to search for it until she found it again.

The Manhattan Phone Book (Abridged)

This is the best story and the worst story anybody ever wrote.

There's lots of ways to judge the merit of a story, right? One of them is, are there a lot of people in it, and are they real. Well, this story has more people in it than any story in the history of the world. The Bible? Forget it. Ten thousand people, tops. (I didn't count, but I suspect it's less than that, even with all the begats.)

And real? Each and every character is a certified living human being. You can fault me on depth of characterization, no question about it. If I'd had the time and space, I could have told you a lot more about each of these people . . . but a writer has dramatic constraints to consider. If only I had more room. Wow! What stories you'd hear!

Admittedly, the plot is skimpy. You can't have everything. The strength of this story is its people. I'm in it. So are you.

It goes like this:

Jerry L. Aab moved to New York six years ago from his home in Valdosta, Georgia. He still speaks with a southern accent, but he's gradually losing it. He's married to a woman named Elaine, and things haven't been going too well for the Aab family. Their second child died, and Elaine is pregnant again. She thinks Jerry is seeing another woman. He isn't, but she's talking divorce.

Roger Aab isn't related to Jerry. He's a native New Yorker. He lives in a third-floor walk-up at 1 Maiden Lane. It's his first place; Roger is just nineteen, a recent high school graduate, thinking about attending City College. Right now, while he makes up his mind, he works in a deli and tries to date

Linda Cooper, who lives two blocks away. He hasn't really decided what to do with his life yet, but is confident a decision will come.

Kurt Aach is on parole. He served two years in Attica, up-state, for armed robbery. It wasn't his first stretch. He had vague ideas of going straight when he got out. If he could join the merchant marine he figures he just might make it, but the lousy jobs he's been offered so far aren't worth the trouble. He just bought a .38 Smith and Wesson from a guy on the docks. He cleans and oils it a lot.

Robert Aach is Kurt's older brother. He never visited Kurt in prison because he hates the worthless bum. When he thinks of his brother, he hopes the state will bring back the electric chair real soon. He has a wife and three kids. They like to go to Florida when he gets a vacation.

Adrienne Aaen has worked at the Woolworths on East 14th Street since she was twenty-one. She's pushing sixty now, and will be retired soon, involuntarily. She never married. She has a sour disposition, mostly because of her feet, which have hurt for forty years. She has a cat and a parakeet. The cat is too lazy to chase the bird. Adrienne has managed to save a little money. Every night she thanks God for all her blessings, and the City of New York for rent control.

Molly Aagard is thirty, and works for the New York Transit Police. She rides the subway every day. She's charged with stopping the serious crimes that infest the underground city, and she works very hard at it. She *hates* the wall-to-wall grafitti that blooms in every car like a malign fungus.

Irving Aagard is no relation. He's fifty-five, and owns an Oldsmobile dealership in New Jersey. People ask him why he lives in Manhattan, and he is always puzzled by that question. Would they rather he lived in Jersey, for chrissake? To Irving, Manhattan is the only place to live. He has enough money to send his three kids—Gerald, Morton, and Barbara—to good schools. He frets about crime, but no more than anyone else.

Shiela Aagre is a seventeen-year-old streetwalker from St. Paul. Her life isn't so great, but it's better than Minnesota. She uses heroin, but knows she can stop whenever she wants to.

Theodore Aaker and his wife, Beatrice, live in a fine apartment a block away from the Dakota, where John Lennon was killed. They went out that night and stood in the candlelight vigil, remembering Woodstock, remembering the summer of love in the Haight-Ashbury. Theodore sometimes wonders how and why he got into stocks and bonds. Beatrice is pregnant with their first child. She is deciding how much time she should take off from her law practice. It's a hard question.

(162,000 characters omitted)

Clemanzo Cruz lives on East 120th Street. He's unemployed, and has been since he arrived from Puerto Rico. He hangs out in a bar at the corner of Lexington and 122nd. He didn't used to drink much back in San Juan, but now that's about all he does. It's been fifteen years. You might say he is discouraged. His wife, Ilona, goes to work at five P.M. at the Empire State Building, where she scrubs floors and toilets. She's been mugged a dozen times on the way home on the number 6 Lexington local.

Zelad Cruz shares an apartment with two other secretaries. Even with roommates it's hard to make ends meet with New York rents the way they are. She always has a date Saturday night—she's quite a beauty—and she swings very hard, but Sunday morning always finds her at early mass at St. Patrick's. There's this guy who she thinks may ask her to get married. She's decided she'll say yes. She's tired of sharing an apartment. She hopes he won't beat her up.

Richard Cruzado drives a cab. He's a good-natured guy. He's been known to take fares into darkest Brooklyn. His wife's name is Sabina. She's always after him to buy a house in Queens. He thinks one of these days he will. They have six children, and life is tough for them in Manhattan. Those houses out in Queens have back yards, pools, you name it.

(1,250,000 characters omitted)

Ralph Zzyzzmjac changed his name two years ago. His real name is Ralph Zyzzmjac. A friend persuaded him to add a Z to be the last guy in the phone book. He's a bachelor, a librarian working for the City of New York. For a good time he goes to the movies, alone. He's sixty-one.

Edward Zzzzyniewski is crazy. He's been in and out of Bellevue. He spends most of his time thinking about that bastard Zzyzzmjac, who two years ago knocked him out of last place, his only claim to fame. He broods about him—a man he's never met—fantasizing that Zzyzzmjac is out to get him. Last year he added two Z's to his name. Now he's thinking about stealing a march on that bastard Zzyzzmjac. He's sure Zzyzzmjac is adding two more Z's this year, so he's going to add *seven*. Ed Zzzzzzzzzzzzyniewski. That'd be nice, he decides.

Then one day seventeen thermonuclear bombs exploded in the air over Manhattan, The Bronx, and Staten Island, too. They had a yield of between five and twenty megatons each. This was more than enough to kill everyone in this story. Most of them died instantly. A few lingered for minutes or hours, but they *all* died, just like that. I died. So did you.

I was lucky. In less time than it takes for one neuron to nudge another I was turned into radioactive atoms, and so was the building I was in, and the ground beneath me to a depth of three hundred meters. In a millisecond it was all as sterile as Edward Teller's soul.

You had a tougher time of it. You were in a store, standing near a window. The huge pressure wave turned the glass into ten thousand slivers of pain, one thousand of which tore the flesh from your body. One sliver went into your left eye. You were hurled to the back of the store, breaking a lot of bones and suffering internal injuries, but you still lived. There was a big piece of plate glass driven through your body. The bloody point emerged from your back. You touched it carefully, trying to pull it out, but it hurt too much.

On the piece of glass was a rectangular decal and the message "Mastercard Gladly Accepted."

The store caught fire around you, and you started to cook slowly. You had time to think "Is this what I pay my taxes for?" and then you died.

This story is brought to you courtesy of The Phone Company. Copies of the story can be found near every telephone in Manhattan, and thousands of stories just like it have been compiled for every community in the United States. They make interesting reading. I urge you to read a few pages every night. Don't forget that many wives are listed only under their husband's name. And there are the children to consider: very few have their own phone. Many people—such as single women—pay extra for an unlisted number. And there are the very poor, the transients, the street people, and folks who were unable to pay the last bill. Don't forget any of them as you read the story. Read as much or as little as you can stand, and ask yourself if this is what you want to pay your taxes for. Maybe you'll stop.

Aw, c'mon, I hear you protest. *Some*body will survive. Perhaps. Possibly. Probably.

But that's not the point. We all love after-the-bomb stories. If we didn't, why would there be so many of them? There's something attractive about all those people being gone, about wandering in a depopulated world, scrounging cans of Campbell's pork and beans, defending one's family from marauders. Sure, it's horrible, sure we weep for all those dead people. But some secret part of us thinks it would be good to survive, to start all over.

Secretly, we know we'll survive. All those *other* folks will die. That's what after-the-bomb stories are all about.

All those after-the-bomb stories were lies. Lies, lies, lies.

This is the only true after-the-bomb story you will ever read.

Everybody dies. Your father and mother are decapitated and crushed by a falling building. Rats eat their severed heads. Your husband is disemboweled. Your wife is blinded, flashburned, and gropes along a street of cinders until fear-crazed dogs eat her alive. Your brother and sister are incinerated in their homes, their bodies turned into fine powdery ash by firestorms. Your children . . . ah, I'm sorry, I hate to tell you this, but your children live a *long* time. Three eternal days. They spend those days puking their guts out, watching the flesh fall from their bodies, smelling the gangrene in their lacerated feet, and asking you why it happened. But you aren't there to tell them. I already told you how you died.

It's what you pay your taxes for.

The Unprocessed Word

John Varley
555 Mozart Place
Eugene, Oregon 97444

Susan Allison
Editor, Berkley Books
The Berkley Building
1 Madison Avenue
New York, New York 10010

Dear Susan,

You and I have talked before about word processors, and how I'm one of the last science fiction writers who doesn't use one. Now I feel it is time to take aggressive action against the blight of computers.

What I want you to do is run the following notice right before the title page of the new book, and in all books after this, and in any re-print editions of previous books written by me. Though this kind of self-promotion is personally repugnant to me, I feel it is time to speak out before it is Too Late. Also, it might help to sell books to people who feel the same way I do.

You may be wondering just what VarleyYarns

is. Well, I've re-organized, partly for tax purposes, partly for other reasons. I've formed a corporation called VarleyYarns, Inc., to market and promote my books. It's a step that's been long overdue. From now on, you can make out all my royalty checks to VarleyYarns.

Best,
John

THE UNPROCESSED WORD

INTRODUCING VARLEYYARNS®

This symbol is your assurance that the following yarn was composed entirely without the assistance of a word processor.

Each VarleyYarn® is created using only natural ingredients: The purest paper, carbon typewriter ribbons, pencils, ballpoint pens, thought, and creativity. Manuscript corrections are done entirely by hand. Final drafts are lovingly re-typed, word by word, in the finest typefaces available—no dot-matrix printers allowed!

The manuscript of each VarleyYarn® is then carried by the United States Postal Service—First Class!—to the good offices of the Berkley/Putnam Publishing Group in Manhattan, New York City, New York. Not a word is ever phoned in via modem.

Not One Word!

Here the VarleyYarn® is given to skilled artisans, men and woman who learned their craft from their parents, and from their parents before them . . . many of them using the tools and even the same offices their grandparents used. Crack teams of proofreaders pore over the manuscript, penciling corrections into the wide margins left for that purpose. Messengers hand-carry the VarleyYarn® from floor to floor of the vast Berkley Building, delivering it to deft Editors, clever Art Directors, and lofty Vice-Presidents.

When all is in readiness, the VarleyYarn® is rushed to the typesetter, who once again re-types the manuscript— *word by word!*— on the typesetting machine. Then the bulky lead plates are trucked to New Jersey and given to the printer, who uses technologies essentially unchanged from the days of Gutenberg.

And the end result? The book you now hold in your hands, as fine a book as the economic climate will allow.

So look for the sign of the twin typewriter keys—your symbol of quality in

100% guaranteed non-processed fiction!

John Varley
555 Mozart Place
Eugene, Oregon 97444

Dear John,

You asked to hear from me as soon as we had some concrete sales figures on the new

book. As you know, we ran your ''promo-
tional'' notice as you instructed, just
after the title page. The book has been out
for a month now, and I'm sorry to say
there's no measurable impact. It's selling about as well as the previous collection.

We have received some rather strange mail,
though, which I am forwarding to you under a separate cover.

John, I'm not completely sure the public
cares whether fiction was written on a
typewriter, a word processor, or with a
quill pen and ink. I know this is an important issue with you and I was happy to help
you try and get your message across, but
maybe it's best for now if we just forget
it. Unless I hear back from you soon, I'm
going ahead with the twenty-eighth printing of WIZARD without the VarleyYarn seal
of approval in front.

                          Yours,
                          Susan Allison

Susan Allison
Berkley

Dear Susan,

Of *course* they care. You can't tell me people can't
tell the difference when it is so obvious to any

literate person. They just haven't been given the choice in recent years ... and more importantly, they haven't heard the message. I'm afraid putting it in just my books was a mistake, as that is simply preaching to the converted. What I want you to do now is use the advertising budget for the new book and, instead of running the standard promo, use the following material instead. I'd like to see it in all the trade publications and as many national magazines as we can afford. And, far from letting you remove the original message from the new printing of WIZARD, I want to keep it, and run this new one on stiff paper—like you used to use for cigarette ads—somewhere in the middle of the book. Full color won't be necessary; just print the underlined parts in red caps.

John

WHY VARLEYYARNS®?

Perhaps you asked yourself: "Why should I buy and read Berkley's VarleyYarns® when cheaper, more plentiful 'processed' fiction puts me to sleep just as quickly?"

Here are some things we at VarleyYarns® think you should know:

Processed fiction can contain harmful additives.

When fiction is produced on a Word Processor each keystroke is first converted to a series of "on" and "off" signals in the microprocessor unit. Some of these signals go to the video screen and are displayed. The rest are "tagged" by various electronic additives and stored in the "memory" for later retrieval. Inevitably, these tags cling to the words themselves, and no amount of further processing can wash them away. Even worse, while in the memory these words are subject to outside interference such as power surges, changes in the Earth's magnetic field, sun spots, lightning discharges, and the passage of Halley's Comet—due back in 1986 . . . *and every 76 years thereafter!* VarleyYarns® are guaranteed to contain no sorting codes, assemblers, inelegant "languages" like FORTRAN or C.O.B.O.L., and to be free of the fuzzy edges caused by too much handling (more commonly known as "hacker's marks").

Floppy disks lack sincerity.

Think about it. When the "word processor" turns off his or her machine . . . *the words all go away!* The screen goes blank. The words no longer exist except as encoded messages on a piece of plastic known as a floppy disk. These words cannot be retrieved except by whirling the disk at great speed—a process that can *itself* damage the words. Words on a floppy disk are un-loved words, living a forlorn half-life in the memory until they are suddenly spewed forth at great and debilitating speed by a dot-matrix printer *that actually burns them into the page!*

VarleyYarn® words go directly from the writer's mind onto the printed page, with no harmful intermediate steps. At night, when the typewriter is turned off, they repose peacefully in cozy stacks of paper on the writ-

er's desk, secure in the knowledge they are cherished
as *words*.

Microprocessors are Un-American.

That's right, we said Un-American. At the heart of
every word processor is something called a microchip.
Due to cheap labor costs, these chips are made in
places like Taiwan, Singapore, Hong Kong, and Japan.
Now, we at VarleyYarns® have nothing against the Japanese (though Pearl Harbor *was* a pretty cowardly attack,
don't you think?), but ask yourself this: Do you want to
entrust your precious fiction to a machine *that doesn't
even speak English?*

So ask your grocer, druggist, airport manager, and book-
seller to stock up on Berkley's VarleyYarns® today. And
next time someone offers to let you read processed
fiction, you can say:

> *"No thanks! I'd rather read a VarleyYarn®!"*

John Varley
555 Mozart Place
Eugene, Oregon 97444

Dear John,

As you must have seen by now, I did as you
asked. But let me tell you, it was a struggle. I fought pretty hard for that ad budget, such as it was, and it was quite a trick

to turn around and tell everyone you now
want this other material to run in place of
the ads we'd prepared.

A word to the wise, my friend. You're
not the only author on the Berkley list.
I called in a lot of favors on this
one.

And I'm sorry to tell you it doesn't seem
to have worked. All of them—*The Times,
Rolling Stone, Publishers Weekly, Variety,
USA Today, Locus*—report negative responses
to the ad as run. Maybe this will convince
you that people really aren't concerned—as
I know you are—about the spread of word
processors.

One more thing you might not have considered. All the other Berkley authors use
word processors. More than a few of them
have called or written about your ad. So
far the tone has been more puzzled than
anything else, but I'm afraid that if we
went on with this it could only get worse.
See, they're beginning to think you're
saying something negative about *their*
fiction.

For this reason, if for no other, I'm pulling
your ad from all the printed media, and
canceling the upcoming radio and television campaign. The forty-third printing of
TITAN goes to the presses next week, and
it will do so without either the Varley-

Yarns ''symbol of quality'' or the two-color
slick paper insert.

Yours truly,
Susan

Dear Susan,

You can't do this to me! You're simply not giving this a chance to work. Naturally there's going
to be some initial resistance. It's a new idea to
most people out there that word additives can be
harmful to one's fiction. Remember how people
fought the idea of ecology in the late 60's? Remember how the AEC used to tell us that radiation was good for you? This is just like that. The
word has to get out now, before it's too late.

So here's what I want you to do. Forget all the
book advertising. I want to go right on to direct mail. See if you can obtain the lists of everyone who ever voted for Eugene McCarthy, and
send them all a copy of the enclosed exposé. It's
time their eyes were really opened.

I have gone to a great deal of trouble obtaining
these testimonials. I expect you to do your part.
And, oh, sure, I know the lawyers on your end are
going to give you a hard time about some of this,
but you'll notice I've concealed the names of the
people involved.

Here's to an unprocessed future ...

John

JOHN VARLEY
The Shame of MacWrite
Brought To You By

VarleyYarns®

Home Of The Unprocessed Word

Almost without our realizing it, a generation has grown up in America that has never read an unprocessed word, never heard an unprocessed line of dialogue. This is tragic enough . . . but have you ever considered the effect of the Word Processor upon today's writers? Many of them have never seen a typewriter. Their familiarity with pen and ink extends only to the writing of checks to pay for a new addition to their computer systems.

And now, slowly, insidiously, hidden from public view, the results of their new toys are beginning to be felt.

We at VarleyYarns® feel it is time for someone to speak out, to rip away the veil of secrecy that has, until now, prevented these writers from coming forward to speak of their shame, their anguish, their heartbreak. You probably don't know any writers personally. Most people don't. Here are some facts you should know:

Fact # 1: Writers can't handle money, and are suckers for shiny new toys.

Writers are a simple folk, by and large. Awkward in social situations, easily deceived, childishly eager to please, the typical writer never had the advantages of a normal childhood. He was the dreamy one, the friend-less one, object of scorn and ridicule to his class-mates. Living in his own fantasy world, writing his "fiction," he is ill-equipped for the pitfalls of money or technology.

Fact #2: Writers come in two types—compulsives, and procrastinators.

The Type A writer will labor endlessly without food, water, or sleep. His output of fiction is prodigious. Many claim they would write fiction even if they were not being paid for it—a sure danger signal.

Type B writers live to sharpen pencils, straighten their desks, create elaborate filing systems, and answer the telephone and the doorbell. A productive day for the Type B writer consists of half a paragraph—which may end up in the wastepaper basket at the end of the day. This writer will work only under dead-line pressure. Any excuse to leave the typewriter is welcomed.

Conclusion: The Word Processor is precisely the <u>wrong</u> tool to put into a writer's hands!!

If you don't believe it, listen to these unsolicited testi-monials from some of the most pitiful cases of comput-aholism:

"SK," Jerusalem's Lot, Maine

I was one of the first writers to get a word processor. My God, if only I had known ... if only ... I was always prolific. I write every day but Guy Fawkes Day, Bastille Day, and the anniversary of the St. Valentine's

Day Massacre. When I got my computer my output increased dramatically. My family didn't see me for days at a time . . . then weeks at a time! I was sending in novels at the rate of three a month . . . and in addition, was writing and selling dozens of short stories every day. Thinking of pseudonyms became a major task in itself, a task I faced with a deepening sense of horror. Have you ever heard of John Jakes? That's really me! And what about Arthur Hailey, I'll bet you've heard of him. That's me, too! And Colleen McCullough, and William Goldman, and Richard Bachman . . . John D. MacDonald really died in 1976 . . . but nobody knows it, because I took over his name! Soon I was writing movie scripts. (Have you heard of Steven Spielberg? That's me, too.) In 1980 I began writing the entire line of Harlequin Romances. I was making money faster than General Dynamics . . . but my kids didn't know me. As I sat at my Word Processor, a strange change would come over me. I would become these other people. Friends would mistake me for Truman Capote, or J. D. Salinger. But I could have lived with that . . . if not for the children. I can hear them now, crying in the kitchen. "Mommy, mommy," they weep. "Who is daddy today?" If only I could save another writer from this nightmare . . . if only . . . if only . . .

"SR," Halifax, Nova Scotia

I used to write with a pencil and paper—I never even used a typewriter for my first drafts . . . until the day someone convinced me to buy a MacIntosh Computer, known in the industry as a Fat Mac. I loved it! In only three or four months I taught myself to type and wrote seventy or eighty letters. I purchased a MacPaint program, and soon was turning out wonderful dot-matrix artwork to amuse my friends. Then I brought a MacAlien program and had hours of fun every day eluding the space monsters that tried to eat me alive. (The MacWrite program still had a few glitches, but I knew I'd work them out . . . one of these days . . . when I got around to it . . . mañana . . . what's the rush?) In the meantime, I was having too much fun . . .

Well, you've probably guessed I'm a Type B writer. It was always easy enough to find an excuse not to write . . . and the Mac made it even easier! Now winter is coming on, I've missed a dozen deadlines, my family is starving, and bill collectors are pounding on the door.

<u>Thank God for the people at VarleyYarns®!</u>

When they heard of my plight they rushed over with a typewriter, reams of paper, and a package of pencils.

I know it will be a long hard path back to sanity . . .
. . . but with the help of VarleyYarns®, I think I can lick it!

<u>"DT" Oakland, California</u>

<u>Born Again!</u>

That's what I told my friends when I finally "made the switch" to a word processor. The ease, the speed, the versatility . . . I began buying new programs as quickly as they came out. I even got to "road-test" a few of them, developed by friends in the industry, before they were available to the general public. I really liked the MacPlot at first. When you "Booted it up, " MacPlot would suggest alternate story lines . . . while at the same time conducting a global search of all stories *written by anyone, anywhere, at any time, to see if an idea was "old hat." Soon all my friends had copied it and were using it, too. Then came MacClimax!, which analyzed your prose for the "high points," and added words and phrases here and there to "punch it up." You've all heard how a word processor can aid you if you decide to change a character's name in the course of a story. With MacCharacter, I was able to change a whimp into a hero, a Presbyterian into an alien suffering from existential despair, or a fourteenth century warlord into a Mexican grape-picker ... all with only a few keys ... all without lapses in story logic! Before long I had them all: MacConflict, MacDialogue, MacMystery, MacWestern, Adverb-Away, VisiTheme, MacDeal-With-The-Devil ...*

Then I noticed a strange thing.

I'm a Type A writer, like Mr. "SK/Bachman/Goldman/ ETC." I'm not happy unless I'm writing most of the day. And now, writing was so easy I could simply write a first line, punch a few keys, and sit back and watch the story write itself. It was so easy, I was miserable. Now, in today's mail, comes MacFirstline, but I don't think I'll run it. I think I'll kill myself instead.

Now where's the MacHara-Kiri suicide-note-writing program ... ?

Sad, isn't it? And there isn't even enough time to tell you of the incalculable amounts of money squandered by writers on expensive systems that were obsolete within a few weeks' time, or to print the countless other testimonials that have been pouring into VarleyYarns® since this crusade of salvation began.

We're trying to help. Won't you? Only with your support can we stamp out this dread killer, this hidden disease called Computaholism. Write your Congressperson today. Form a committee. Give generously. Be sure to vote.

And don't forget . . . to buy and read Berkley's Varley-Yarns®.

Dear John,

All right, enough is enough. I don't think you realize it, but I put my career on the line over your *last* insane request. If you think I'm going to publish and mail that diatribe, you've got another think coming.

I went so far as to show it to our lawyers. You said you disguised the names, but how many writers do you think there *are* in Halifax, Nova Scotia? Or in *Maine,* for that matter. And do you have any idea how much money that guy has? Enough to keep you in court for the next twenty years.

Maybe I'll regret this later, but there are a few things I've been dying to get off my chest, so here goes. First . . . was that some kind of crack, back in your first ad? Something like ''as fine a book as the economic climate will allow''? Let me tell you, we editors work *hard* and we do the best job we can. So we don't usually have

much of an advertising budget. So DEMON *was*
printed on newsprint. So *sue* me, okay?

As for your horror stories about exces-
sively prolific authors . . . boy, don't
I *wish!* I could say a thing or two about
missed deadlines, that's for sure. And
did you read what Norman Spinrad and Algis
Budrys had to say about your last two epics?
So much for the inherent superiority of
the typewriter.

TITAN parts four, five, and six are due at
the end of the month, don't forget. You may
not find the editors here at Berkley quite
so forgiving the next time you ask for a
deadline extension.

                              Yours,
                              Susan

SUSAN ALLISON
BERKLEY PUBLISHING
NEW YORK

DEAR SUSAN,

HOLD EVERYTHING! NO NEED TO
GET UPSET. HELL, YOU DIDN'T
THINK I WAS SERIOUS, DID YOU?
THE THING IS, SEE, I WAS TALK-
ING TO HARLAN ELLISON THE
OTHER DAY, AND WHILE HE AGREED
WITH MY STAND AGAINST THE WORD

PROCESSOR, HE FELT THE WHOLE
VARLEYYARNS BUSINESS SMACKED
OF TOO MUCH SELF-PROMOTION.

BUT BEYOND THAT, AS YOU MIGHT
HAVE GUESSED FROM THE HOLES
ALONG THE SIDE OF THE PAPER,
I'VE BOUGHT A WORD PROCESSOR.
(SORRY ABOUT THIS TYPEFACE:
MY LETTER-QUALITY PRINTER IS
''DOWN'' AGAIN. I'M USING AN
OLD ''WORDSPITTER'' PRINTER I
BORROWED FROM THE E   STATE
OF ''DT'' IN OAKLAND.)

I'M WRITING THIS ON AN EXXON
OFFICE SYSTEMS ''ANNIE'' COM-
PUTER. AS YOU MAY HAVE HEARD,
EXXON GOT OUT OF THE COMPUTER
BUSINESS AFTER A FEW YEARS OF
POOR SALES, SO I GOT THIS MA-
CHINE AT A BARGAIN-BASEMENT
PRICE! FOR ONLY $5000 I GOT A
MAINFRAME MORE POWERFUL THAN
THE ONE NASA USED TO SEND MEN
TO THE MOO   N IN 1969, A DISK
DRIVE, A ''SANDY'' PRINTER, A
''PUNJAB'S CRYSTAL'' MONITOR
SC   REEN, AND A LITTLE DEVICE
SIMILAR TO THE APPLE MOUSE,
WHICH EXXON CALLS AN ''ASP.''
I'VE BEEN TOLD THIS IS WHAT IS
KNOWN AS AN ORPHAN COMPUTER,
BUT IT SHOULDN'T MATTER, AS IT
WILL RUN SOME OF THE APPLE
SOFTWARE, AND THE SALESMAN--A

MR . PANGLOSS--ASSURES ME
EXXON WILL CONTINUE TO SER-
VICE IT AND PRODU   CE MORE
PROGRAMS .

SO FAR HE'S BEEN AS GOOD AS HIS
WORD . THE LASER-DRIVEN
HYPERSPEED WHIRL-WRITE
''SANDY'' PRINTER HAS BROKEN
DOWN EIGHT TIMES SO FAR, AND
THE SERVICE MANAGER, MR .
GOLDBERG, IS ALWAYS HERE
WITHIN A WEEK OR TWO .
(HE'S HERE RIGHT NOW--HEY,
RUBE!--SO PRETTY SOON I CAN
PUT THE PRINTER ''ON-LINE''
AG AIN . HE SAYS IT'S JUST RUN
OUT OF PHOTONS AGAIN .)

I'VE BEEN HAVING A BALL . I'VE
USED THE MACWARBUCKS PROGRAM
TO BALANCE MY CH   ECKBOOK AND
PLAN MY FINANCIAL FUTURE . MY
OUTPUT OF FICTION HAS REALLY
INCREASED . YOU'LL RECEIVE
SHORTLY, UNDER SEPARATE
COVER, TWO TRILOGIES AND FIVE
OTHER NOVELS . JUST THIS MORN-
ING I TRIED PHONING ANOTHER
NOVEL TO YOUR OFFICE VIA MO-
DEM, BUT EITHER MY MACHINE OR
YOUR COMPUTER ROOM OR POOR OLD
MA BELL SEEM TO HAVE LOST IT .
OH, WELL, NO BIG DEAL, THERE'S
PLENTY MORE WHERE THAT ONE
CAME FROM!

TO FACILITATE YOUR ACCOUNTING
DEPARTMENT'S WRITING OF MY
CHECKS, IN THE FUTURE I SHALL
SIGN MYSELF WITH THE UNIVER-
SAL WRITERS CODE (UWC) SYMBOL
YOU SEE BELOW, RECENTLY AP-
PROVED BY THE WRITERS GUILD.
SO IT'S GOODBYE, JOHN VARLEY,
HELLO 2100061161 . . . BUT YOU
CAN CALL ME 210, IF WE'RE
STILL FRIENDS.

21000 61161

Press Enter ■

"This is a recording. Please do not hang up until—"

I slammed the phone down so hard it fell onto the floor. Then I stood there, dripping wet and shaking with anger. Eventually, the phone started to make that buzzing noise they make when a receiver is off the hook. It's twenty times as loud as any sound a phone can normally make, and I always wondered why. As though it was such a terrible disaster: "Emergency! Your telephone is off the hook!!!"

Phone answering machines are one of the small annoyances of life. Confess, do you really *like* to talk to a machine? But what had just happened to me was more than a petty irritation. I had just been called by an automatic dialing machine.

They're fairly new. I'd been getting about two or three such calls a month. Most of them come from insurance companies. They give you a two-minute spiel and then a number to call if you are interested. (I called back, once, to give them a piece of my mind, and was put on hold, complete with Muzak.) They use lists. I don't know where they get them.

I went back to the bathroom, wiped water droplets from the plastic cover of the library book, and carefully lowered myself back into the water. It was too cool. I ran more hot water and was just getting my blood pressure back to normal when the phone rang again.

So I sat through fifteen rings, trying to ignore it.

Did you ever try to read with the phone ringing?

On the sixteenth ring I got up. I dried off, put on a robe,

walked slowly and deliberately into the living room. I stared at the phone for a while.

On the fiftieth ring I picked it up.

"This is a recording. Please do not hang up until the message has been completed. This call originates from the house of your next-door neighbor, Charles Kluge. It will repeat every ten minutes. Mister Kluge knows he has not been the best of neighbors, and apologizes in advance for the inconvenience. He requests that you go immediately to his house. The key is under the mat. Go inside and do what needs to be done. There will be a reward for your services. Thank you."

Click. Dial tone.

I'm not a hasty man. Ten minutes later, when the phone rang again, I was still sitting there thinking it over. I picked up the receiver and listened carefully.

It was the same message. As before, it was not Kluge's voice. It was something synthesized, with all the human warmth of a Speak'n'Spell.

I heard it out again, and cradled the receiver when it was done.

I thought about calling the police. Charles Kluge had lived next door to me for ten years. In that time I may have had a dozen conversations with him, none lasting longer than a minute. I owed him nothing.

I thought about ignoring it. I was still thinking about that when the phone rang again. I glanced at my watch. Ten minutes. I lifted the receiver and put it right back down.

I could disconnect the phone. It wouldn't change my life radically.

But in the end I got dressed and went out the front door, turned left, and walked toward Kluge's property.

My neighbor across the street, Hal Lanier, was out mowing the lawn. He waved to me, and I waved back. It was about seven in the evening of a wonderful August day. The shadows were long. There was the smell of cut grass in the air. I've always liked that smell. About time to cut my own lawn, I thought.

It was a thought Kluge had never entertained. His lawn was brown and knee-high and choked with weeds.

I rang the bell. When nobody came I knocked. Then I

sighed, looked under the mat, and used the key I found there to open the door.

"Kluge?" I called out as I stuck my head in.

I went along the short hallway, tentatively, as people do when unsure of their welcome. The drapes were drawn, as always, so it was dark in there, but in what had once been the living room ten television screens gave more than enough light for me to see Kluge. He sat in a chair in front of a table, with his face pressed into a computer keyboard and the side of his head blown away.

Hal Lanier operates a computer for the L.A.P.D., so I told him what I had found and he called the police. We waited together for the first car to arrive. Hal kept asking if I'd touched anything, and I kept telling him no, except for the front door knob.

An ambulance arrived without the siren. Soon there were police all over, and neighbors standing out in their yards or talking in front of Kluge's house. Crews from some of the television stations arrived in time to get pictures of the body, wrapped in a plastic sheet, being carried out. Men and women came and went. I assumed they were doing all the standard police things, taking fingerprints, collecting evidence. I would have gone home, but had been told to stick around.

Finally I was brought in to see Detective Osborne, who was in charge of the case. I was led into Kluge's living room. All the television screens were still turned on. I shook hands with Osborne. He looked me over before he said anything. He was a short guy, balding. He seemed very tired until he looked at me. Then, though nothing really changed in his face, he didn't look tired at all.

"You're Victor Apfel?" he asked. I told him I was. He gestured at the room. "Mister Apfel, can you tell if anything has been taken from this room?"

I took another look around, approaching it as a puzzle.

There was a fireplace and there were curtains over the windows. There was a rug on the floor. Other than those items, there was nothing else you would expect to find in a living room.

All the walls were lined with tables, leaving a narrow aisle down the middle. On the tables were monitor screens, keyboards, disc drives—all the glossy bric-a-brac of the new age. They were interconnected by thick cables and cords. Beneath the tables were still more computers, and boxes full of electronic items. Above the tables were shelves that reached the ceiling and were stuffed with boxes of tapes, discs, cartridges . . . there was a word for it which I couldn't recall just then. It was software.

"There's no furniture, is there? Other than that . . ."

He was looking confused.

"You mean there was furniture here before?"

"How would I know?" Then I realized what the misunderstanding was. "Oh. You thought I'd been here before. The first time I ever set foot in this room was about an hour ago."

He frowned, and I didn't like that much.

"The medical examiner says the guy had been dead about three hours. How come you came over when you did, Victor?"

I didn't like him using my first name, but didn't see what I could do about it. And I knew I had to tell him about the phone call.

He looked dubious. But there was one easy way to check it out, and we did that. Hal and Osborne and I and several others trooped over to my house. My phone was ringing as we entered.

Osborne picked it up and listened. He got a very sour expression on his face. As the night wore on, it just got worse and worse.

We waited ten minutes for the phone to ring again. Osborne spent the time examining everything in my living room. I was glad when the phone rang again. They made a recording of the message, and we went back to Kluge's house.

Osborne went into the back yard to see Kluge's forest of antennas. He looked impressed.

"Mrs. Madison down the street thinks he was trying to contact Martians," Hal said, with a laugh. "Me, I just thought he was stealing HBO." There were three parabolic dishes. There were six tall masts, and some of those things you see on telephone company buildings for transmitting microwaves.

Osborne took me to the living room again. He asked me to describe what I had seen. I didn't know what good that would do, but I tried.

"He was sitting in that chair, which was here in front of this table. I saw the gun on the floor. His hand was hanging down toward it."

"You think it was suicide?"

"Yes, I guess I did think that." I waited for him to comment, but he didn't. "Is that what you think?"

He sighed. "There wasn't any note."

"They don't always leave notes," Hal pointed out.

"No, but they do often enough that my nose starts to twitch when they don't." He shrugged. "It's probably nothing."

"That phone call," I said. "That might be a kind of suicide note."

Osborne nodded. "Was there anything else you noticed?"

I went to the table and looked at the keyboard. It was made by Texas Instruments, model TI-99/4A. There was a large bloodstain on the right side of it, where his head had been resting.

"Just that he was sitting in front of this machine." I touched a key, and the monitor screen behind the keyboard immediately filled with words. I quickly drew my hand back, then stared at the message there.

PROGRAM NAME: GOODBYE REAL WORLD

DATE: 8/20

**CONTENTS: LAST   WILL   AND   TESTAMENT;
MISC. FEATURES**

PROGRAMER: "CHARLES KLUGE"

TO RUN

PRESS ENTER ■

The black square at the end flashed on and off. Later I learned it was called a cursor.

Everyone gathered around. Hal, the computer expert, explained how many computers went blank after ten minutes of no activity, so the words wouldn't be burned into the television screen. This one had been green until I touched it, then displayed black letters on a blue background.

"Has this console been checked for prints?" Osborne asked. Nobody seemed to know, so Osborne took a pencil and used the eraser to press the *ENTER* key.

The screen cleared, stayed blue for a moment, then filled with little ovoid shapes that started at the top of the screen and descended like rain. There were hundreds of them in many colors.

"Those are pills," one of the cops said, in amazement. "Look, that's gotta be a Quaalude. There's a Nembutal." Other cops pointed out other pills. I recognized the distinctive red stripe around the center of a white capsule that had to be a Dilantin. I had been taking them every day for years.

Finally the pills stopped falling, and the damn thing started to play music at us. "Nearer My God To Thee," in three-part harmony.

A couple people laughed. I don't think any of us thought it was funny—it was creepy as hell listening to that eerie dirge—but it sounded like it had been scored for pennywhistle, calliope, and kazoo. What could you do but laugh?

As the music played a little figure composed entirely of squares entered from the left of the screen and jerked spastically toward the center. It was like one of those human figures from a video game, but not as detailed. You had to use your imagination to believe it was a man.

A shape appeared in the middle of the screen. The "man" stopped in front of it. He bent in the middle, and something that might have been a chair appeared under him.

"What's that supposed to be?"

"A computer. Isn't it?"

It must have been, because the little man extended his arms, which jerked up and down like Liberace at the piano. He was typing. The words appeared above him.

SOMEWHERE ALONG THE LINE I MISSED SOMETHING. I SIT HERE, NIGHT AND DAY, A SPIDER IN THE CENTER OF A COAXIAL WEB, MASTER OF ALL I SURVEY ... AND IT IS NOT ENOUGH. THERE MUST BE MORE.

ENTER YOUR NAME HERE ■

"Jesus Christ," Hal said. "I don't believe it. An interactive suicide note."

"Come on, we've got to see the rest of this."

I was nearest the keyboard, so I leaned over and typed my name. But when I looked up, what I had typed was VICT9R.

"How do you back this up?" I asked.

"Just enter it," Osborne said. He reached around me and pressed ENTER.

DO YOU EVER GET THAT FEELING, VICT9R? YOU HAVE WORKED ALL YOUR LIFE TO BE THE BEST THERE IS AT WHAT YOU DO, AND ONE DAY YOU WAKE UP TO WONDER WHY YOU ARE DOING IT? THAT IS WHAT HAPPENED TO ME.

DO YOU WANT TO HEAR MORE, VICT9R? Y/N ▮

The message rambled from that point. Kluge seemed to be aware of it, apologetic about it, because at the end of each forty- or fifty-word paragraph the reader was given the Y/N option.

I kept glancing from the screen to the keyboard, remembering Kluge slumped across it. I thought about him sitting here alone, writing this.

He said he was despondent. He didn't feel like he could go on. He was taking too many pills (more of them rained down the screen at this point), and he had no further goal. He had done everything he set out to do. We didn't understand what he meant by that. He said he no longer existed. We thought that was a figure of speech.

ARE YOU A COP, VICT9R? IF YOU ARE NOT, A COP WILL BE HERE SOON. SO TO YOU OR THE COP: I WAS NOT SELLING NARCOTICS. THE DRUGS IN MY BEDROOM WERE FOR MY OWN PERSONAL USE. I USED A LOT OF THEM AND NOW I WILL NOT NEED THEM ANYMORE.

PRESS ENTER ▮

Osborne did, and a printer across the room began to chatter, scaring the hell out of all of us. I could see the carriage zipping back and forth, printing in both directions, when Hal pointed at the screen and shouted.

"Look! Look at that!"

The compugraphic man was standing again. He faced us. He had something that had to be a gun in his hand, which he now pointed at his head.

"Don't do it!" Hal yelled.

The little man didn't listen. There was a denatured gunshot sound, and the little man fell on his back. A line of red dripped down the screen. Then the green background turned to blue, the printer shut off, and there was nothing left but the little black corpse lying on its back and the word ****DONE**** at the bottom of the screen.

I took a deep breath, and glanced at Osborne. It would be an understatement to say he did not look happy.

"What's this about drugs in the bedroom?" he said.

We watched Osborne pulling out drawers in dressers and beside the tables. He didn't find anything. He looked under the bed, and in the closet. Like all the other rooms in the house, this one was full of computers. Holes had been knocked in walls for the thick sheaves of cables.

I had been standing near a big cardboard drum, one of several in the room. It was about thirty gallon capacity, the kind you ship things in. The lid was loose, so I lifted it. I sort of wished I hadn't.

"Osborne," I said. "You'd better look at this."

The drum was lined with a heavy-duty garbage bag. And it was two-thirds full of Quaaludes.

They pried the lids off the rest of the drums. We found drums of amphetamines, of Nembutals, of Valium. All sorts of things.

With the discovery of the drugs a lot more police returned to the scene. With them came the television camera crews.

In all the activity no one seemed concerned about me, so I slipped back to my own house and locked the door. From time to time I peeked out the curtains. I saw reporters interviewing the neighbors. Hal was there, and seemed to be having a good time. Twice crews knocked on my door, but I didn't answer. Eventually they went away.

I ran a hot bath and soaked in it for about an hour. Then I turned the heat up as high as it would go and got in bed, under the blankets.

I shivered all night.

Osborne came over about nine the next morning. I let him in. Hal followed, looking very unhappy. I realized they had been up all night. I poured coffee for them.

"You'd better read this first," Osborne said, and handed me the sheet of computer printout. I unfolded it, got out my glasses, and started to read.

It was in that awful dot-matrix printing. My policy is to throw any such trash into the fireplace, un-read, but I made an exception this time.

It was Kluge's will. Some probate court was going to have a lot of fun with it.

He stated again that he didn't exist, so he could have no relatives. He had decided to give all his worldly property to somebody who deserved it.

But who was deserving? Kluge wondered. Well, not Mr. and Mrs. Perkins, four houses down the street. They were child abusers. He cited court records in Buffalo and Miami, and a pending case locally.

Mrs. Radnor and Mrs. Polonski, who lived across the street from each other five houses down, were gossips.

The Andersons' oldest son was a car thief.

Marian Flores cheated on her high school algebra tests.

There was a guy nearby who was diddling the city on a freeway construction project. There was one wife in the neighborhood who made out with door-to-door salesmen, and two having affairs with men other than their husbands. There was a teenage boy who got his girlfriend pregnant, dropped her, and bragged about it to his friends.

There were no fewer than nineteen couples in the immediate area who had not reported income to the IRS, or who padded their deductions.

Kluge's neighbors in back had a dog that barked all night.

Well, I could vouch for the dog. He'd kept me awake often enough. But the rest of it was *crazy!* For one thing, where did a guy with two hundred gallons of illegal narcotics get the right to judge his neighbors so harshly? I mean, the child abusers were one thing, but was it right to tar a whole family because their son stole cars? And for another . . . how did he *know* some of this stuff?

But there was more. Specifically, four philandering husbands. One was Harold "Hal" Lanier, who for three years had been seeing a woman named Toni Jones, a co-worker at the L.A.P.D. Data Processing facility. She was pressuring him for a divorce; he was "waiting for the right time to tell his wife."

I glanced up at Hal. His red face was all the confirmation I needed.

Then it hit me. What had Kluge found out about *me?*

I hurried down the page, searching for my name. I found it in the last paragraph.

". . . for thirty years Mr. Apfel has been paying for a mistake he did not even make. I won't go so far as to nominate him for sainthood, but by default—if for no other reason—I hereby leave all deed and title to my real property and the structure thereon to Victor Apfel."

I looked at Osborne, and those tired eyes were weighing me.

"But I don't *want* it!"

"Do you think this is the reward Kluge mentioned in the phone call?"

"It must be," I said. "What else could it be?"

Osborne sighed, and sat back in his chair. "At least he didn't try to leave you the drugs. Are you still saying you didn't know the guy?"

"Are you accusing me of something?"

He spread his hands. "Mister Apfel, I'm simply asking a question. You're never one hundred per cent sure in a suicide. Maybe it was a murder. If it was, you can see that, so far, you're the only one we know of that's gained by it."

"He was almost a stranger to me."

He nodded, tapping his copy of the computer printout. I looked back at my own, wishing it would go away.

"What's this . . . mistake you didn't make?"

I was afraid that would be the next question.

"I was a prisoner of war in North Korea," I said.

Osborne chewed that over a while.

"They brainwash you?"

"Yes." I hit the arm of my chair, and suddenly had to be up and moving. The room was getting cold. "No. I don't . . . there's been a lot of confusion about the word. Did they 'brainwash' me? Yes. Did they succeed? Did I offer a confession of my war crimes and denounce the U.S. Government? No."

Once more, I felt myself being inspected by those deceptively tired eyes.

"You still seem to have . . . strong feelings about it."

"It's not something you forget."

"Is there anything you want to say about it?"

"It's just that it was all so . . . no. No, I have nothing further to say. Not to you, not to anybody."

"I'm going to have to ask you more questions about Kluge's death."

"I think I'll have my lawyer present for those." Christ. Now I was going to have to get a lawyer. I didn't know where to begin.

Osborne just nodded again. He got up and went to the door.

"I was ready to write this one down as a suicide," he said. "The only thing that bothered me was there was no note. Now we've got a note." He gestured in the direction of Kluge's house, and started to look angry.

"This guy not only writes a note, he programs the fucking thing into his computer, complete with special effects straight out of Pac-Man.

"Now, I know people do crazy things. I've seen enough of them. But when I heard the computer playing a hymn, that's when I knew this was murder. Tell you the truth, Mr. Apfel, I don't think you did it. There must be two dozen motives for murder in that printout. Maybe he was blackmailing people around here. Maybe that's how he bought all those machines. And people with that amount of drugs usually die violently. I've got a lot of work to do on this one, and I'll find who did it." He mumbled something about not leaving town, and that he'd see me later, and left.

"Vic . . ." Hal said. I looked at him.

"About that printout," he finally said. "I'd appreciate it . . . well, they said they'd keep it confidential. If you know what I mean." He had eyes like a basset hound. I'd never noticed that before.

"Hal, if you'll just go home, you have nothing to worry about from me."

He nodded, and scuttled for the door.

"I don't think any of that will get out," he said.

It all did, of course.

It probably would have even without the letters that began arriving a few days after Kluge's death, all postmarked Trenton, New Jersey, all computer-generated from a machine no

one was ever able to trace. The letters detailed the matters
Kluge had mentioned in his will.

I didn't know about any of that at the time. I spent the rest of
the day after Hal's departure lying in my bed, under the
electric blanket. I couldn't get my feet warm. I got up only to
soak in the tub or to make a sandwich.

Reporters knocked on the door but I didn't answer. On the
second day I called a criminal lawyer—Martin Abrams, the
first in the book—and retained him. He told me they'd probably call me down to the police station for questioning. I told
him I wouldn't go, popped two Dilantin, and sprinted for the
bed.

A couple of times I heard sirens in the neighborhood. Once
I heard a shouted argument down the street. I resisted the
temptation to look. I'll admit I was a little curious, but you
know what happened to the cat.

I kept waiting for Osborne to return, but he didn't. The
days turned into a week. Only two things of interest happened
in that time.

The first was a knock on my door. This was two days after
Kluge's death. I looked through the curtains and saw a silver
Ferrari parked at the curb. I couldn't see who was on the
porch, so I asked who it was.

"My name's Lisa Foo," she said. "You asked me to drop
by."

"I certainly don't remember it."

"Isn't this Charles Kluge's house?"

"That's next door."

"Oh. Sorry."

I decided I ought to warn her Kluge was dead, so I opened
the door. She turned around and smiled at me. It was blinding.

Where does one start in describing Lisa Foo? Remember
when newspapers used to run editorial cartoons of Hirohito
and Tojo, when the *Times* used the word "Jap" without
embarrassment? Little guys with faces wide as footballs, ears
like jug handles, thick glasses, two big rabbity buck teeth,
and pencil-thin moustaches . . .

Leaving out only the moustache, she was a dead ringer for
a cartoon Tojo. She had the glasses, and the ears, and the
teeth. But her teeth had braces, like piano keys wrapped in
barbed wire. And she was five-eight or five-nine and couldn't
have weighed more than a hundred and ten. I'd have said a

hundred, but added five pounds for each of her breasts, so improbably large on her scrawny frame that all I could read of the message on her T-shirt was "POCK LIVE."

It was only when she turned sideways that I saw the esses before and after.

She thrust out a slender hand.

"Looks like I'm going to be your neighbor for a while," she said. "At least until we get that dragon's lair next door straightened out." If she had an accent, it was San Fernando Valley.

"That's nice."

"Did you know him? Kluge, I mean. Or at least that's what he called himself."

"You don't think that was his name?"

"I doubt it. 'Kluge' means clever in German. And it's hacker slang for being tricky. And he sure was a tricky bugger. Definitely some glitches in the wetware." She tapped the side of her head meaningfully. "Viruses and phantoms and demons jumping out every time they try to key in, software rot, bit buckets overflowing onto the floor . . ."

She babbled on in that vein for a time. It might as well have been Swahili.

"Did you say there were demons in his computers?"

"That's right."

"Sounds like they need an exorcist."

She jerked her thumb at her chest and showed me another half-acre of teeth.

"That's me. Listen, I gotta go. Drop in and see me anytime."

The second interesting event of the week happened the next day. My bank statement arrived. There were three deposits listed. The first was the regular check from the V.A., for $487.00. The second was for $392.54, interest on the money my parents had left me fifteen years ago.

The third deposit had come in on the twentieth, the day Charles Kluge died. It was for $700,083.04.

A few days later Hal Lanier dropped by.

"Boy, what a week," he said. Then he flopped down on the couch and told me all about it.

There had been a second death on the block. The letters had stirred up a lot of trouble, especially with the police going

house to house questioning everyone. Some people had confessed to things when they were sure the cops were closing in
on them. The woman who used to entertain salesmen while
her husband was at work had admitted her infidelity, and the
guy had shot her. He was in the County Jail. That was the
worst incident, but there had been others, from fistfights to
rocks thrown through windows. According to Hal, the IRS
was thinking of setting up a branch office in the neighborhood, so many people were being audited.

I thought about the seven hundred thousand and eighty-
three dollars.

And four cents.

I didn't say anything, but my feet were getting cold.

"I suppose you want to know about me and Betty," he
said, at last. I didn't. I didn't want to hear *any* of this, but I
tried for a sympathetic expression.

"That's all over," he said, with a satisfied sigh. "Between
me and Toni, I mean. I told Betty all about it. It was real bad
for a few days, but I think our marriage is stronger for it
now." He was quiet for a moment, basking in the warmth of
it all. I had kept a straight face under worse provocation, so I
trust I did well enough then.

He wanted to tell me all they'd learned about Kluge, and
he wanted to invite me over for dinner, but I begged off on
both, telling him my war wounds were giving me hell. I just
about had him to the door when Osborne knocked on it.
There was nothing to do but let him in. Hal stuck around,
too.

I offered Osborne coffee, which he gratefully accepted. He
looked different. I wasn't sure what it was at first. Same old
tired expression . . . no, it wasn't. Most of that weary look
had been either an act or a cop's built-in cynicism. Today it
was genuine. The tiredness had moved from his face to his
shoulders, to his hands, to the way he walked and the way he
slumped in the chair. There was a sour aura of defeat around
him.

"Am I still a suspect?" I asked.

"You mean should you call your lawyer? I'd say don't
bother. I checked you out pretty good. That will ain't gonna
hold up, so your motive is pretty half-assed. Way I figure it,
every coke dealer in the Marina had a better reason to snuff
Kluge than you." He sighed. "I got a couple questions. You
can answer them or not."

"Give it a try."

"You remember any unusual visitors he had? People coming and going at night?"

"The only visitors I *ever* recall were deliveries. Post Office, Federal Express, freight companies . . . that sort of thing. I suppose the drugs could have come in any of those shipments."

"That's what we figure, too. There's no way he was dealing nickel and dime bags. He must have been a middle man. Ship it in, ship it out." He brooded about that for a while, and sipped his coffee.

"So are you making any progress?" I asked.

"You want to know the truth? The case is going in the toilet. We've got too many motives, and not a one of them that works. As far as we can tell, nobody on the block had the slightest idea Kluge had all that information. We've checked bank accounts and we can't find evidence of blackmail. So the neighbors are pretty much out of the picture. Though if he were alive, most people around here would like to kill him *now*."

"Damn straight," Hal said.

Osborne slapped his thigh. "If the bastard was alive, *I'd* kill him," he said. "But I'm beginning to think he never *was* alive."

"I don't understand."

"If I hadn't seen the goddam body . . ." He sat up a little straighter. "He said he didn't exist. Well, he practically didn't. PG&E never heard of him. He's hooked up to their lines and a meter reader came by every month, but they never billed him for a single kilowatt. Same with the phone company. He had a whole exchange in that house that was *made* by the phone company, and delivered by them, and installed by them, but they have no record of him. We talked to the guy who hooked it all up. He turned in his records, and the computer swallowed them. Kluge didn't have a bank account anywhere in California, and apparently he didn't need one. We've tracked down a hundred companies that sold things to him, shipped them out, and then either marked his account paid or forgot they ever sold him anything. Some of them have check numbers and account numbers in their books, for accounts or even *banks* that don't exist."

He leaned back in his chair, simmering at the perfidy of it all.

"The only guy we've found who ever heard of him was the guy who delivered his groceries once a month. Little store down on Sepulveda. They don't have a computer, just paper receipts. He paid by check. Wells Fargo accepted them and the checks never bounced. But Wells Fargo never heard of him."

I thought it over. He seemed to expect something of me at this point, so I made a stab at it.

"He was doing all this by computers?"

"That's right. Now, the grocery store scam I can understand, almost. But more often than not, Kluge got right into the basic programming of the computers and wiped himself out. The power company was never paid, by check or any other way, because as far as they were concerned, they weren't selling him anything.

"No government agency has ever heard of him. We've checked him with everybody from the Post Office to the CIA."

"Kluge was probably an alias, right?" I offered.

"Yeah. But the FBI doesn't have his fingerprints. We'll find out who he was, eventually. But it doesn't get us any closer to whether or not he was murdered."

He admitted there was pressure to simply close the felony part of the case, label it suicide, and forget it. But Osborne would not believe it. Naturally, the civil side would go on for some time, as they attempted to track down all Kluge's deceptions.

"It's all up to the dragon lady," Osborne said. Hal snorted.

"Fat chance," Hal said, and muttered something about boat people.

"That girl? She's still over there? Who is she?"

"She's some sort of giant brain from Cal Tech. We called out there and told them we were having problems, and she's what they sent." It was clear from Osborne's face what he thought of any help she might provide.

I finally managed to get rid of them. As they went down the walk I looked over at Kluge's house. Sure enough, Lisa Foo's silver Ferrari was sitting in his driveway.

I had no business going over there. I knew that better than anyone.

So I set about preparing my evening meal. I made a tuna casserole—which is not as bland as it sounds, the way I make it—put it in the oven and went out to the garden to pick the

makings for a salad. I was slicing cherry tomatoes and thinking about chilling a bottle of white wine when it occurred to
me that I had enough for two.

Since I never do anything hastily, I sat down and thought it
over for a while. What finally decided me was my feet. For
the first time in a week, they were warm. So I went to
Kluge's house.

The front door was standing open. There was no screen.
Funny how disturbing that can look, the dwelling wide open
and unguarded. I stood on the porch and leaned in, but all I
could see was the hallway.

"Miss Foo?" I called. There was no answer.

The last time I'd been here I had found a dead man. I
hurried in.

Lisa Foo was sitting on a piano bench before a computer
console. She was in profile, her back very straight, her brown
legs in lotus position, her fingers poised at the keys as words
sprayed rapidly onto the screen in front of her. She looked up
and flashed her teeth at me.

"Somebody told me your name was Victor Apfel," she
said.

"Yes. Uh, the door was open . . ."

"It's hot," she said, reasonably, pinching the fabric of her
shirt near her neck and lifting it up and down like you do
when you're sweaty. "What can I do for you?"

"Nothing, really." I came into the dimness, and stumbled
on something. It was a cardboard box, the large flat kind used
for delivering a jumbo pizza.

"I was just fixing dinner, and it looks like there's plenty
for two, so I was wondering if you . . ." I trailed off, as I
had just noticed something else. I had thought she was wearing shorts. In fact, all she had on was the shirt and a pair
of pink bikini underpants. This did not seem to make her
uneasy.

". . . would you like to join me for dinner?"

Her smile grew even broader.

"I'd love to," she said. She effortlessly unwound her legs
and bounced to her feet, then brushed past me, trailing the
smells of perspiration and sweet soap. "Be with you in a
minute."

I looked around the room again but my mind kept coming
back to her. She liked Pepsi with her pizza; there were dozens
of empty cans. There was a deep scar on her knee and upper

thigh. The ashtrays were empty . . . and the long muscles of her calves bunched strongly as she walked. Kluge must have smoked, but Lisa didn't, and she had fine, downy hairs in the small of her back just visible in the green computer light. I heard water running in the bathroom sink, looked at a yellow notepad covered with the kind of penmanship I hadn't seen in decades, and smelled soap and remembered tawny brown skin and an easy stride.

She appeared in the hall, wearing cut-off jeans, sandals, and a new T-shirt. The old one had advertised BURROUGHS OFFICE SYSTEMS. This one featured Mickey Mouse and Snow White's Castle and smelled of fresh bleached cotton. Mickey's ears were laid back on the upper slopes of her incongruous breasts.

I followed her out the door. Tinkerbell twinkled in pixie dust from the back of her shirt.

"I like this kitchen," she said.

You don't really look at a place until someone says something like that.

The kitchen was a time capsule. It could have been lifted bodily from an issue of *Life* in the early fifties. There was the hump-shouldered Frigidaire, of a vintage when that word had been a generic term, like Xerox or Coke. The counter tops were yellow tile, the sort that's only found in bathrooms these days. There wasn't an ounce of Formica in the place. Instead of a dishwasher I had a wire rack and a double sink. There was no electric can opener, Cuisinart, trash compacter, or microwave oven. The newest thing in the whole room was a fifteen-year-old blender.

I'm good with my hands. I like to repair things.

"This bread is terrific," she said.

I had baked it myself. I watched her mop her plate with a crust, and she asked if she might have seconds.

I understand cleaning one's plate with bread is bad manners. Not that I cared; I do it myself. And other than that, her manners were impeccable. She polished off three helpings of my casserole and when she was done the plate hardly needed washing. I had a sense of a ravenous appetite barely held in check.

She settled back in her chair and I re-filled her glass with white wine.

"Are you sure you wouldn't like some more peas?"

"I'd bust." She patted her stomach contentedly. "Thank you so much, Mister Apfel. I haven't had a home-cooked meal in ages."

"You can call me Victor."

"I just love American food."

"I didn't know there was such a thing. I mean, not like Chinese or . . . you *are* American, aren't you?" She just smiled. "What I meant—"

"I know what you meant, Victor. I'm a citizen, but not native-born. Would you excuse me for a moment? I know it's impolite to jump right up, but with these braces I find I have to brush *instantly* after eating."

I could hear her as I cleared the table. I ran water in the sink and started doing the dishes. Before long she joined me, grabbed a dish towel, and began drying the things in the rack, over my protests.

"You live alone here?" she asked.

"Yes. Have ever since my parents died."

"Ever married? If it's none of my business, just say so."

"That's all right. No, I never married."

"You do pretty good for not having a woman around."

"I've had a lot of practice. Can I ask you a question?"

"Shoot."

"Where are you from? Taiwan?"

"I have a knack for languages. Back home, I spoke pidgen American, but when I got here I cleaned up my act. I also speak rotten French, illiterate Chinese in four or five varieties, gutter Vietnamese, and enough Thai to holler 'Me wanna see American Consul, pretty-damn-quick, you!' "

I laughed. When she said it, her accent was thick.

"I been here eight years now. You figured out where home is?"

"Vietnam?" I ventured.

"The sidewalks of Saigon, fer shure. Or Ho Chi Minh's Shitty, as the pajama-heads re-named it, may their dinks rot off and their butts be filled with jagged punjee-sticks. Pardon my French."

She ducked her head in embarrassment. What had started out light had turned hot very quickly. I sensed a hurt at least as deep as my own, and we both backed off from it.

"I took you for a Japanese," I said.

"Yeah, ain't it a pisser? I'll tell you about it some day.

Victor, is that a laundry room through that door there? With
an electric washer?''

''That's right.''

''Would it be too much trouble if I did a load?''

It was no trouble at all. She had seven pairs of faded jeans,
some with the legs cut away, and about two dozen T-shirts. It
could have been a load of boys' clothing except for the frilly
underwear.

We went into the back yard to sit in the last rays of the
setting sun, then she had to see my garden. I'm quite proud of
it. When I'm well, I spend four or five hours a day working
out there, year-round, usually in the morning hours. You can
do that in southern California. I have a greenhouse I built
myself.

She loved it, though it was not in its best shape. I had spent
most of the week in bed or in the tub. As a result, weeds were
sprouting here and there.

''We had a garden when I was little,'' she said. ''And I
spent two years in a rice paddy.''

''That must be a lot different than this.''

''Damn straight. Put me off rice for *years*.''

She discovered an infestation of aphids, so we squatted
down to pick them off. She had that double-jointed Asian
peasant's way of sitting that I remembered so well and could
never imitate. Her fingers were long and narrow, and soon
the tips of them were green from squashed bugs.

We talked about this and that. I don't remember quite how
it came up, but I told her I had fought in Korea. I learned she
was twenty-five. It turned out we had the same birthday, so
some months back I had been exactly twice her age.

The only time Kluge's name came up was when she mentioned how she liked to cook. She hadn't been able to at
Kluge's house.

''He has a freezer in the garage full of frozen dinners,'' she
said. ''He had one plate, one fork, one spoon, and one glass.
He's got the best microwave oven on the market. And that's
it, man. Ain't nothing else in his kitchen at *all*.'' She shook
her head, and executed an aphid. ''He was one weird dude.''

When her laundry was done it was late evening, almost
dark. She loaded it into my wicker basket and we took it out
to the clothesline. It got to be a game. I would shake out a
T-shirt and study the picture or message there. Sometimes I

got it, and sometimes I didn't. There were pictures of rock groups, a map of Los Angeles, Star Trek tie-ins . . . a little of everything.

"What's the L5 Society?" I asked her.

"Guys that want to build these great big farms in space. I asked 'em if they were gonna grow rice, and they said they didn't think it was the best crop for zero gee, so I bought the shirt."

"How many of these things do you have?"

"Wow, it's gotta be four or five hundred. I usually wear 'em two or three times and then put them away."

I picked up another shirt, and a bra fell out. It wasn't the kind of bra girls wore when I was growing up. It was very sheer, though somehow functional at the same time.

"You like, Yank?" Her accent was very thick. "You oughtta see my sister!"

I glanced at her, and her face fell.

"I'm sorry, Victor," she said. "You don't have to blush." She took the bra from me and clipped it to the line.

She must have mis-read my face. True, I had been embarrassed, but I was also pleased in some strange way. It had been a long time since anybody had called me anything but Victor or Mr. Apfel.

The next day's mail brought a letter from a law firm in Chicago. It was about the seven hundred thousand dollars. The money had come from a Delaware holding company which had been set up in 1933 to provide for me in my old age. My mother and father were listed as the founders. Certain long-term investments had matured, resulting in my recent windfall. The amount in my bank was *after* taxes.

It was ridiculous on the face of it. My parents had never had that kind of money. I didn't want it. I would have given it back if I could find out who Kluge had stolen it from.

I decided that, if I wasn't in jail this time next year, I'd give it all to some charity. Save The Whales, maybe, or the L5 Society.

I spent the morning in the garden. Later I walked to the market and bought some fresh ground beef and pork. I was feeling good as I pulled my purchases home in my fold-up wire basket. When I passed the silver Ferrari I smiled.

She hadn't come to get her laundry. I took it off the line and folded it, then knocked on Kluge's door.

"It's me. Victor."

"Come on in, Yank."

She was where she had been before, but decently dressed this time. She smiled at me, then hit her forehead when she saw the laundry basket. She hurried to take it from me.

"I'm sorry, Victor. I meant to get this—"

"Don't worry about it," I said. "It was no trouble. And it gave me the chance to ask if you'd like to dine with me again."

Something happened to her face which she covered quickly. Perhaps she didn't like "American" food as much as she professed to. Or maybe it was the cook.

"Sure, Victor, I'd love to. Let me take care of this. And why don't you open those drapes? It's like a tomb in here."

She hurried away. I glanced at the screen she had been using. It was blank, but for one word: intercourse-p. I assumed it was a typo.

I pulled the drapes open in time to see Osborne's car park at the curb. Then Lisa was back, wearing a new T-shirt. This one said A CHANGE OF HOBBIT, and had a picture of a squat, hairy-footed creature. She glanced out the window and saw Osborne coming up the walk.

"I say, Watson," she said. "It's Lestrade of the Yard. Do show him in."

That wasn't nice of her. He gave me a suspicious glance as he entered. I burst out laughing. Lisa sat on the piano bench, poker-faced. She slumped indolently, one arm resting near the keyboard.

"Well, Apfel," Osborne started. "We've finally found out who Kluge really was."

"Patrick William Gavin," Lisa said.

Quite a time went by before Osborne was able to close his mouth. Then he opened it right up again.

"How the hell did you find that out?"

She lazily caressed the keyboard beside her.

"Well, of course I got it when it came into your office this morning. There's a little stoolie program tucked away in your computer that whispers in my ear every time the name Kluge is mentioned. But I didn't need that. I figured it out five days ago."

"Then why the . . . why didn't you tell me?"

"You didn't ask me."

They glared at each other for a while. I had no idea what events had led up to this moment, but it was quite clear they didn't like each other even a little bit. Lisa was on top just now, and seemed to be enjoying it. Then she glanced at her screen, looked surprised, and quickly tapped a key. The word that had been there vanished. She gave me an inscrutable glance, then faced Osborne again.

"If you recall, you brought me in because all your own guys were getting was a lot of crashes. This system was brain-damaged when I got here, practically catatonic. Most of it was down and your guys couldn't get it up." She had to grin at that.

"You decided I couldn't do any worse than your guys were doing. So you asked me to try and break Kluge's codes without frying the system. Well, I did it. All you had to do was come by and interface and I would have downloaded N tons of wallpaper right in your lap."

Osborne listened quietly. Maybe he even knew he had made a mistake.

"What did you get? Can I see it now?"

She nodded, and pressed a few keys. Words started to fill her screen, and one close to Osborne. I got up and read Lisa's terminal.

It was a brief bio of Kluge/Gavin. He was about my age, but while I was getting shot at in a foreign land, he was cutting a swath through the infant computer industry. He had been there from the ground up, working at many of the top research facilities. It surprised me that it had taken over a week to identify him.

"I compiled this anecdotally," Lisa said, as we read. "The first thing you have to realize about Gavin is that he exists nowhere in any computerized information system. So I called people all over the country—interesting phone system he's got, by the way; it generates a new number for each call, and you can't call back or trace it—and started asking who the top people were in the fifties and sixties. I got a lot of names. After that, it was a matter of finding out who no longer existed in the files. He faked his death in 1967. I located one account of it in a newspaper file. Everybody I talked to who had known him knew of his death. There is a paper birth certificate in Florida. That's the only other evidence I found of him. He was the only guy so many people in the field knew who left no mark on the world. That seemed conclusive to me.''

Osborne finished reading, then looked up.

"All right, Ms. Foo. What else have you found out?''

"I've broken some of his codes. I had a piece of luck, getting into a basic rape-and-plunder program he'd written to attack *other* people's programs, and I've managed to use it against a few of his own. I've unlocked a file of passwords with notes on where they came from. And I've learned a few of his tricks. But it's the tip of the iceberg.''

She waved a hand at the silent metal brains in the room.

"What I haven't gotten across to anyone is just what this *is*. This is the most devious electronic weapon ever devised. It's armored like a battleship. It has to be; there's a lot of very slick programs out there that grab an invader and hang on like a terrier. If they ever got this far Kluge could deflect them. But usually they never even knew they'd been burgled. Kluge'd come in like a cruise missile, low and fast and twisty. And he'd route his attack through a dozen cut-offs.''

"He had a lot of advantages. Big systems these days are heavily protected. People use passwords and very sophisticated codes. But Kluge helped *invent* most of them. You need a damn good lock to keep out a locksmith. He helped install a lot of the major systems. He left informants behind, hidden in the software. If the codes were changed, the computer *itself* would send the information to a safe system that Kluge could tap later. It's like you buy the biggest, meanest, best-trained watchdog you can. And that night, the guy who *trained* the dog comes in, pats him on the head, and robs you blind.''

There was a lot more in that vein. I'm afraid that when Lisa began talking about computers, ninety percent of my head shut off.

"I'd like to know something, Osborne," Lisa said.

"What would that be?''

"What is my status here? Am I supposed to be solving your crime for you, or just trying to get this system back to where a competent user can deal with it?''

Osborne thought it over.

"What worries me," she added, "is that I'm poking around in a lot of restricted data banks. I'm worried about somebody knocking on the door and handcuffing me. *You* ought to be worried, too. Some of these agencies wouldn't like a homicide cop looking into their affairs.''

Osborne bridled at that. Maybe that's what she intended.

"What do I have to do?" he snarled. "Beg you to stay?"

"No. I just want your authorization. You don't have to put it in writing. Just say you're behind me."

"Look. As far as L.A. County and the State of California are concerned, this house doesn't exist. There is no lot here. It doesn't appear in the tax assessor's records. This place is in a legal limbo. If anybody can authorize you to use this stuff, it's me, because I believe a murder was committed in it. So you just keep doing what you've been doing."

"That's not much of a commitment," she mused.

"It's all you're going to get. Now, what else have you got?"

She turned to her keyboard and typed for a while. Pretty soon a printer started, and Lisa leaned back. I glanced at her screen. It said: osculate posterior-p. I remembered that osculate meant kiss. Well, these people have their own language. Lisa looked up at me and grinned.

"Not you," she said, quietly. *"Him."*

I hadn't the faintest notion of what she was talking about.

Osborne got his printout and was ready to leave. Again, he couldn't resist turning at the door for final orders.

"If you find anything to indicate he didn't commit suicide, let me know."

"Okay. He didn't commit suicide."

Osborne didn't understand for a moment.

"I want proof."

"Well, I have it, but you probably can't use it. He didn't write that ridiculous suicide note."

"How do you know that?"

"I knew my first day here. I had the computer list the program. Then I compared it to Kluge's style. No *way* he could have written it. It's tighter'n a bug's ass. Not a spare line in it. Kluge didn't pick his alias for nothing. You know what it means?"

"Clever," I said.

"Literally. But it means . . . a Rube Goldberg device. Something overly complex. Something that works, but for the wrong reason. You 'kluge around' bugs in a program. It's the hacker's Vaseline."

"So?" Osborne wanted to know.

"So Kluge's programs were really crocked. They were full of bells and whistles he never bothered to clean out. He was a genius, and his programs worked, but you wonder why they did. Routines so bletcherous they'd make your skin crawl. Real crufty bagbiters. But good programming's so rare, even his diddles were better than most people's super-moby hacks."

I suspect Osborne understood about as much of that as I did.

"So you base your opinion on his programming style."

"Yeah. Unfortunately, it's gonna be ten years or so before that's admissable in court, like graphology or fingerprints."

We eventually got rid of him, and I went home to fix the dinner. Lisa joined me when it was ready. Once more she had a huge appetite.

I fixed lemonade and we sat on my small patio and watched evening gather around us.

I woke up in the middle of the night, sweating. I sat up, thinking it out, and I didn't like my conclusions. So I put on my robe and slippers and went over to Kluge's.

The front door was open again. I knocked anyway. Lisa stuck her head around the corner.

"Victor? is something wrong?"

"I'm not sure," I said. "May I come in?"

She gestured, and I followed her into the living room. An open can of Pepsi sat beside her console. Her eyes were red as she sat on her bench.

"What's up?" she said, and yawned.

"You should be asleep, for one thing," I said.

She shrugged, and nodded.

"Yeah. I can't seem to get in the right phase. Just now I'm in day mode. But Victor, I'm used to working odd hours, and long hours, and you didn't come over here to lecture me about that, did you?"

"No. You say Kluge was murdered."

"He didn't write his suicide note. That seems to leave murder."

"I was wondering why someone would kill him. He never left the house, so it was for something he did here with his computers. And now you're . . . well, I don't know *what* you're doing, frankly, but you seem to be poking into the same things. Isn't there a danger the same people will come after you?"

"People?" She raised an eyebrow.

I felt helpless. My fears were not well-formed enough to make sense.

"I don't know . . . you mentioned agencies . . ."

"You notice how impressed Osborne was with that? You think there's some kind of conspiracy Kluge tumbled to, or you think the CIA killed him because he found out too much about something, or . . ."

"I don't know, Lisa. But I'm worried the same thing could happen to you."

Surprisingly, she smiled at me.

"Thank you so much, Victor. I wasn't going to admit it to Osborne, but I've been worried about that, too."

"Well, what are you going to do?"

"I want to stay here and keep working. So I gave some thought to what I could do to protect myself. I decided there wasn't anything."

"Surely there's something."

"Well, I got a gun, if that's what you mean. But think about it. Kluge was offed in the middle of the day. Nobody saw anybody enter or leave the house. So I asked myself, who can walk into a house in broad daylight, shoot Kluge, program that suicide note, and walk away, leaving no traces he'd ever been there?"

"Somebody very good."

"Goddamn good. So good there's not much chance one little gook's gonna be able to stop him if he decides to waste her."

She shocked me, both by her words and by her apparent lack of concern for her own fate. But she had said she was worried.

"Then you have to stop this. Get out of here."

"I won't be pushed around that way," she said. There was a tone of finality to it. I thought of things I might say, and rejected them all.

"You could at least . . . lock your front door," I concluded, lamely.

She laughed, and kissed my cheek.

"I'll do that, Yank. And I appreciate your concern. I really do."

I watched her close the door behind me, listened to her lock it, then trudged through the moonlight toward my house. Halfway there I stopped. I could suggest she stay in my spare bedroom. I could offer to stay with her at Kluge's.

No, I decided. She would probably take that the wrong way.

I was back in bed before I realized, with a touch of chagrin and more than a little disgust at myself, that she had every reason to take it the wrong way.

And me exactly twice her age.

I spent the morning in the garden, planning the evening's menu. I have always liked to cook, but dinner with Lisa had rapidly become the high point of my day. Not only that, I was already taking it for granted. So it hit me hard, around noon, when I looked out the front and saw her car gone.

I hurried to Kluge's front door. It was standing open. I made a quick search of the house. I found nothing until the master bedroom, where her clothes were stacked neatly on the floor.

Shivering, I pounded on the Laniers' front door. Betty answered, and immediately saw my agitation.

"The girl at Kluge's house," I said. "I'm afraid something's wrong. Maybe we'd better call the police."

"What happened?" Betty asked, looking over my shoulder. "Did she call you? I see she's not back yet."

"Back?"

"I saw her drive away about an hour ago. That's quite a car she has."

Feeling like a fool, I tried to make nothing of it, but I caught a look in Betty's eye. I think she'd have liked to pat me on the head. It made me furious.

But she'd left her clothes, so surely she was coming back.

I kept telling myself that, then went to run a bath, as hot as I could stand it.

When I answered the door she was standing there with a grocery bag in each arm and her usual blinding smile on her face.

"I wanted to do this yesterday but I forgot until you came over, and I know I should have asked first, but then I wanted to surprise you, so I just went to get one or two items you didn't have in your garden and a couple of things that weren't in your spice rack . . ."

She kept talking as we unloaded the bags in the kitchen. I said nothing. She was wearing a new T-shirt. There was a big V, and under it a picture of a screw, followed by a hyphen and a small-case "p." I thought it over as she babbled on. V, screw-p. I was determined not to ask what it meant.

"Do you like Vietnamese cooking?"

I looked at her, and finally realized she was very nervous.

"I don't know," I said. "I've never had it. But I like Chinese, and Japanese, and Indian. I like to try new things." The last part was a lie, but not as bad as it might have been. I do try new recipes, and my tastes in food are catholic. I didn't expect to have much trouble with southeast Asian cuisine.

"Well, when I get through you *still* won't know," she laughed. "My momma was half-Chinese. So what you're gonna get here is a mongrel meal." She glanced up, saw my face, and laughed.

"I forgot. You've been to Asia. No, Yank, I ain't gonna serve any dog meat."

There was only one intolerable thing, and that was the chopsticks. I used them for as long as I could, then put them aside and got a fork.

"I'm sorry," I said. "Chopsticks happen to be a problem for me."

"You use them very well."

"I had plenty of time to learn how."

It was very good, and I told her so. Each dish was a revelation, not quite like anything I had ever had. Toward the end, I broke down halfway.

"Does the V stand for victory?" I asked.

"Maybe."

"Beethoven? Churchill? World War Two?"

She just smiled.

"Think of it as a challenge, Yank."

"Do I frighten you, Victor?"

"You did at first."

"It's my face, isn't it?"

"It's a generalized phobia of Orientals. I suppose I'm a racist. Not because I want to be."

She nodded slowly, there in the dark. We were on the patio again, but the sun had gone down a long time ago. I can't recall what we had talked about for all those hours. It had kept us busy, anyway.

"I have the same problem," she said.

"Fear of Orientals?" I had meant it as a joke.

"Of Cambodians." She let me take that in for a while, then went on. "I fled to Cambodia when Saigon fell. I walked across it. I'm lucky to be alive really. They had me in labor camps."

"I thought they called it Kampuchea now."

She spat. I'm not even sure she was aware she had done it.

"It's the People's Republic of Syphilitic Dogs. The North Koreans treated you very badly, didn't they, Victor?"

"That's right."

"Koreans are pus suckers." I must have looked surprised, because she chuckled.

"You Americans feel so guilty about racism. As if you had invented it and nobody else—except maybe the South Africans and the Nazis—had ever practiced it as heinously as you. And you can't tell one yellow face from another, so you think of the yellow races as one homogeneous block. When in fact Orientals are among the most racist peoples on the earth. The Vietnamese have hated the Cambodians for a thousand years. The Chinese hate the Japanese. The Koreans hate everybody. And *everybody* hates the 'ethnic Chinese.' The Chinese are the Jews of the east."

"I've heard that."

She nodded, lost in her own thoughts.

"And I hate all Cambodians," she said, at last. "Like you, I don't wish to. Most of the people who suffered in the camps were Cambodians. It was the genocidal leaders, the Pol Pot scum, who I should hate." She looked at me. "But sometimes we don't get a lot of choice about things like that, do we, Yank?"

The next day I visited her at noon. It had cooled down, but was still warm in her dark den. She had not changed her shirt.

She told me a few things about computers. When she let me try some things on the keyboard I quickly got lost. We decided I needn't plan on a career as a computer programmer.

One of the things she showed me was called a telephone modem, whereby she could reach other computers all over the world. She "interfaced" with someone at Stanford whom she had never met, and who she knew only as "Bubble Sorter." They typed things back and forth at each other.

At the end, Bubble Sorter wrote "bye-p." Lisa typed T.

"What's T?" I asked.

"True. Means yes, but yes would be too straightforward for a hacker."

"You told me what a byte is. What's a byep?"

She looked up at me seriously.

"It's a question. Add p to a word, and you make it a question. So bye-p means Bubble Sorter was asking if I wanted to log out. Sign off."

I thought that over.

"So how would you translate 'osculate posterior-p'?"

" 'You wanna kiss my ass?' But remember, that was for Osborne."

I looked at her T-shirt again, then up to her eyes, which were quite serious and serene. She waited, hands folded in her lap.

Intercourse-p.

"Yes," I said. "I would."

She put her glasses on the table and pulled her shirt over her head.

We made love in Kluge's big waterbed.

I had a certain amount of performance anxiety—it had been a long, *long* time. After that, I was so caught up in the touch and smell and taste of her that I went a little crazy. She didn't seem to mind.

At last we were done, and bathed in sweat. She rolled over, stood, and went to the window. She opened it, and a breath of air blew over me. Then she put one knee on the bed, leaned over me, and got a pack of cigarettes from the bedside table. She lit one.

"I hope you're not allergic to smoke," she said.

"No. My father smoked. But I didn't know you did."

"Only afterwards," she said, with a quick smile. She took a deep drag. "Everybody in Saigon smoked, I think." She stretched out on her back beside me and we lay like that, soaking wet, holding hands. She opened her legs so one of her bare feet touched mine. It seemed enough contact. I watched the smoke rise from her right hand.

"I haven't felt warm in thirty years," I said. "I've been hot, but I've never been warm. I feel warm now."

"Tell me about it," she said.

So I did, as much as I could, wondering if it would work this time. At thirty years' remove, my story does not sound so horrible. We've seen so much in that time. There were people in jails at that very moment, enduring conditions as bad as any I encountered. The paraphernalia of oppression is still pretty much the same. Nothing physical happened to me that would account for thirty years lived as a recluse.

"I *was* badly injured," I told her. "My skull was fractured. I still have . . . problems from that. Korea can get very cold, and I was never warm enough. But it was the other stuff. What they call brainwashing now.

"We didn't know what it was. We couldn't understand that even after a man had told them all he knew they'd keep on at us. Keeping us awake. Disorienting us. Some guys signed confessions, made up all sorts of stuff, but even that wasn't enough. They'd just keep on at you.

"I never did figure it out. I guess I couldn't understand an evil that big. But when they were sending us back and some of the prisoners wouldn't go . . . they really didn't *want* to go, they really believed . . ."

I had to pause there. Lisa sat up, moved quietly to the end of the bed, and began massaging my feet.

"We got a taste of what the Vietnam guys got, later. Only for us it was reversed. The G.I.'s were heroes, and the prisoners were . . ."

"You didn't break," she said. It wasn't a question.

"No, I didn't."

"That would be worse."

I looked at her. She had my foot pressed against her flat belly, holding me by the heel while her other hand massaged my toes.

"The country was shocked," I said. "They didn't understand what brainwashing was. I tried telling people how it was. I thought they were looking at me funny. After a while, I stopped talking about it. And I didn't have anything else to talk about.

"A few years back the Army changed its policy. Now they don't expect you to withstand psychological conditioning. It's understood you can say anything or sign anything."

She just looked at me, kept massaging my foot, and nodded slowly. Finally she spoke.

"Cambodia was hot," she said. "I kept telling myself when I finally got to the U.S. I'd live in Maine or someplace, where it snowed. And I did go to Cambridge, but I found out I didn't like snow."

She told me about it. The last I heard, a million people had died over there. It was a whole country frothing at the mouth and snapping at anything that moved. Or like one of those sharks you read about that, when its guts are ripped out, bends in a circle and starts devouring itself.

She told me about being forced to build a pyramid of severed heads. Twenty of them working all day in the hot sun finally got it ten feet high before it collapsed. If any of them stopped working, their own heads were added to the pile.

"It didn't mean anything to me. It was just another job. I was pretty crazy by then. I didn't start to come out of it until I got across the Thai border."

That she had survived it at all seemed a miracle. She had gone through more horror than I could imagine. And she had come through it in much better shape. It made me feel small. When I was her age, I was well on my way to building the prison I have lived in ever since. I told her that.

"Part of it is preparation," she said, wryly. "What you expect out of life, what your life has been so far. You said it yourself. Korea was new to you. I'm not saying I was ready for Cambodia, but my life up to that point hadn't been what you'd call sheltered. I hope you haven't been thinking I made a living in the streets by selling apples."

She kept rubbing my feet, staring off into scenes I could not see.

"How old were you when your mother died?"

"She was killed during Tet, 1968. I was ten."

"By the Viet Cong?"

"Who knows? Lot of bullets flying, lot of grenades being thrown."

She sighed, dropped my foot, and sat there, a scrawny Buddha without a robe.

"You ready to do it again, Yank?"

"I don't think I can, Lisa. I'm an old man."

She moved over me and lowered herself with her chin just below my sternum, settling her breasts in the most delicious place possible.

"We'll see," she said, and giggled. "There's an alternative sex act I'm pretty good at, and I'm pretty sure it would make you a young man again. But I haven't been able to do it for about a year on account of these." She tapped her braces. "It'd be sort of like sticking it in a buzz saw. So now I do this instead. I call it 'touring the silicone valley.' " She started

moving her body up and down, just a few inches at a time.
She blinked innocently a couple times, then laughed.

"At last, I can see you," she said. "I'm awfully myopic."

I let her do that for a while, then lifted my head.

"Did you say silicone?"

"Uh-huh. You didn't think they were real, did you?"

I confessed that I had.

"I don't think I've ever been so happy with anything I
ever bought. Not even the car."

"Why did you?"

"Does it bother you?"

It didn't, and I told her so. But I couldn't conceal my
curiosity.

"Because it was safe to. In Saigon I was always angry that
I never developed. I could have made a good living as a
prostitute, but I was always too tall, too skinny, and too ugly.
Then in Cambodia I was lucky. I managed to pass for a boy
some of the time. If not for that I'd have been raped a lot
more than I was. And in Thailand I knew I'd get to the West
one way or another, and when I got there, I'd get the best car
there was, eat anything I wanted any time I wanted to, and
purchase the best tits money could buy. You can't imagine
what the West looks like from the camps. A place where you
can buy tits!"

She looked down between them, then back at my face.

"Looks like it was a good investment," she said.

"They do seem to work okay," I had to admit.

We agreed that she would spend the nights at my house.
There were certain things she had to do at Kluge's, involving
equipment that had to be physically loaded, but many things
she could do with a remote terminal and an armload of
software. So we selected one of Kluge's best computers and
about a dozen peripherals and installed her at a cafeteria table
in my bedroom.

I guess we both knew it wasn't much protection if the
people who got Kluge decided to get her. But I know I felt
better about it, and I think she did, too.

The second day she was there a delivery van pulled up
outside, and two guys started unloading a king-size waterbed.
She laughed and laughed when she saw my face.

"Listen, you're not using Kluge's computers to—"

"Relax, Yank. How'd you think I could afford a Ferrari?"

"I've been curious."

"If you're really good at writing software you can make a lot of money. I own my own company. But every hacker picks up tricks here and there. I used to run a few Kluge scams, myself."

"But not anymore?"

She shrugged. "Once a thief, always a thief, Victor. I told you I couldn't make ends meet selling my bod."

Lisa didn't need much sleep.

We got up at seven, and I made breakfast every morning. Then we would spend an hour or two working in the garden. She would go to Kluge's and I'd bring her a sandwich at noon, then drop in on her several times during the day. That was for my own peace of mind; I never stayed more than a minute. Sometime during the afternoon I would shop or do household chores, then at seven one of us would cook dinner. We alternated. I taught her "American" cooking, and she taught me a little of everything. She complained about the lack of vital ingredients in American markets. No dogs, of course, but she claimed to know great ways of preparing monkey, snake, and rat. I never knew how hard she was pulling my leg, and didn't ask.

After dinner she stayed at my house. We would talk, make love, bathe.

She loved my tub. It is about the only alteration I have made in the house, and my only real luxury. I put it in—having to expand the bathroom to do so—in 1975, and never regretted it. We would soak for twenty minutes or an hour, turning the jets and bubblers on and off, washing each other, giggling like kids. Once we used bubble bath and made a mountain of suds four feet high, then destroyed it, splashing water all over the place. Most nights she let me wash her long black hair.

She didn't have any bad habits—or at least none that clashed with mine. She was neat and clean, changing her clothes twice a day and never so much as leaving a dirty glass on the sink. She never left a mess in the bathroom. Two glasses of wine was her limit.

I felt like Lazarus.

•   •   •

Osborne came by three times in the next two weeks. Lisa met him at Kluge's and gave him what she had learned. It was getting to be quite a list.

"Kluge once had an account in a New York bank with nine *trillion* dollars in it," she told me after one of Osborne's visits. "I think he did it just to see if he could. He left it in for one day, took the interest and fed it to a bank in the Bahamas, then destroyed the principal. Which never existed anyway."

In return, Osborne told her what was new on the murder investigation—which was nothing—and on the status of Kluge's property, which was chaotic. Various agencies had sent people out to look the place over. Some FBI men came, wanting to take over the investigation. Lisa, when talking about computers, had the power to cloud men's minds. She did it first by explaining exactly what she was doing, in terms so abstruse that no one could understand her. Sometimes that was enough. If it wasn't, if they started to get tough, she just moved out of the driver's seat and let them try to handle Kluge's contraption. She let them watch in horror as dragons leaped out of nowhere and ate up all the data on a disc, then printed "You Stupid Putz!" on the screen.

"I'm cheating them," she confessed to me. "I'm giving them stuff I *know* they're gonna step in, because I already stepped in it myself. I've lost about forty percent of the data Kluge had stored away. But the others lose a hundred percent. You ought to see their faces when Kluge drops a logic bomb into their work. That second guy threw a three thousand dollar printer clear across the room. Then tried to bribe me to be quiet about it."

When some Federal agency sent out an expert from Stanford, and he seemed perfectly content to destroy everything in sight in the firm belief that he was *bound* to get it right sooner or later, Lisa let him get tangled up in the Internal Revenue Service's computer. He couldn't get out, because some sort of watchdog program noticed him. During his struggles, it seemed he had erased all the tax records from the letter S down into the W's. Lisa let him think that for half an hour.

"I thought he was having a heart attack," she told me. "All the blood drained out of his face and he couldn't talk. So I showed him where I had—with my usual foresight—arranged for that data to be recorded, told him how to put it back where he found it, and how to pacify the watchdog. He couldn't get out of that house fast enough. Pretty soon he's gonna realize you *can't* destroy that much information with anything short of dynamite because of the backups and the limits of how much can be running at any one time. But I don't think he'll be back.''

"It sounds like a very fancy video game," I said.

."It is, in a way. But it's more like Dungeons and Dragons. It's an endless series of closed rooms with dangers on the other side. You don't dare take it a step at a time. You take it a *hundredth* of a step at a time. Your questions are like, 'Now this isn't a question, but if it entered my mind to *ask* this question—which I'm not about to do—concerning what might happen if I looked at this door here—and I'm not touching it, I'm not even in the next room—what do you suppose you might do?' And the program crunches on that, decides if you fulfilled the conditions for getting a great big cream pie in the face, then either throws it or allows as how it *might* just move from step A to step A Prime. Then you say, 'Well, maybe I *am* looking at that door.' And sometimes the program says 'You looked, you looked, you dirty crook!' And the fireworks start.''

Silly as all that sounds, it was very close to the best explanation she was ever able to give me about what she was doing.

"Are you telling him everything, Lisa?" I asked her.

"Well, not *every*thing. I didn't mention the four cents."

Four cents? Oh my god.

"Lisa, I didn't want that, I didn't ask for it, I wish he'd never—"

"Calm down, Yank. It's going to be all right."

"He kept records of all that, didn't he?"

"That's what I spend most of my time doing. Decoding his records.''

"How long have you known?"

"About the seven hundred thousand dollars? It was in the first disc I cracked.''

"I just want to give it back."

She thought that over, and shook her head.

"Victor, it'd be more dangerous to get rid of it now than it would be to keep it. It was imaginary money at first. But now it's got a history. The IRS thinks it knows where it came from. The taxes are paid on it. The State of Delaware is convinced that a legally chartered corporation disbursed it.

An Illinois law firm has been paid for handling it. Your bank had been paying you interest on it. I'm not saying it would be impossible to go back and wipe all that out, but I wouldn't like to try. I'm good, but I don't have Kluge's touch.''

"How could he *do* all that? You say it was imaginary money. That's not the way I thought money worked. He could just pull it out of thin air?''

Lisa patted the top of her computer console, and smiled at me.

"This is money, Yank,'' she said, and her eyes glittered.

At night she worked by candlelight so she wouldn't disturb me. That turned out to be my downfall. She typed by touch, and needed the candle only to locate software.

So that's how I'd go to sleep every night, looking at her slender body bathed in the glow of the candle. I was always reminded of melting butter dripping down a roasted ear of corn. Golden light on golden skin.

Ugly, she called herself. Skinny. It was true she was thin. I could see her ribs when she sat with her back impossibly straight, her tummy sucked in, her chin up. She worked in the nude these days, sitting in lotus position. For long periods she would not move, her hand lying on her thighs, then she would poise, as if to pound the keys. But her touch was light, almost silent. It looked more like yoga than programming. She said she went into a meditative state for her best work.

I had expected a bony angularity, all sharp elbows and knees. She wasn't like that. I had guessed her weight ten pounds too low, and still didn't know where she put it. But she was soft and rounded, and strong beneath.

No one was ever going to call her face glamorous. Few would even go so far as to call her pretty. The braces did that, I think. They caught the eye and held it, drawing attention to that unsightly jumble.

But her skin was wonderful. She had scars. Not as many as I had expected. She seemed to heal quickly, and well.

I thought she was beautiful.

I had just completed my nightly survey when my eye was caught by the candle. I looked at it, then tried to look away.

Candles do that sometimes. I don't know why. In still air, with the flame perfectly vertical, they begin to flicker. The flame leaps up then squats down, up and down, up and down, brighter and brighter in regular rhythm, two or three beats to the second—

—and I tried to call out to her, wishing the candle would stop its flickering, but already I couldn't speak—

—I could only gasp, and I tried once more, as hard as I could, to yell, to scream, to tell her not to worry, and felt the nausea building . . .

I tasted blood. I took an experimental breath, did not find the smells of vomit, urine, feces. The overhead lights were on.

Lisa was on her hands and knees leaning over me, her face very close. A tear dropped on my forehead. I was on the carpet, on my back.

"Victor, can you hear me?"

I nodded. There was a spoon in my mouth. I spit it out.

"What happened? Are you going to be all right?"

I nodded again, and struggled to speak.

"You just lie there. The ambulance is on its way."

"No. Don't need it."

"Well, it's on its way. You just take it easy and—"

"Help me up."

"Not yet. You're not ready."

She was right. I tried to sit up, and fell back quickly. I took deep breaths for a while. Then the doorbell rang.

She stood up and started to the door. I just managed to get my hand around her ankle. Then she was leaning over me again, her eyes as wide as they would go.

"What is it? What's wrong now?"

"Get some clothes on," I told her. She looked down at herself, surprised.

"Oh. Right."

She got rid of the ambulance crew. Lisa was a lot calmer after she made coffee and we were sitting at the kitchen table. It was one o'clock, and I was still pretty rocky. But it hadn't been a bad one.

I went to the bathroom and got the bottle of Dilantin I'd hidden when she moved in. I let her see me take one.

"I forgot to do this today," I told her.

"It's because you hid them. That was stupid."

"I know." There must have been something else I could have said. It didn't please me to see her look hurt. But she was hurt because I wasn't defending myself against her attack, and that was a bit too complicated for me to dope out just after a grand mal.

"You can move out if you want to," I said. I was in rare form.

So was she. She reached across the table and shook me by the shoulders. She glared at me.

"I won't take a lot more of that kind of shit," she said, and I nodded, and began to cry.

She let me do it. I think that was probably best. She could have babied me, but I do a pretty good job of that myself.

"How long has this been going on?" she finally said. "Is that why you've stayed in your house for thirty years?"

I shrugged. "I guess it's part of it. When I got back they operated, but it just made it worse."

"Okay. I'm mad at you because you didn't tell me about it, so I didn't know what to do. I want to stay, but you'll have to tell me how. Then I won't be mad anymore."

I could have blown the whole thing right there. I'm amazed I didn't. Through the years I've developed very good methods for doing things like that. But I pulled through when I saw her face. She really did want to stay. I didn't know why, but it was enough.

"The spoon was a mistake," I said. "If there's time, and you can do it without risking your fingers, you could jam a piece of cloth in there. Part of a sheet, or something. But nothing hard." I explored my mouth with a finger. "I think I broke a tooth."

"Serves you right," she said. I looked at her, and smiled, then we were both laughing. She came around the table and kissed me, then sat on my knee.

"The biggest danger is drowning. During the first part of the seizure, all my muscles go rigid. That doesn't last long. Then they all start contracting and relaxing at random. It's *very* strong."

"I know. I watched, and I tried to hold you."

"Don't do that. Get me on my side. Stay behind me, and watch out for flailing arms. Get a pillow under my head if you can. Keep me away from things I could injure myself on." I looked her square in the eye. "I want to emphasize this. Just *try* to do all those things. If I'm getting too violent, it's better you stand off to the side. Better for both of us. If I knock you out, you won't be able to help me if I start strangling on vomit."

I kept looking at her eyes. She must have read my mind, because she smiled slightly.

"Sorry, Yank. I am not freaked out. I mean, like, it's totally gross, you know, and it barfs me out to the max, you could—"

"—gag me with a spoon, I know. Okay, right, I know I was dumb. And that's about it. I might bite my tongue or the inside of my cheek. Don't worry about it. There is one more thing."

She waited, and I wondered how much to tell her. There wasn't a lot she could do, but if I died on her I didn't want her to feel it was her fault.

"Sometimes I have to go to the hospital. Sometimes one seizure will follow another. If that keeps up for too long, I won't breathe, and my brain will die of oxygen starvation."

"That only takes about five minutes," she said, alarmed.

"I know. It's only a problem if I start having them frequently, so we could plan for it if I do. But if I don't come out of one, start having another right on the heels of the first, or if you can't detect any breathing for three or four minutes, you'd better call an ambulance."

"Three or four minutes? You'd be dead before they got here."

"It's that or live in a hospital. I don't like hospitals."

"Neither do I."

The next day she took me for a ride in her Ferrari. I was nervous about it, wondering if she was going to do crazy things. If anything, she was too slow. People behind her kept honking. I could tell she hadn't been driving long from the exaggerated attention she put into every movement.

"A Ferrari is wasted on me, I'm afraid," she confessed at one point. "I never drive it faster than fifty-five."

We went to an interior decorator in Beverly Hills and she bought a low-watt gooseneck lamp at an outrageous price.

I had a hard time getting to sleep that night. I suppose I was afraid of having another seizure, though Lisa's new lamp wasn't going to set it off.

Funny about seizures. When I first started having them, everyone called them fits. Then, gradually, it was seizures, until fits began to sound dirty.

I guess it's a sign of growing old, when the language changes on you.

There were rafts of new words. A lot of them were for things that didn't even exist when I was growing up. Like software. I always visualized a limp wrench.

"What got you interested in computers, Lisa?" I asked her.

She didn't move. Her concentration when sitting at the machine was pretty damn good. I rolled onto my back and tried to sleep.

"It's where the power is, Yank." I looked up. She had turned to face me.

"Did you pick it all up since you got to America?"

"I had a head start. I didn't tell you about my Captain, did I?"

"I don't think you did."

"He was strange. I knew that. I was about fourteen. He was an American, and he took an interest in me. He got me a nice apartment in Saigon. And he put me in school."

She was studying me, looking for a reaction. I didn't give her one.

"He was surely a pedophile, and probably had homosexual tendencies, since I looked so much like a skinny little boy."

Again the wait. This time she smiled.

"He was good to me. I learned to read well. From there on, anything is possible."

"I didn't actually ask you about your Captain. I asked why you got interested in computers."

"That's right. You did."

"Is it just a living?"

"It started that way. It's the future, Victor."

"God knows I've read that enough times."

"It's true. It's already here. It's power, if you know how to use it. You've seen what Kluge was able to do. You can make money with one of these things. I don't mean earn it, I mean *make* it, like if you had a printing press. Remember Osborne mentioned that Kluge's house didn't exist? Did you think what that means?"

"That he wiped it out of the memory banks."

"That was the first step. But the lot exists in the county plat books, wouldn't you think? I mean, this country hasn't *entirely* given up paper."

"So the county really does have a record of the house."

"No. That page was torn out of the records."

"I don't get it. Kluge never left the house."

"Oldest way in the world, friend. Kluge looked through the L.A.P.D. files until he found a guy known as Sammy. He sent him a cashier's check for a thousand dollars, along with a letter saying he could earn twice that if he'd go to the hall of records and do something. Sammy didn't bite, and neither did McGee, or Molly Unger. But Little Billy Phipps did, and he got a check just like the letter said, and he and Kluge had a wonderful business relationship for many years. Little Billy drives a new Cadillac now, and hasn't the faintest notion who Kluge was or where he lived. It didn't matter to Kluge how much he spent. He just pulled it out of thin air."

I thought that over for a while. I guess it's true that with enough money you can do just about anything, and Kluge had all the money in the world.

"Did you tell Osborne about Little Billy?"

"I erased that disc, just like I erased your seven hundred thousand. You never know when you might need somebody like Little Billy."

"You're not afraid of getting into trouble over it?"

"Life is risk, Victor. I'm keeping the best stuff for myself. Not because I intend to use it, but because if I ever needed it badly and didn't have it, I'd feel like such a fool."

She cocked her head and narrowed her eyes, which made them practically disappear.

"Tell me something, Yank. Kluge picked you out of all your neighbors because you'd been a boy scout for thirty years. How do you react to what I'm doing?"

"You're cheerfully amoral, and you're a survivor, and you're basically decent. And I pity anybody who gets in your way."

She grinned, stretched, and stood up.

" 'Cheerfully amoral.' I like that." She sat beside me, making a great sloshing in the bed. "You want to be amoral again?"

"In a little bit." She started rubbing my chest. "So you got into computers because they were the wave of the future. Don't you ever worry about them . . . I don't know, I guess it sounds corny . . . do you think they'll take over?"

"Everybody thinks that until they start to use them," she said. "You've got to realize just how stupid they are. Without programming they are good for nothing, literally. Now, what I do believe is that the people who *run* the computers will take over. They already have. That's why I study them.''

"I guess that's not what I meant. Maybe I can't say it right.''

She frowned. "Kluge was looking into something. He'd been eavesdropping in artificial intelligence labs, and reading a lot of neurological research. I think he was trying to find a common thread.''

"Between human brains and computers?''

"Not quite. He was thinking of computers and neurons. Brain cells." She pointed to her computer. "That thing, or any other computer, is light-years away from being a human brain. It can't generalize, or infer, or categorize, or invent. With good programming it can appear to do some of those things, but it's an illusion.

"There's an old speculation about what would happen if we finally built a computer with as many transistors as the brain has neurons. Would there be self-awareness? I think that's baloney. A transistor isn't a neuron, and a quintillion of them aren't any better than a dozen.

"So Kluge—who seems to have felt the same way—started looking into the possible similarities between a neuron and a 16-bit computer. That's why he had all that consumer junk sitting around his house, those Trash-80's and Atari's and TI's and Sinclair's, for chrissake. He was used to *much* more powerful instruments. He ate up the home units like candy.''

"What did he find out?''

"Nothing, it looks like. A 16-bit unit is more complex than a neuron, and no computer is in the same galaxy as an organic brain. But see, the words get tricky. I said an Atari is more complex than a neuron, but it's hard to really compare them. It's like comparing a direction with a distance, or a color with a mass. The units are different. Except for one similarity.''

"What's that?''

"The connections. Again, it's different, but the concept of networking is the same. A neuron is connected to a lot of others. There are trillions of them, and the way messages pulse through them determine what we are and what we think and what we remember. And with that computer I can reach a million others. It's bigger than the human brain, really, because the information in that network is more than all humanity could cope with in a million years. It reaches from Pioneer

Ten, out beyond the orbit of Pluto, right into every living room that has a telephone in it. With that computer you can tap tons of data that has been collected but nobody's even had the time to look at.

"That's what Kluge was interested in. The old 'critical mass computer' idea, the computer that becomes aware, but with a new angle. Maybe it wouldn't be the size of the computer, but the *number* of computers. There used to be thousands of them. Now there's millions. They're putting them in cars. In wristwatches. Every home has several, from the simple timer on a microwave oven up to a video game or home terminal. Kluge was trying to find out if critical mass could be reached that way."

"What did he think?"

"I don't know. He was just getting started." She glanced down at me. "But you know what, Yank? I think you've reached critical mass while I wasn't looking."

"I think you're right." I reached for her.

Lisa liked to cuddle. I didn't, at first, after fifty years of sleeping alone. But I got to like it pretty quickly.

That's what we were doing when we resumed the conversation we had been having. We just lay in each other's arms and talked about things. Nobody had mentioned love yet, but I knew I loved her. I didn't know what to do about it, but I would think of something.

"Critical mass," I said. She nuzzled my neck, and yawned.

"What about it?"

"What would it be like? It seems like it would be such a vast intelligence. So quick, so omniscient. God-like."

"Could be."

"Wouldn't it . . . run our lives? I guess I'm asking the same questions I started off with. Would it take over?"

She thought about it for a long time.

"I wonder if there would be anything to take over. I mean, why should it care? How could we figure what its concerns would be? Would it want to be worshipped, for instance? I doubt it. Would it want to 'rationalize all human behavior, to eliminate all emotion,' as I'm sure some sci-fi film computer must have told some damsel in distress in the fifties.

"You can use a word like awareness, but what does it mean? An amoeba must be aware. Plants probably are. There may be a level of awareness in a neuron. Even in an intergrated circuit chip. We don't even know what our own awareness really is. We've never been able to shine a light on it, dissect it, figure out where it comes from or where it goes when we're dead. To apply human values to a thing like this hypothetical computer-net consciousness would be pretty stupid. But I don't see how it could interact with human awareness at all. It might not even notice us, any more than we notice cells in our bodies, or neutrinos passing through us, or the vibrations of the atoms in the air around us.''

So she had to explain what a neutrino was. One thing I always provided her with was an ignorant audience. And after that, I pretty much forgot about our mythical hyper-computer.

''What about your Captain?'' I asked, much later.

''Do you really want to know, Yank?'' she mumbled sleepily.

''I'm not afraid to know.''

She sat up and reached for her cigarettes. I had come to know she sometimes smoked them in times of stress. She had told me she smoked after making love, but that first time had been the only time. The lighter flared in the dark. I heard her exhale.

''My Major, actually. He got a promotion. Do you want to know his name?''

''Lisa, I don't want to know any of it if you don't want to tell it. But if you do, what I want to know is did he stand by you?''

''He didn't marry me, if that's what you mean. When he knew he had to go, he said he would, but I talked him out of it. Maybe it was the most noble thing I ever did. Maybe it was the most stupid.

''It's no accident I look Japanese. My grandmother was raped in '42 by a Jap soldier of the occupation. She was Chinese, living in Hanoi. My mother was born there. They went south after Dien Bien Phu. My grandmother died. My mother had it hard. Being Chinese was tough enough, but being half Chinese and half Japanese was worse. My father was half French and half Annamese. Another bad combination. I never knew him. But I'm sort of a capsule history of Vietnam.''

The end of her cigarette glowed brighter once more.

''I've got one grandfather's face and the other grandfather's height. With tits by Goodyear. About all I missed was some American genes, but I was working on that for my children.

"When Saigon was falling I tried to get to the American Embassy. Didn't make it. You know the rest, until I got to Thailand, and when I finally got Americans to notice me, it turned out my Major was still looking for me. He sponsored me over here, and I made it in time to watch him die of cancer. Two months I had with him, all of it in the hospital."

"My god." I had a horrible thought. "That wasn't the war, too, was it? I mean, the story of your life—"

"—is the rape of Asia. No, Victor. Not that war, anyway. But he was one of those guys who got to see atom bombs up close, out in Nevada. He was too Regular Army to complain about it, but I think he knew that's what killed him."

"Did you love him?"

"What do you want me to say? He got me out of hell."

Again the cigarette flared, and I saw her stub it out.

"No," she said. "I didn't love him. He knew that. I've never loved anybody. He was very dear, very special to me. I would have done almost anything for him. He was fatherly to me." I felt her looking at me in the dark. "Aren't you going to ask how old he was?"

"Fiftyish," I said.

"On the nose. Can I ask you something?"

"I guess it's your turn."

"How many girls have you had since you got back from Korea?"

I held up my hand and pretended to count on my fingers.

"One," I said, at last.

"How many before you went?"

"One. We broke up before I left for the war."

"How many in Korea?"

"Nine. All at Madame Park's jolly little whorehouse in Pusan."

"So you've made love to one white and ten Asians. I bet none of the others were as tall as me."

"Korean girls have fatter cheeks too. But they all had your eyes."

She nuzzled against my chest, took a deep breath, and sighed.

"We're a hell of a pair, aren't we?"

I hugged her, and her breath came again, hot on my chest.

I wondered how I'd lived so long without such a simple miracle as that.

"Yes. I think we really are."

Osborne came by again about a week later. He seemed subdued. He listened to the things Lisa had decided to give him without much interest. He took the printout she handed him, and promised to turn it over to the departments that handled those things. But he didn't get up to leave.

"I thought I ought to tell you, Apfel," he said, at last. "The Gavin case has been closed."

I had to think a moment to remember Kluge's real name had been Gavin.

"The coroner ruled suicide a long time ago. I was able to keep the case open quite a while on the strength of my suspicions." He nodded toward Lisa. "And on what she said about the suicide note. But there was just no evidence at all."

"It probably happened quickly," Lisa said. "Somebody caught him, tracked him back—it can be done; Kluge was lucky for a long time—and did him the same day."

"You don't think it was suicide?" I asked Osborne.

"No. But whoever did it is home free unless something new turns up."

"I'll tell you if it does," Lisa said.

"That's something else," Osborne said. "I can't authorize you to work over there anymore. The county's taken possession of house and contents."

"Don't worry about it," Lisa said, softly.

There was a short silence as she leaned over to shake a cigarette from the pack on the coffee table. She lit it, exhaled, and leaned back beside me, giving Osborne her most inscrutable look. He sighed.

"I'd hate to play poker with you, lady," he said. "What do you mean, 'Don't worry about it'?"

"I bought the house four days ago. And its contents. If anything turns up that would help you re-open the murder investigation, I will let you know."

Osborne was too defeated to get angry. He studied her quietly for a while.

"I'd like to know how you swung that."

"I did nothing illegal. You're free to check it out. I paid good cash money for it. The house came onto the market. I got a good price at the Sheriff's sale."

"How'd you like it if I put my best men on the transaction? See if they can dig up some funny money? Maybe fraud. How about I get the F.B.I. in to look it all over?"

She gave him a cool look.

"You're welcome to. Frankly, Detective Osborne, I could have stolen that house, Griffith Park, and the Harbor Freeway and I don't think you could have caught me."

"So where does that leave me?"

"Just where you were. With a closed case, and a promise from me."

"I don't like you having all that stuff, if it can do the things you say it can do."

"I didn't expect you would. But that's not your department, is it? The county owned it for a while, through simple confiscation. They didn't know what they had, and they let it go."

"Maybe I can get the Fraud detail out here to confiscate your software. There's criminal evidence on it."

"You could try that," she agreed.

They stared at each other for a while. Lisa won. Osborne rubbed his eyes and nodded. Then he heaved himself to his feet and slumped to the door.

Lisa stubbed out her cigarette. We listened to him going down the walk.

"I'm surprised he gave up so easy," I said. "Or did he? Do you think he'll try a raid?"

"It's not likely. He knows the score."

"Maybe you could tell it to me."

"For one thing, it's not his department, and he knows it."

"Why did you buy the house?"

"You ought to ask *how*."

I looked at her closely. There was a gleam of amusement behind the poker face.

"Lisa. What did you do?"

"That's what Osborne asked himself. He got the right answer, because he understands Kluge's machines. And he knows how things get done. It was no accident that house going on the market, and no accident I was the only bidder. I used one of Kluge's pet councilmen."

"You bribed him?"

She laughed, and kissed me.

"I think I finally managed to shock you, Yank. That's gotta be the biggest difference between me and a native-born

American. Average citizens don't spend much on bribes over here. In Saigon, everybody bribes.''

"Did you bribe him?''

"Nothing so indelicate. One has to go in the back door over here. Several entirely legal campaign contributions appeared in the accounts of a State Senator, who mentioned a certain situation to someone, who happened to be in the position to do legally what I happened to want done.'' She looked at me askance. "Of *course* I bribed him, Victor. You'd be amazed to know how cheaply. Does that bother you?''

"Yes,'' I admitted. "I don't like bribery.''

"I'm indifferent to it. It happens, like gravity. It may not be admirable, but it gets things done.''

"I assume you covered yourself.''

"Reasonably well. You're never entirely covered with a bribe, because of the human element. The councilman might geek if they got him in front of a grand jury. But they won't, because Osborne won't pursue it. That's the second reason he walked out of here without a fight. *He* knows how the world wobbles, he knows what kind of force I now possess, and he knows he can't fight it.''

There was a long silence after that. I had a lot to think about, and I didn't feel good about most of it. At one point Lisa reached for the pack of cigarettes, then changed her mind. She waited for me to work it out.

"It is a terrific force, isn't it,'' I finally said.

"It's frightening,'' she agreed. "Don't think it doesn't scare me. Don't think I haven't had fantasies of being superwoman. Power is an awful temptation, and it's not easy to reject. There's so much I could do.''

"Will you?''

"I'm not talking about stealing things, or getting rich.''

"I didn't think you were.''

"This is political power. But I don't know how to wield it . . . it sounds corny, but to use it for good. I've seen so much evil come from good intentions. I don't think I'm wise enough to do any good. And the chances of getting torn up like Kluge did are large. But I'm not wise enough to walk away from it. I'm still a street urchin from Saigon, Yank. I'm smart enough not to use it unless I have to. But I can't give it away, and I can't destroy it. Is that stupid?''

I didn't have a good answer for that one. But I had a bad feeling.

My doubts had another week to work on me. I didn't come to any great moral conclusions. Lisa knew of some crimes, and she wasn't reporting them to the authorities. That didn't bother me much. She had at her fingertips the means to commit more crimes, and that bothered me a lot. Yet I really didn't think she planned to do anything. She was smart enough to use the things she had only in a defensive way—but with Lisa that could cover a lot of ground.

When she didn't show up for dinner one evening, I went over to Kluge's and found her busy in the living room. A nine-foot section of shelving had been cleared. The discs and tapes were stacked on a table. She had a big plastic garbage can and a magnet the size of a softball. I watched her wave a tape near the magnet, then toss it in the garbage can, which was almost full. She glanced up, did the same operation with a handful of discs, then took off her glasses and wiped her eyes.

"Feel any better now, Victor?" she asked.

"What do you mean? I feel fine."

"No you don't. And I haven't felt right, either. It hurts me to do it, but I have to. You want to go get the other trash can?"

I did, and helped her pull more software from the shelves.

"You're not going to wipe it all, are you?"

"No. I'm wiping records, and . . . something else."

"Are you going to tell me what?"

"There are things it's better not to know," she said, darkly.

I finally managed to convince her to talk over dinner. She had said little, just eating and shaking her head. But she gave in.

"Rather dreary, actually," she said. "I've been probing around some delicate places the last couple days. These are places Kluge visited at will, but they scare the hell out of me. Dirty places. Places where they know things I thought I'd like to find out."

She shivered, and seemed reluctant to go on.

"Are you talking about military computers? The C.I.A.?"

"The C.I.A. is where it starts. It's the easiest. I've looked around at NORAD—that's the guys who get to fight the next war. It makes me shiver to see how easy Kluge got in there. He cobbled up a way to start World War Three, just as an exercise. That's one of the things we just erased. The last two days I was nibbling around the edges of the big boys. The Defense Intelligence Agency and the National Security . . . something. DIA and NSA. Each of them is bigger than the CIA. Something knew I was there. Some watchdog program. As soon as I realized that I got out quick, and I've spent the last five hours being sure it didn't follow me. And now I'm sure, and I've destroyed all that, too.''

"You think they're the one who killed Kluge?"

"They're surely the best candidates. He had tons of their stuff. I know he helped design the biggest installations at NSA, and he'd been poking around in there for years. One false step is all it would take.''

"Did you get it all? I mean are you sure?"

"I'm sure they didn't track me. I'm not sure I've destroyed all the records. I'm going back now to take a last look.''

"I'll go with you.''

We worked until well after midnight. Lisa would review a tape or a disc, and if she was in any doubt, toss it to me for the magnetic treatment. At one point, simply because she was unsure, she took the magnet and passed it in front of an entire shelf of software.

It was amazing to think about it. With that one wipe she had randomized billions of bits of information. Some of it might not exist anywhere else in the world. I found myself confronted by even harder questions. Did she have the right to do it? Didn't knowledge exist for everyone? But I confess I had little trouble quelling my protests. Mostly I was happy to see it go. The old reactionary in me found it easier to believe There Are Things We Are Not Meant To Know.

We were almost through when her monitor screen began to malfunction. It actually gave off a few hisses and pops, so Lisa stood back from it for a moment, then the screen started to flicker. I stared at it for a while. It seemed to me there was an image trying to form in the screen. Something three-dimensional. Just as I was starting to get a picture of it I happened to glance at Lisa, and she was looking at me. Her face was flickering. She came to me and put her hands over my eyes.

"Victor, you shouldn't look at that.''

"It's okay," I told her. And when I said it, it was, but as soon as I had the words out I knew it wasn't. And that is the last thing I remembered for a long time.

I'm told it was a very bad two weeks. I remember very little of it. I was kept under high dosages of drugs, and my few lucid periods were always followed by a fresh seizure.

The first thing I recall clearly was looking up at Doctor Stuart's face. I was in a hospital bed. I later learned it was in Cedars-Sinai, not the Veteran's Hospital. Lisa had paid for a private room.

Stuart put me through the usual questions. I was able to answer them, though I was very tired. When he was satisfied as to my condition he finally began to answer some of my questions. I learned how long I had been there, and how it had happened.

"You went into consecutive seizures," he confirmed. "I don't know why, frankly. You haven't been prone to them for a decade. I was thinking you were well under control. But nothing is ever really stable, I guess."

"So Lisa got me here in time."

"She did more than that. She didn't want to level with me at first. It seems that after the first seizure she witnessed she read everything she could find. From that day, she had a syringe and a solution of Valium handy. When she saw you couldn't breathe she injected you, and there's no doubt it saved your life."

Stuart and I had known each other a long time. He knew I had no prescription for Valium, though we had talked about it the last time I was hospitalized. Since I lived alone, there would be no one to inject me if I got in trouble.

He was more interested in results than anything else, and what Lisa did had the desired result. I was still alive.

He wouldn't let me have any visitors that day. I protested, but soon was asleep. The next day she came. She wore a new T-shirt. This one had a picture of a robot wearing a gown and mortarboard, and said "Class of 11111000000." It turns out that was 1984 in binary notation.

She had a big smile and said "Hi, Yank!" and as she sat on the bed I started to shake. She looked alarmed and asked if she should call the doctor.

"It's not that," I managed to say. "I'd like it if you just held me."

She took off her shoes and got under the covers with me. She held me tightly. At some point a nurse came in and tried to shoo her out. Lisa gave her profanities in Vietnamese, Chinese, and few startling ones in English, and the nurse left. I saw Doctor Stuart glance in later.

I felt much better when I finally stopped crying. Lisa's eyes were wet, too.

"I've been here every day," she said. "You look awful, Victor."

"I feel a lot better."

"Well, you look better than you did. But your doctor says you'd better stick around another couple of days, just to make sure."

"I think he's right."

"I'm planning a big dinner for when you get back. You think we should invite the neighbors?"

I didn't say anything for a while. There were so many things we hadn't faced. Just how long could it go on between us? How long before I got sour about being so useless? How long before she got tired of being with an old man? I don't know just when I had started to think of Lisa as a permanent part of my life. And I wondered how I could have thought that.

"Do you want to spend more years waiting in hospitals for a man to die?"

"What do you want, Victor? I'll marry you if you want me to. Or I'll live with you in sin. I prefer sin, myself, but if it'll make you happy—"

"I don't know why you want to saddle yourself with an epileptic old fart."

"Because I love you."

It was the first time she had said it. I could have gone on questioning—bringing up her Major again, for instance—but I had no urge to. I'm very glad I didn't. So I changed the subject.

"Did you get the job finished?"

She knew which job I was talking about. She lowered her voice and put her mouth close to my ear.

"Let's don't be specific about it here, Victor. I don't trust any place I haven't swept for bugs. But, to put your mind at ease, I did finish, and it's been a quiet couple of weeks. No one is any wiser, and I'll never meddle in things like that again.''

I felt a lot better. I was also exhausted. I tried to conceal my yawns, but she sensed it was time to go. She gave me one more kiss, promising many more to come, and left me.

It was the last time I ever saw her.

At about ten o'clock that evening Lisa went into Kluge's kitchen with a screwdriver and some other tools and got to work on the microwave oven.

The manufacturers of those appliances are very careful to insure they can't be turned on with the door open, as they emit lethal radiation. But with simple tools and a good brain it is possible to circumvent the safety interlocks. Lisa had no trouble with them. About ten minutes after she entered the kitchen she put her head in the oven and turned it on.

It is impossible to say how long she held her head in there. It was long enough to turn her eyeballs to the consistency of boiled eggs. At some point she lost voluntary muscle control and fell to the floor, pulling the microwave down with her. It shorted out, and a fire started.

The fire set off the sophisticated burglar alarm she had installed a month before. Betty Lanier saw the flames and called the fire department as Hal ran across the street and into the burning kitchen. He dragged what was left of Lisa out onto the grass. When he saw what the fire had done to her upper body, and in particular her breasts, he threw up.

She was rushed to the hospital. The doctors there amputated one arm and cut away the frightful masses of vulcanized silicone, pulled all her teeth, and didn't know what to do about the eyes. They put her on a respirator.

It was an orderly who first noticed the blackened and bloody T-shirt they had cut from her. Some of the message was unreadable, but it began, ''I can't go on this way any-more . . .''

There is no other way I could have told all that. I discovered it piecemeal, starting with the disturbed look on Doctor Stuart's face when Lisa didn't show up the next day. He wouldn't tell me anything, and I had another seizure shortly after.

The next week is a blur. Betty was very good to me. They gave me a tranquilizer called Tranxene, and it was even better. I ate them like candy. I wandered in a drugged haze, eating only when Betty insisted, sleeping sitting up in my chair, coming awake not knowing where or who I was. I returned to the prison camp many times. Once I recall helping Lisa stack severed heads.

When I saw myself in the mirror, there was a vague smile on my face. It was Tranxene, caressing my frontal lobes. I knew that if I was to live much longer, me and Tranxene would have to become very good friends.

I eventually became capable of something that passed for rational thought. I was helped along somewhat by a visit from Osborne. I was trying, at that time, to find reasons to live, and wondered if he had any.

"I'm very sorry," he started off. I said nothing. "This is on my own time," he went on. "The department doesn't know I'm here."

"Was it suicide?" I asked him.

"I brought along a copy of the . . . the note. She ordered it from a shirt company in Westwood, three days before the . . . accident."

He handed it to me, and I read it. I was mentioned, though not by name. I was "the man I love." She said she couldn't cope with my problems. It was a short note. You can't get too much on a T-shirt. I read it through five times, then handed it back to him.

"She told you Kluge didn't write his note. I tell you she didn't write this."

He nodded reluctantly. I felt a vast calm, with a howling nightmare just below it. Praise Tranxene.

"Can you back that up?"

"She saw me in the hospital shortly before the . . . accident. She was full of life and hope. You say she ordered the shirt three days before. I would have felt that. And that note is pathetic. Lisa was never pathetic."

He nodded again.

"Some things I want to tell you. There were no signs of a struggle. Mrs. Lanier is sure no one came in the front. The crime lab went over the whole place and we're sure no one was in there with her. I'd stake my life on the fact that no one entered or left that house. Now, *I* don't believe it was suicide, either, but do you have any suggestions?"

"The NSA," I said.

I explained about the last things she had done while I was still there. I told him of her fear of the government spy agencies. That was all I had.

"Well, I guess they're the ones who could do a thing like that, if anyone could. But I'll tell you, I have a hard time swallowing it. I don't know why, for one thing. Maybe you believe those people kill like you and I'd swat a fly." His look made it into a question.

"I don't know what I believe."

"I'm not saying they wouldn't kill for national security, or some such shit. But they'd have taken the computers, too. They wouldn't have left her alone, they wouldn't even have let her *near* that stuff after they killed Kluge."

"What you're saying makes sense."

He muttered on about it for quite some time. Eventually I offered him some wine. He accepted thankfully. I considered joining him—it would be a quick way to die—but did not. He drank the whole bottle, and was comfortably drunk when he suggested we go next door and look it over one more time. I was planning an visiting Lisa the next day, and knew I had to start somewhere building myself up for that, so I agreed to go with him.

We inspected the kitchen. The fire had blackened the counters and melted some linoleum, but not much else. Water had made a mess of the place. There was a brown stain on the floor which I was able to look at with no emotion.

So we went back to the living room, and one of the computers was turned on. There was a short message on the screen.

IF YOU WISH TO KNOW MORE

PRESS ENTER ▪

"Don't do it," I told him. But he did. He stood, blinking solemnly, as the words wiped themselves out and a new message appeared.

YOU LOOKED

The screen started to flicker and I was in my car, in darkness, with a pill in my mouth and another in my hand. I spit out the pill, and sat for a moment, listening to the old engine ticking over. In my hand was the plastic pill bottle. I felt very tired, but opened the car door and shut off the engine. I felt my way to the garage door and opened it. The air outside was fresh and sweet. I looked down at the pill bottle and hurried into the bathroom.

When I got through what had to be done there were a dozen pills floating in the toilet that hadn't even dissolved. There were the wasted shells of many more, and a lot of other stuff I won't bother to describe. I counted the pills in the bottle, remembered how many there had been, and wondered if I would make it.

I went over to Kluge's house and could not find Osborne. I was getting tired, but I made it back to my house and stretched out on the couch to see if I would live or die.

The next day I found the story in the paper. Osborne had gone home and blown out the back of his head with his revolver. It was not a big story. It happens to cops all the time. He didn't leave a note.

I got on the bus and rode out to the hospital and spent three hours trying to get in to see Lisa. I wasn't able to do it. I was not a relative and the doctors were quite firm about her having no visitors. When I got angry they were as gentle as possible. It was then I learned the extent of her injuries. Hal had kept the worst from me. None of it would have mattered, but the doctors swore there was nothing left in her head. So I went home.

She died two days later.

She had left a will, to my surprise. I got the house and contents. I picked up the phone as soon as I learned of it, and called a garbage company. While they were on the way over I went for the last time into Kluge's house.

The same computer was still on, and it gave the same message.

PRESS ENTER ■

I cautiously located the power switch, and turned it off. I had the garbage people strip the place to the bare walls.

I went over my own house very carefully, looking for anything that was even the first cousin to a computer. I threw out the radio. I sold the car, and the refrigerator, and the stove, and the blender, and the electric clock. I drained the waterbed and threw out the heater.

Then I bought the best propane stove on the market, and hunted a long time before I found an old icebox. I had the garage stacked to the ceiling with firewood. I had the chimney cleaned. It would be getting cold soon.

One day I took the bus to Pasadena and established the Lisa Foo Memorial Scholarship fund for Vietnamese refugees and their children. I endowed it with seven hundred thousand eighty-three dollars and four cents. I told them it could be used for any field of study except computer science. I could tell they thought me eccentric.

And I really thought I was safe, until the phone rang.

I thought it over for a long time before answering it. In the end, I knew it would just keep on going until I did. So I picked it up.

For a few seconds there was a dial tone, but I was not fooled. I kept holding it to my ear, and finally the tone turned off. There was just silence. I listened intently. I heard some of those far-off musical tones that live in phone wires. Echoes of conversations taking place a thousand miles away. And something infinitely more distant and cool.

I do not know what they have incubated out there at the NSA. I don't know if they did it on purpose, or if it just happened, or if it even has anything to do with them, in the end. But I know it's out there, because I heard its soul breathing on the wires. I spoke very carefully.

"I do not wish to know any more," I said. "I won't tell anyone anything. Kluge, Lisa, and Osborne all committed suicide. I am just a lonely man, and I won't cause you any trouble."

There was a click, and a dial tone.

Getting the phone taken out was easy. Getting them to remove all the wires was a little harder, since once a place is wired they expect it to be wired forever. They grumbled, but when I started pulling them out myself, they relented, though they warned me it was going to cost.

PG&E was harder. They actually seemed to believe there was a regulation requiring each house to be hooked up to the grid. They were willing to shut off my power—though hardly pleased about it—but they just weren't going to take the wires away from my house. I went up on the roof with an axe and demolished four feet of eaves as they gaped at me. Then they coiled up their wires and went home.

I threw out all my lamps, all things electrical. With hammer, chisel, and handsaw I went to work on the drywall just above the baseboards.

As I stripped the house of wiring I wondered many times why I was doing it. Why was it worth it? I couldn't have very many more years before a final seizure finished me off. Those years were not going to be a lot of fun.

Lisa had been a survivor. She would have known why I was doing this. She had once said I was a survivor, too. I survived the camp. I survived the death of my mother and father and managed to fashion a solitary life. Lisa survived the death of just about everything. No survivor expects to live through it all. But while she was alive, she would have worked to stay alive.

And that's what I did. I got all the wires out of the walls, went over the house with a magnet to see if I had missed any metal, then spent a week cleaning up, fixing the holes I had knocked in the walls, ceiling, and attic. I was amused trying to picture the real-estate agent selling this place after I was gone.

It's a great little house, folks. No electricity . . .

Now I live quietly, as before.

I work in my garden during most of the daylight hours. I've expanded it considerably, and even have things growing in the front yard now.

I live by candlelight, and kerosene lamp. I grow most of what I eat.

It took a long time to taper off the Tranxene and the Dilantin, but I did it, and now take the seizures as they come. I've usually got bruises to show for it.

In the middle of a vast city I have cut myself off. I am not part of the network growing faster than I can conceive. I don't even know if it's dangerous to ordinary people. It noticed me, and Kluge, and Osborne. And Lisa. It brushed against our minds like I would brush away a mosquito, never noticing I had crushed it. Only I survived.

But I wonder.

It would be very hard . . . Lisa told me how it can get in through the wiring. There's something called a carrier wave that can move over wires carrying household current. That's why the electricity had to go.

I need water for my garden. There's just not enough rain here in southern California, and I don't know how else I could get the water.

Do you think it could come through the pipes?

BESTSELLING

Science Fiction
and
Fantasy